IN ● THE
LONG ● RUN

N. J. Crisp

VIKING

VIKING
Viking Penguin Inc., 40 West 23rd Street,
New York, New York 10010, U.S.A.
Penguin Books Ltd, Harmondsworth,
Middlesex, England
Penguin Books Australia Ltd, Ringwood,
Victoria, Australia
Penguin Books Canada Limited, 2801 John Street,
Markham, Ontario, Canada L3R 1B4
Penguin Books (N.Z.) Ltd, 182–190 Wairau Road,
Auckland 10, New Zealand

First published in 1987 by Viking Penguin Inc.
Published simultaneously in Canada

LIBRARY OF CONGRESS CATALOGING IN PUBLICATION DATA
Crisp, N. J.
In the long run.
I. Title.
PR6053.R49715 1987   823'.914   86-40324
ISBN 0-670-81321-4

Printed in the United States of America by
R.R. Donnelley & Sons Company, Harrisonburg, Virginia
Set in Trump Mediaeval
Designed by Robert Bull

IN ● THE
LONG ● RUN

Also by N. J. Crisp

The Gotland Deal
The London Deal
The Odd Job Man
A Family Affair
Festival
The Brink
Yesterday's Gone

"In the long run we are all dead."
—John Maynard Keynes

" . . . the shooting has started . . . history has recorded
who fired the first shot. In the long run, however,
all that will matter is who fires the last shot."
—Franklin D. Roosevelt

*From his Navy and Total Defense Day
address, October 27, 1941, following
two attacks by German U-boats on
American destroyers, September 4, 1941,
and October 17, 1941.*

ACKNOWLEDGMENTS

This story is imaginary, as are all the characters, but there has been more than one real life *Fluchthelfer*, literally "escape-helper" (including one Hans Ulrich Lenzlinger, who was shot to death by an unknown assailant at his home in Switzerland in February 1979), and I am most grateful to the several West German and Swiss journalists who freely and generously provided background information; and to Kate Lowe for studying the mass of original material in German and translating into impeccable English the most informative and interesting sections.

It was Dr. Joy Osborne, my daughter-in-law, who researched the medical information I required, as she has done for several other works of mine, vetted the manuscript and suggested necessary changes to ensure accuracy. She patiently endures these demands on her busy doctor's time, and says that she enjoys doing it, but I am much in her debt just the same.

Finally, a much overdue tribute is due Janice Jarmain, who for more than a decade has combined with her family commitments the production of faultless typescripts, from often heavily and illegibly amended drafts, of all my novels, screenplays, and stage plays. My working life has been made a good deal easier by her willing assistance and initiative, and it is high time I recorded my grateful thanks and appreciation.

N. J. CRISP
London
November 1985

IN
● THE
LONG ●
RUN

ONE

The blond young man lazily ate breakfast. His eyelids had flicked open at 7 A.M. exactly; he had risen at once, showered, dressed, and packed his bags before phoning room service.

He had arrived in the city six days before, checked into the carefully selected hotel, and ridden up in the elevator to the pre-booked room on the top floor which faced toward the lake. Since then, he had spent the greater part of his time in his room, although he had briefly absented himself before the chambermaid's daily visit, and had taken dinner each evening in the dining room, a meal over which, without showing undue haste, he did not linger. Before lunch each day, he had left the hotel, carrying his briefcase, immaculately dressed, exchanging a few casual words with the polite doorman on each occasion. The doorman, had he been required to search his memory at some later date, would have gained the impression that the blond young man, like most of the hotel guests, nearly all of whom carried the *Wall Street Journal* or the *Financial Times*, had business in the financial quarter of the city which entailed a series of meetings and lunches, although he would have been hard-pressed to recall which banks or financial institutions the blond young man had mentioned, if any.

Once out of the hotel, the blond young man had walked briskly for an hour or so, stretching his legs, eaten a light lunch in a different café each day while he read the *Neue Zürcher Zeitung*, and returned to the hotel where, in his room, he resumed his vigil.

The city was beautiful if oddly dull, with its staid, respectable face, a discreetly secretive place, coupled with a certain degree of expensive hypochondria, serviced by the health clinics dotted along the lakeside.

Throughout the six days, the blond young man had made no telephone calls, and received only one. That had come through late the previous afternoon, when he was beginning to wonder if he might be obliged to extend his stay. The message he received was satisfactory. He thanked the caller, and hung up.

Despite the phone call confirming the arrangements, he had no intention of moving unless everything this morning matched his previous observations. In his view success depended not only on extensive training and experience but also on care and extreme caution.

The blond young man was sitting comfortably in an armchair set back a little way from the casement windows. The house was just over half a mile away, but the military binoculars he raised brought it so close that it seemed he could have reached out and touched the Mercedes station wagon parked in the short driveway outside the front door. The house itself, although large, was stolidly unassuming, matching its neighbors, soberly masking the money which it required to live in that fashionable suburb. A suitable home for someone who had ingeniously built up a flourishing enterprise and preferred to conduct its affairs in seclusion and privacy.

Behind the house, blurring out of focus, glints of sunlight sparkled from the still waters of the lake. Foreshortened by the powerful lenses, the house appeared to stand on the lakeside itself, although in fact it was several hundred yards away. Just the same, from the principal living rooms and bedrooms which were at the rear of the house, the owner would have enjoyed an idyllic view of the lake, with its passing traffic of small steamers and ferry boats, and the panorama of gentle mountains rising beyond.

The blond young man carefully scanned the windows facing him, searching for any indication that today's routine might be different in even the smallest degree. He paid particular attention to the two rooms which were furnished as offices. One was used as a general office and incorporated a comfortable waiting area. The typewriters were shrouded. No one sat at the desks or stood beside the telex. The other was an executive office. That was empty too. The recessed safe built into one wall could not be seen, but he knew exactly where it was situated, as he knew everything about that house he had never entered.

Just before 8:35 A.M. the front door opened, and the neat and not unattractive woman secretary whose name was Carli came out with the two German shepherds. The dogs' muzzles were lifted in excitement, their tails wagging furiously. For the next hour, they were off duty, and they knew it. The secretary opened the rear door of the Mercedes, and the dogs bounded in joyously.

The blond young man kept his binoculars focused, but he relaxed a little. He was not concerned about the sophisticated electronic and video security systems which protected the house, but the dogs were another matter. For all their handsome cheerfulness as they sat upright in the Mercedes, bright-eyed and panting in anticipation, they were powerful guard dogs, trained to attack as well as give warning. Dogs like that were a nuisance.

However, even such vigilant and deadly animals had to be exercised and their natural functions taken care of.

Their owner was a wary man, but even the wariest of men tended imperceptibly to fall into a routine, especially one which seemed to be both safe and convenient; in this case, allowing the dogs their run each morning after they had guarded the house during the hours of darkness, and

•

taken by the secretary, her departure timed so that, when she returned an hour later, her employer would have spent twenty-five minutes or so at his desk dealing with any private and confidential mail.

The binoculars followed the secretary as she rounded the Mercedes and climbed into the driver's seat. The blond young man noted the line of her breasts under her white blouse as she leaned forward and inserted the ignition key into the lock. The picture of full, soft breasts conjured up by the momentary glimpse reminded him of the monastic nature of his six-day stay.

In that sedate city, so conscious of its own image, where money was the principal commodity, money could also buy entertainment and amusement for businessmen weary after a hard day's toil and tourists after a hard day's sightseeing. The blond young man, who was not quite as young as he looked, preferred girls of tender years, before the freshness of childhood had entirely evaporated. In his mind he had more than once constructed a picture of the teenage hostess he could choose who would assuage his appetite. She remained a disturbing mental image. All his professional instincts rejected any such unauthorized expedition. Aside from that, he valued his job. Given his seniority, his success rate, and the trust reposed in him, it was unlikely that his assignment would be supervised by someone unknown to him, but not inconceivable. It would be foolish in the extreme to risk the ruin of his career. Just the same, although the secretary was too old to appeal to him, her breasts were reminiscent of those he had assigned to the imaginary teenage hostess, and turned his thoughts to his increasingly urgent needs. Tonight, his task completed, he would attend to them.

He became aware that several seconds had passed. The secretary still had only one hand on the steering wheel, and she was still leaning forward, her other hand on the ignition key. In his mind, the blond young man could hear what she could, half a mile away: the sound of an engine revving continually and declining to fire. The various possibilities flashed through the blond young man's mind, including postponement.

Inside the house, the noise would have been real, not imagined. The front door opened, and Stephen Haden came out. The secretary looked at him, said something, and gestured.

Haden waved her out of the car, slid into the driver's seat, and bent over the ignition switch. Moments later, he gave the secretary a smile. Words passed between them, she shrugged, and got back in again.

As she drove slowly along the short drive and paused at the road, the blond young man's binoculars remained on Stephen Haden. He had never been closer to Haden than half a mile, but the man's appearance was as familiar to him as though they were lifelong friends. He was to some extent acquainted with his background as well.

Stephen Haden was a little less than six feet tall, heavily built, but carried no excess weight, and moved easily and lightly. He took care of his body, and was a powerful and formidable man. In repose, his face, with its high cheekbones, widely spaced cool blue eyes, and hard-edged jaw, wore a set, unfathomable expression which, since he appeared to blink less often than most people, gave the impression that he should be handled with caution. When it suited him he had another face, when a broad smile erased the hardness, and the blue eyes crinkled and grew warm.

Haden's father had been English, and his mother Swiss. He was bilingual in English and German, and spoke fluent French and passable Italian. As a young man, he had begun to train as an architect, but had soon abandoned that and, after spending two or three years in England, had returned to work in a small garage, which carried out general repairs including patching up bodywork. Later, using money borrowed from his mother, he had set up on his own, specializing in crash repairs. That business failed, leaving him penniless but with certain contacts. Part of his trade had come from specially modifying high-priced cars which were subsequently exported, and which the police rather suspected had been stolen.

For a few years, Haden flirted with a number of enterprises of the kind where precise definitions of legality were arguable, and often required the services of an able lawyer. He dabbled in antiques, some of which proved to be debatably less than genuine. A combined import and courier agency was hastily wound up when detectives at police headquarters became interested in what they regarded as a front for smuggling.

There were others, but it was all small-time stuff, although he tasted temporary success when he started a club which quickly attracted an enthusiastic, free-spending clientele. Again, Stephen Haden fell foul of bureaucratic definitions. The police maintained that it was a brothel. Haden made certain changes to rectify this misunderstanding, but his clients lost interest. The club closed six months after Stephen Haden had married his elegant manageress, a divorcée with a small daughter.

But Stephen Haden was nothing if not persistent, and eventually he hit upon the right outlet for his varied talents, which had brought him success to the point of notoriety and supported the agreeable life-style he frankly enjoyed.

Along the way, his wife, Anna, divorced him, probably with his enthusiastic consent. Anna now lived in a small pleasant villa, and spent a good deal of time on the Italian Riviera, where she felt much at home. The divorce settlement had been generous. Haden could be generous, at least with money; less so in giving of himself. He was a complex and contradictory man. Some found him likeable, some hated him. He was clever and arrogant. He was self-centered and suspicious. He was strong and courageous; he was paranoid about security.

The sketchy collection of facts and suppositions comprised all the blond young man knew about Stephen Haden as a person. It was more than he needed. He was not interested in Haden's soul, for want of a better term, since patently no such thing existed. Some information, but not much, came from his six days' vigil, the remainder from the dossier he had studied and memorized as a matter of routine.

The blond young man recalled one more item, culled from press clippings attached to Haden's dossier, which had induced a smile.

Stephen Haden used paid advertising sparingly; he preferred the free variety and cultivated journalists in a way which kept his business in the news, and hence in potential clients' minds. The press had gladly seized on it when he said that he did not expect to live to a great age. He was convinced that he would die a violent death. That piece of bravado had made a good quote.

The binoculars had remained unwaveringly on Stephen Haden. The blond young man, who liked to dress well himself, admired in passing the unobtrusively perfect cut of Haden's pearl-gray lightweight suit. Now Haden turned and went back into the house. The front door closed behind him.

The blond young man glanced at his watch. The unexpected delay before the secretary's final departure had seemed endless even to a man of his serene temperament, but in reality only an additional two minutes had been consumed. He telephoned Reception, and asked for his bill and a taxi at once.

The taxi dropped him, as instructed, outside a lawyer's office which, like many in the city, was also the business address of a long string of companies, listed on a sign beside the entrance. The blond young man inquired about a taxi to the airport around lunchtime when his business inside would be concluded, accepted the proffered phone number with thanks, and paid the driver.

He watched the taxi until it was lost in the traffic, crossed the road, and entered the multi-story car park

•

where he had left his car on the top deck six days before, having decided to eschew the hotel car park. He stowed his bags in the trunk, but placed his briefcase on the passenger seat ready for his meeting, assured himself that the flat package was still underneath the driver's seat, drove down the ramp, and paid at the barrier.

Minutes later, he parked his car on the quiet road, fifty yards short of Stephen Haden's house. A gardener was crouched beside a flower bed as he walked past one of the gardens, but otherwise he saw no one before he turned into the drive.

The blond young man moved easily around the side of the house to the rear, and immediately descended the steps which led down into the basement area where he was shielded from overlooking windows.

He paused for just a moment before gently trying the basement door, poised and ready to retreat again if all was not as it should be. But the door was not locked, it opened smoothly and soundlessly, and no alarm broke the silence. In a second, he was inside. He glanced up. The individual door alarm was in the "Off" position.

He was in a storeroom. He threaded his way through the clutter into an unlighted corridor, and along it. He passed the open door to a room inside which the pump of a large central heating boiler was humming away monotonously to itself, turned right, and came to the stairs beside which were steps leading down to the nuclear fallout shelter.

The blond young man moved up the stairs with the delicate precision of a cat, and slowly eased open the door at the top. He was facing a large hall, bright in the morning light. His eyes sought the front door. A bundle of letters lay behind the lattice of the mail box. The morning's work had not yet begun. Eyes narrowed, he searched for the neat panel inset at the top-right-hand side of the front door, and found it. The control governing the door audio alarm system was still in the "On" position. When Haden's office manager, Anton Weiss, arrived he would not be able to use his key to let himself in. He would have to ring the doorbell and be identified. Only then would the system be turned "Off."

The blond young man remained where he was for another half a minute, his ears alert, still ready to postpone his meeting should there be the slightest indication of anything untoward. But he could hear nothing. Not a sound interrupted the silence, not so much as the ticking of a clock.

The blond young man made no sound either, as he moved into the hall. He ignored the main staircase, and went up a shorter flight of stairs which led to a galleried mezzanine floor, where there was only one door. He opened it, and entered the empty general office.

He angled a comfortable, padded chair in the waiting area until it suited his purposes, and sat down, relaxed.

He placed his briefcase on his knees, and looked at his watch again. It was 9:08 A.M. He had approximately seven minutes to wait.

The forthcoming meeting would be the culmination of a great deal of preparation, thought, and planning, but the blond young man's pulse rate remained even. He was completely at ease, quietly confident of his ability to handle the encounter. Chance could never be entirely eliminated, but the difficult part had been achieved. He was in position. He would see Haden alone, off guard, and without anyone else present. Others had pondered such an arrangement before now and decided that it was less easy than it sounded.

As the minute hand crept imperceptibly forward around the face of his watch, the blond young man slowed his breathing, listening intently for the first faint sound which would soon intrude on the blank silence, his head cocked in the direction of the hall whence it would come.

The telex beside the window began to chatter furiously.

After the complete absence of any noise save the blond young man's soft breathing, it sounded like a manic pneumatic drill clamoring away unceasingly.

The blond young man stared at the telex. The printer rattled across the paper with monotonous speed, again and again, over and over, paper spilling upwards, apparently inexorably determined to clatter on indefinitely.

The telex stopped, as abruptly as it had begun.

The blond young man strained his ears in the sudden silence. Nothing. Several inches of paper extruded from the telex. He thought for a moment, and then changed the position of his chair slightly.

Ninety seconds later, he heard what he was waiting for: a slight, brief metallic click from the falling flap of the lattice mail box. The blond young man began to count silently, having timed his own ascent of the stairs at a measured pace. He was not confident that he would be able to detect soft footfalls muffled by the thick pile of the carpet on the stairs and landing.

The blond young man was right. He did not hear Stephen Haden approaching, but his ears, sensitive as a wild animal's, picked up the rustle of paper against paper, and a moment later the door behind which he was concealed swung open toward him, and Stephen Haden entered the room.

Haden was shuffling the bunch of letters in his hands as he walked in. He moved forward a couple of steps, during which he took the keys to his private office and safe from his pocket, when he saw the paper protruding from the telex. As the blond young man had rather expected, Haden changed direction and crossed toward the machine.

At the moment when Haden began to bend down and read the message, the blond young man shot him in the back twice, paired shots from his silenced automatic, the two muffled *"phuts"* so close together as to be almost one.

Stephen Haden's body fell forward onto the telex. The

machine's innards jangled, the fitment rocked. Envelopes and keys spilled from Haden's limp fingers.

For a moment, he hung there, face down. The blond young man, still comfortably seated, saw the dark blood-stain over Haden's heart, the random, oozing ugly shape disfiguring the immaculate pearl-gray suit.

Then Haden slithered to the floor as though seeking final repose, his body twisting sideways as it fell. A thump as the carpeted floor accepted its burden, and there was dead silence again.

The blond young man stood up, the briefcase from which he had taken his gun in one hand, the automatic in the other. Stephen Haden was motionless, his head twisted sideways at an unnatural angle, his face the pasty color of death.

The blond young man was about to move forward to the body when, suddenly, he froze. For the first time, his composure was seriously disturbed, his breathing became shallow.

Somewhere, downstairs in that house which should now have contained only one living being, himself, a radio had been switched on. The thudding rhythm of heavy metal pop music was distant but distinct.

The blond young man edged cautiously to the door and looked down into the hall. It was empty, but the radio played on. His heartbeat slowed back to normal as he took in and accepted this new, unexpected factor.

Moving his head from side to side in an attempt to locate the source of the music, he inched along the galleried landing until he was at the head of the short flight of stairs, the automatic in his hand ready in case anyone appeared. No one did, but as he changed position, he became certain that the music was coming from behind one of the doors beneath the gallery, probably the kitchen.

The blond young man was mystified. After six days of keeping watch, he knew the routine of this house inside out. Once the secretary had left with the dogs, it should have been empty, except for Stephen Haden, until Anton Weiss arrived at about 9:30 A.M.

Moreover, to eliminate the possibility of unexpected callers, he had kept the house under observation with his night glasses the previous evening, as during every evening, until the lights had been extinguished at 11:22 P.M. He had continued to study the house until long after midnight before finally going to bed, but it had remained shrouded in darkness.

The blond young man could not account for the presence of this unknown individual who had switched on a radio. He had no idea who it might be. Nor had he any desire to find out. His job was done. The safe was secondary, not imperative. His business now was to remove himself from the scene, not to linger. The blond young man had no taste for unplanned encounters if they could be avoided. By definition, they might be risky, might carry unknown dangers.

He slipped the hand holding the automatic into his pocket, ready for instant use if absolutely necessary. He decided to take the quickest route out of the house, rather than use up time by making his way back to the basement door, as he had intended.

With quick but feather-light steps, he descended the stairs. He had been right about the source of the music. It was coming from the kitchen.

He crossed the hall with long quiet strides. Releasing his grip on the gun, he reached up to the inset panel, and punched the door security system off, killing the audio alarm.

The blond young man opened the door wide. The heavy metal music was still playing, but the kitchen door remained closed.

He had half crossed the threshold when, without warning, the heavy, thudding beat doubled in volume. He stopped and swung around.

The door was open and no one was within his range of

vision, but the music was coming toward him, the track approaching its frenzied climax.

And then he saw her, a sleepy-eyed teenage girl, wandering slowly across the hall. She was wearing fluffy slippers, a padded dressing gown, and carried a radio/cassette player. Her head was rocking dreamily in time to the music.

Momentarily, the blond young man considered going back inside and killing her, as the half-open door attracted the teenage girl's attention, and her head turned.

Their eyes met. The blond young man was poised, ready to step back across the threshold, had her eyes begun to widen in fear, had her lips parted to cry out.

The teenage girl's face remained immobile, and registered neither alarm nor surprise. The blond young man changed his mind, smiled, nodded a friendly good-bye, and slammed the door closed.

His task was to kill Stephen Haden, not some unknown girl—unless that was essential for his own safety. His razor-sharp instant judgment told him it was not. The fact that she had seen him did not much concern him. In broad daylight, someone was bound to notice and remember him later anyway. He had taken that as a certainty from the beginning, and allowed for it.

The gardener appeared with a wheelbarrow as he walked past the next house but one. The blond young man cast a swift look at his watch. It was 9:18 A.M.

He glanced at the house as he drove past it, and studied his rearview mirror when he slowed down before turning right, but everything remained peaceful and quiet. No alarm had been raised.

Ten minutes later, he was leaving the city of Zurich. He settled down to enjoy the drive. He was safe. His job was done.

At 9:29 A.M. Anton Weiss rang the front doorbell. After a while, he rang the doorbell again. Eventually, the teenage girl in the dressing gown opened the door.

He smiled his surprise, went in, and chatted with her briefly before he trotted up the stairs.

At 9:33 A.M., he pushed open the door of the general office and saw Stephen Haden's crumpled body lying on the floor.

Downstairs, he could hear the thud of heavy metal music.

TWO

It was as regular as a metronome; a mechanical sound, monotonous in its exactness; a deep hiss dying away and then a distinct click, on and on, repeated unendingly, as if something was being inflated, over and over again.

Then voices overlaid, speech, but no identifiable words, no meaning, mere background against the interminable *shush-click, shush-click, shush-click* . . .

Both soothing and wearying in the comfortable darkness, masking other odd sensations, slight but potentially less pleasant if dwelt upon. Drifting now, weightless, drifting away, back to welcoming, warm eternity . . .

*T*he telephone ringing in the darkness. Fumbling for the receiver.

"Hullo."

"Hullo. I'm at the airport."

"Who is that?"

"Christa. I didn't wake you, did I?"

Groping for the switch. The flare of light. Blinking.

"Do you know what time it is?"

"Sorry. I sent Mother a cable . . . "

"Why aren't you at school?"

"It's half term. I was going to stay, but everyone else was going home, so I decided . . . "

"At the last minute, as usual."

"I asked her to meet me, but I've been waiting here for hours. I keep phoning her, but there's no reply."

"Since she's away, there wouldn't be."

"Where is she?"

"Rapallo . . . or Santa Margherita . . . I forget."

"Oh, God. Didn't she get my cable?"

"I don't know! Why can't you plan things properly, for Christ's sake?"

The aftertaste of cognac harsh in the sluggishness after being awakened from deep sleep.

"Can I come and stay with you overnight? Then I can probably track her down tomorrow. I think I know where she might be. Can I? I don't know what else to do. I shan't get in your way."

"Yes, all right. Get a taxi."

"I don't think I've got enough money with me. I thought she'd be meeting me."

"Get a taxi, and I'll pay him when you get here. I'm not turning out."

"Thanks. Sorry to be a nuisance . . . "

"Just hurry up. I've got an important meeting in the morning. I don't want to be up all night waiting for you."

Replacing the receiver. The click.

Shush-click, shush-click, shush-click . . .

A lifetime later, more, perhaps eons, floating in this dark, unknown void, the mechanism was still performing its strange, mysterious function, taken for granted, familiar, on this return visit to the place of mechanical sound.

The voices again, octaves apart, a soothing lullaby without words, lapping in and out of the eternal counterpoint . . .

Shush-click, shush-click . . .

Perhaps were there light, the sounds might have sources, but there was no light, merely a gentle pressure on the source from which light might have been perceived, slight, almost imperceptible, yet firm, impossible to shift or penetrate. A sense of stickiness too, sealing off that source. Odd, that.

Voices becoming louder, insistent. Disturbing. Too much trouble. Switch off. Perpetual motion, heartening, reliable, always there. Not insistent, not disturbing. Hear that, ignore the voices.

Shush-click, shush-click . . .

Familiar and comforting as the rocking of a cradle, the soft crooning of a mother bending over, unseen but always there. "Go to sleep, my baby. . . . "

*F*ather.

The face, the eyes, the smile. Him. Here. Talking.

But the smile not the one, twisted, teeth bared, a snarl of anger and pain.

Father?

Don't look at me like that. Don't be angry with me. It's so good to see you, to be walking with you again.

Across the meadow. The sun shining. That's my bow and arrow, the one you made for me. Where have you been?

The white open-necked shirt, the broad chest, the powerful forearms, the crinkled eyes, the deep voice, unchanged after all these years. When did you get back?

Father?

It's your voice, your face, the rough feel of your tweed jacket, but you can't be here. It's impossible.

Go away! Please go away. You're not real.

You are dead.

You know you are dead. You know you don't exist.

Your remains have decayed in the cemetery for decades. Why won't you listen to me? Can't you hear me? I can hear you. You are real, I can see you, I can touch you, you are here.

But you are dead.

Father?

Stop looking at me like that. You are dead.
Don't you know you are dead?

*I*n the spacious cubicle, the doctor glanced at the large, continually updated chart. He scarcely noticed the continuous sound of the ventilator.

The life-support paraphernalia had been in place for five days since the emergency operation. Five days was a lengthier period than the doctor would have wished. Unless the present deterioration could be checked, unless there was some response to the treatment the doctor had ordered, the patient's prospects were negligible.

Tubes fed into the mouth and up the nose. There was a drip in the left arm, and a continuous monitor attached to the right arm, measuring the blood pressure.

Three chest leads were connected to a portable ECG. A catheter led into a graduated bag from which the hourly urine output was measured. A tube running into a main vein above the righthand clavicle was the CVP line, by means of which the central venous pressure was read off against a column of mercury. The doctor's mind took in all the readings and their deeply worrying implications automatically.

Over the patient's eye sockets were small gauze pads to prevent the eyes from drying out. The pads were daubed with Vaseline, and were checked hourly.

The nurse lifted the pads in anticipation as the doctor turned. Using a pencil torch, he examined the pupil reflexes, and straightened up.

"Thank you, nurse."

She replaced the pads.

A tall dark-haired woman had come into the cubicle. The worldly poise and self-possession which she wore as naturally as her elegant clothes were tinged with hesitant nervousness. Beside her was the slim, young girl with the wavy fair hair, her face sober and pale, the young skin taut over the high cheekbones. The doctor, disguising his concern, produced a brief smile of recognition.

"I'm sorry . . . ," the woman said. Her face was perfectly made-up, but the underlying strain showed through. "If you'd rather we waited . . . "

"It's all right," the doctor said.

"Is there . . . ," the woman began. She paused, frowning slightly, as though the choice of words was important. " . . . any change?" she finished at last, uncertainly.

"None to speak of," the doctor said, steadily. "At best, it'll be a long job, even if all goes well."

"You see, darling?" she said to the slender young girl. "It wouldn't serve any purpose, you staying. I can always phone you if . . . if necessary. He's in good hands," the woman said. "There's nothing we can do."

The girl moved a chair, and sat down beside the immobile figure.

"Can he hear anything, doctor?" she asked, at last, her voice light and girlish. "Does he even know we're here?"

"We talk to him," the doctor said. "But he doesn't respond. Whether he can hear us or not, I can't say."

The woman drew the doctor aside, away from the girl. Her eyes, enlarged by mascara, were unblinking, her gaze firm and forceful.

"Is there any chance he'll recover?" she asked.

"It's a critical period," the doctor said carefully. This one was not looking for facile optimism. "Everything possible is being done."

"It's a miracle he's survived this long, isn't it?"

"His injuries were extremely serious," the doctor said. "In most men, they would have proved fatal."

"Yes, he's strong," the woman said, reflectively. "But he's not immortal."

"He could pull through," the doctor said. "We'll know in the very near future."

•

"But he could die soon," she said.

The girl looked at her blank-faced.

*F*ather?

He's gone. Strange, that. Everyone thought he was dead, but he came back, alive, talking, reproachful. The recollection of his presence real, but receding.

Father?

No. No answer. No one there.

He's died at last, then. The first time must have been a mistake. But now he's dead. That's who they were talking about.

A sense of relief. The dead should remain dead. Where could he have been all those years?

*"W*hat would the price be?"

It's that bar where it all began, pools of light over the tables, the face of the man opposite shadowed, the signet ring on his right hand glinting as he lifted the glass to his lips. An expensive signet ring. A discreet, well-tailored suit. A man with money.

"Ten thousand dollars, American." Price it in American dollars, like oil. It sounds impressive. A moment of worry. He didn't mind that, his head half nodding already. Damn. Pitched it too low, guessed at the wrong round figure. Put that right fast. "In advance. The second half when it's done."

The head stopped nodding. He minded that all right.

"That adds up to a lot of money . . . " The shadowed eyes glimpsed, wary, watchful.

"Please yourself. It's your father, not mine." Was he going to get up and walk away, taking his much-needed dollars with him? The nervous contraction in the pit of the stomach. Never mind the second half, just the advance would be a godsend, enough to survive for another month. Next month could look after itself. A month was forever.

Perhaps it would be better to bargain, settle for less. No, sod him. The mean bastard had money, you only had to look at him.

"Suppose it fails?"

"It never has yet." Quite right. Never done it before.

"Things can go wrong." The elbows on the table as he leaned forward, the lamp illuminating the thinning, neatly brushed back hair, the sharp face. "In that case, it would have cost me ten thousand dollars for nothing."

"There'll be a formal contract. If the contract isn't fulfilled, the advance would be refunded." The man liked that, but it was going too far. Once he thought about it, he'd get suspicious. "Less necessary expenses incurred." That sounded better. Less eager.

"A formal contract." Thoughtful. Impressed.

"Ready for signature tomorrow morning." There would be no refunds, the small print would take care of that.

"Very well." The hand extended across the table. Taking it. The flesh clammy.

"Give me the addresses of the friends you mentioned on both sides. And it is understood, the balance paid on delivery, in cash."

The head nodding in acceptance. The signet ring glinting as the hand was raised, gesturing and pointing at the empty glasses.

"Waiter."

One of those unwanted voices again. Muffled, a blur of sound, high-pitched but insistent.

Go away. Leave me alone.

Something else. Something moving of its own accord. What? Studied with momentary detached interest. A leg? Not walking, not running. Just one leg, belonging to no one. Firm yet gentle rhythmical movements. Is there some sort of pattern?

It's stopped.

Now another leg. A different one. The same thing. Forget it. Nothing to do with me.

*T*he back-street workshop cluttered, but the big Opel should do. Ageing, but sound enough. Tires okay. Nothing to attract attention.

The man in white overalls watching, expressionless. Good contacts pay off. No curiosity, no questions. Laconic. Kurt Gabler. A tough customer, but useful.

It'll mean working most of the night. The whole thing improvised, off the cuff. No choice, had to seize that unexpected chance. Inspecting tools . . . oxyacetylene equipment . . . Kurt Gabler only too ready to help—and cheap.

"Anything to screw those bastards." The big Opel sitting under the unshaded, glaring lights. Kurt Gabler waiting, impassive.

Time to start work . . .

*T*he long queue of vehicles at the checkpoint. Yawning at first, but the tiredness draining away as the queue edges forward. Adrenaline taking over as the military uniforms come near, the young, unsmiling faces. Keyed up, the sense of excitement extinguishing nervousness and growing into pleasure.

Handing over papers. Cold eyes studying them carefully.

"Business?"

That properly registered company which had never traded had come in useful at last. The notepaper was impressive. They were keen on trade and hard currency.

*W*here's this? Oh, yes, the other side, the reverse image. Same people, same language, but what a difference across the divide.

Less traffic, huge apartment blocks like barracks. No bustle, no neon lights, no night clubs. The chill winter daylight fading. The street map memorized. Across the city, no mistakes, no hesitation. A few interested glances at the registration plates now and then, but that was all.

Dark now. The street ill-lit. The final turning. Slowing. There's the house, on the corner. Swinging the wheel, through the open gates, and into the courtyard.

The farewells, the good wishes. Waiting impatiently, beginning to shiver. At last, the little group moving to the Opel, opening the capacious trunk.

"Not in there!"

"What?" The look of puzzlement.

"The first bloody place they'll look."

Opening the rear passenger door, pulling out the rear seat back cushion, pointing.

The old man's look of horror as he leaned forward stiffly.

"I can't get in there."

Suppressing the spurt of anger. A sleepless night spent, helped by Kurt Gabler, moving the trunk partition back that few centimeters which would not be noticed, enlarging the cavity over one wheel arch, testing the resulting space, making sure a body could be squeezed in, restoring, making good, ensuring there were no signs of any work carried out, even checking the underside of the wheel arch and carefully replacing the fragments of mud which had been dislodged. And now this silly old fool . . .

Trying to be patient.

"You've no idea how small a human being can make himself, when necessary."

Helping him, guiding him, easing and pushing his old bones into place, ignoring his complaining grunts, until he was lying in position on his side in the shape of a flat *V*, his legs draped over one wheel arch.

"There you are. Now, I'm going to secure this cushion. Try and relax. A touch of cramp the other end, but you'll be all right. One thing. If we stop and the engine's switched off, and you hear them poking about, don't make a sound, or we're both for it. Understood?"

A last glimpse of the old man's face, pale, apprehensive, tongue passing over thin, dry lips, jamming the cushion back into place, securing it, testing it with a rough heave. Satisfied. Okay, here we go.

"*O*ver there."

Shit. Pulling out of the line of vehicles, aligning the hood with the pointing finger, stopping beside the waiting group.

"Switch off. Out."

Engine dying, door slamming, out into the bitter cold, hands jammed in pockets, eyes narrowed and blinking against the wind-borne snowflakes.

Three of them, one with a powerful flashlight, sizing up the car, no hurry. Trunk lid raised, rummaging inside, suitcase flung open, contents tipped out. Banging on the floor of the trunk with some implement, the partition.

Keep quiet, old man. Don't lose your head.

Heart thumping, shoulders hunched, the thin, icy wind numbing. Don't these bastards feel the bloody cold?

Why did they pick on me? Have they been tipped off?

The one with the flashlight crouching, the bright beam methodically traveling across the underside of the car. Now shining it up underneath the wheel arch.

God, what's he looking at so intently? Did I overlook something?

The third one inside, pulling the back seat out, poking about, tapping. Bracing himself, grasping the back cushion.

"How much longer is this going to take?" The irate tone of an innocent businessman in a hurry. Trying to distract him.

Deaf and dumb for all the effect it has.

Jesus, if he goes on like that, brute force is going to rip the whole thing out . . .

It's not my car, and I don't know anything about it. All I can say. Might as well save my breath. What happens now? Prison? Or just disappear? Never heard of again?

---

*T*he heater blasting out hot air, the car warm and cozy. Boxed in, jostling for position in the lanes of traffic, and enjoying it. Loving it. The cars, the people, the crowded shops.

Savoring the sense of exhilaration. Made it, brought it off, fooled them.

Wonder how the old man is?

"You all right back there? Can you hear me? Not long now."

Just a routine search after all, picked out at random, not a tip-off. Looking for anything, some poor bastard curled up under a rug in the trunk, smuggled currency, smuggled all sorts, anything forbidden, anything that upsets them, and there's plenty of that.

Déjà vu, this good feeling, close to triumph, familiar, sought for, cherished, experienced on many occasions, always the same. No, this is the first time, the others come later, that's right.

Threading across the city, finding the handsome, low-built apartment block, pulling up outside. A few words on the entry phone, and back to the car, gently easing the old man out from his cramped hiding place, finally lifting him bodily out of the car.

The poor old bugger rigid, joints locked, but cheerful, grinning idiotically and groaning with pain at the same time, hardly able to believe it.

Relatives running out, neighbors, passersby gathering in a little circle, realizing what's happened.

And they start clapping happily, all smiling, and applauding!

The nice-looking middle-aged woman with the envelope in her hand crying over the old man, and then turning and hugging me, tears of pure joy running down her face.

"Thank you . . . thank you . . . God bless you and keep you . . . " A bloody hero!

And inside the envelope, another ten thousand dollars, American. Christ. There's real money to be made at this game. Need someone in West Berlin, though. Kurt Gabler maybe? He learns fast. Why not? Think about Kurt Gabler, sound him out.

*T*he young, rather pretty physiotherapist was moving the right arm in a predetermined pattern. She had already completed similar passive exercises on the legs, talking at intervals as she did so.

"... nearly finished ... keep the joints supple ... helps to prevent the muscles wasting ... there ... all done ... "

Gently, she replaced the limp arm, and bent forward over the face with the gauze pads over the eyes and the tubes running into mouth and nose.

"Right. One more thing, Mr. Haden. If you can hear me, we've done this before. Now you've had your chest physio, I'm going to pass a tube down your throat to suck out any secretions which may have gathered in your lungs. You won't feel much, and it will soon be over. Ready, Mr. Haden? I'm starting now."

Steadily, the sterile tube slipped down his throat. When it was in position, the physiotherapist switched on the suction pump.

*T*he words penetrating, the memory of the frequent hateful sensation returning. Not again. No. Don't.

The thing being forced in. Rebelling. Fighting against it. Summoning up every ounce of strength to resist the assault. But nothing happens. Can't move, can't see, can't prevent it.

Oh, God, what's happened to me? Who's doing this?

*T*he physiotherapist switched off the suction pump, and withdrew the tube.

"There. All over, Mr. Haden. Has to be done, I'm afraid. I'll come and see you again later. All right?"

She noticed that the detective was standing behind her in the cubicle, watching. As on a previous occasion, his presence startled her slightly. The man had a knack of silent movement, drifting in casually, unseen and unheard, as if stealth were second nature to him.

He smiled at her and nodded a greeting.

"How's he doing? Does he know what's going on yet?"

"We don't believe so."

The detective's smile lingered thoughtfully.

"I wouldn't be too sure of that. If I know him, he's lying there listening to everything, taking it all in, biding his time. That's his style, always has been. The games he plays, most questions he'd rather not answer."

"I doubt if you're right," the physiotherapist said. She lowered her voice to a soft murmur. "His condition's still critical. If he doesn't improve soon, he'll die. I should think he'd be only too anxious to help you, if he could."

"You don't know him very well," the detective observed mildly. He drew a chair up to the bed. "All right if I have another go?"

It was a rhetorical question. The detective was one of the very few who were allowed access to this patient, critical condition or not.

"His mother usually comes to see him about this time," the physiotherapist said, but he was deaf to such trifles.

"Haden," the detective said clearly. "Haden. You know who I am. Can you hear me? If you can, try and lift one fingertip. Just one finger, all right? Haden. Can you hear me?"

Only the relentless, inexorable *shush-click* of the ventilator signaled that, with its aid, the apparently lifeless body was still breathing.

*T*he doctor was in his office, studying the latest discouraging X-rays.

It was infuriating. They had come a long way since the ambulance had arrived at 9:51 A.M. that day, the trolley

•

rushed in, the patient delivered to the alerted, waiting emergency team. So much had been achieved, against all odds.

Resuscitation was the first urgent step before the faint, residual flicker of life ceased and the serious chest and abdominal wounds proved fatal.

An endotracheal tube provided an airway. It was immediately apparent that, as so often with gunshot wounds, not only had air entered the pleural cavity and caused the left lung to collapse, but the lips of the wound were producing a valvular effect, allowing more and more air to be sucked in, resulting in a tension pneumothorax. The patient's increasingly severe breathlessness was all too obvious, and very serious.

A pack of thick gauze was hurriedly applied to close the sucking chest wound. To further relieve the condition, a chest drain was inserted into the chest, a tube connected to an underwater seal which let the air out of the pleural cavity. This allowed air to escape from the pleural cavity on expiration, but prevented it from being sucked back through the water seal on inspiration.

There had been serious loss of blood, both from the chest and abdominal injuries, and two drips were put up, one in each arm, and, initially, O Negative blood, which suited all blood types, transfused.

A nasogastric tube was threaded down the nose and into the stomach contents, which prevented the unconscious patient from vomiting and inhaling the vomit into the lungs, while a cardiac monitor was set up, and a CVP line inserted above the right collarbone.

Meanwhile, blood had been taken for cross-matching and routine tests, the patient connected to an ECG, and chest and abdominal X-rays carried out.

And the patient's slender connection to life had been maintained, although he was certainly due to die shortly without urgent surgery.

The problems were daunting indeed. The patient's injuries were so serious that it was surprising he had survived thus far.

One bullet had actually lacerated the heart, causing bleeding into the pericardium, and producing cardiac tamponade, a condition in which the blood-filled space around the heart was exerting pressure on the heart itself. A pericardiocentesis, a fine needle passed into the pericardial space, had confirmed the diagnosis and temporarily relieved the pressure during the initial period of resuscitation.

As well as the air entering the pleural cavity on the left, blood coming from the chest wall, lung, and heart had also entered, and there was both air and blood in the space, producing a hemopneumothorax, while there was a ruptured diaphragm as well.

The structure dividing the chest from the abdomen had been torn by the gunshot wound, and the abdominal contents had moved up into the chest, further embarrassing the patient's breathing.

The expected surgical emphysema had been present: air which had entered the tissues just under the skin. The patient's face and neck appeared swollen, and when the doctor had felt the skin over the trunk and neck, there had been a crackling sensation under his fingers. He had actually been feeling the air under the skin.

In the abdomen, the ruptured spleen had caused rapid blood loss. The patient was pale, his blood pressure dropping, pulse rate rising, respiration rapid. The only course open was to remove the spleen.

As for the penetrating wound of the left kidney, it was hoped that a partial nephrectomy would suffice. It seemed that the damage was limited to a small laceration. However, it was very difficult to stitch kidneys, hence the decision that part of it would have to be removed.

In the theater, the patient would undergo a thoracotomy, a laparotomy, and the entry and exit wounds would be treated, but with a delayed primary closure.

The latter technique involved leaving the entry and exit wounds, once treated, open for a minimum of three days before being sutured, which dramatically cut down on the infection rate, always a major hazard with gunshot wounds.

Surgery had gone well. Once the patient's chest wall had been opened, the pericardium had been opened and the blood and clots drained out; the heart laceration had been stitched; the blood loss stopped from the bleeding vessels in the chest; and the hole in the diaphragm repaired after putting the abdominal contents back down into the abdomen.

The abdomen had been opened, and the spleen and part of the left kidney removed.

Finally, the entry and exit wounds had been excised well, and then left open.

Nothing had gone wrong. Textbook stuff, the doctor had reflected, pleased.

The textbook, however, contained other entries, including a particularly common complication with penetrating injuries.

By the time the entry and exit wounds were sutured, the patient was developing a fever and anemia. The diagnosis of this worrying condition was confirmed by a chest X-ray. Empyema.

The initial treatment was by antibiotics, both by mouth and directly into the pleural cavity, and by drawing off the pus causing the problem by putting a needle into the chest.

Antibiotics and repeated aspirations. however, were not working. There was no sign of the patient's condition improving. And further surgery now to deal with the empyema would certainly kill him. He was too weak.

The doctor shook his head, disheartened, laid the X-rays aside, left his office, and made his way toward the doctors' dining room. Halfway, he changed his mind, returned to the patient, examined him, conferred with the nurse, and checked the updated chart. But there was no perceptible change.

He stood for a while looking at the patient, searching

his mind for some other step which could be taken, and failing to find one.

All the known weapons of medicine and technology had been used. The only remaining hope lay outside his power, and rested in that once powerful, unconscious body connected to all the life-support paraphernalia; whether within it somewhere there remained sufficient invisible residue of the strongest human instinct, to live, or whether the faint flicker was already expiring. The answer, either way, could not be long delayed, and was beyond the doctor's control anyway.

"I shall be at lunch, nurse," he said.

THREE

Stephen Haden's eyelids lifted like two blinds snapping open. He knew immediately who he was, he knew that for some unknown reason he was in a hospital. Lurking somewhere was the dim recollection of disagreeable dreams, but he could not identify them; they remained out of reach.

It could have been soon after that he found a face looking down at him, or it might have been hours later, he could not tell. The face belonged to a dark-haired man in his thirties wearing a white coat, and was rather serious and withdrawn. As their eyes met, a nice smile pleasantly modified his expression.

"Hullo, Mr. Haden. I'm Dr. Hensler. How are you feeling?"

Haden became aware that his body appeared to be composed of a collection of various discomforts and pains, one of which was excruciating.

"My throat . . ." he began. It hurt even more when he spoke, and he stopped.

Dr. Hensler nodded sympathetically.

"Most patients complain of that" he said. "I know it's unpleasant, but we'll give you something for it, and it'll soon go away. You've been in intensive care," he explained. "We moved you out last night."

"Why . . .?" Haden managed, and left it at that.

"You'd been shot," Dr. Hensler said.

"Don't . . . remember . . ." Haden found it hard to concentrate on anything but his throat, which appeared to be on fire.

"We believe that the gun used was almost certainly fitted with a silencer, which would reduce the muzzle velocity of the bullets. But for that, your chances of survival would have been nil."

Haden knew about the effect of a silencer on muzzle velocity, but his mind was woolly and in no state to consider such details.

"What's . . . the damage?" he managed.

"Nothing you can't live with," Dr. Hensler assured him. "Or without," he added dryly. "I'll explain what was done later. At present, you're very weak. We want you to get plenty of rest." He eyed Haden as if assessing something. "Your mother's here. She's been desperately worried about you, naturally. Do you feel up to seeing her for a moment?"

Haden nodded dully. Really, he just wanted to be left alone.

*H*aden's throat had improved considerably by the time the barrel-chested figure of Schlunegger appeared, and although feeling very unwell in himself, his limbs were stronger.

Haden said, "I thought you'd turn up sometime."

"What? I've haunted this bloody hospital," Schlunegger said, as he sat down. "We've held many a one-sided conversation."

Haden shook his head.

"Don't remember you," he said. "None of it, come to that. Who shot me?"

"I was hoping you'd tell me," Schlunegger said.

"I wish I knew," Haden said.

"Yes," Schlunegger said dubiously. "Let's hear what you do know."

That was easy. First, Haden had spent some time in careful reflection since regaining his senses. Second, he knew practically nothing.

"The same as any other morning. Took a handful of letters from the mail box. Walked upstairs looking at the envelopes, and into the outer office. There was a message on the telex. Went over to look at it. After that—nothing."

"You were shot twice in the back," Schlunegger said. "Found lying beside the telex. What about the keys to your private office and the safe?"

"I think I had them in my hand," Haden said.

"That fits. They were on the floor." He gazed at Haden, speculatively. "Your private office was still locked."

Haden said, "Those keys could have been used, and put back beside me."

"No fingerprints," Schlunegger said. "Not anywhere. Always gloves, of course, but inside the safe was ten thousand American dollars, five thousand English pounds, eight thousand German marks, and twenty-five thousand Swiss francs. Enough for a few groceries. Or maybe cash to square people who don't like checks."

Haden wished that Schlunegger, always a boring individual, would stick to the point.

"Whoever shot me, then," he said, "it was personal. Not for the money in the safe."

"Robbery could still have been the motive," Schlunegger said. "Can't rule it out. We think he might have been interrupted."

"He?" Haden queried. "You know who it was?"

Schlunegger said, "We'd like to interview a blond young man, age about twenty-five, clean-shaven, medium height, smartly dressed, carrying a briefcase. Not much of a description, but it's all we've got. Fit anyone you know?"

Haden shook his head slowly.

"Not that I can think of. Who saw him?"

"Your step-daughter caught a glimpse of him as he was leaving, and the gardener next door but one saw him drive away in a white BMW with Zurich license plates."

"There can't be too many cars of that description around," Haden said.

"He didn't notice the number," Schlunegger said. "No reason to. And the plates could have been phoney anyway. We tried to trace it, of course, and it seems that a white BMW did cross the frontier at about the right time that morning, but it had Frankfurt plates. Thanks to my colleagues in the Federal Republic," Schlunegger continued, staring at Haden very hard, "we understand that it was a rented car, returned that day. The hirer gave the name of Schmidt, and a nonexistent address."

Stephen Haden studied the ceiling. The convoluted workings of Schlunegger's mind were becoming visible.

"You're ferreting in a blind alley, Franz," he said.

"You had an appointment that morning at 10 A.M.," Schlunegger said, "with someone Carli referred to as Schmidt, although she professed to know nothing about him."

"She doesn't," Haden said.

"Perhaps he arrived early," Schlunegger suggested.

"He didn't," Haden said.

"I was there at 10 A.M. No Schmidt turned up."

"He wouldn't," Haden said. "Not with police cars outside."

Schlunegger said, "You had an appointment with a man known as Schmidt. Someone using the name of Schmidt returns a distinctive car similar to one seen earlier outside your house. In between, you come within a fraction of an inch of being murdered."

Haden said, "It's too simple."

"I'm a simple fellow," Schlunegger said. "I like simple answers."

"The man I was expecting," Haden said, "his name isn't Schmidt." During Karl Kordt's secret visit to Zurich, self-protection required that he remain strictly incognito.

"You astound me," Schlunegger said.

Haden said, "He's not blond, and he's certainly not young. There's no connection."

"Excuse me if I prefer to corroborate that for myself," Schlunegger said. "His real name and address."

Haden shook his head.

"Our business was private and confidential," he said.

"One thing you're not is a bloody priest," Schlunegger said. "All I want to do is eliminate him from the case. So what's the big problem?"

"If you attempted to contact him about me, he could face prison or worse. And he might not be the only one. Where he comes from, I'm an enemy of the state."

"Times have changed. They're letting them out now. Who needs to hire the Mercenary Pimpernel any more?"

"Stop acting naive," Haden said. "All sorts. Special cases. Even those they don't want can wait years for permission."

Schlunegger cocked his head and nibbled his lower lip, before changing track.

"While you've been in here, waited on hand and foot, some of us have been working," he said. "More than two hundred statements have been taken in a dozen cities spread over half Europe. Your associates, your contacts, your so-called 'agents,' except a couple we haven't traced yet, that hooligan Kurt Gabler and Christian Weber. Carli vaguely thinks they might be on holiday." He snorted derisively. "Where are they? Doing their stuff smuggling some poor bastards so you can get even richer?"

Haden shrugged and yawned.

Schlunegger sighed, and resumed. "We've followed up every anonymous tip-off. We've offered a reward for information." He nodded at some newspapers on the bedside locker. "I see you've been reading about yourself."

"Yes. How I opened the front door, let in someone I obviously knew, and was found later, shot several times in the chest, anything between four and six shots. Planted by you, I suppose."

"It saves time later," Schlunegger said, derisively. "Some nut case rings up to confess, I just ask him how many times he shot you. No one's said twice, and in the *back*. The same goes for so-called information. None of it checks out with what really happened. This investigation is in the doldrums. I'm no closer to the blond young man than you are to eternal salvation." He studied the stubby fingernails on his stubby hands.

"No one rang the doorbell," Haden said. "Christa was still in the guest room. I reset the alarm when Carli took the dogs out. So how could anyone have got in?"

"The basement door at the rear of the house was open," Schlunegger reflected.

"That's how he must have left. You said that Christa caught sight of him. Didn't she think it was strange, someone going out the back way?"

"He didn't," Schlunegger said, patiently. "Your stepdaughter saw him as he was closing the front door. She says he nodded to her, and smiled. She thought he'd had an appointment with you."

"That basement door is always kept locked and bolted," Haden said. "If it was open, I'd have heard the alarm."

"It wasn't locked, it wasn't bolted, and the door alarm was switched off," Schlunegger said. "You're a careful man. When did you last check it?"

"I'm not sure," Haden said. It was increasingly difficult to dispel the fuzziness invading his brain. "It's hardly ever used."

"Perhaps the intruder had opened it, intending to leave that way, and your step-daughter disturbed him," Schlunegger said. "I'm still not convinced you're telling me the truth about your man Schmidt."

Haden said, "If I thought it was him, I'd tell you."

"You might have other ideas," Schlunegger said.

"It's *your* job to find the bastard," Haden said, lethargically.

"We'll talk again," Schlunegger said. He stood up. "Unless you find yourself talking to your Maker. The papers say you're worth five million Swiss francs."

"They'll say anything," Haden told him. "You should know that."

Schlunegger said, "I hope you've made your will. Someone went to a great deal of trouble to get you. If you walk out of here, they might decide to try again." He nodded cheerfully. "Take care of yourself."

The shambling yet strangely light-footed man drifted silently away. Haden's drooping eyelids had closed before he had left the ward. Just before he reached the comforting embrace of a deep sleep, a nurse woke him up to take his temperature and blood pressure.

"**H**ey, Rudi," Stephen Haden called. "When do I get out of here?"

He was sitting up in bed, bored with radio, television, and reading. At first when, after overcoming the initial dizziness, he had weaved his way to the bathroom and back on his own, he had been glad to crawl back between the sheets. Now the world outside the windows beckoned invitingly, and bed was no longer a welcome refuge, but an imposed constraint from which his chief ambition was to escape.

Dr. Rudolf Hensler, hailed by Haden as he passed the open door, came in and perched himself amicably on the bed. A kind of friendship had sprung up between the two men, on the patient's side from simple gratitude, and on the doctor's from pride in a prize patient, living evidence of the skill and effort which had confounded all the odds and presented with life a man who should have been dead. Dr. Hensler had quite forgotten that there had been a time when he had despaired. Rudolf Hensler was a wise and clever doctor, but he was only human.

He said, "After what you've been through, you need plenty of rest. Let's think in terms of another week or ten days."

Haden said, "Forget it. This weekend. Final offer, or I release myself tomorrow."

"Well, we'll see," Hensler said, reluctantly. "But whenever it is . . . "

"I know. A long convalescence. I shall go abroad," Haden said. "Florida, Barbados, I don't know. Lie in the sun and do nothing."

"It would be preferable if we continued to see you here," Hensler said. "We're completely familiar with all the possible problems."

"Rudi," Haden said, "when you gave me all that technical garbage, you didn't mention possible problems."

"They may arise from the laceration to the left kidney," Hensler said.

"You said part of it had been removed, and that'd fix it."

"There is the possibility, no more, let me emphasize that, of some further complications. But there's really no point in worrying about something which may never happen, you know."

Haden said, "Never mind the pep talk. Give me the facts. I need to know exactly where I stand."

Dr. Hensler sighed. His ideal patient was a trusting soul who remained within easy reach of the hospital, not one who asked too many questions prior to gallivanting around the world.

"Very well," he said. "As a result of the kidney injury, you may go on to develop hypertension, high blood pressure. If that were very severe, you may require a total nephrectomy, the removal of the damaged kidney."

"Anything else?" Haden asked.

"You could develop kidney stones, which may or may not be a serious problem, depending on the type of calculi which might form. Or the kidney may become swollen, which is known as hydronephrosis. These are the reasons,"

Dr. Hensler said, heavily, "why you will require the most careful follow-up after your discharge, and it would be much better if that took place here. It is essential that you have regular IVPs, kidney X-rays, together with blood tests."

"Put it all down on paper, please, Doc, ready for the weekend," Haden said. "I want to head for the sun."

"Well, it's not ideal," Hensler said, unhappily. "And only on the understanding that you put yourself in the hands of a good local physician at once, who will place you under the supervision of the nearest hospital. I'll recommend a sensible diet for you, and get all the sleep you can. Two or three months, complete rest and relaxation is what you need. No late nights, no undue exertion, no stress. Give your body a chance. It's taken one hell of a hammering. You *must* take extra care of yourself. Do you understand me?" he insisted.

Haden said, "You can be a very convincing fellow, Rudi."

"Well, I'd hate to lose you now," Dr. Hensler said dryly.

"I don't suppose a good cognac will appear on your sensible diet," Haden remarked.

"In the long run we're all dead," Dr. Hensler said. "It depends on whether you'd prefer it were sooner rather than later."

*T*he warm air of early summer brushed Stephen Haden's face as, having shaken Dr. Hensler by the hand and repeated his promises to be a good boy, he walked out of the hospital and climbed into Franz Schlunegger's car.

Schlunegger was in a surly mood.

"They wanted to keep you in," he complained. "What's the hurry? Outside, you're just a nuisance. I gave you fair warning. What do you expect? Police protection?"

"No," Haden said. "I'm going abroad to convalesce."

"Not until we've talked properly," Schlunegger said. "I still think you're withholding information."

He braked, and the car pulled up outside police headquarters.

Two hours later, Haden left with his personal possessions, which the police had retained, including the key to his safe, and took a taxi. Schlunegger was still obsessed with Haden's appointment with the unknown "Schmidt," probably for no better reason than lack of anything else to worry away at, but in the face of Haden's persistent refusal to identify him, Schlunegger had finally given up.

"Oh, get out, you're wasting my time," he had said. "Go abroad. I like the idea. But let me know where you'll be. Just me. In my professional opinion you're a walking target. Don't broadcast your whereabouts is my advice."

Carli's smile was wide, and she hugged him and kissed him on the cheek, while Anton Weiss wrung his hand and slapped him on the back.

"Working overtime, Toni?" Haden inquired. As a rule Weiss preferred to keep his weekends clear.

"Catching up," Anton said. "Things have been rather hectic."

Haden said, "Let's go to the office, and you can bring me up-to-date." He led the way upstairs.

As he walked into the outer office, a momentary irrational shiver of apprehension seized him, and he paused and glanced over his shoulder toward where his assailant must have been waiting.

"Show me exactly where you found me, Toni," he said.

"Just here," Weiss said, indicating.

Haden stared down at the floor.

"We had the carpet cleaned," Carli said, subdued. "The bloodstains . . ."

Haden turned and faced the telex. Behind him, the blond young man had been standing, or perhaps sitting. In his mind, he reconstructed those few seconds yet again, groping for some recollection which might have eluded him until now, some sound, some smell, some forgotten glimpse, anything, no matter how trivial. He stood, willing his senses to search the room as it had been that morning, but from the moment he had bent toward the telex message, he remembered nothing. Not the bullets thudding into his back, not falling to the floor. If a man had approached his body and looked down at him, Haden's eyes had seen no part of him, not his shoes, not his clothes, certainly not his face. After the sheet of paper protruding from the telex machine, there was a blank.

Carli's hand touched his arm.

"Stephen. Are you all right?"

"Fine," Haden said. "I think I'll have a cognac."

"Should you? I mean . . ."

"Approved by the doctor," Haden told her. "He said it would be good for me."

He went into his office, and sat in his padded swivel chair behind the large desk.

"It's good to have you back," Weiss said.

Carli, at the drinks cabinet, glanced her smiling confirmation.

Haden slid open the right-hand top drawer beside him and groped inside. His fingers brushed the cool steel of the loaded automatic which was clipped to the roof of the desk inside the drawer. He took his cheroots from the drawer, and lit one.

Haden sipped his cognac and puffed at the cheroot, while Weiss assembled files and folders, found telex messages and notes of telephone conversations, explained actions taken, results, events in progress.

Haden found that he was experiencing a slight dizziness, due he supposed to the unaccustomed alcohol combined with the cheroot, but it soon passed.

Weiss was saying, ". . . we had so many inquiries after the . . . er . . . incident. Of course, it was in all the West German newspapers, as well as here, and I suppose people . . ."

"At least it was good for business, then," Haden said.

"We thought you'd want us to keep going as best we

could," Anton Weiss said. "But we had to open a new bank account as money came in. We did ask you to authorize us to draw on one of the usual trading accounts when we came to see you, but you seemed not to understand."

Haden shook his head.

"I was in a bad way," he said. "Don't remember that."

"The police took the key to the safe away after they'd examined the contents," Carli said.

"For forensic examination. I got it back today," Haden said.

"I couldn't find the second key anywhere," Carli said. "I tried the bank and the lawyers, but no one knew where it was."

"But you got by," Haden said. The point of a spare key, as he saw it, was that no one knew where it was but himself.

Weiss said, "Once the advance payments came in. Some of our agents are still owed money, however . . ." He glanced at the safe. "They expect to be paid promptly, so now that you're back . . ."

"I shall need that money myself," Haden said. "I'm leaving on Monday for Miami, to recuperate."

"For how long?"

Haden said, "Certainly weeks, possibly months. I'll transfer adequate funds to the new account to keep you going in my absence."

"We shall miss you," Carli said. "But I'm sure it's the best thing."

"The doctor insisted," Haden said. "Perhaps you'd book my flight. Say I'll pick up the ticket Monday morning."

"I'll do it now," Carli said.

She went into the outer office, and Haden heard the murmur of her voice speaking on the telephone.

". . . I believe you had an appointment that morning with a Herr Schmidt," Weiss was saying. "He hasn't called us, but no doubt you know how to contact him should it be a matter which could be dealt with during your absence?"

"That one's gone away," Haden said. "It's too late now." It might not be, but he was no longer interested in Karl Kordt's proposal.

Weiss nodded acceptance and did not refer to it again. He was good at not asking unwanted questions.

*R*udi Hensler's warnings were proving entirely accurate. Already, the day seemed to have lasted an intolerably long time. By nine o'clock, bed was an absolute necessity.

He was lying propped up against the pillows, thinking about the phone call he should make, when Carli came into his room.

"Would you rather be alone?" she asked. "Or . . . ?"

In the shaded half-light of the bedside lamp, she looked very attractive. The observation was a dispassionate one, in which Haden felt no personal involvement.

"I just need to sleep, Carli," he said.

She nodded understandingly.

"Well, I'll say good-night."

"Carli," Haden said. "Where are the dogs?"

"I had to put them in the kennels. I'm just the one who takes them out once a day. I can't have them back while you're away, Stephen. I just can't manage them on my own."

"Good-night, Carli," Haden said.

He lay staring for a while at the floor-length draped curtains. They were used to being in kennels during his absences. They'd be okay.

Carli was right. The two German shepherds tolerated Carli and the others, but they were unswerving one-man dogs. When he was at home, they followed him around, padding at his heels. Had they been with him that morning, they would have torn the blond young man to pieces the moment they saw a gun in his hand, and before he had time to pull the trigger.

He reached for the telephone, dialed his mother's number, and told her that he was leaving at once, on doctor's orders, to convalesce. She was patently glad to hear his voice.

"I'm sorry I couldn't be there when you came out of hospital, but I've been a bit under the weather . . ."

"What's wrong?" Haden asked. "Have you seen the doctor?"

"Oh, yes . . . it's nothing to worry about . . . just the usual aches and pains . . ."

But she went on to tell him about them in detail anyway.

Haden listened, making appropriately consoling noises. His mother often had aches and pains.

". . . still, all that's not important . . . ," she said into the phone. ". . . the main thing is you're so much better . . . do they know who did it yet? . . . so awful . . . he should be made to pay . . ."

"I'm sure he will, Mother," Haden said. "I'll come and see you when I get back."

". . . yes, do, please . . . perhaps you could stay for a while . . . if you're not too busy . . ."

"I'll arrange not to be," Haden said. "Look after yourself." He replaced the receiver and switched off the light. He felt unnaturally weak and listless, strength drained. A good night's sleep would rectify that, he told himself, and from now on he would grow stronger by the day.

What was more tiresome was the lack of clarity in his mind. His usual fast thought processes had deserted him; his brain was working only in lethargic fits and starts.

He had found considerable difficulty in concentrating on Weiss's comprehensive, if somewhat rambling, exposition. Nevertheless, he had a feeling that the new bank account had been skillfully milked to some degree by Weiss, or Carli, or more probably both. Such a feeling might be born of an oversuspicious nature, but he thought not. Nor would he be unduly surprised should such be the case. He would have been more surprised if, with himself safely out of the way, they had not.

For the time being, he had limited whatever damage there might be. So long as they could only get at current income, not too much could leak away. When he returned, he would put matters right, recover whatever they might have siphoned off. Just now, all he cared about was getting away.

Behind closed eyelids, he thought about the blond young man. He assembled a picture from what he had been told. Medium height, well-cut clothes, easy unhurried movements. But the picture was shadowy and incomplete. Stephen Haden yawned, and surrendered to sleep.

The front door of his house was wide open. He could see the dogs looking back at him as Carli drove off with them.

He walked inside. Christa was there. Lipstick glistened redly, her face was a mask of makeup, full breasts overflowed from a tight dress. She looked like an old whore, but he knew it was Christa. She ran downstairs, and he followed her. The basement door was open, and she had disappeared.

He was standing in the hall. He took the gun from his pocket, and clicked his fingers. The dogs appeared. Blood ran from their open jaws.

He walked upstairs. He knew who was up there. The dogs followed him, panting blood-stained saliva, but there was no sound.

He was in his private office looking at the back of a man who was crouched in front of his safe. His head was bare, and his hair was yellow. Haden attempted to raise the gun and aim at his back. The gun was leaden; he could scarcely lift it.

The figure at the safe stood up and turned around. It had no face.

Under the yellow hair was nothing but a parchment-white oval, yet Haden knew that he was smiling.

Haden tried to pull the trigger, but he had no strength: it would not move.

The figure advanced toward Haden, ballooning in size. He was choking, suffocating. With his last breath, he screamed an order to the dogs.

The two animals, bloody jaws agape, turned and sprang at Haden's face.

Stephen Haden came awake in the dark bedroom. Perspiration drenched his face and ran down his chest. His heart raced in pounding thuds as though it would burst through his rib cage. His pillow was wet with sweat.

FOUR

The gardener eyed Stephen Haden with the speculative interest due a man who had traveled to the threshold of death and turned back, and strove to be as helpful as his cautious, inward nature allowed.

He had only recalled the car in retrospect when the police arrived. As for the driver, well, blond hair, certainly, young, well-dressed, but try as he might he had been unable to remember anything else when the police questioned him, nor could he now. His mind had been on his work, and he had scarcely noticed the man at all. The police had shown him all kinds of photographs, but he had recognized none of them.

Stephen Haden retraced his footsteps. The blond young man had walked this way. Haden went back inside the house and fetched the suitcases from his bedroom. The money from the safe was in his briefcase.

Carli saw him as he was coming downstairs, and looked at her watch.

"You don't have to go yet."

"I'm seeing Anna on the way, to say good-bye and to thank her for coming to the hospital."

"Well, I'd better come with you, and bring the car back from the airport."

Haden shook his head.

"I'm leaving it with Anna. You can use the Fiat while I'm away."

Carli's face softened.

"We'll take care of things here. You look after yourself." She hugged him, and then looked at him. "Let us know where you're staying, won't you."

Haden drove to the airline office, where he canceled his flight to Miami. He took the motorway, and crossed the frontier into West Germany. This could have been the route the blond young man had taken. If so, somewhere along it he had stopped and switched the license plates.

Soon enough, if anyone was sufficiently interested to make inquiries, it would come to light that he had changed his plans, but a certain temporary confusion was all he needed. In this instance, Haden agreed with Schlunegger. He was not anxious to broadcast his whereabouts.

After a while, he found the autobahn tiring, with its lurching juggernauts and thrusting, speeding streams of traffic. He turned off, and crossed into France. He had toyed with the idea of going as far as Frankfurt, but he doubted if he would learn anything which Schlunegger had not already gleaned from the Federal police. In any case, to use his contacts in Frankfurt would reveal his whereabouts— and someone had betrayed him; perhaps more than one, knowingly or not. Even by making inquiries at the car-rental office, he would draw attention to himself. He had discarded the notion.

Again, Haden found that he was tiring fast. He stopped in Rheims, found a hotel, went to bed early, and slept for twelve hours. Tomorrow would do.

The following day, he took the car ferry from Calais to Dover, where he chose to show his Swiss, rather than his British, passport. As a Swiss tourist entering the U.K., the formalities were negligible.

In London, Haden opted for a large hotel near Holland Park which, besides the facilities of its kind, possessed the

additional advantages of being well away from the West
End, convenient car parking, and easy exit from London to
the south and west. He registered, entering "British" under
"Nationality," and was shown to his room. When parking
the car, he had removed his gun from its hiding place, and
felt more comfortable now that it was about his person.

Haden did not expect his telephone call to be unreser-
vedly welcomed, and the neutral, guarded tone at the other
end was no great surprise.

"You have recovered, then. I read about it in the German press."

"You once offered to be of service if I needed it," Haden
said.

"Did I? . . . perhaps at the time, yes, but . . ."

Haden said, "Don't spoil it. This evening."

"I have an engagement."

"A drink first," Haden said. He could hear the soft
sound of breathing. "I'll be sitting in the foyer, outside the
dining room. Any time after six."

Haden lay on the bed and dozed. He woke at five-thirty,
and reached for the telephone again.

He listened to the ringing tone for a long time. Eventually, a woman's voice answered.

"Hullo?"

"This is Stephen Haden. Who's speaking?"

"Oh, Mr. Haden, hullo." Surprise underlay her brisk,
businesslike tone. "I'm Mary Turner. We've never spoken
before, I believe."

"No," Haden agreed. "Is Christa there?"

"I'm not sure. Hold on, please."

The phone was put down. Distantly, there was a bubble
of girlish voices, the words indecipherable. Somewhere, a
door banged, and someone called. Haden yawned.

"Hullo. Who is that?"

"Stephen. Didn't she tell you?"

"Sorry, I wasn't expecting to hear from you. I thought
someone was playing a joke." She sounded confused. "I'm a

bit out of breath. I've just run upstairs. Where are you? How are you feeling?"

"Fine. I'm in London."

"London? Why?"

"Business," Haden said. "I thought I'd come and see you tomorrow. About two o'clock. Okay?"

"I wish you could have let me know you were coming." She was ill at ease, her lack of response evident. "How long are you staying?"

"I thought Wednesday was a half day," Haden said.

"It is, but I've arranged to do some extra studying, and it'd be difficult to cancel it now."

"All right," Haden said. "How about Thursday teatime? We'll go out somewhere. Is that allowed?"

"Oh, that'll be fine." She was relieved. "I'll fix it with Mary. See you then. Must rush . . . someone's calling me . . . oh, I'd better give you directions . . ."

"I've got the address," Haden said. "I'll find it."

He hung up. It was like making an appointment with a stranger. Well, that was the way it was.

However, he supposed, since on this occasion he wanted something, he would have to put himself out a bit on Thursday, make an effort.

*I*t was twenty past six when Stephen Haden saw the rather short, overweight man whose stomach stretched his charcoal-gray suit, and whose round face nature had cast in a cheerful, hail-fellow-well-met mold. His eyes skated past Haden as he looked around.

Haden raised his hand, embracing the man and a waiter. A beaming smile creased the affable features as the man crossed to Haden, shook hands damply, and sat down beside him.

"Didn't recognize you at first, Stephen," he said. "Fully restored, I hope?"

"Pretty well," Haden said. The waiter arrived. "Another cognac. What's yours, Harry?"

"Nothing for me, old chap," Harry said. "I can't stay . . . I did explain on the phone . . ." The waiter glided away. "I'm catching a plane first thing in the morning, and it'll be a week or so before I'm back. You were lucky to catch me in London. All go, you know, no peace for the wicked. What brings you here?"

"This and that," Haden said. The disconcerted surprise on the phone had been assiduously banished, but he was talking too much. "I heard you were in town until Wednesday."

"Ah, via my answerphone on Sunday, I expect," Harry said tolerantly. "The one who hung up. I supposed someone had dialed a wrong number. You should have left a message."

"I wanted to talk to you," Haden said. "Not a machine."

"If I'd known you were going to be around, I'd have set some time aside. As it is, I have this rather important appointment, and I'll have to leave soon."

"It won't take long," Haden said.

Harry's eyes followed the waiter as he approached the table. Haden took his glass and lifted it.

"Your continued good health and prosperity, Harry," he said. "How is young Heinz Meyer? Well and happy?"

"I believe so," Harry said, with a courteously disguised touch of impatience. "I hate to rush you, Stephen, I'd love to stay and have a good talk, but I simply can't. You mentioned a service you needed. Could we come to that?"

"We have," Haden said.

*H*arold Leyton had previously figured in Haden's life only as a client by proxy. He had telephoned, and they had met for the first time over dinner in a Zurich restaurant.

Leyton was a sales consultant operating out of London who specialized in trade with the Eastern European countries. An accomplished linguist, he traveled extensively behind the Iron Curtain, had cordial contacts with the state trading organizations in Prague, Budapest, Bucharest, and Moscow, always attended the Leipzig Fair and, a born salesman, did extremely well for himself by acting on behalf of smaller British, European, and American companies who wanted a specialist in the somewhat different marketing skills required. In Dresden, he had got to know a young man called Heinz Meyer.

"I felt sorry for him," Harold Leyton had confided. "Nice chap, but lonely, and unhappy. Familiar story, I suppose," he went on, helping himself to more vegetables. "Divided family. Father got out somehow years ago, but wife and son refused permission to join him. Recently, Heinz's mother died." Leyton waved his fork. "I gather they were very close. He asked me if I would go and see his father the next time I was in Munich. So I did. He's done well. Could afford to pay to have his son with him again. So that's why I'm here. On his father's behalf."

His small eyes peered at Haden hopefully. Haden leaned back, toying with his wine. He had finished eating, sometime before.

"You're often in and out of the D.D.R., Mr. Leyton," he said. "You must have friendly contacts there. Any chance you could pull the right strings?"

"Dear God, I can't get involved," Leyton said, alarmed. "It's my bread and butter, they trust me, I couldn't risk spoiling that. I don't mind being the go-between, but that's all. Using your organization, how much would it cost his father?"

"That depends on how difficult it is," Haden said. "Before I can assess the royalty on such a commission, I need all the details."

Harold Leyton nodded his understanding.

"There could be one minor snag, I suppose." Reluctantly, he pushed his gleaming plate aside. "He's an actor. I don't think he's terribly good, to be candid." He laughed. "Which he knows himself. He's told me he's tired of the whole thing."

"Where does he work? The theater? Movies?" The snag struck Haden as rather more major than minor.

"Neither, very much," Leyton said. "He gets by as an occasional presenter on East German television."

"A well-known face is not an ideal piece of merchandise in my business," Haden said.

"He's not on all that often," Leyton protested. "And is it so important?" He leaned forward intently. "I've seen occasional newspaper items about people you've got out. True, they're pretty cagey about your methods, but don't you often use specially adapted cars? If so, no one's going to see his face anyway."

"The State Security Service over there read the same papers," Haden said. "Even so, with all the traffic over a dozen transit routes, it can still be done . . ."

"Well, fine," Leyton said, eagerly. "Once in the car . . ."

"There's the problem," Haden said. "A pickup point, or a rendezvous, he's liable to be recognized, the car noticed and remembered."

"His father asked me to say," Leyton said quietly, "that if special arrangements were necessary, he'd be willing to pay—within reason, of course."

"Give me some time," Haden had said. "Let me have a photograph of him and I'll look into it."

They had met two weeks later, on a café terrace overlooking the lake, where they drank coffee.

"I've talked to some people of mine who've been there recently," Haden had said. By then, he rarely crossed into East Germany himself. He had become something of a bête noire with the State Security Service. A somewhat indifferent photograph of himself, culled from an old newspaper, hung on a "Wanted" poster at Checkpoint Charlie which offered a reward of 500,000 East German marks for his capture. It was an impressive-sounding sum but, except for citizens of the D.D.R., the currency lacked allure. His original one-man escapades had evolved over a period into a business concerned with the efficient transport of human cargo.

The fieldwork was usually carried out by a team of agents, mostly politically committed young men who were happy to combine a dislike of the communist system with interesting if dangerous work for which they were well paid. Occasionally, one of them got caught, was tried, and sentenced to a long term of imprisonment, anything from seven to fifteen years.

"What do they say?" Leyton asked. "Can it be done?"

"His name isn't well known, but his face is," Haden said. "In the D.D.R., that is. Not elsewhere. Can this Heinz Meyer keep a cool head?"

"Cool describes him," Leyton said. "What will he have to do?"

"Not panic," Haden said. "It'll mean using forged documents, which we'll provide. It's a method I don't much like, as a rule. False papers are only as good as the refugee's nerves. People can get overexcited."

"He's not that bad an actor," Leyton said, smiling. "I have to be in Dresden soon. What can I tell him?"

"The next time he can take a long weekend off without comment," Haden said, "he's to spend it in Prague. No one'll query that. Prague's an okay place for him to go. He won't even need a visa."

Leyton nodded.

"Who does he contact?"

"No one. We'll contact him. He's to wear Western-made clothes, suit, shirt, shoes, everything. He's to carry nothing made in the East. Wristwatch, pen, cigarette lighter, that kind of thing. He'll be given the right props in Prague."

Leyton nodded. "Can I tell his father everything's going to be all right?"

"You can," Haden said. "If he's willing to pay fifty thousand dollars, plus all expenses."

"You mean Deutschmarks," Leyton suggested.

"Dollars," Haden said. "American."

"That's a lot more than he expected," Leyton said

slowly. "I'm not sure he can find that kind of money."

"Up to him," Haden said. "Special case."

"Well, I'll speak to him," Harold Leyton said.

"Let me know," Haden said.

Haden approached a compliant coach operator with whom he had done business before. A price was struck. The date was left open.

Haden met Harold Leyton several times when their paths crossed as they went about their mutual business, at Berne Airport, a hotel in Dusseldorf, and Leyton's office base in London, little more than a cubbyhole, part of a large anonymous suite. The occupants shared reception and secretarial facilities. Evidently Leyton's business did not call for too much paperwork. The portly, cheerful man was friendly, and they progressed to first-name terms. The arrangements progressed too, and finally Haden received a coded telex. The date was fixed.

Haden recalled one of his agents from West Berlin. Christian Weber was about the same general build and age as Heinz Meyer, and facially was not unlike him. The photographs on the forged passports had been carefully doctored to create a resemblance. The blank passports were authentic, cost five thousand marks each, and had been obtained from a reliable if unofficial source in Stuttgart, an underworld trader in such items. They were filled in and suitable stamps added in Zurich.

Haden and Christian Weber traveled to the pickup point in Regensburg, and joined the coach which was taking a group of tourists on a long weekend trip to Prague. The tour was legitimate but, on this occasion, subcontracted to Haden, who provided the driver, one of his own men. Their reserved seats were at the back of the coach, Haden rebuffed any attempts at conversation by his fellow travelers, and Christian passed the journey huddled up in the corner, asleep. The frontier crossing was routine. Coaches were passing to and fro all the time. The passengers were traveling on a collective visa.

Haden and Weber were the last off the coach, and the last to check into the hotel. Thereafter, Christian spent most of the time in his room "with a severe cold."

Haden dutifully saw the sights of Prague, which he knew well anyway. In the evening, he went out for a stroll. After more sightseeing on the second day, he took the air again after dinner. Once certain that still no one displayed any interest in him, he turned into a particular bar, sat down at an empty table, ordered a beer, and idly glanced at his magazine. Ten minutes later, Heinz Meyer walked in, looked around, and crossed to the table where the broad-shouldered man was reading a copy of *Der Spiegel*.

"Would it disturb you if I sat here?" he inquired politely.

Haden shook his head and continued reading. Heinz Meyer asked for a glass of Riesling, sipped it when it arrived, and studied the other customers casually.

"I was here last night," he said softly. "I thought you weren't coming."

"I saw you when I walked past," Haden said. "You were told one evening—not which one."

Heinz Meyer's smile had the attractive confidence of the young. "There is nothing to worry about. I too am careful."

Haden thought that his self-possession had better be justified. He had largely abandoned the use of forged papers since one woman, booked on a flight out of East Berlin and equipped with a carefully contrived cover story and documents, had become flustered at the airport, and been detained by the State Security Service.

Haden took a tourist guide to Prague from his pocket, turned to the street map, and indicated a point roughly halfway between their respective hotels.

"Do you know this street?" he asked.

No one was within earshot of their table. Anyone who happened to be looking at them would see a couple of tourists discussing tomorrow's itinerary.

Heinz Meyer nodded. Haden's finger traced the course of the long, narrow street.

"Start walking in this direction at seven-twenty exactly on Monday morning. Don't be late. We shan't wait. You'll be left behind. Don't be early, either." His eyes rested on Heinz Meyer's gold wristwatch.

"Swiss, and so highly reliable," Heinz Meyer said slyly. "Western clothes, pen, et cetera, et cetera."

"Double-check your pockets before you leave," Haden said. He was beginning to find the young man's tolerant air of cocksureness irritating. "No luggage. You leave everything behind except yourself."

"A pleasant prospect," Heinz Meyer said. "But how? Our mutual friend said you wouldn't tell him. What about my papers?"

Haden closed the guide and returned it to his pocket.

He said, "Just be at the right place at the right time. If I think it's still safe, well and good. If not, there's no harm done, and you can go home again."

"It is not my home," Heinz Meyer said. He was no longer smiling. "I loathe the place."

"Then keep your fingers crossed, or pray, or whatever you do," Haden said. "I'll say good-night."

He pushed his chair back, and stood up.

"Your magazine," Heinz Meyer said.

"I've finished with it," Haden said.

Heinz Meyer said, knowingly, "Then perhaps I'll take it."

He drew the folded copy of *Der Spiegel* toward him. His face changed as the magazine crumpled under his fingers.

Haden bent forward, smiling, and shook Heinz Meyer's free hand, a man saying good-bye to an acquaintance.

"No, Mr. Meyer," he said, in a soft undertone. "You don't take a passport in someone else's name back to your approved hotel, nor wander around Prague with it. Besides, it cost money. If you have to go back after all, it could come in for someone else."

He released Heinz Meyer's hand, and walked out.

On Monday morning, Haden and Christian Weber, luggage packed and ready for collection, left the hotel while the other members of the party were having breakfast. The coach was due to depart at 8 A.M.

They walked along the broad shopping street. Haden carried a briefcase. The early morning traffic was building up. Now and then, they paused, interested in something or another in one of the shop windows.

At 7:20 A.M., Haden paused and lit a cheroot. Christian Weber continued on, and turned into a narrow street some fifty meters ahead.

Haden stood on the pavement, puffing his cheroot reflectively. The pedestrians passing by were in a hurry, and took no notice of him.

He eyed a queue waiting at a nearby bus stop with some reserve, but a bus drew up, and they all climbed on. Those who got off did not linger. The minute hand of his watch was approaching 7:22 A.M. Christian Weber was a reliable and experienced operative. If anything around that corner was not to his taste, it would be Christian who would reappear and not Heinz Meyer.

It was Heinz who entered the shopping street. Haden saw him and turned away. He was glad to notice that Heinz Meyer merely lengthened his stride a little in order to catch up to him, giving no impression of any hurry. They walked along side by side.

Haden was not concerned about Christian Weber, who frequently operated in Czechoslovakia. He would cross into Austria by his own route, using his own papers, and return to West Berlin from there. Christian had the kind of initiative which Haden liked. Engaged to a girl in the West, he also claimed two "fiancées" in East Berlin. One or another of these ladies was used to account for his frequent visits to that part of the divided city. At around 15,000 Deutschmarks and upwards per successful escape, Christian was well-paid. But he earned his money.

The empty coach was outside the hotel. The driver was busy loading the luggage. He did not look at them.

Haden and Heinz Meyer boarded the coach and took their seats at the rear. Haden handed his companion the briefcase.

"Your papers," he said. "Memorize who you are, where you come from, everything."

Heinz Meyer opened the briefcase, and studied the contents. Haden gave him five minutes, and then questioned him closely. Heinz was word perfect. Haden asked to see everything in his pockets, checked them, and was satisfied.

"Do they usually upset tourists by searching them?" Heinz Meyer asked.

"No," Haden said. "Hard currency's important to them. But if suspicions are aroused, they might. It's a precaution; worthwhile, against the risk of some ten years in jail, wouldn't you say?"

Through the window, he saw a few passengers drifting toward the coach. "Go to sleep," he said. "The less your face is noticed, the better."

Heinz Meyer curled sideways in his seat, buried his head in the corner, and feigned sleep. Haden closed his eyes too. He heard the engine start, and the doors close. The coach jolted into motion.

Once the steady, even drumming told him that they were outside the city, he opened his eyes. Most of the other passengers he could see were either sitting blank-faced or dozing after their early start. Haden watched the pleasant countryside pass by.

When the coach ground to a stop at the frontier, they were told to disembark. Haden and Heinz Meyer were last off, and joined the end of the queue inside the adjoining building. The passengers had been counted as they got off; the total checked against the number who had entered the country.

The coach was being searched, including the luggage

compartment, in a routine fashion. Heinz Meyer was breathing steadily and appeared calm.

Haden watched the other passengers as the queue shortened, and those who had been dealt with moved away from the desk and hung about waiting until they were permitted to rejoin the coach.

Most of them were middle-aged West Germans, unlikely to say or do anything untoward, even had any of them noticed that Haden's companion was not the same one with whom he had entered the country. Moreover, he was pretty certain that none of them had got a clear sight of Christian Weber, who had either been sleeping, face covered, or confined to his room, but he studied them carefully anyway. One woman was glancing at Heinz now and then, but Haden decided, from the light in her eyes, that she simply found him an extremely handsome young man.

The coach driver was outside, smoking a cigarette, and engaging one of the frontier guards in cordial conversation.

Heinz Meyer reached the desk, handed over his papers, and answered the questions, which sounded routine, but could catch the unwary—like the woman at East Berlin Airport who, in response to the simple question "Name?" had, from ingrained force of habit, given her real surname. Heinz Meyer's replies, however, were immediate and faultless, and his papers were stamped and returned to him.

A man in the background, however, wearing plainclothes, was eyeing Heinz thoughtfully and moved forward, hand outstretched, before he could return his papers to the briefcase. Heinz was led to one side.

Haden took his place and went through his own formalities, answering casually as though nothing were amiss. Silently, he urged Heinz to keep his self-possession. He could do nothing to help Heinz now. To intervene would only be to draw attention to himself. All he could do was rejoin the coach, and leave Heinz to whatever awaited him. They would know that Heinz must have had help, but they were not likely to detain a whole coachload of Western tourists, and there was nothing immediately to associate Haden with Heinz. Unless, of course, the young man's facade cracked, and he said or did something which would give Haden away.

The coach driver had noticed, and seemed to be suggesting to the frontier guard that time was getting on. They moved together toward the coach.

And then, as he took his papers and turned away from the desk, Haden saw that the object of the plainclothesman's suspicions was the briefcase, which he was probing intently, presumably in search of a false compartment that might contain, for example, some subversive statement to the Western press from a member of the Charter 77 group.

Haden breathed more easily. He could vouch for the innocence of that briefcase. He left the building. The luggage compartment of the coach was closed. The passengers were climbing on board. Haden joined them.

The coach driver started the engine when he saw Heinz coming. Heinz skipped up the steps, and made his way along the gangway. The doors hissed shut.

Heinz squeezed past Haden and sank into his seat. The coach rolled forward, the customs barrier opened, and they were through.

Heinz looked at Haden with raised sculptured eyebrows. There was a peculiar smile on his lips.

At the end of the journey, they collected their luggage. Haden had left his car in a car park nearby. Heinz gazed with interest at the Romantic and Gothic buildings as they passed through and out of the old Imperial German city. After a brief stop later, they drove into Switzerland, which Heinz entered—technically illegally—concealed when they crossed the frontier, and on to Zurich, where the West German Consul's office registered the "fugitive" as an official refugee from the D.D.R. and provided him with the requisite temporary travel documents.

It was of little importance whether a forged passport had

been used or, indeed, the crossing made without any papers at all. West German policy maintained the right to freedom of movement for all Germans, and under West German law, it was not illegal for a German from the Eastern Bloc countries to cross the border.

Official government spokesmen, however, had in the past regretted that commercial enterprises "make their profits from the particularly difficult situation of those affected," adding for good measure, "a business is being made from people's troubles."

Stephen Haden regarded such pronouncements, made in his view more with an eye to official relations with East Berlin than any regard for the refugees, as hypocritical in the extreme. As he saw it, the traffic he and his kind handled largely consisted of those who, for various reasons, stood next to no chance of benefiting from the cumbersome "official" scheme operating at the time between the two Germanies under which West Germany "bought" a restricted number of refugees from the East, with its annual quotas, interminable waiting list, and the effective veto exercised by East Berlin on individual applicants.

Haden saw nothing wrong in providing a short circuit for those whose relatives could afford to pay, or who could borrow the money against expected earnings. Nevertheless, he was forced to recognize as a fact of life that Germany was obliged to live divided, an imperative which perhaps accounted for the decidedly ambivalent West German attitude toward such a "Fluchthelfer" as himself.

There had been other occasions which led those engaged in such "commercial operations" to wonder uneasily if ambivalence concealed downright hostility. It had become known, for example, that a register had been drawn up by the Federal Office in Cologne for the "Defense of the Constitution" of commercial escape helpers and their contacts. Given the existence of such a list, it was perhaps not surprising that a claim appeared in the press that "some people have been denounced by name to the D.D.R." This was forcefully denied, but it remained the case that the "Defense of the Constitution" handed over their findings about escape-aid operations to the Ministry of the Interior, to be passed on to the Chancellor's Office. For what purpose was not entirely clear.

It was largely with an eye to West German official sensitivities that Haden often arranged a detour across Switzerland with refugees, which usually did something to forestall D.D.R. protests against "misuse of transit routes."

The D.D.R. might protest to the Swiss authorities instead, of course, and Berne had let it be known that they were "embarrassed" by Haden's activities and, perhaps with an eye to diplomatic niceties, officially "took a skeptical view" of Haden's ventures on the grounds that they were incompatible with "primary humanitarian interests worthy of protection in accordance with Swiss traditions."

On the other hand, there was no law in Switzerland which forbade escape aid and when, on two separate occasions, the D.D.R. had lodged official diplomatic protests, asking the Swiss government to put an end to Haden's operations, the Swiss Foreign Office had passed them on to the district solicitors responsible in Zurich—but nothing had happened, at least directly.

So long as he was, in practice, left alone, calculated statements, designed to signal official distance from Haden's "commercial enterprise" for consumption outside rather than inside the democratic countries from which they originated, did little real harm. Haden sometimes wondered sourly, though, why his efforts received so little appreciation. Except, of course, from those refugees whom his organization brought out.

Heinz Meyer wore a slightly dazed look when he joined Haden again.

"I can hardly believe it," he said. "I'm free. Free!"

"I thought you seemed pretty confident all along," Haden said.

"That was a front," Heinz said. "An act. Inside . . ." He

took Haden's hand and shook it. "I can't tell you how grateful I am."

"It's what I do, that's all," Haden said. "My trade." They were nearly all like this when they finally realized that they had actually escaped, for good.

"And the people you help . . . like me . . . ," Heinz said earnestly, ". . . nothing's ever said . . . their names . . . where they settle . . . there might still be problems . . . for me, that is . . . I'm sure you understand . . ."

"It remains a completely confidential matter," Haden said. "I need protection too. Harold Leyton's waiting outside. He'll take you to Munich. After that, I forget everything. I've never even heard of Heinz Meyer, much less met him."

Harold Leyton beamed broadly when he saw Heinz, gripped him by the shoulders, and shook him playfully.

Haden stood to one side, watching them. Only one formality remained, and it was done. Harold Leyton came over and provided it, handing over the briefcase which Heinz had used. Inside was the balance owed, twenty-five thousand dollars.

"I've just telephoned his father," Leyton said. "He's beside himself. Sends his grateful thanks. You have mine too. Meyer senior has built up a very nice little export agency. He's offered me exclusive marketing rights in Eastern Europe."

"I wondered what was in it for you," Haden said.

"Everyone wins," Harold Leyton said jovially. "And if I can ever be of service, don't hesitate to let me know."

Haden had not seen Harold Leyton since. Until now.

A woman was sitting alone, abstractedly turning the pages of a magazine. She had come in soon after Harold Leyton, and a part of Haden was conscious of her. Tall and slim, with glossy hair and fine, well-boned features, there was nothing revealing about her fashionable clothes, yet her long crossed legs gave promise of a singularly well proportioned body.

She glanced up, saw that the man she was waiting for had entered the foyer, rose, and walked toward him. Haden watched the way she moved. He was interested to find that she aroused interest in him. It seemed a long time since he had looked at any woman as a woman. Staying alive had been all. It was, he reflected in passing, perhaps a good sign that his eyes had even strayed past the figure of Harold Leyton, that he was even aware of the presence of the attractive stranger.

Harold Leyton said, "What do you want from me, Stephen?"

"An introduction," Haden said.

Leyton leaned his elbows on his chubby knees, and stared across the low table.

"Who? In particular?"

Haden said, "There's a type of fellow who could be a member of some Western underground group happy to do a job for the cause; he could be from the D.D.R., a specialist. There are those who take an interest in such people. One of them, that's who—in particular."

"I'm just a businessman," Leyton said. "Why on earth ask me?"

"In your business," Haden said, "I'd be surprised if you haven't come across one or two."

"I can't afford to get mixed up with people like that," Leyton said. "If some fool starts putting out feelers just because I travel a lot in the East, I run a mile. I'm sorry, Stephen, I can't help you."

Haden said, equably, "I'm a businessman, too, and I'm not much interested in my clients' motives. You can't bank curiosity. I did wonder, Harry, about you, about Heinz Meyer, but it wasn't my concern. Now it is."

"I haven't the first idea what you're talking about," Leyton said, a baffled expression on his mustached moon face. He pulled back his cuff, and looked at his watch. "And I can't wait to find out."

Haden's hand shot forward, clamped Leyton's wrist, and twisted it as he was about to stand up. Leyton drew in breath sharply.

"Two minutes, Harry. You can be two minutes late." He released the fleshy wrist. Leyton rubbed it, his face set.

"I formed an impression about Heinz Meyer. I think that, once he'd got his final West German papers, he joined you here in London. If so, some people might take exception."

Harold Leyton laughed. "How quaintly old-fashioned. Do you imagine anyone cares about my private life?"

Haden said, "Not if they believe he's West German." Harold Leyton was breathing heavily. His cheeks wore an angry flush. Haden continued, "One or two of the West German news agencies might think it worth a few lines, touching story about international businessman who took pity on boy in Dresden and had him smuggled to the West."

"You swore . . . absolute silence . . . ," Harold Leyton breathed, ". . . the contract . . . complete confidentiality . . ."

Haden said, "I'm waiving that clause. Sue me after the story's appeared if you like."

"You bastard," Leyton whispered. "You corrupt, evil bastard."

"Love is a terrible thing, Harry," Haden said. "It can get you into all kinds of trouble."

"I am just a businessman," Harold Leyton said again. "I don't know the kind of people you want."

Haden said, "Ask around. You have until midday tomorrow. If I haven't heard by then, I'll assume you don't care if I talk to the press."

Harold Leyton rose, and walked away. Haden followed him along the foyer, and through the revolving doors. Leyton was climbing into a taxi. Haden held the door open, leaned into the cab, and looked deep into Harold Leyton's eyes.

"Harry," he said. "You just have someone call me. That's all you do. No loose talk to Heinz. You behave, and I won't interfere with your domestic bliss. Do anything I don't like, and it's open house."

Haden slammed the door closed. Harold Leyton leaned forward and spoke to the driver. The taxi turned into the road, and drove off, its diesel engine rattling.

Haden went back into the hotel. He needed another drink. He was gambling on an unproven hunch, that Leyton was a courageous man, his chubby good nature concealing a capacity to resist almost any threat, save in one respect. Haden swallowed his cognac in one, and walked into the dining room. He could not afford to feel sorry for Harold Leyton.

The telephone call came through at eleven-thirty the following morning.

"Mr. Haden? I believe we have a mutual acquaintance . . . ?"

It was a woman's voice, soft velvet American, amusement tinging the rising lilt at the end of the sentence.

FIVE

The London office of the International Information Institute occupied the first floor of a gracious Georgian building, a private mansion in bygone days, and was situated in a quiet square near Curzon Street.

Haden had declined the hotel doorman's offer, "Taxi, sir?" when he emerged from the hotel, choosing to walk toward Holland Park, backtrack along Addison Gardens, cross the road, and take the underpass to Shepherds Bush Underground Station. He bought his ticket and descended the escalator in the knowledge that where he was going was of no interest to anyone.

He got off at Marble Arch, turned off Park Lane, and strolled in the warm sunshine along the streets of Mayfair and into the square. Inside, the porter, his desk incongruous in the magnificent entrance hall, inquired politely if he had an appointment, verified it on one of his telephones, and directed him. Haden walked up the grand, sweeping staircase, and into the discreetly indicated reception office, where he was asked to wait.

Considerable pains had been taken to preserve the original fabric. The Conference Room to the right of the armchair in which Haden was sitting retained the huge double

•

doors which had once led, he supposed, to the drawing room, and the furnishings were chosen to blend with the paneled walls. But within all that was the busy atmosphere of any office, anywhere, with all its trappings.

The double doors of the Conference Room opened slightly. Haden heard the velvet American voice say, "Frank, I feel we have to look at that Rome material again," and she came out, closing the doors behind her.

Haden stood up, and took her outstretched hand, as she turned toward him.

"Mr. Haden, I'm Helen Lloyd. I'm sorry to have to keep you waiting, but my meeting is running late."

She seemed smaller and younger than last night's stranger, perhaps thirty or a little over, but even more striking. She wore her dark hair short, and either no makeup or so skillfully applied that it did not show, and no jewelry of any kind. Her eyes were hazel, her nose delicately straight, her mouth wide and full, although her welcoming smile had something impish about it. Her expensive blouse and skirt might have been an executive uniform on most women; on Helen Lloyd, with her erect carriage, tapering waist, and slender legs, it looked like it had been created for her. He released her slim, firm fingers.

"It's all right," Haden said. "I've nothing else to do."

"Fine," Helen Lloyd said. "I'll try to get through soon. My secretary will look after you. Stephanie, would you arrange that, please?"

The receptionist nodded, and spoke into a phone briefly. Helen Lloyd went back into the Conference Room.

Moments later, a fresh-faced, youthful, tailored Englishman appeared, introduced himself as Jeremy, Helen's secretary, and inquired solicitously if Haden would like tea or coffee, or perhaps some particular Institute publication. Haden declined all offers, and the young man returned to his office.

Haden sat and waited. Stephanie, a statuesque girl who sounded like an efficient Sloane Ranger, answered telephones, took messages, transferred calls, and typed in the brief intervals. Jeremy had left his office door open, and Haden could see him using a word processor. Another visitor arrived for an appointment with the Director, and was at once ushered along a corridor.

After twenty minutes, Helen Lloyd reemerged from the Conference Room and closed the doors decisively behind her.

"Okay, Mr. Haden," she said. "They can get along without me now."

"Messages, Helen," Stephanie said.

Helen Lloyd took the message slips, separated them at a glance, and handed them back to the receptionist.

"Jeremy can deal with those. These two I'll handle later. I think I deserve a break." She turned to Haden. "Suppose we go and have tea at the Dorchester?"

They walked along side by side, while Helen Lloyd conversed, easily and naturally, about nothing very much. Not for the first time, Haden reflected that most Americans seemed to have a remarkable gift for small talk.

"What does the International Information Institute do?" he inquired, as they paused at some traffic lights before crossing.

"We're a commercial information and research organization," Helen Lloyd said. "I'm assistant to the London director."

"Is that how you know Harold Leyton?"

"Harry's an occasional client," she said. "We believe he has potential."

"He's not short of money now," Haden remarked.

They made it across the road.

"I've never met a businessman yet who didn't want to grow."

"Is tea obligatory?" Haden asked.

"No," she said glancing at him. "It's somewhere to talk without telephones ringing."

"They don't ring in Hyde Park, either," Haden said.

Once across Park Lane it was surprising, as they walked on the grass deeper into the park, how quickly the constant grumble of the six lanes of traffic faded into little more than a background murmur. A good many Londoners had had the same idea: the grass was sprinkled with sunbathers in various stages of undress, but the great park easily absorbed them all, and there were plenty of open spaces.

"Have you worked in London long?" Haden asked.

"Three years, after spells in Bonn and Paris. Originally, I studied languages and history, did some postgraduate work after my master's degree, considered an academic career, but the opportunity with the Institute came along at around the same time, so here I am."

From a European, such an unsolicited C.V. would have carried with it more than a hint of bragging. From this quietly contained American, it was a mere casual statement of fact. He glanced from side to side.

"What are you looking for?" she asked.

"An unoccupied seat," Haden said.

"What's wrong with here?"

She sank onto the grass carelessly, and leaned back on her elbows.

Haden sat beside her, hugging his knees. Their nearest neighbors were two teenagers, lying alongside each other, clamped together.

"Maybe we should move," Helen Lloyd said, her eyes following his gaze.

"They don't even know we're here," Haden said. The couple were well out of earshot.

Helen Lloyd turned her face to the sun, and closed her eyes.

"This is nice," she murmured. "But I do have to return a couple of calls this afternoon."

"How much do you know about me?"

"I scan the West German press. It's part of my job. You're a *Fluchthelfer*."

"Anything else?"

"Someone tried to kill you in Zurich, not long ago."

"I want to know who," Haden said.

She opened her eyes then, and turned her face toward him.

"That's what this is about?"

"I doubt if Harold Leyton misunderstood me, Miss Lloyd," Haden said.

She let the implication pass.

"The Swiss police are very highly regarded. They won't let an attempted murder case drop."

"Switzerland's neutral," Haden said. "The information I need will probably have to come from a source which isn't."

"This conversation has taken a really unexpected twist," Helen Lloyd said.

It was Haden's turn to let something pass.

"The police have no good description of the man concerned. I may be able to get hold of a rather better idea of his general apearance . . ."

"How?" she asked.

"It doesn't matter. With luck, it might just be good enough for the right person to suggest a few possible candidates."

"If you can get a description of him, why not simply give it to the police?"

"Miss Lloyd," Haden said, "by your own account, you're a very bright lady. The kind of files it might be compared with are in other hands."

"I see," Helen Lloyd said. "Or I think I do. But if so, why should these other people help you?"

Haden said, "I'm looking for an unofficial contact. Money might be a good reason."

Helen Lloyd laughed, with a mixture of amusement and puzzlement.

"This is getting to be like *Alice Through the Looking*

Glass. Suppose you did find a White Rabbit who could help to identify the man who shot you, what then?"

"He knows me," Haden said, "but since we didn't get to meet face to face, I don't know him. I'd like to, that's all."

"Up to that point, you've been fairly convincing," Helen Lloyd said. "If more than a little bizarre. Or perhaps I mean irrational. Does it occur to you that you're trying to fish in dirty waters? And that could be dangerous?"

"There's a Swiss copper called Franz Schlunegger," Haden said. "He's no friend of mine, but he knows his job. He thinks they'll try again. I may have less to lose this way."

"You could lose your life."

"Everyone does," Haden said.

"Who are 'they'?"

"I want to know that, too," Haden said.

"What I can't understand," Helen Lloyd said, "is why Harry Leyton involved me, for God's sake?"

"I asked him for a contact," Haden said. "You phoned me. That's all I know."

She shook her head.

"Harry has a weird sense of humor. Or else he was trying to pass the buck, get you off his back." She glanced at him sideways with a smile which had passed from impish to the verge of mocking. "If that sounds insulting, I'm sorry."

"Harry didn't think it was in the least funny," Haden said. "And I believe he knows better than to try and evade my request." Helen Lloyd did not reply, and he studied her face in the silence. "Are you an *Alice* buff?" he asked. "Your smile lingers, like the Cheshire Cat's."

"Are you surprised? You talk quite matter-of-factly about an absurd topsy-turvy world. 'Off with his head!' Presumably, you believe it, but Harry's got it wrong," Helen Lloyd said flatly. "I'm certainly not in touch with the sort of people you're after." The trace of a frown touched her eyes. "Unless . . . I wonder . ..."

"Unless what?"

"There are FBI men stationed at the American Embassy," Helen Lloyd said slowly. "I've gotten to know one of them at various embassy functions. I may have talked about him, I can't remember. Do you suppose that's what Harry had in mind?"

Haden said, "If that's all you can think of."

"I must go," Helen Lloyd said.

She stood up quickly. Haden got to his feet as well.

"I'll walk you back to the office," he said.

"Women have the vote in Switzerland these days, I believe," Helen Lloyd said. "They're also quite capable of walking alone, you know. I'll say one thing about this afternoon; it's been different."

"I'll phone you tomorrow morning," Haden said.

"I shan't be in the office," Helen Lloyd said.

She turned and walked away, skirting the oblivious teenagers.

Haden watched her until her supple figure grew small. He made his way across the park to Bayswater Road, and hailed a taxi.

He watched the shops and restaurants of Notting Hill Gate pass by, and felt discouraged. He thought of Harold Leyton, who would be in Budapest by now, and wondered whether to ring Der Spiegel, whose London office was in the Daily Telegraph building, as soon as he got back to the hotel.

He paid the driver, went inside, and collected his key. He was not expecting any messages, and there were none. In his room, he eyed the telephone, and decided to have a cold shower instead.

He had no faith in the FBI man, but there was always the other, if unlikely, possibility. The phone call could wait for twenty-four hours.

As he stepped under the shower, as cold as the water was the chill reflection that his guesswork about Harold Leyton could have been wrong from beginning to end.

*I*t was another fine, warm day. Just before noon, Stephen Haden put in a personal call to Helen Lloyd at the International Information Institute. She was not in the office. He left it until just after three o'clock before trying again. The result was the same. This time, he left a message, saying that he would be out for a while, but expected to be back around seven.

Once on the M.3 motorway, he made good time. North of Basingstoke, he turned off and drove along the tangle of minor roads he had memorized. He overshot the lane outside the village and had to turn back, but when he parked outside the large mullioned windows, he was still early.

Trees shaded the paths which led to the scattered low classroom blocks. He could see the sports fields, beyond which were wooded hills. It was a pleasant scene.

Haden went into the main building, at one time, apparently, some rich man's country house, found the school secretary's office, and made his presence known, after which he wandered around, killing time.

The central feature was a mock baronial hall in which now stood two ping-pong tables. Behind the closed doors of the music room someone was playing the piano. At the rear, glass doors opened out onto a balustraded terrace overlooking formal gardens. The fees for Christa's education began to seem less extortionate. Haden could see where the money went.

To one side of the French windows was an open area, where pictures hung in neat, methodical rows. Haden glanced at them casually. They were a mixture of water colors, oils, and pen and ink, and ran the gamut from conventional to challenging abstract. Each bore a gold star, and a name, "Roger Ellis, 6th Form," "Andrea Pearson, 3rd Form," and so on, an exhibition of pupils' outstanding work.

Haden paused at two of them, and was studying them

more closely, when a short, round woman bustled in.

"Mr. Haden? I'm Mary Turner. She'll be along in a few minutes, but I think we should have a chat first."

"How do you do," Haden said. She had a pleasant if unremarkable face, and was younger than she had sounded on the telephone, still in her twenties.

"I see you've found her portraits."

"Yes." Both were head and shoulders, one done in pen and ink, one in oil pastels. The former was of a boy, his face serious, the features lean, hair falling over his forehead; the latter was softer and more romantic, an exceptionally pretty, smiling young girl. "They seem pretty good to me."

The discovery was a surprising one. He had no idea what her abilities might be.

"She has a considerable talent for art," Mary Turner said. "But her talents are less apparent in other directions. Her oral German is excellent, as one would expect, but her grammar lets her down badly in her written work. The same is true of her English. Math, slapdash, she won't work at the basics. Science, she enjoys the practical work, but skates over the theory. I could go on. She is not doing herself justice, Mr. Haden."

Mary Turner was gazing at him sharply, as if she expected some response. From her point of view, of course, Haden was a visiting parent, if only of the proxy kind, and presumably concerned.

"It's early days," he said. "She's only fourteen."

"When she should be establishing the groundwork for the future," Mary Turner said tartly. "She's a very nice girl, well-behaved and cooperative in the House. Unless we're all mistaken, she also has considerable academic potential, but she quite simply is not working hard enough, Mr. Haden. Unless she changes her attitude, she will not gain the results of which she is capable."

"I think she realizes that, Miss Turner," Haden said, hoping to placate the woman. Why was this blast being directed at him? It was not his responsibility. "I had intended to come and see her yesterday afternoon, but she had some extra studying to do."

"The only thing she was studying yesterday afternoon," Mary Turner said, "was biology in the woods." Her eyes flickered toward the pen-and-ink portrait of the boy.

Somewhere outside was the sound of voices and laughter, the girls' high-pitched, the boys', in the course of breaking, hoarse. Lessons must be over. Where the hell was Christa? Did this determined female imagine that what she was talking about had something to do with him?

"While she's here, you're responsible for her welfare, Miss Turner," he said. "I'm sure you have firm views on the subject."

"Indeed," Mary Turner said. "I myself don't believe that indiscriminate sex between children is in their own best interests. We keep them under supervision but we are not their parents, Mr. Haden. This school is not a receptacle for the children of broken marriages, even if it sometimes feels like it."

"I don't see her very often, Miss Turner," Haden said. The woman was like a battering ram. "She lives with her mother, naturally. I'm only her step-father."

"Yes, but you're here, so I'm having a go at you," Mary Turner said, with a sudden disarming smile. "I'd speak in the same way to her mother, but she hasn't found it possible to visit her yet."

"She does live in Switzerland," Haden pointed out.

"So do you," Mary Turner said. "I know you're in England on business, but at least you've taken the trouble to come and see her." She sighed. "I'm aware of the difficulties," she said. "But as I understand it, she was only four years old when you married your wife. She never sees her real father. You're the only father figure available." She paused, and looked up at him speculatively. "Do you know that she's very proud of you, Mr. Haden?"

"Me?" He shook his head. "No."

"She talks about you sometimes," Mary Turner said. "She is. When her mother telephoned to say that you were going to recover, she cried."

From the direction of the hall, there was the sound of hurried footsteps on the floorboards.

Mary Turner moved to the open door and called. "Your step-father's in here."

Christa came in pink-faced, clutching a large, flat folder.

"I hope we'll meet again, Mr. Haden," Mary Turner said. "Good-bye."

She smiled at Christa and walked away, her heels clicking busily.

Christa blew a stray wisp of hair away from her mouth.

"Sorry . . . I've been finishing something off in Art, and I forgot the time . . ." She indicated the folder. "I'll just take this up to the dorm . . . shan't be long . . ."

"Bring it with you," Haden said. He took her slender arm. "Let's go."

Outside, they walked toward the Mercedes. Some boys and girls wearing jeans and T-shirts were perched in a row on a low brick wall like so many inquisitive birds. Haden recognized one of the boys.

"Who's the serious-looking youth with the hair?"

"Paul. I said you might let him come with us."

"Not today," Haden said. "Get in."

The car drifted easily along the winding drive, toward the lane.

"He was hoping to meet you," Christa said. "He thinks you're a sort of Robin Hood."

Haden laughed.

"There's more profit in robbing the rich than the poor," he said. "Robin Hood was probably a good thief with a better P.R. man."

"I like to think that it might have been true," Christa said. "Helping the victims of tyranny."

"If so, I expect it was for his own ends," Haden said. "Your Miss Turner cornered me. I had quite a lecture."

"I thought she might," Christa said. "She's all right, though. She means well."

"Do you like it at this school?" Haden asked.

"Yes," Christa said. "It's fun."

"Her boiled-down message is," Haden said, "that there should be more work and less fun."

He was satisfied that he had done his duty, more in fact than the circumstances demanded. Christa's future was her mother's problem.

Christa was sitting gazing silently through the windshield. He wondered briefly what was going on in her mind. Recollections of biology studied in the woods? Perhaps because, although tall for her age, she was delicately slender, her breasts, although forming, little more than a gentle swell as yet even when she wore a sweater, Mary Turner's implication had taken him by surprise. That the Christa who had peripherally entered his life as a doll-like little girl in ankle socks might be crossing the threshold into womanhood had never entered his mind. He studied the idea in a detached fashion as they sped along a stretch of dual carriageway, and disposed of it into some mental dustbin. That was definitely her mother's business.

"Where are we going?" Christa inquired.

"Frensham Ponds."

"Oh, good, I like it there. Paul's father took us one Sunday. He's a TV director. Paul's going to be in the school play next year. He thinks he might like to be an actor, but he's brilliant at science as well, so he's not sure." Abstractedly, she smoothed the neat dress she was wearing, presumably in honor of the occasion. "The cream cakes were lovely," she said reflectively.

Haden parked outside the hotel beside an inlet from the lake, and got out.

"Bring that with you," he said, indicating the folder on the back seat.

"Why? It's only my sketchpad and things."

"Bring it," Haden said.

They were served tea at a table outside on the terrace overlooking the sunlit expanse of water, surrounded by sandy pine-clad dunes. Christa was able to cope effortlessly with strawberries and cream, delicate sandwiches, a chocolate eclair, and, finally, a cream doughnut. The appetite of the active young was a wonderful thing.

"Ooh." She dabbed her lips with a napkin, and smiled at him with simple pleasure. "That was wonderful. Thanks, Stephen."

"I'd like you to do something for me in return," Haden said. "Tell me about the young man you saw the day I was shot."

Her smile faded. With care, she folded her napkin.

"I try not to think about that." Momentarily, she wore the vulnerable look of a small child. "It was only for a second or two, I hadn't been up long, I'm never properly awake until I've had a shower . . ."

"Until today, I hadn't realized you were something of an artist. Could you draw his face for me?"

She thought for a moment, and then closed her eyes.

"I don't know," she said, slowly, her eyes still closed.

"Have a try," Haden said.

"Why? For the police?"

"It might help," Haden said, "in tracking him down."

"Well, all right. Don't look, though, in case it turns out to be a mess."

Haden shook his head, and leaned back in his chair. Christa took a sketchpad, a pencil, and a soft eraser from her folder. She turned sideways in her chair away from him, balanced the pad on her knee, and bent over it.

The English climate was on its best behavior, the sky uncommonly, almost Mediterranean deep blue, its usual trace of milkiness, even on a fine day, absent for once. The still waters reflected the bright sun in glittering shimmers, and Haden put on his sunglasses.

In the distance, small dinghies with multicolored sails were tacking slowly across the lake, sometimes losing the gentle breeze and drifting, sails flapping. A little nearer, on the broad stretch of dunes, families were sunbathing, while toddlers splashed in the shallow water, their excited cries scarcely audible from the terrace. The idea of attempted murder in cold blood, of killing in return, seemed very remote.

Christa ripped a page from her pad, and crumpled it.

"False start," she said. "Trying to be too clever."

"More tea?" She shook her head. Haden drained the teapot for himself.

"You look different," Christa said.

"The sunglasses, I expect."

"No. You've lost weight. Your face is thinner. And without your mustache . . ."

"It came off in hospital," Haden said. "Like the weight. I decided I could do without both."

"Oh, it suits you. You look younger."

She went back to her sketchpad. Haden smoked thoughtfully. He too had reached the conclusion that the missing mustache, the leaner features, the lost weight, had modified his appearance to a slight degree which could yet be significant—although the reflection in the mirror was always going to be the face of Stephen Haden to him, no matter how it changed or aged. Christa's casual remark, though, was of considerable interest. Someone to whom he had never spoken, and knew him less well, might possibly fail to recognize him immediately. One day that moment would come. A man with only one objective in life, given sufficient money and determination, a man careless of the consequences, such a man, in Haden's estimation, was likely to achieve his aim, eventually.

Meanwhile, he could only take one step at a time, and hope that any false starts might be as temporary and fleeting as Christa's had evidently been.

She was working busily now, bent over her pad, absorbed, her hair falling over her face, sometimes brushing it aside impatiently, sketching, using her eraser, sketching again.

Haden could see nothing of Anna in the girl, either in appearance or in nature. From what little he knew of her real father, now thought to be resident somewhere in Brazil for good reasons of his own, while she might have inherited something of his good looks, he doubted if that dubious individual had contributed anything to her character. The permutation of genes could produce surprising results.

Christa straightened up, held the pad before her at arm's length, and studied it doubtfully.

"Is Paul your boyfriend?" Haden asked.

"Mmm. Sort of. He has problems. I try and give him advice."

Haden suppressed a smile.

"What kind of problems?"

"Parent problems. A lot of kids do. That's the best I can manage."

Haden took the sketchpad and looked at it.

"It's not much more than a cartoon, really," Christa said, defensively.

The face was that of a young man, head half-turned, as if gazing out of the paper. The lips curved in a small, polite smile. A few deft lines and a little shading indicated that he was very fair. It was a face not easy to describe in words, the kind that would merge easily into a crowd. And yet . . .

"I'd know him if I saw him," Haden said.

"Do you like it?" Her eyes lit up with pleasure.

"It's marvelous," Haden said. "Congratulations."

Eagerly, she pulled her chair around the table and sat beside him, bending over the pad, pointing. He could smell the faint fragrance of her hair.

"The first time, I tried to do him full face. That's why I went wrong. I only saw him for a moment, and from this angle. When I concentrated, as if it were an exercise for Terry—that's my art teacher—I found that I could *see* him, even though I couldn't describe him. But only like that. I couldn't do him full face, or profile."

"It's not how he looks," Haden said.

She stared at him, her eyes puzzled and hurt, like those of a dog rebuked for no reason.

"You just said . . . ," she began.

"It's how he looked then," Haden interrupted. "Christa, he thought I was dead. He ran into you. He smiled as if he belonged there, and walked out. He didn't care that he'd been seen."

"Oh, you mean he'd changed his appearance."

"I believe so."

"Then trying to draw him was a waste of time," Christa said, discouraged.

"I'm not talking about anything melodramatic like stage makeup. Was his hair really blond, for instance?"

"I don't know," Christa said, still put out.

"Suppose his hair was dark? Suppose he usually wore a beard? Things like that."

Christa's expression lightened. She became interested again.

"May I . . . ?"

She took the sketchpad and began doodling small outline faces in the margin.

"Or . . . ," Haden said slowly. Christa's sketch had done much to change the abstract concept of a blond young man into a series of possible living human beings, based on the single glimpse she had caught of him. With that advance in perspective had arrived a possibility which had not occurred to him before. ". . . might he have been rather older than you thought he was?"

Christa shook her head definitely.

"That's how he looked," she said.

"Have you ever seen a man who usually wears a hairpiece, when he takes it off?"

She grasped the idea at once, and giggled delightedly.

"I like it! I love it! Just a minute."

A few quick, bold lines appeared on the cartridge paper, some rapid shading, and she showed him the result, proudly.

"Brilliant," Haden said softly.

It was little more than an impression, smaller in size than a cigarette packet, the face outlined with the indication of a smile, recognizably derived from the same subject. But now the fair hair was dark and receding halfway to the crown, giving him a very high forehead. It was the face of a man well into his thirties.

"Give it to me, and I'll do him again properly," Christa said, her hand outstretched eagerly.

"It's time I took you back to school," Haden said.

"Already?" She looked at her wristwatch. "God, I didn't realize . . . "

Haden gave her his car keys.

"You go and get in. I'll pay the bill."

He tucked the sketchpad under his arm, met the waitress as he entered the hotel, paid her, walked on through to Reception, and spoke to the girl behind the desk. She nodded agreement, took the sketchpad, and disappeared into the inner office.

When she came back, Haden thanked her warmly, pocketed the photocopy, went outside, and slid into the car, now uncomfortably hot after standing in the sun.

Christa handed him the keys and spoke at the same time as he was settling himself behind the steering wheel.

"I've been thinking. What I could do is a whole series of sketches, different ones, how he might look, with a beard or mustache or without, balding or not, and so on. Would that help, do you think?"

Haden gave her the sort of smile she deserved, and the sketchpad. This girl required no persuasion. She had become fascinated and intrigued by the whole thing.

"You're a honey," he said.

"How soon do you want them?"

"As soon as possible," Haden said.

Stephen Haden chose the A.3 back to London. He was in a mood to take his time. He felt both exhilarated and oddly relaxed. The exhilaration was easily accounted for; the day had proved far more promising than he had expected. For the first time, the tantalizing veil which separated him from the blond young man had, if not parted, at least thinned a little, like drifting fog, revealing a vague shape which, if Christa's enthusiasm persisted, could soon become more clearly defined.

The other feeling was less easy to analyze. He had positively enjoyed the afternoon for some curious reason, in a way which was unlike any other sense of pleasure he could recall.

He was prodding at this curious phenomenon when he became aware that there was a cream-colored Ford Sierra in his rearview mirror some distance behind, that it could have been there for some time, and that he did not know for how long.

For a while, he watched it as he allowed his speed marginally to increase. The Sierra dropped back a little, but did not disappear from view.

There was a filling station coming up. Haden suddenly at the last moment braked and pulled in beside the pumps. The Sierra went past as he was getting out, too fast for him even to distinguish if the driver was a man or a woman. The Ford had accelerated hard.

When his tank was full, Haden pulled into the car park of the adjoining Little Chef restaurant and killed half an hour eating a steak and salad before driving on.

He saw no similar Sierra nor, as he made his way into London by an indirect route, did any other car become attached to him, the second of the pair which might be expected, but he was irritated and annoyed with himself.

The chances were that the Sierra was just another innocent vehicle, but he had not seen it early; his concentration
had lapsed. He could not pursue his quest without revealing
where he was to those he had no reason to trust, which
included Harold Leyton and Helen Lloyd.

No car had tailed him to the school, he was confident of
that, which almost certainly made his nervousness about
the cream Ford Sierra a symptom of mild paranoia. Almost
certainly, but not quite. Which school his step-daughter attended was hardly a state secret. Suppose it was known that
he had traveled to England, but not where he was staying?
Might "they" have placed Christa under surveillance, in
case he contacted her? Would "they" go to so much
trouble?

Stephen Haden possessed a considerable degree of self-
awareness. He knew that ninety-nine percent of the time
he saw danger where none existed. He did not keep cats in
view of his dogs' disposition to regard them as natural prey,
but he identified with them. He recognized the nervous
caution, eyes and ears alert, bodies tense, the creeping war-
iness of movement ready for instant avoiding action, the
conviction that danger lurked behind every unfamiliar object no matter how seemingly innocent.

Haden reversed into a space in the car park and walked
into the hotel. In his business, risks were of the essence,
neutralized so far as was humanly possible by a ruthlessly
exercised degree of caution. This, Haden believed, given his
hazardous trade, was why he was still around. But only just
still around. On the morning when it had mattered, he had
failed to detect danger, lulled by familiar day-to-day routine. His antennae had not responded to any signals, diverted perhaps by the mild irritant of Christa's unexpected
arrival, and his mind's attention on the forthcoming interview with Karl Kordt, the "Schmidt" who had not turned
up. "Schmidt" was the one among several who had known
exactly where he would be that morning. "Schmidt" had

insisted that 10 A.M. was the only time when he could meet Haden. "Schmidt," with his financially attractive proposition, could have been part of the whole careful setup.

There were no messages. Haden took his key and turned away.

Helen Lloyd was sipping a drink in a corner outside the bar, where she could see the elevators. Haden sat down beside her.

"You said seven o'clock," she said accusingly. "I'd nearly given you up."

"My psychic powers are limited," Haden said. "I didn't know you'd be here."

"Then why leave messages? What kept you?"

"Traffic," Haden said. "The M.4 was up. My grandparents used to live near Reading. I didn't meet them until I was grown up. They're both long since dead, of course. But I always liked it there. I thought I'd go and have another look."

His eyes rested on hers as she listened. Making such a sentimental journey had not crossed his mind. But all he could detect was a trace of impatience; not so much as the tiniest flicker or waver betrayed that she might know otherwise.

"I don't like waiting," she said.

Haden said, "I'm here now." This was a subtly different Helen Lloyd, but all women were chameleons, he had long ago decided. She finished her Campari and put the glass down. "Another one?" Haden asked.

Helen Lloyd shook her head.

"I suggest we either have dinner or go to your room," she said.

"I've eaten," Haden said.

"Fine. I'm not hungry. I'd rather go to bed anyway."

Haden regarded her curiously. The mocking amusement had returned to her eyes.

He said, "Someone changed the rules when I wasn't looking."

"The rules are very simple. That's my inclination. What's yours?"

"My inclination," Haden said, "is to wonder why."

"Why what?" She seemed to be enjoying herself. "Women have desires as well, you know."

"There should be an award for the most blindingly obvious statement of the year," Haden said.

"Debating tricks cut no ice with me," Helen Lloyd said. "If equality means anything, women should be free to make up their minds, too."

"They always have been," Haden said, "short of rape, which was never in the cards, I promise you. It's known as saying 'yes' or 'no.'"

Helen Lloyd laughed delightedly.

"A response truly worthy of being preserved in aspic," she said. "I'd say you put yourself about when you feel like it. But now you're embarrassed. You're not used to a woman asking you, I guess."

"They do it all the time," Haden said. "For money."

"I don't insult easily," Helen Lloyd said mildly. "Stop being defensive."

"Curious," Haden corrected. "We met once, we shook hands, we talked for half an hour. Suddenly, I'm someone a clever and beautiful woman wants to climb into bed with. Pretty but dumb, or clever but desperate, I might buy. It's the combination bothers me."

Helen Lloyd sighed.

"Pretend our eyes met across a crowded room and not a word was spoken, if it makes you feel better," she said. "Listen, I'm thirty-two years old. For reasons which don't concern you, I've been celibate for quite a while. I am in fact choosy. I find you, physically, a very attractive man. Also, interesting. The Horay Henrys who infest this town I can do without. You're a male chauvinist, sexist to the core, but since I don't have to live with that, it's just amusing. In short, an agreeable sexual attraction is present. On my part, anyway. You either share it, or you don't. I am not asking to be serviced. Mutual enthusiasm is required, but if lacking, will not be taken amiss. So get off the fence. I don't propose to sit here and argue about it any more."

Haden laughed.

*H*e came out of the bathroom, and slipped into bed. The sun had declined behind a rim of cloud, but the curtains were not drawn, and fading daylight entered the room.

Her face, dark-framed by her hair on the pillow, was serious, incredibly innocent, and lovely in the half-light. She reached out a hand, her fingers, gossamer light, touched his body.

"Your scars," she murmured.

For a while, he just looked at her, taking in the perfection of her, while her fingers traced the thin, whitish lines. Then he bent over her, a hand cupping one breast, and they kissed, lips tentatively exploring at first, becoming familiar. He felt the nipple stiffening into his palm.

She twisted, ducked her head, and began to kiss his body.

"Those scars . . . ," she whispered again.

She kissed them in turn, her tongue following each line, while with mouth and fingers he explored her magnificent body.

" . . . those awful scars . . . "

He paused for breath.

"The doctors were very proud of them," he told her. "Model scars. Healed splendidly."

"No . . . ," her voice said indistinctly. ". . . no . . . terrible . . . "

She twisted again, and lay back. She seemed moved. Her wide eyes were misted. Her arms lifted and embraced him. Her lips opened.

Pounding heartbeats slowed. The soaring dizziness

passed. Breathing was easier. Outside, the lights of the city glowed.

"You need a shave," she said. "My face will be raw in the morning."

"You should have made an appointment," he said. "I'd have attended to it."

She switched on her bedside lamp, turned, and looked at him. Her eyes were dark pools in which glimmered tiny lights.

"Let's do it again," she said.

Something half woke him. Outside the night sky was black, but there was sufficient reflected light for him to see the shape emerging from the bathroom. Still befuddled by sleep, it took a moment or two to remember where he was, who the woman was. She was fully dressed.

"Where are you going?" His mouth was dry, the words drowsily blurred.

"Home. I like to wake up in my own bed." He groped for the light switch. "Don't turn on the light." She sat on the edge of the bed, and took his hand.

"I'll come down with you. See you into a taxi."

"No. Stay where you are. I don't need an escort." Her fingers interlocked with his. "I did speak to my friend. He can't help, personally. He said it's no use going through channels."

"I know that already."

"He knows people, but wouldn't say who. Semiofficial, was how he put it."

"Front organizations, you mean?"

"I wouldn't know. I didn't ask. He wouldn't have told me anyway. He couldn't see what might be in it for anyone except you."

"I told you. Money."

"I said that. He just smiled. He'll talk to these people. If anyone's interested, you may be contacted." She released his hand and stood up. "But it's not a promise. You may hear nothing."

"If you happen to be speaking to Harold Leyton, tell him I'd better hear."

"Harry's in Hungary. I've no reason to speak to him. I don't even know where he's staying."

"You never know. He may call you."

"Why this harping on Harry? It's nothing to do with him."

"He'll understand."

"I'm too tired for cryptic utterances. Good-night. Sleep well."

Her shape crossed the room. As she opened the door and moved into the lighted corridor, he saw her face clearly, but she did not look back. The door clicked closed.

He got up, went into the bathroom, and drank a glass of water. His clothes were hanging up where he had left them, after undressing. He checked his pockets and examined his wallet.

Even though fierce desire had begun to rage from just looking at her as they had ridden up in the elevator together, he had thought it desirable not to leave his gun and holster hanging up in full view. Together with the photocopy of Christa's sketches, he had laid them in the cupboard under the wash basin, and covered them with a hand towel, laid in a particular way, carefully memorized.

He opened the door, crouched, studied the hand towel for a few moments, and then lifted it. The sketch, gun, and holster were still there. He stood up and closed the door. He was reasonably certain that the towel had been disarranged, although the other articles had not been moved.

He went into the bedroom, closed the curtains, straightened the crumpled bedclothes, and got back into bed. There was still a trace of her perfume lingering on the pillow.

He wondered what Helen Lloyd had wanted to learn

about him, and whether she had done so, but his mind wandered to what he had learned about her body and the pleasure it gave. Thinking about that, he fell into a deep, dreamless sleep.

He awoke late, rested and feeling good. It caught his eye as soon as he got out of bed.

An envelope had been pushed under his door. It was not sealed. There was no name on it.

S I X

Stephen Haden waited until after breakfast before dialing. He wished that someone would come out from the woodwork. He counted the ringing tones: fifteen times before a man's voice answered.

"Mermaid Cars, good morning."

"This is Stephen Haden."

"One moment, sir." There was a silence, during which he could hear nothing. He looked at the card in his hand. "Mermaid Cars. Chauffeur driven limousines. 24-hour service. Airports. Ports. Tours. Continental travel." It was not the shoddy kind of card pushed through letter boxes by minicab firms. The card was white, high quality, expensively engraved. When he had first taken it from the envelope, he had immediately turned it over, but nothing was written on the back. The same man's voice came on the line. "Would one hour's time be convenient, sir?"

"Perfectly," Haden said.

"Thank you very much, sir."

The line went dead. Haden replaced the receiver. He glanced through the *Daily Telegraph*, then rang Mermaid Cars again. Once more the same voice answered after fifteen ringing tones.

Haden hung up, called Directory Enquiries, and told the

operator that he had the number of Mermaid Cars but needed their address, which he had mislaid. There was a pause during which, he supposed, the information came up on a display screen.

"I'm sorry, but that number is ex-directory."

"I've got the number. All I want is the address."

"We're not allowed to give that information. I suggest you ring them and ask for the address."

"With that number, the office would be somewhere in the Victoria district, wouldn't it?"

"I'm afraid I couldn't say."

The line went dead. Haden gave up and went through the Zurich newspapers, which he had asked the hall porter to obtain. They were yesterday's editions.

Only one of them carried any reference to his attempted murder. The report, while an "exclusive," bore the slightly desperate stamp of a reporter flogging into life a story which had run its natural course. He skimmed through it.

"Disturbing speculations arise from investigation into Haden shooting . . . unsupported claims that Haden was involved in all kinds of transactions besides smuggling refugees . . . said to be associated with another organization dealing in pictures and antiques . . . police spokesman denies knowledge of allegations . . . refugees' property confiscated by D.D.R. authorities after successful escapes . . . some believe valuable items have turned up in the West and been sold by unknown vendors . . . absolutely no proof of collusion with D.D.R. State Security Service . . . sources close to Public Prosecutor believe possible motives for attempted murder include revenge, either by relatives of 'escape-clients' who failed to gain freedom, or a former employee . . . Interpol in Paris have issued worldwide warrant for arrest of unnamed West Berliner . . . Public Prosecutor denies 'any question of strong suspicion,' maintains man being sought only 'because we would very much like to check his alibi' . . . according to Zurich examining magistrate, 'If Inspector Chance doesn't intervene, the assassin's

identity may well remain unknown' . . . Stephen Haden,
who prefers to be described as an entrepreneur . . . regarded
by some as a James Bond of humanity . . . a Paris news-
paper called his organization 'a band of robbers' . . . now
said to be convalescing from his near-fatal wounds . . . po-
lice and his Zurich office deny any knowledge of his pres-
ent whereabouts . . . believed to be in hiding, still in fear of
his life . . . "

Haden went back to the beginning and read the report
again, carefully, from beginning to end. The "disturbing
speculations" remained vague innuendoes. The various
sources seemed to be singing different tunes but, to Haden's
ear, orchestrated in concert. The sympathetic appraisal
when his life hung by a thread had evaporated. He was no
longer being portrayed as a rather admirable figure. The ter-
mites were nibbling at the foundations. That could be
Schlunegger's doing. Schlunegger, for all his devious methods, was an uncomplicated copper. Actions were either
lawful or they were not. The way Haden blurred the edges
had always bothered him. Or it might not be Schlunegger.
The problem was elimination, not possibilities.

The telephone rang. Haden lifted the receiver.

"Your car is here, Mr. Haden" the hall porter said.

*T*he Jaguar was waiting outside. The chauffeur,
a neatly suited, bareheaded man in his thirties, was holding
the door open. Haden got into the back seat.

"I didn't tell your operator where I was staying," Haden
said. "How did you know where to pick me up?"

"The office is very efficient, sir," the chauffeur said. "I
expect they had a note of your hotel."

"How? I've never phoned your people before."

"You must have been personally recommended, sir,"
the chauffeur said, patiently. "All our clients are."

He was keeping to the main roads, content to drift along
in the traffic stream. They seemed to be heading in the general direction of Kingston.

"A peculiar firm you work for," Haden said, "with an ex-directory telephone number."

"Not at all, sir," the driver said, tolerantly amused. "We specialize in a very high class clientele who demand personal service. We don't want just anybody ringing up. That wouldn't do at all, sir."

"Then why was your card shoved under my door?"

"As I've said, sir, you must have been recommended."

This was going to be a waste of time.

"Where's your office?"

"The garage is in West London, sir."

"The office isn't. It's a Victoria number."

"That doesn't signify, sir. When we moved office, we took the phone number with us, to avoid inconvenience." In the rearview mirror, Haden saw the chauffeur's eyes flick toward him. "Do you have a complaint, sir? If so, I can call in on the radio at once."

"Forget it," Haden said tiredly.

The car drew up outside Hampton Court Palace.

"I'm afraid this is as close as I can get, sir," the chauffeur said.

"Close to what?"

"The rose garden, sir," the chauffeur said, as though it was obvious.

Haden got out.

"How much do I owe you?"

"It's on the account, sir," the driver said, his stock of infuriating patience limitless. "Including gratuity. A car will be sent to pick you up later."

"When?" Haden demanded.

"It'll be here, sir," the driver said. He nodded respectfully and drove away.

Haden circled the rose garden and finally settled on an unoccupied bench close to a wall, facing King Henry VIII's palace. There was a steady flow of visitors, but most headed for the maze, or went inside to see those rooms open to the public.

The businessman who arrived five minutes later, carrying a briefcase, was alone. He strolled along the paths appreciatively, a man with time to spare. Haden watched him. He was around forty, hair fashionably graying at the temples, fashionably cut, wearing fashionably large glasses, the successful executive for all seasons commonly to be seen in most Western capitals. He disappeared from view, having at no time glanced in Haden's direction.

A casually dressed young man lingered nearby in a hesitant fashion, then seemed to change his mind and walked toward the palace.

The businessman reappeared, wandered along the path, and sat on the bench. He opened his briefcase, took out a sheaf of papers and, using the lid of the briefcase as a miniature desk, began to study them intently in silence, making occasional quick notes with a gold pen.

Haden looked around for another vacant bench.

"You needn't move, Mr. Haden," the businessman said, his head still bowed.

Haden thought that he spoke with a New England accent.

"Who might you be?" he inquired.

"The one who has been asked to interview you."

"About what?"

"The purpose is not my concern. The result will be assessed elsewhere. By whom, I don't know."

"It's very strange," Haden said, "how no one knows anything."

"That's the way it is, Mr. Haden." The eyes behind the glasses were pale and expressionless.

"Somewhere, there has to be an organ grinder," Haden said. "Pass a message back, via the people you don't know. Say I'm bored with this. I'll talk to whoever arranges meetings. Face to face, or nothing. Okay?"

"I'll certainly pass on your message, if you wish, Mr. Haden. If I do, the certain result will be nothing. You won't hear again. But you're a free man. You initiated the process.

You can end it at this point if you so desire. It is entirely in your hands."

Just at that moment, Haden would have much preferred to use his hands on this dusty American automaton's throat.

Two little boys raced past, shrieking at the tops of their voices.

"Do you know what I want?" Haden asked, his voice tight.

"I simply do as I'm requested." The large glasses glimmered in the sunshine. "May we begin?"

He rearranged the sheaf of papers, and glanced at Haden questioningly.

"Is all that stuff about me?" Haden asked.

"The computer has much to answer for. It spews out more paper than any bureaucracy."

He reversed the order of the top two sheets.

"I didn't realize I was worth that much space on anyone's computer," Haden said.

"No disrespect, Mr. Haden, but you're probably not. Create an empire based on the storage of information, and information gets stored, most of it useless. Much of this, I think, we may ignore."

"Thank Christ for that," Haden said with feeling.

"From which countries have you smuggled refugees to the West?"

"Most from the D.D.R. A lot from Czechoslovakia, a few from Poland and Rumania."

"There is a note that you took a group, two at a time, across Lake Neusiedler from Hungary to Austria."

"They were East Germans. It had been arranged that they should take a holiday in Hungary."

"Is it really the case that you used a miniature submarine to convey them across the lake?"

"Some fool invented that yarn," Haden said contemptuously. "It was a small inflatable dinghy. That's why it took several nights to get them all across."

"Do you work in collusion with the State Security Service of East Germany?"

Haden stared at him bleakly. A plane on its way into Heathrow whined overhead.

"If interrogation is your trade, mister," he said, "you should take a refresher course."

"It would explain your immunity for several years," the man observed mildly.

"My immunity ended with two bullets in the back."

"You believe the attempt was carried out by a D.D.R. agent?"

"I don't know. It's one possibility. They've consistently tried to infiltrate my organization."

"You're referring to Gottfried Keller, whom two of your men took by force to your house in Zurich, where he was beaten up, and a loaded revolver held to his head until he signed a confession."

Haden said, "He confessed of his own free will."

"Not according to Keller, who retracted later, on the grounds that it was obtained by force. You were arrested by a detective called Schlunegger, and charged under articles 181 and 182 of the Swiss Criminal Code, concerning coercion and wrongful deprivation of personal liberty. For which you were convicted and fined."

Haden shrugged. The memory still rankled.

"Keller wasn't the only one."

"When you have meted out the same rough justice, perhaps?"

"I protect myself to the best of my ability," Haden said. "The police can't. Or won't."

"Referring back a little, 'collusion' may have been too strong a term. But I have to tell you that there are indications, admittedly of a circumstantial nature, of some connection between yourself and the State Security Service. You may wish to reconsider your answer. The parties concerned will wish reasonable doubt to be allayed. It is entirely up to you, of course."

The man's bespectacled eyes had never left Haden's face, and although he was still holding his pen, he had not used it.

"Do you have total recall?" Haden asked. "Or is this being recorded?"

"I do have a fairly good memory, but it's also being recorded. Do you have any objection?"

"Tape can be edited," Haden said, "to make it appear I'd said any goddamn thing you wanted."

"That isn't the purpose."

"What is, for Christ's sake?"

"To establish whether you are reliable. To explain, for example, indirect evidence of collusion with the State Security Service." If persistence was a virtue, this one had it.

"There is no collusion," Haden said, slowly. "There's a reward out for me. They use sympathizers to plant smear stories."

"They'd do that if there were collusion, in order to conceal it."

"I have contacts," Haden said. "Not with anyone in the State Security Service itself, that would be far too dangerous. But people outside it, who can come up with information."

"Such as?"

"Density of traffic on the various transit routes. Special checks. Any of my people attracting suspicion. Units manning the 'green frontier.' When they're changed. Where they're spread thin. I need that kind of information. Organizing an escape is like planning a military operation."

"The names of these contacts?"

"That's one answer you're not getting," Haden said flatly.

"Who is Kurt Gabler?"

"He's in charge of the West Berlin branch."

"Describe the kind of man he is."

"Flashy. A braggart, likes to be seen as a man of action. But he really is a tough customer. The most highly paid man I've got. Ambitious. Knows his job. Needs careful handling. Not a fellow it would be wise to cross. Does that match *your* description of him?"

The American ignored the sarcasm.

"He's being sought by the West Berlin police, on charges of tax evasion. An unknown informant laid information. Your doing, Mr. Haden?"

"No," Haden said. "Why should I try and get rid of Kurt? He's too important, too good an operator."

"You'd save the money owing to him, royalties I believe you term it, an estimated one hundred thousand Swiss francs. You'd get rid of a dangerous rival, a man who might like to take over your organization."

"I wonder where you get your information," Haden said.

"He has friends. Friends gossip. Is it true?"

"I didn't rat on him," Haden said.

"Maybe he thought you did. He hasn't been seen since ten days before you were shot."

So it was Kurt Gabler that Interpol had a warrant out for.

"He doesn't fit the description," Haden said.

"I didn't suggest he might have pulled the trigger. Men can be hired for that." He looked down at his papers, scanned a couple rapidly, and discarded them, slipping them into his briefcase. "At one time, the Public Prosecutor in Zurich opened inquiries concerning fraud and profiteering on your part."

"That was when the Swiss government were under pressure from the D.D.R. My business isn't illegal under Swiss law. They tried that instead, but dropped it when some of my clients came forward."

"Saying what?"

"In effect, that the smuggling of human beings was a perfectly normal business."

"Perfectly normal?" The rather heavy eyebrows rose.

"At one time, there were twenty-odd organizations engaged in escape aid. Mine wasn't the only one."

"No. Although it was certainly the most peculiar. How many refugees have you smuggled to the West since you began operations?"

"Just over eight hundred."

"The fees you charge, that would represent a gross of upwards of twenty million U.S. dollars. Not bad, even allowing for overhead. Not bad at all. The official scheme, under which Bonn paid the D.D.R. to release people, secured the freedom of well over *twelve thousand* at no cost to themselves."

"It cost the Federal government over half a billion Deutschmarks," Haden said. "Taxpayers' money. Someone always pays."

"The suggestion would be, I guess, that you and your kind profiteered from human misery, while making very little impact on the problem."

"Crap," Haden said. "Each individual has his or her own problem. I solve it without red tape. There's a market. I didn't create it. All the D.D.R. has to do is open the doors of its paradise, and people like me are out of business."

"The logic of that is that you would prefer the doors not to open. You seek profits. Maybe the easier they come the better?"

"I can't change Eastern Bloc policy," Haden said. "I'm not a charity. I'm not an idealist. If a difficult job turns out easy, fine. That makes up for the easy ones which turn difficult. You seem to be asking me to defend myself. Against what?"

"It is said that you betrayed many, possibly hundreds, to the D.D.R. State Security Service for blood money of up to ten thousand, fifteen thousand Swiss francs per head."

"Who says?"

"Informed sources suggest that your operations were carried out with the D.D.R.'s knowledge and consent. That is, you were allowed to keep up appearances, to take out to the West would-be refugees of lesser interest to the D.D.R."

"Disinformation designed to discredit," Haden said. "'Informed sources' sounds like Zurich . . . although why now, I don't know . . . I can't think . . . " Yesterday, and earlier today, his brain had been clear and sharp, or so he had imagined. Now the deadening fogginess was returning, threatening to clog his thoughts. The result, he supposed, of concentrating on this quiet man's apparently random questions, the deadly object of which had now emerged. He closed his eyes and took deliberate deep breaths, searching for the halfway convincing reply which he knew must be there, could he but find it.

"Are you feeling okay, Mr. Haden?"

Haden opened his eyes.

"Some of my people have been arrested. Why would they do that if it was all a setup?"

"The same sources indicate that you tipped off the D.D.R. about two of those men yourself because, as it was put, they were 'inconvenient' for you."

Haden said, "Both had been planted on me. So I sent them back where they belonged."

"Betraying refugees would make good commercial sense. Easy money, no risk. You've no political motives. You're not an idealist."

"It's a lie," Haden said. "But it's a good lie. The kind a character like you seizes on. Well, good lies are bloody hard to disprove, so buy it if you must. I can't stop you."

"It would look better if you tried, Mr. Haden."

"I can't swear to the figures," Haden said, after a long pause, "but I'd say some thirty to forty percent of the men and women I've brought out have been in the medical field, doctors, dentists, research workers, that kind of thing. They're the last people the D.D.R. would let go 'to keep up appearances.'"

"I guess they invested a lot of money in their training,"

the American said. "But it's a good rebuttal, if it stands up. A few names might help."

"Give you names?" Haden said. "A man who won't say who he is, or who he represents?"

"You're the one who needs the references. I don't."

"Quite often, medical organizations in the Federal Republic will advance the fee to the escaper, and have it paid back to them later, out of his earnings in the West. They might not deny that, if they were asked."

"That'll be decided elsewhere. Mr. Haden, I'm going to read a quotation to you."

He extracted the right piece of paper from the sheaf.

"My driver's here," Haden said.

The same man had appeared and was standing patiently some twenty yards away.

"We haven't finished yet. Ready? 'One can therefore hardly comprehend how very inwardly happy a man feels whenever he observes signs of other people's favorable opinion; his vanity is somehow flattered.' Do you recognize that?"

"Schopenhauer," Haden said. Nothing surprised him any more.

"The volume was found open on your desk when the police searched your office. That passage was marked."

"Another newspaper item," Haden said. "I was reading, the night before. It caught my attention."

"Interesting." The American returned the papers to his briefcase.

"If I'd applied for a job," Haden said, "and this was the interview, I don't think I'd get it."

"I'm not an expert in these matters, Mr. Haden, but I'd say you need to offer something better."

"Like what?"

"Information of some kind. Anything which might establish your credentials. Your goodwill, even."

"I think the International Information Institute is a

C.I.A. front organization," Haden said. "Will that do?"

For the first time, the American smiled.

"Some people see Reds under every bed. Others think the C.I.A. runs everything."

Haden produced the expensive white business card.

"Mermaid Cars doesn't trade. I think it's the transport section of some secret service outfit." He glanced at the patient driver, who was examining a fine bloom with great interest. "Maybe British, he is, but maybe not. When you dial, the phone rings fifteen times before it's answered. I think that's while the incoming call is identified and switched through to some duty officer. Could be in Victoria. Where do you hang out?"

The American shook his head.

"Demonstrating an ability to conjure up a fantasy world like that may be amusing, Mr. Haden, or even significant to a psychiatrist, I wouldn't know. Gain Brownie points, it does not."

Haden said, "Harold Leyton is a highly successful marketing man. He's an Institute client. He spends half his life traveling behind the Iron Curtain. I think he's also a spy, working for British Intelligence, or American, or West German, or perhaps all three. As a guess, I'd say he makes contact with agents over there, acts as a mobile combined messenger and courier."

"You're doing it again, Mr. Haden," the American said regretfully. "This delightful garden is not nearly so colorful as your imagination."

Haden said, "Leyton is a homosexual. He has a boy friend called Heinz Meyer. Supposed to come from Munich. He doesn't. He's East German. Probably planted on Leyton by the D.D.R. secret service."

"Exactly what leads you to believe this, Mr. Haden?" The voice was whisper soft.

"Heinz Meyer lived in Dresden. I got him out, via Prague. Harold Leyton said he was acting for Heinz's father. I think he'd fallen in love with the boy."

The large glasses swiveled as the American gazed thoughtfully across the garden, and then back at Haden.

"Were this true, Mr. Haden, you knowingly smuggled into the West a man you suspected of being an East German agent, whose objective, in your belief, was to infiltrate Allied intelligence. How many points do you think that would score on a scale of zero to zero?"

"The same as you," Haden said. "If I'd realized it at the time. I didn't. Only when I came to think about it, much later."

"But you've done nothing about it until now."

"Now I'm asked for evidence of goodwill. I've delivered."

"Mr. Haden, if you've provided one foreign agent with cover as a refugee, what makes you imagine the D.D.R. haven't used you for the same purpose on other occasions?"

"Perhaps they have," Haden snapped. "And maybe, for all I know, *your* mob have used me or someone like me to get one or two of your own people *out* when you couldn't manage it yourselves."

"A display of aggression will impress no one, Mr. Haden. It can be used to hide something, as well as to vent righteous anger."

"Piss off," Haden said.

He stood up and walked away along the path.

"I'll show you where the car's parked, Mr. Haden," the driver said.

"Take him," Haden said. He pointed back at the American. "Or deliver the tape he's got, I don't care which."

*H*aden jumped on the first bus he saw, which proved to be going the wrong way. He got off, and providentially found a taxi.

Stephen Haden privately considered his speculations about the Institute and Mermaid Cars pretty fantastic too. He was far from certain that his guesses about Harold Leyton were not mere wild nonsense. The possibility had first occurred to him during the endless days spent lying in a hospital bed when, considering the drug regime he had been on, weird ideas were only too likely to masquerade as reasonable.

The telephone inquiries which had failed to elicit any trace of a Meyer in Munich, a man of the right age to be Heinz's father who had escaped from East Germany some years before and set up a business, were necessarily cursory. Munich was a big city, and Meyer was a common name. The fact that he had been unable to track down the right Meyer senior who lived and worked in or near Munich did not signify that he did not exist.

Harold Leyton had certainly been alarmed and did not want the truth about Heinz Meyer broadcast. Yet even that could bear another interpretation. Leyton might have some other, long-standing, stable relationship going, about which Haden knew nothing. Harold Leyton could simply have been reacting like a married man who had a mistress on the side, and did not want his wife to find out.

Haden felt no compunction about informing on Harold Leyton, if indeed he had, which was beginning to seem increasingly dubious. If he was right, Leyton deserved limited sympathy. If he was wrong, it did not matter.

Most of the information the bespectacled American had used might have come from a computer, but if so, the machine had largely stored press clippings. The attempt on Haden's life had made news in Switzerland and West Germany. Fact had been vigorously stirred with rumor and the outright fanciful in a proportion of about one to four. The American had also possessed, though, scattered fragments of information which could not have come from any newspaper, and ought to have been known only to Haden himself and a few close associates.

He considered Kurt Gabler. For all his flashiness, Kurt was dangerous, perfectly capable of using a hired killer. Kurt was also the kind who would prefer to do the job himself, and not in the back either. He would want to watch his victim's face.

Carli and Anton Weiss would certainly have known that Kurt Gabler had not been seen since ten days before Haden was shot. Kurt did not exactly live in the open and ten days would have passed unnoticed, but his prolonged absence would have seriously inconvenienced the organization while Haden was in the hospital. They would have had to put in someone else quickly to run the West Berlin branch. Yet Anton had not included Kurt's disappearance and replacement during his briefing. Nor had Carli referred to such a major problem, even though she was frequently in touch with Kurt Gabler as a matter of course. Perhaps they had considerately withheld anything which would worry him in his weakened condition. Perhaps there was another reason.

He became aware that the taxi was drawing up outside the hotel.

With his key, Haden was handed a message from Christa, timed at 12:35 P.M., asking him to call back. He did so at once, using one of the phones in the foyer, but she was in class.

It was nearly 6:30 P.M. before he finally reached her on the house telephone.

"Can't stop," Christa said, cheerfully, "must start my prep. The things we were talking about'll be finished by Sunday."

"Fine," Haden said. "I'll drive down and collect them."

"No, I'll catch the train. I feel like a day in London anyway. And will it be all right if Paul comes along as well?"

"Can you find the hotel? I'll give you lunch."

"Oh, lovely, thank you, but the thing is, we have to get permission, and it's supposed to be in writing, and by Thursday, so you'll have to talk to Mary nicely about it. And that includes Paul, of course, only his parents are away, and someone has to vouch for him."

"All right, all right," Haden said. "Put her on."

Mary Turner spoke crisply and with some coolness. She pointed out the irregularity of such a late arrangement, inquired if he was fully aware that he was committing himself to be responsible for Paul as well as Christa, and emphasized that it was his duty arising therefrom to ensure that they arrived back at school safely, and in time for supper.

Haden promised to meet the specified requirements and banged the phone down. He felt like one of the formidable Mary Turner's pupils.

Since there was little he could usefully do on Saturday, he decided that he might as well treat it as a rest day and enjoy his enforced leisure.

The International Information Institute yielded an answerphone which informed him that the office was closed until 9 A.M. on Monday morning, and invited him to leave a message.

"Tell Helen Lloyd there's been no result, I can't wait any longer, I'm going ahead, and the consequences are not my pigeon," Haden said.

He did not bother with his name and telephone number.

Stephen Haden had taken unfailing good health for granted, until the unseen gunman shot him down. Being aware of his own condition, much less checking it all the time, he found distasteful. By former attitudes, it smacked of hypochondria. But he could not help but note certain changes in himself which he did not like.

He was conscious that recovery in the general sense, far from being full, was patchy and uncertain. In some respects, it had gone into reverse. Only two days before, with Christa, he had felt good, really good. It was since then that he had noticed a vague feeling of general malaise. It was indefinable, yet all-pervading. He could not pinpoint anything, he only knew it was there.

The remainder of the day passed. Nothing happened. Had the Institute carried on the kind of covert activities

Haden had dealt to the American in the hope of denting the man's relaxed impermeability, he doubted if it would have operated on a five-days-a-week, nine-to-five basis. Messages on the answerphone would be checked frequently when the Institute's overt business ceased, and passed on. But Helen Lloyd did not call him. He remained ignored by the rest of the world.

Just before he went to bed, Haden remembered to book a table for Sunday lunch.

It was while he was sitting in the foyer, lethargically glancing through the *Observer* and waiting for Christa and Paul to arrive, that the soft, feminine voice on the loudspeaker intoned his name.

Stephen Haden dropped the *Observer*, jumped to his feet, and made for the nearest phone. He felt better at once, the adrenaline flowing. His message had done its work after all.

The operator put him through.

"Hullo?"

"Stephen, this'll have to be quick, only I haven't got any more change, and I'm in a call box . . . "

"A call box where?" Haden demanded irritably. "Christa, you're supposed to be here."

"I know, I'm sorry . . . shut up you two, I'm trying to talk . . . ," she said to someone else. "The thing is, first of all the train was late, and then we discovered some friends are going to be in Chelsea, and I wondered if you'd mind very much if we spent an hour or two with them, had a snack somewhere, and came over to you later . . . "

"Now, listen," Haden began ominously. The repeated tone, indicating that more money should be inserted, bleeped into his ear.

"Oh, hell," he heard her say, in the few seconds which followed. "Someone must have some change. Come on . . . "

"Three o'clock," Haden shouted. "No later. Do you hear me?"

But the phone had gone dead.

Moodily, Haden found the head waiter and canceled his reservation. He did not feel hungry. The bar beckoned. He supposed he should drink something like orange juice. Rudi Hensler had been specific. He ordered a cognac.

One of the porters came in as he was sitting at a table, looked around, and came across.

"This has just been delivered, Mr. Haden," he said.

Haden took the envelope.

"Who by?"

"A messenger, sir. He said there'd be no answer."

"Thank you," Haden said.

He examined the envelope. "BY HAND. URGENT." it was headed, in typed capitals. His name and hotel followed. There was no return address.

Inside was a return air ticket to Gothenburg, and confirmation of a hotel booking.

SEVEN

Christa hurried in, saw him, and came over to the table, smiling tentatively. Paul ambled after her.

"Hullo," she said. "This is Paul. We're not late, are we?"

"Yes," Haden said.

"I'm sorry. It's Paul's fault . . . "

"I didn't tell Paul," Haden said. "I told you."

"I knew you'd be angry," she said, blinking. "Only we just didn't notice the time . . . "

"Oh, sit down," Haden said. "I've ordered tea."

"Oh, good, I like teas."

"I've noticed," Haden said. "What have you been doing, anyway?"

"Nothing much, really, but it's been lovely. We met the other kids in Sloane Square, and wandered along the Kings Road, and then we had a McDonald's, and then two soldiers tried to pick us up, me and another girl, in Leicester Square, at least they said they were soldiers, they were wearing jeans . . . "

"What the devil were you doing in Leicester Square?"

"Some dimwit thought Covent Garden station closed on Sundays," Christa explained logically. "That's where we were going. We were sitting on a seat, the others had wandered off somewhere . . . "

"It was you two who'd wandered off," Paul said. "We were looking for you."

"We knew you'd find us," Christa said. "Then these soldiers came along, they were only about eighteen . . . " She giggled. " . . . and asked us to go to the pictures with them. Oh, muffins!" she said with delight, as the muffins arrived.

"I'm beginning to sympathize with Mary Turner," Haden said.

Paul smiled faintly, and politely offered Haden the plate.

"Not for me," Haden said.

"While we're stuffing ourselves," Christa said, "you can look at this."

She handed Haden a small envelope and started eating with relish. "Oh, these are super."

Haden lifted the flap of the unsealed envelope. Into his hand fell what looked to be, at first glance, several passport photographs. Closer inspection showed that they were, in fact, carefully drawn pen-and-ink sketches, transferred and reduced onto small, glossy prints. Each was from the same angle, the face half turned toward "camera," a neutral polite smile on the lips. Otherwise, although the shape of the face and head was the same, as were the eyes and nose, the various permutations of hairline and coloring, bearded and clean-shaven, could have belonged to different men: the other faces he might have worn. In all, there were eight.

"This must have taken you forever," Haden said.

"Not once I'd got the hang of it." She licked her fingers. "It's always the same bone structure. Luckily, I had double art on Friday, work of our own choice, so I did that, and a free period in the afternoon, and all day yesterday, of course, I skipped games . . . "

"How did you get them to look like photographs?"

"Paul did that. He's a photographic nut. It was his idea.

He thought it would be more convenient if the police were showing them around to people, and somehow they'd look more realistic."

"They do," Haden said. "Paul, thank you very much indeed. And you, young lady."

"Well, if you're really sure you like them . . . "

She left it hanging, her eyes large and expectant. Haden was learning something else about her, although "signs of other people's favorable opinion" could be a weakness, a view the American had quite evidently shared, with his dry remark, "Interesting."

He rewarded her with a warm, affectionate smile.

"You're a love." He reached for his wallet. "Look, suppose you buy yourself something . . . "

"Gosh, no, I don't want money . . . "

That was a mistake.

"Quite right, money grows on trees," he said. It did like hell. Money was a man's life. "Something even better, as a sign of appreciation. Another plate of muffins? Or sandwiches, I see they've all gone too. Get fat instead."

She laughed.

"I shall never get fat."

Haden smiled at her fourteen-year-old confidence that a tall, pencil-slim body was a permanent gift of nature, and only other people got fat. How easy it was to make this girl "inwardly happy" with a few of the words she wanted to hear.

"I think I might be able to cope with a cream cake, though," Christa mused. "Oh . . . before I get my fingers sticky again . . . Paul thought some copies could come in useful . . . three of each . . . "

She fumbled in her shoulder bag, and gave Haden a rather fatter envelope.

"Paul was right," Haden said.

Paul smiled his acknowledgment, a contained, reserved smile. This boy was not one of those who needed much approval. Haden slid the two envelopes into his inside breast pocket. Past Paul's head, he had seen Helen Lloyd. He waved and stood up as she came over.

"Hullo," he said, "this is a surprise."

"I'm sorry. I guess I'm intruding."

"Not at all," Haden said. "My step-daughter, Christa, her friend Paul. This is Helen Lloyd."

"Hi. Glad to know you."

"Sit down and join us. Would you like some tea?"

"Thank you. I happened to be nearby, and I thought I'd drop by and see if you were at home."

Haden ordered another pot of tea. Helen Lloyd fell into conversation with the two youngsters with enviable ease. Both responded to her friendliness almost instantly. Paul became animated and talkative. With Christa, she struck an immediate rapport, and they gossiped away about anything from fashions to films, as if they had known each other for years.

Haden said little, content to sit and watch. If it was an act, it was a very good one indeed. As if by instinct, she found the level which would accommodate both herself and the teenage girl. He admired the sheer technique of the performance, whether it was genuine or not. As a chameleon, Helen Lloyd was in a class of her own.

She listened with every appearance of interest, laughing at girlish anecdotes, interjecting questions, and Stephen Haden learned more about the school and its people in twenty minutes than he had in the three years since Anna had flown with Christa to England for the beginning of her first term.

"Oh, yes, there are lots of foreign kids there," Christa was saying to Helen Lloyd. "Well, I'm foreign, too, of course . . . "

"Yes, but you don't act like it," Paul told her. "You're like an English girl."

"The idiot thinks that's a compliment," Christa said,

affectionately. "I sometimes wish I could be both British and Swiss, like Stephen, though . . . "

"How does that come about, Mr. Haden?" Paul asked. "I thought you had to renounce one or the other."

"My father was British," Haden said, "which made me a British national, but my mother was Swiss and we lived in Switzerland. She wanted me to become a Swiss subject, especially after my father died, so I did. At that point, I lost my British nationality. But later I came to England and worked here for a couple of years . . . "

"What was that?" Helen Lloyd asked. "To find out where half of you belonged?"

"A little perhaps, although my father never wanted to come back. More simple restlessness, I think. Anyway, while I was here, I discovered that, because my father was English, it was possible for me to have a British passport as well, so I applied and got one. That's how, Paul."

"Having two, I expect that's sometimes been an asset, in your business," Paul said.

"It's had its uses," Haden said.

"But as a Swiss citizen, wouldn't you have had to do National Service?" Paul asked. "Weapons training, and so on?"

"I did it when I got back," Haden said. The boy was well informed.

"A pity they don't have conscription here," Christa told Paul. "It would do you good."

"You two are never going to get back in time by train now," Haden said, looking at his watch. "I'd better take you. Ready?"

"Can I come along too?" Helen Lloyd asked. "I've never seen an English boarding school. Or why don't I drive you? My car's right outside, in the road."

"If it hasn't been towed away," Christa said.

"Not on a Sunday, she's safe" Haden said. He glanced at Helen Lloyd. "What have you got?"

"Something *huge*," Christa said. "A Cadillac."

Helen Lloyd laughed, and shook her head.

"American staff are asked to use British-made cars," she said. "Public relations, I guess. It's a Sierra." She glanced at Haden sideways. "I can deliver them, if you'd rather stay here."

"Christa's housemistress thinks I've been in charge of them all day," he said. "God help her naivete. I'd better show my face."

Outside, wryly amused at his own instant, mistaken deduction, he climbed into the front seat. The Sierra was dark green.

Haden gave Helen Lloyd monosyllabic directions from time to time. The youngsters in the back were talking quietly to each other, mostly, as far as Haden could gather, about a sixth former who was to be expelled for smoking pot.

They left the motorway, drove along the maze of country lanes, and passed through the village.

"Next turning right," Haden said.

Christa said suddenly, "You can go in here, it's quicker."

"What?" Haden glimpsed what looked like a track leading into the woods. A five-bar gate was propped open.

"It's the back way in," Christa said. "A shortcut. It's supposed to be for staff, but no one minds."

"I think I'd better keep going, honey," Helen Lloyd said toward Christa. "There's a van up my tail."

"Sorry," Christa apologized. "My fault."

"It's okay." Helen Lloyd said. "Let's arrive in style. Around the back are trashcans in my experience. I didn't come to see trashcans."

They turned right and, three hundred yards along the lane, turned right again into the school grounds, and followed the drive which wound through the lawns, studded with trees and rhododendron bushes, toward the school.

"Hey, this is nice," Helen Lloyd said approvingly, as she parked.

Paul gravely asked her if she would like to be shown around, she accepted at once, and they walked off together.

Haden and Christa stood by the car, watching them. Clouds covered the sky, but it was still pleasantly warm with a slight breeze, which ruffled Christa's hair.

"Helen's smashing," she said. "Is she your girlfriend?"

"We've only just met."

"Oh." There was a touch of disappointment. Then she smiled fondly. "I think Paul's got a crush on her."

Two more cars arrived. Parents and children got out. Christa waved to the youngsters. Haden folded his arms, and leaned against the trunk.

"Do you have a crush on Paul?"

"I'm not sure," Christa said. "I'm thinking about it. I suppose Mary brought this up."

"Among your other shortcomings."

"Which are legion, we all know that," Christa said.

"It's her job," Haden said. "What does your mother say?"

The parents got back into one of the cars, a Volvo, and it drove off.

"I don't think she's noticed that I'm not a child any more," Christa said. "We get sex lessons at school, if that's what you're asking."

Haden sighed.

"Not really." He looked down at his feet. He had forgotten to put his shoes out the night before, and they needed cleaning. "It's not my place. You didn't ask for me as a step-father."

"Lots of the kids here have step-fathers or step-mothers," Christa said. "Half of them are absolute horrors. You've never been like that. You pay for me to come here. That means a lot. Perhaps I haven't been working hard enough. I will try, Stephen, honestly."

Since the girl had arrived with Anna, he had agreed to meet the school fees for the English education which Anna wanted for her, when Anna departed; part of the price to be paid to end the marriage. Gratitude scarcely seemed called for.

"This afternoon," Haden said, "I'd taken on responsibility for you, just for once, even if only for half a day. And I didn't know where you were, or what you were doing."

"I told you what we did."

"You don't always speak the truth," Haden said.

Her cheeks flushed.

"I do about important things."

Haden wondered what the hell he was doing. It was absurd. Somewhere, there was a man he intended to find and kill. Later, perhaps, those who had helped him. To the girl beside him, it was "important" that she had told the truth concerning her whereabouts for two hours. The gulf between them was immeasurable.

Christa said, "I know there are things about me you don't approve of. I've said I'll try."

"For yourself, not for me," Haden said. "Make your own decisions. You like approval, that's one aspect of you, or so it seems to me." She smiled half-heartedly and did not deny it. "It's a nice attribute," he went on. "It's engaging. Be aware of it, that's all. There's one easy way to gain a boy's approval, for instance."

"I know that already," Christa said.

"It's your life, not mine. I'd rather you didn't get hurt too much. That's all."

"I'm not ready yet, anyway," Christa said. "Girls talk . . . " She shrugged. ". . . but I don't want to be talked into something, just to keep up with the others. When I'll decide, I don't know. But it won't be yet."

"Do you come under much pressure from the boys here?"

"A few of the older ones, fifth and sixth formers. Not Paul."

"How do you handle it?"

"Laugh them out of it, try and do it without putting them down or hurting their feelings."

Haden smiled.

"You'll be all right," he said. "You'll do the choosing."

Something struck him about that remark, some echo he could not immediately place.

Helen Lloyd had emerged from the school with Paul.

"Shall I see you again next weekend?" Christa asked.

"I may not be here," Haden said.

"Oh . . . well, anyway, thanks for everything . . . I've enjoyed it . . . "

"I should be thanking you for all your hard work," Haden said.

"That's nothing. It was fun." She glanced at Helen Lloyd and Paul. They had paused a few yards away, and he was pointing something out to her. Christa turned back to Haden. "I'm glad you talked to me about things."

Haden said, "You're okay. It was a waste of time."

"No, it wasn't . . . I like you to worry about me . . . " To Haden's surprise, she flung her arms around him.

"My pleasure," Haden said awkwardly.

She hugged him fiercely, her slim, firm young body pressed against him. Somewhat embarrassed, he returned her embrace, and lightly stroked her smooth hair.

Christa kissed him quickly on the cheek, broke away, and called to Paul.

"Come on, lover boy, we'll be late for supper."

The two youngsters hared off, racing each other toward the school. Haden got into the car. Helen Lloyd drove back along the winding drive and into the lane.

"Christa's sweet," she said. "Half child, half woman, outgoing, knows her own worth. Sometimes very together and mature, and then she'll relapse into being a little girl. It's an enchanting combination. It makes me feel old."

"Were you ever like that?"

"A little, I guess. It seems a long time ago. One thing did

surprise me, though. Somehow, I hadn't expected she'd be so fond of you."

Haden shifted in his seat.

"She's just polite, that's all."

Helen Lloyd glanced at him, a small, odd smile on her lips.

"Like it or not, Stephen Haden, that girl adores you."

"You turn left now," Haden said, brusquely.

"I know."

There was no oncoming traffic. She swung the wheel, and began to accelerate toward the village.

"Pull up!" Haden said suddenly.

"What?"

"I want to go back."

"To the school? Why?"

"For Christ's sake, back up."

He was twisted around, trying to see over the hedge. As they had passed the track and the open five-bar gate, he was almost certain that he had caught sight, from the corner of his eye, of the gleam of cream bodywork somewhere in the trees.

Helen Lloyd had brought the car to a stop. She reversed, looking back over her shoulder.

"Would you mind telling me . . . ," she began.

"Not now. Do as I ask. Drive in here. The back way."

She engaged forward gear and drove slowly along the bumpy track. There was no car parked among the trees. They lurched on along the uneven surface and came to macadam, where half a dozen pleasant houses, staff quarters perhaps, were scattered in a semicircle around a small green. There were several cars parked outside the houses. None of them was cream.

"What now?" Helen Lloyd inquired.

"Keep going. It should lead us back to the school."

It did. There was the predicted row of dustbins outside the kitchens, from which came the busy clatter of crockery.

She followed the narrow strip of macadam. It circled the main buildings and came out into the parking area at the front. There were a couple of late arrivals, a Ford Granada and an Audi.

Haden told her to wait, and got out.

On one of the lawns near the main drive, some older boys were engaged in catching practice with a cricket ball. They looked at him blankly when first interrupted, but then tried to be helpful. A cream-colored car? One might have driven away a few minutes before, but if so none of them could remember what make it had been.

He slid in beside Helen Lloyd, and strapped himself in. "We can go now," he said. "Sorry."

They were passing through the village before Helen Lloyd spoke.

"What was all that about?"

"I'm neurotic," Haden said. "Seeing things."

Her lips pursed momentarily, but she did not pursue the subject.

They sat in one corner of the large but almost empty hotel lounge, drinking coffee.

"When did you get my message?" Haden asked.

"What message?"

"I left one on your office answerphone. Sunday afternoon, you've nothing better to do with your life than turn up here."

"I'd had lunch with some friends who live off Campden Hill. We sat talking afterwards, and when I left I decided to call in on the offchance. It was an impulse. There's no one in the office weekends. I shall get it tomorrow morning. What was it about?"

"Ignore it," Haden said. "Friday I was taken to Hampton Court and interviewed. Or perhaps I mean vetted."

"Who by?"

"He wouldn't say. Suppose you tell me."

"I spoke to my friend in the embassy. I guess he contacted someone, but if so, I don't know who."

"You go through that door," Haden said, pointing, "turn right, and there's a phone on the left. Call him, and ask."

"He wouldn't tell me, Stephen," she said quietly. "He may not know himself. He could have spoken to someone, who spoke to someone else . . . "

"Yes, I've heard the ground rules," Haden said. "No one knows anyone or anything. That's the way it is." He stared at her unblinkingly, holding her eyes. "I'm being passed around like a football, but I don't know who's playing, nor what game. I don't like it."

"It's no use looking at me like that," she said. "I've told you everything I know."

"Really? Having screwed me into exhaustion, you searched my bathroom. Tell me about that."

"Let's take it one at a time, Haden," she said tartly. "Most women can fake a good orgasm, including me. It saves those boring discussions afterwards when it doesn't work. On that occasion, I didn't have to fake. It worked."

"That's not what I asked," Haden said, impatiently.

"You implied I was using sex for some other reason. I wasn't. Right? Okay. Next. I have my share of natural curiosity. In the elevator, I thought I'd felt something under your shoulder. I wasn't sure. Candidly, at that moment, I didn't care. Later, I checked. You'd hidden it under a towel. Being in bed with a man who goes around armed is a new experience. It tells me something about him which I feel I should know."

"What it tells you should be no surprise," Haden said. "I don't intend to get caught again. What did you make of the sketch?"

"You're beginning to really annoy me," Helen Lloyd said. "What sketch?"

"Let's say you don't know. This came, this afternoon."

She took out the air ticket to Gothenburg and the hotel

reservation, looked at them, and then felt inside the envelope.

"Just these? No note? No phone call?"

"Just that," Haden said. "No explanation."

"Why Sweden? How are you supposed to know what to do when you get there?"

"If it's kosher, someone will contact me," Haden said. "There's another possibility. Taking a gun into a country inside a car is one thing. By air, it's another matter. You can try concealing it in your luggage, but it only needs an anonymous tip-off and you get the works from Customs the other end." He gestured. "Someone who knows I go around armed may want to get me someplace where I won't be."

"I follow the drift," Helen Lloyd said. "I think I'm entitled to take offense. Your suspicious nature could be screwing up something rather nice."

"You've never been shot in the back," Haden said.

"I wish you felt you could trust me," Helen Lloyd said.

"So do I, but there's no point in trying to con you."

"I'd go along with a certain decent pretense," Helen Lloyd said.

"You're involved. How, I don't know. Perhaps you don't either. But when I see you, things happen afterwards. I don't believe in that much random chance."

"If you were right," Helen Lloyd said, "you'd be taking a risk in admitting your suspicions. I'd report in that you know they're using me, and you think Gothenburg could be a setup, and whatever else you think I've done . . . I've lost count."

"Why all the hole-and-corner stuff? I can pay. We either do business or we don't. What's going on? What are they playing at? Show me someone else I can ask, and I will."

"You know everything I've been told," Helen Lloyd said. That, he thought, stood a sporting chance of being true. "Who's been in touch with you, I don't know," she went on. He considered the truth of that to be rather less likely. "This afternoon," she said, "for a couple of hours, watching you and Christa together, you were someone I liked a lot. I was glad I'd dropped in. Now I wish I hadn't."

She was very convincing. He wished he was convinced.

"Christa liked you," he said. "She was trying to pair us off."

Helen Lloyd smiled.

"Imitations of normality," she said wryly. She returned the air ticket and hotel booking. He put them away. "Will you go?" she asked.

"I haven't decided."

"I think you have, but you're not going to tell me," Helen Lloyd said. She stood up. "Thanks for the coffee. Good-bye and good luck, in case we don't meet again."

"You're my only contact," Haden said. "I expect we'll be in touch."

"Don't stake your life on it," Helen Lloyd said.

Next morning, Stephen Haden packed his bags, went downstairs, and paid his bill.

"And to confirm that there is a hold on your room from Wednesday night onwards," the girl said.

"I didn't ask for a hold," Haden said.

"Are you sure, sir?" She turned up her records worriedly. "No, there's no mistake . . . we have a definite request . . . "

"Who from?"

"I don't know, sir. I've only just come on duty. Would you like us to cancel it?"

"No," Haden said. "Leave it."

Someone expected him to come back. Or possibly to persuade him he was expected back.

The hall porter intercepted him as he turned away.

"Your car's waiting, sir."

The same driver was standing by the revolving doors. He nodded respectfully as Haden approached.

"Good morning, sir. Nice day."

"Are you the only driver they've got?" Haden inquired.

"Oh, no, sir" the man said with a smile. "It's simply that I have to meet a client at the airport later, so it fits in nicely. Empty mileage is the bane of this business, sir."

"Tough luck," Haden said. "Your office has got it wrong. I'm not going to the airport."

"I don't understand this, sir. My booking chit says 'Mr. Haden—Airport.'"

"Your car's in the way out there," Haden said.

An arriving taxi was hooting belligerently. Haden sat down and watched through the plate-glass windows. The driver got into his Jaguar, moved it a few yards out of the taxi's way, and spoke into his radio. After that, he drove off.

Traffic was dense along the M.4, the airport spur, and into the tunnel, where Haden was boxed in by buses which obscured his rear view, but he was fairly certain that no cream-colored car remained behind him.

He drove into the short-term car park, which was deliberately prohibitively expensive as a matter of policy, but close to the terminal. On the top deck, he chose a far corner, parked, switched off, and sat for a few minutes, watching, before he stowed his gun in the special compartment underneath the carpeting, inside which it had traveled into the country. He had decided not to run the risk of detection by taking it with him.

After a moment's hesitation, he took Rudi Hensler's letter from the glove compartment and placed it in his wallet. The feeling that he might need it was probably imagination, but if he did, it would be of no use in his car when he was somewhere else. Having it on him made him feel better.

One small suitcase was all he was taking with him. In the terminal, he checked in just as his flight was being called. On his way to the departure lounge, he saw a familiar figure, drinking tea and reading a newspaper. He changed direction.

The Jaguar driver looked up.

"Oh, hullo, Mr. Haden." He folded his newspaper. "I'm waiting for my next client's plane to arrive. I thought you said you weren't going to the airport, sir."

"You can tell them they guessed right, and I'm catching the flight after all," Haden said.

"Sorry, sir?"

"See you when I get back," Haden said pleasantly.

At Gothenburg airport, Haden was one of three passengers stopped while passing through the green channel. Which could have been coincidence. His suitcase and briefcase duly searched, he walked through into the terminal building and waited about for a while, but no one took the slightest notice of him, much less approached him. He decided that he was not to be met, and took a Mercedes taxi into the city.

The hotel was an imposing building at the head of the broad, tree-lined boulevard which constituted the main shopping area.

Inside, it was spacious and welcoming, an agreeable combination of Swedish efficiency and comfort. Haden checked in, and handed over his booking confirmation slip. In return, he received his key, and a card with a time written on it.

"What's this?" he asked. He spoke in English. His Swedish was negligible, although he understood a few words when the language veered toward German.

"That is your booking for the sauna which you requested, sir."

"Did I?"

"It says so here, sir," the tall, blond girl said. "When your reservation was made from London."

"Of course," Haden said. "Thank you."

He followed the porter up to his well-designed and fitted room, and unpacked. A folder on the writing desk contained much information about the hotel facilities and the amenities of Gothenburg, but nothing else. He skimmed through the material, and learned about the hotel's sauna, swimming pool, masseur, and rooftop cocktail bar, with "magnificent views" across the city. In his spare time, he could visit the nearby art gallery, theater, or concert hall.

At the appointed time, he took the elevator down to the lower ground floor and followed the signs. Through an open door, he could see the swimming pool. A couple of people were determinedly ploughing up and down, more were relaxing around the pool. It looked inviting.

The receptionist took his card, gave him a towel, and showed him where to change. His towel draped around him, he headed for the sauna.

"Not that one, sir," the receptionist said. "Your booking is for the small sauna. That way, and on your right."

Haden padded the few extra steps into a sort of alcove, opened the indicated door, and went in.

The hot, dry air as the door closed behind him was like stepping into the Sahara. The cubicle was almost in darkness, lit only by a shielded, low-power bulb tucked away on the floor underneath the slatted seat. On the seat was a large dim shape. The shape shuffled sideways, making room for him.

"Tak," Haden said, spread his towel, and sat down.

Slowly, his eyes adjusted to the near-darkness. The sauna was large enough for two occupants, just about. Perspiration began to prickle his skin.

The bulk of the dim shape beside him grew clearer. The sagging belly, streaming with sweat, the slack genitals between the spread-apart, once powerful thighs, could have belonged to any ageing businessman, hopefully attempting to sweat off the excesses of a late lunch.

The outline of the head, topped with cropped gray hair,

was, however, somewhat familiar. Haden turned and looked into the face, with its cordial, bucolic jowls and prominent nose. A chuckle issued from the mouth.

"Good afternoon, Mr. Haden," said "Schmidt."

"Schmidt," who had failed to keep his appointment on the day of the shooting, and whose real name was Karl Kordt.

EIGHT

"I am glad you survived," Kordt said, sympathetically. "That day, I arrived by taxi—and went on past by taxi without stopping, I can tell you, when I saw all the police activity. I am grateful to you, Mr. Haden, for remaining silent. An appointment with you might have proved rather difficult to explain."

"Yet here we are now," Haden said. "I doubt if you're in Sweden alone."

"Oh, come, really," Kordt said in a genial, schoolmasterly fashion. "You've traveled inside the D.D.R. yourself . . . even if not *as* yourself," he added, with a sly grin. "You know that we're not really shadowed everywhere by the secret police. That's a Western myth. My delegation are here to work, not spy on me. And they know I'm the boss."

"They have eyes in their heads," Haden said. "I don't care about your neck. I do care about mine."

Karl Kordt bent down and slid the lamp sideways a little. A faint beam shafted between the slats and onto Haden's face.

"Your ordeal improved you," Kordt remarked. "To the casual eye, you look quite unlike your press photographs."

"I'm registered under my own name," Haden said, tiredly. He wiped sweat from his face. Kordt had the advan-

•

tage. He knew what he was doing here, and perhaps
Haden's purpose too. "Sweden has lost its appeal. I think
I'll check out."

Karl Kordt laughed.

"Relax, Mr. Haden, and enjoy yourself," he said. "My
colleagues are elsewhere. They won't be back until half
past seven. Phew, I've had enough." He slid off the seat, and
flung his towel over his shoulder. "I shall look forward to a
glass of beer in the roof bar, but I make it a rule not to drink
before six o'clock."

The door banged shut behind him. Haden stuck it out
for another ten minutes, made his way to the swimming
pool, and dived in. He surfaced and swam several lengths,
thinking about Karl Kordt.

Most of the tables were strung out beside the
large windows. At five to six, the roof bar was nearly empty.
Haden chose a corner table and found himself looking down
at some distant playing fields. It was rather like being in a
stationary airship. He ordered a lager from the waiter, lit a
cheroot, and waited.

From behind him, he heard Karl Kordt make his entrance, talking in German to the waiter in his hail-fellow-
well-met way.

"Hullo, there, young fellow. You know what I'm thirst-
ing for, don't you."

"I do indeed, Herr Kordt," the waiter said, also in German. "Coming up, at once."

Kordt plumped himself down opposite Haden.

"Excellent German, he speaks, eh?" he said. "Some English too, but not so hot. Clever people, these Swedes. Most
of them have a second language, and sometimes more."

The waiter was on his way with a dewy glass of lager.

"We need to if we're to do business in the world, Herr
Kordt," he said. "No one speaks Swedish but the Swedes."

Kordt rumbled with laughter.

"Pragmatic yet independent, and a high standard of living," he said. "Admirable. Listen," he continued more quietly, "we wish to talk business so—the usual arrangement, and I shall be grateful."

"I'll see to it, Herr Kordt," the young waiter promised.

Within seconds, "Reserved" signs had appeared on the adjoining tables.

Kordt smiled at Haden, and winked.

"They're very obliging. I like this place," he said, very much at home. He gulped down half his cold lager. "Ah, that's better."

"What are you doing here?" Haden asked, speaking in English.

"Fishing for a shipbuilding order for one of our Baltic yards. Coals to Newcastle, the English would say, I think. They have good yards here, short of work. But we are cheaper, so we shall see. Also, we shall be talking to Volvo." He shrugged. "Everyone talks to Volvo. Maybe we shall lay some groundwork for the future."

Before their previous cautious discussions had begun, Stephen Haden had warily considered it prudent to ask Christian Weber, one of the few men in the world he actively liked and trusted, to make discreet inquiries concerning Karl Kordt during his next visit to the D.D.R. to see one of his "fiancées."

Weber's verbal report, conveyed during a meeting at his comfortable West Berlin apartment, had been reasonably full, although he prefaced it by dryly remarking that it should be regarded in much the same light as a set of company accounts which the auditors felt obliged to qualify heavily in the absence of supporting evidence.

An engineer by training, Kordt had served in the Wehrmacht during the Second World War and, so it was believed, had been a junior staff officer at the Bendlerstrasse in 1944 at the time of the attempt on Hitler's life. Posted immediately afterwards to the Eastern Front, he had avoided the death by strangulation with piano wire which overtook a good many of his fellow officers at a time when the slightest association with any of the plotters was proof enough of treason.

In a minor skirmish, Kordt had been slightly wounded, and left behind by his retreating unit. His contention during questioning that he had been a long-time secret socialist anti-Nazi and deeply involved in the July Plot had stood up during lengthy subsequent interrogation, and he had received privileged treatment from his Russian captors.

Christian Weber, a diligent and careful operator, had tried to verify Kordt's service record in West Berlin but could not trace the relevant documents, which neither proved nor disproved any of it. In the chaos of collapse and defeat, many official records had been destroyed or gone missing. What was easier to establish was that it had been nearly two years after the end of the war when Karl Kordt had returned to his home in what became East Germany, where he flung all his considerable talents into helping to rebuild its shattered industrial base. He revealed a flair for organization and, later, an ability to inspire confidence in those who were increasingly looking for trade with the East, and especially with the advent of the policy of détente.

No longer regarded as merely a technician, Kordt gained respect in Western business circles as not only a skillful if tough negotiator but a man who understood the free-market system and knew how to play his own so that, for the purposes of a deal, the two ran in concert. He had become something of a trouble-shooter, often conducting business negotiations outside his own specialty, and had played a significant, if quiet, part in smoothing the way for the gas pipeline project against American objections.

Given the importance of the role he played in securing contracts and hard currency, Karl Kordt was, not surprisingly, a man of considerable importance inside his own country, even though he took good care to maintain a discreet distance from official political activities. This, perhaps, lent some credence to his sighs about government interference and red tape which struck a responsive chord with Western businessmen, who were prone to complain about the same thing, free-market economy notwithstanding.

Nevertheless, genuine maverick or not, Karl Kordt had all the right contacts inside the D.D.R., and confidential access to anyone he chose. His standing was high, he was rewarded with special privileges by a grateful government as one of those who had played a leading part in proving that a modern, industrial, efficient state with a high standard of living could be established under the communist system, a model to be upheld and admired.

Stephen Haden, who had never received any requests to smuggle anyone into rather than out of the D.D.R., suspected that East Germany's comparative industrial success had rather more to do with basic German characteristics of tenacity, application, and skill, which were not much changed by drawing a line on a map. As for Karl Kordt himself, he had no idea if the bluff, clever German was a courageous man of unswerving principle, or a dedicated survivor, a Vicar of Bray. The subject of their previous discussions had led him to lean toward the Vicar of Bray theory, but whether or not that was accurate had not much mattered then.

"You seem disinclined to get to the point, Mr. Haden," Karl Kordt said.

"I'm wondering why I should trust you," Haden said.

"You have the ace up your sleeve," Kordt said. "You can cause serious difficulties for me any time you choose."

"I've no proof," Haden said. "Nothing."

"The allegation would be sufficient," Kordt said.

Haden considered that dubiously. The arrangement they had formerly been inching toward had possessed a simple, appealing charm, namely, that all possessions left behind by refugees smuggled out of East Germany were immediately confiscated. In the case of doctors, dentists, academics, and similar professional people, those possessions could include antique furniture, paintings, silver, and other objects of considerable value. Haden would set up a shell company which would act as a purchasing agent. Kordt would use his influence to authorize the sale. The antique furniture and so on would appear in the West, and be auctioned by unknown vendors.

A Liechtenstein holding company would ensure that neither Haden nor Kordt could be identified as participants. The profits would be equally divided.

"The Zurich press are hinting," Haden said, "that it's something I've been doing for years."

Karl Kordt nodded.

"East Berlin took it seriously. They've started an investigation. That's really buried the idea. A pity," he said, regretfully. "That could have been a really sweet number."

"I think you leaked that little item," Haden said.

"Me? Why should I screw up a great idea?"

Haden said, "If it's already going, and I tried to play my ace, as you put it, East Berlin would think I was trying to divert attention from some other bastard."

Karl Kordt smiled. "You could still embarrass me. Mud sticks. Your ace may have ceased to be a trump, but it's still a good enough card."

"And yet here you are, with me, again," Haden said. "On whose behalf?"

"Initially, someone useful to me who would appreciate a favor. Beyond that I don't know. I don't suppose he does either."

"Your motives for doing this favor?"

"Favors beget favors," Karl Kordt said patiently. "They oil the wheels. Doors open. We want to do business with the West. I have to play the game the Western way. Sometimes, that means not asking too many questions if I see the prospect of advantage. I would commend the same philosophy to you, Mr. Haden. The clock ticks on. Our time is limited."

Haden took the envelope from his pocket and passed it

across the table. Karl Kordt tipped out the passport-sized sketches and studied them.

"Full face and profile would be of more assistance," Kordt said, eventually. "Should he be on file somewhere."

"Not available," Haden said.

"You give me very little to go on," Kordt complained. "Eight different versions of him."

"He dresses well," Haden said. "Likes good clothes. Good cars too. He's a professional. Perhaps a mercenary. Plenty of nerve. Ruthless. A cool head. Cautious and careful, and yet an arrogant bastard too. So self-confident he deliberately takes a few risks, for the hell of it. On the face of it, the BMW was crazy, it was bound to be remembered. Yet he got away with it. That gave him a kick. But the risk was more cosmetic than actual. I think he'd been in Zurich for days, perhaps longer. No one had seen the car before he did the job. He'd stowed it somewhere. Used false license plates too. And in Zurich, he was accepted, passed unnoticed. The police checked hotels, the lot. No one remembered a suspicious blond young man. That's him. A contradiction. A cautious pro, who knows his job; also vain, a man who likes to show off a bit, if only to himself."

Karl Kordt smiled faintly.

"Quite a character sketch, considering you never even saw him."

Haden said, "I've spent a long time thinking about him."

"Someone saw him," Kordt observed, tapping the glossy sketches.

"The gardener two doors away," Haden said. "I hired an artist to draw them from his description."

"And what exactly do you want?"

"His identity, and where he can be found," Haden said. "What do you want?"

"Assuming I can identify him for you? Fifty thousand Swiss francs, deposited according to my instructions."

Haden nodded. "Provided your information's good."

"That's a side deal between you and me," Kordt said calmly. "The major requirement is otherwise."

"Forget it," Haden said. "Fifty thousand Swiss francs is enough."

"Do let me finish," Karl Kordt said gently. "It's only doing what you're good at. A gentleman wishes to leave for the West. By chance, you will be paid in excess of fifty thousand Swiss francs plus expenses for your services. So you see . . . " He spread his hands, beaming. ". . . you will remain well in profit on the deal."

"I don't like your arithmetic," Haden told him.

"There are certain problems which no doubt you will overcome, as usual," Kordt said. "The gentleman concerned is in a wheelchair. You will not be able to use your preferred route, via Prague. He is not free to travel. He might, however, be allowed to take a short holiday at one of our Baltic seaside resorts, such as Sellin or Zinnowitz. There is a ferry service from Trelleborg in Sweden to Sassnitz. You could be provided with the necessary papers—say to visit a relative in the D.D.R. It would be perfectly satisfactory for you to take him to Sweden which, as you know, rarely accedes to demands for the return of refugees." He gazed at Haden inquiringly. "It's only a suggestion," he said mildly. "You have complete discretion as to the actual method you use. To be frank, I would prefer not to know your intentions anyway."

"If he can't travel to Prague," Haden said, "he's in trouble with the State Security Service."

"Nothing serious," Karl Kordt said reassuringly.

"If you're expecting your people to demand that he be handed back, it's serious," Haden said. "Let someone else get your man out, and we'll stick to the side deal."

Kordt returned the sketches to the envelope and tucked it into his breast pocket. "Sadly, the favor I require from elsewhere depends upon the wheelchair-bound person's safe arrival in the West."

"Then you'll have to get by without it," Haden said.

"And you will have to get by without my help," Karl Kordt said, tapping his breast pocket. "My colleagues will be back soon. Our time is up." He rose to his feet. "Think it over."

Haden said, "Fifty thousand Swiss francs and no wheelchair merchant. You think it over."

Karl Kordt smiled, patted his shoulder gently, and walked out of the bar.

The young waiter removed the "Reserved" signs from the adjoining tables.

*H*aden considered returning to London a day early, but it had cost somebody several hundred pounds to send him to this hotel, presumably for some good reason. The ambivalent Karl Kordt was scarcely the most reliable contact he could have wished, but at least the man's ambition to acquire money in a safe haven was a reassuring character constant.

The nearby art gallery helped him pass the morning. Haden spent the afternoon in the hotel gymnasium and eased his aching limbs in the sauna afterwards. His body had far from recovered its former strength. He swam for a while, and lounged beside the pool for an hour. He had made sure that the hotel desk knew his whereabouts, but no one approached him.

At six o'clock, he sat at the former table in the rooftop bar. The young waiter greeted him in a friendly fashion, and brought him a lager. By seven o'clock the bar was full. Haden gestured for his bill.

"Thank you, sir," the young waiter said, accepting the tip. "And Herr Kordt telephoned to apologize, but he is engaged in much paperwork."

Haden was cleaning his teeth when there was a soft knock on his door. He spat toothpaste into the wash basin. When he turned the handle Karl Kordt walked in.

"My colleagues enjoy night clubs," he explained. "So do I, but I have foregone my pleasure on your behalf," he said reprovingly.

"A name," Haden said. "Otherwise, go and have fun."

Karl Kordt smiled agreeably.

"Your man with the variable facial hair and hairstyles presents problems," he said.

"Think about the balance in your Swiss numbered account," Haden said.

"I do," Karl Kordt said. "The problems may not be insuperable, one hopes, but it will take time. I shall be in London in seven or ten days' time. I hope to have something for you then. By a happy chance, the wheelchair-bound gentleman will then be ready for shipment, so it will all fit in nicely."

"The first half interests me," Haden said. "The second doesn't."

"The two are interlocked, Mr. Haden."

"Sixty thousand Swiss francs for you, provided your identification's good, and no funny business with guys in wheelchairs."

"I'd love to do it that way, but I quite simply can't," Karl Kordt said sadly.

"Let the idea gestate," Haden said. "Good-night."

Rain-sodden clouds blanketed London. Rain whipped off the windows of the airliner as it slanted in toward Heathrow. The pure, warm, sunlit clarity of the previous few days might never have existed.

Stephen Haden drove his Mercedes out of the short-term car park. As he entered the tunnel, he caught sight of a cream-colored Ford Sierra turning into the traffic stream some half a dozen vehicles behind him.

Haden joined the M.4 motorway and headed west, away from London. The Sierra was still there. He left the motorway at the Slough turnoff, took an exit from the roundabout at random, made two right turns and then a left along minor roads. The Sierra followed him. He drove steadily, making no attempt to shake the cream car off. Haden had had enough of this Sierra.

Windshield wipers flicking monotonously, he led the Sierra on across country. It remained some distance behind, but the driver must realize that Haden knew it was there.

Finally, at a fork, Haden chose the unmetaled alternative, little more than a car's width wide, its hollows patched with gravel, winding between the trees of a wood studded with undergrowth. It might have been the side entrance into some estate, although there was no house in sight.

Nor was the Sierra, a bend or two behind. Haden turned into the wood, bumping gently across the uneven ground between the trees, swung the wheel, braked, and switched off.

He heard the Sierra before he saw it, the slowing crunch of tires on gravel. Swiftly, his fingers eased the carpet back beside the seat, slid open the compartment, and the revolver was in his hand. He slipped out of the Mercedes, clicked the door gently closed. He heard the squeak of the Sierra's bodywork brushing against undergrowth.

Softly, Haden trod the few yards which took him behind a clump of bushes. The rain had eased a little, but not much. Water from overhanging branches wetted his hair and dripped down his neck. Between the leaves of the bush, cream bodywork slid into view and stopped. The engine died, a door slammed.

Haden inched sideways, trying to see who it was. Rustling sounds told him that the driver of the Sierra was approaching the Mercedes, and then they stopped.

"Stephen? Stephen? Where are you? I need to talk to you. It's about your man."

Haden moved a little more, and the bush was no longer in his line of sight. Harold Leyton was standing near the

Mercedes, his back to Haden. The collar of his trench coat was turned up. He was bareheaded and the steady rain was running from his hair.

"Stephen . . . oh, for Christ's sake . . . I'm in no mood for bloody hide and seek . . . "

His head had been swiveling as he called and, glimpsing or sensing Haden behind him, he turned and stared at the gun in Haden's hand.

"What the devil is that for?"

"I don't like being followed."

"I was waiting for a chance to talk to you."

"You can talk to me anytime."

"We had to be alone . . . what I've heard, I daren't risk anyone knowing I've told you . . . it'd be more than my life's worth . . . "

"What have you heard?"

Harold Leyton took out a large white handkerchief and mopped his face.

"I'm getting drenched," he complained. "Can't we talk in your car?"

"I don't mind getting wet," Haden said. "Talk."

"Dear God, this is ridiculous," Harold Leyton said. "And stop pointing that thing at me. I'm allergic to guns." Haden shoved the offending object in his pocket. "Thank you," Harold Leyton said, ironically. "All right, if you insist on getting soaked . . . this happened in Budapest . . . someone in the know . . . not a Hungarian . . . there'd been an item about you in the papers . . . I can't tell you who told me . . . "

Harold Leyton wiped rainwater from his head, and wrung out the handkerchief.

"Did you get a name?"

"He's based in West Germany. Perfect cover. Lives in Hamburg. Or perhaps just outside. This . . . someone . . . I was talking to let slip the name of a bar your man often uses. But if you go there, Stephen, I must have your word of honor that you'll never tell anyone you got this from me, because if you did . . . "

Harold Leyton shook his head and returned the handkerchief to his trench-coat pocket as he was speaking. Haden was listening intently. A slice of a second too late he saw that Harold Leyton's hand had reappeared from his pocket with quite astonishing speed, and that it was holding a small snub-nosed automatic.

Haden dived forward for the ground as the automatic cracked. He was conscious of the whine of the bullet as he bounced off the ground and hurled himself at Harold Leyton in one movement. A second shot from the automatic ripped through the shoulder pad of his suit and then his head rammed into Harold Leyton's midriff.

Leyton grunted and fell backwards, but grasped Haden's head in a lock with his left arm while trying to bring his automatic to bear with his right. Haden's revolver had fallen from his pocket and was out of reach.

They fought savagely and silently. Haden was the bigger man but Leyton, for all his podgy build, was remarkably strong, and the exertion soon told on Haden in his less-than-perfect condition. His eyes were misting redly before, locked like two animals, the automatic bending toward his temple, he managed to sink his teeth into Harold Leyton's gun hand.

Leyton screeched with pain, the automatic fell from his fingers, but he still clawed at Haden's eyes with his free hand. Haden swayed back and drove his fist into Harold Leyton's face with all his strength.

Harold Leyton's head whipped back and he fell prone, sprawling. He rolled over, pushed at the ground, tried to stand up. His legs buckled under him and he collapsed into a sitting position, sagging at the foot of an oak tree.

Breath labored and rasping, Stephen Haden picked up the automatic, removed the bullet clip, and put it in his pocket, wincing as he did so. His right hand was flaming with pain. He wondered if he had dislocated his knuckles. He found his revolver, picked it up with his left hand, looked at Leyton, and tucked it into his waistband.

Harold Leyton had not moved. His head was bowed. Blood was running from his mouth and staining his trench coat. Mingled with the blood were tears.

Harold Leyton was sobbing uncontrollably, crying like a bereaved child, tears mixing with the rain and running down his face. He remained where he was, racked with misery, while Haden moved stiffly to the Mercedes, took the lightweight raincoat from the rear seat, and put it on. His wet clothes were sticking to him, and spasms of shivering shook him.

He walked back across the grass and stood over the pathetic figure. Harold Leyton's sobs were dying away slowly. Only an occasional gulp convulsed his body. Slowly, as his eyes focused on Haden's legs, he raised his head and looked up into Haden's face. When he spoke, the words were slurred and thick.

"You bastard, Haden . . . you bastard . . . he's gone . . . it's all finished . . . everything . . . because of you . . ."

"Who? Heinz Meyer?"

"You promised . . . if I helped you . . . you'd leave us alone . . . but you told someone . . . you lied to me . . . and now he's gone . . . gone . . ."

"When you were in Budapast, did Heinz Meyer use your car?"

Harold Leyton turned his head away, spat blood onto the grass, and said nothing. Haden knocked the bleeding face in the other direction with a vicious, left-handed slap.

"Was it Heinz?" This time he hit the face back-handed. "Was it?"

Harold Leyton made no attempt to raise his hands to ward off the blows. He leaned back against the tree trunk, looked Haden in the eyes, and said with contempt, "Do you think you can beat answers out of me?"

Haden said, "Come on. Get up."

He heaved Harold Leyton to his feet. Leyton's legs bent under him. Supporting the man's weight, Haden dragged him across to the Mercedes, and propped him against it. Using his own handkerchief, he wiped the blood from Leyton's face. More dribbled down his chin at once.

"Open your mouth and let me have a look," Haden said.

Harold Leyton did as he was told. Haden fetched the First Aid kit from behind the rear seat, and made a plug of cotton.

"You've lost a tooth," he said. "Bite on that and the bleeding'll stop." Leyton complied. Haden led him around the car. "Inside," he said.

With shaking hands he started the engine and turned on the heater. Warm air gushed in. Beads of sweat stood out on Haden's forehead, but they were ice cold. Spasmodic tremors shook his body. His teeth chattered uncontrollably, and dull, sickening pain licked into his loins.

"Heinz Meyer was an agent," Haden said at last, with difficulty. "He was planted on you."

A weary grimace crossed Harold Leyton's face.

"I knew that," he said. "So did they. I'm just a businessman, I'm not involved in espionage. But they told me what to say. Things they wanted Heinz to send back. False information. It was a good arrangement. Suited everybody. I had Heinz. He was pretending at first, of course, but as time went on, I think he came to care for me. And I loved him. Just loved him." Harold Leyton studied the marks on his right hand abstractedly. "Now the whole thing's blown," he said. "You fucked it up. All of it. They daren't risk going on. Not once someone else knew. Too dangerous all around. They've lost a sweet and easy way to channel phoney information to the other side. I've lost Heinz. They were going to arrest him, but he got wind of that somehow." Haden could guess how, but said nothing. "Even my business," Harold Leyton said, "that's gone. I'd be arrested the minute I set foot in any Eastern Bloc country. They think I'm a bloody spy."

"You're a top salesman, Harry," Haden said. "You can sell in the West." Leyton leaned his head against the head rest and closed his eyes. "Feeling better now?" Haden asked.

"No," Harold Leyton said. "It's all your doing. I wanted you dead."

"They'd have known it was you," Haden said. "Life imprisonment for murder, you wouldn't have liked that. You'll get over it in the long run. Everyone does."

"I doubt if you've ever cared for anyone in your life, except yourself," Harold Leyton said. "How would you know?"

The car engine idled gently. The hum of the heater was a whispering sigh. The warm air was caressing and comfortable. Haden's unpredictable shivering spasms were arriving less frequently. The parchment pastiness was leaving Harold Leyton's face, the normal ruddy blush returning.

"I'm sure you know Karl Kordt," Haden said.

"Kordt?" Harold Leyton opened his eyes wide. Head tilted, he stared at Haden. "I've met him . . . Leipzig . . . Berlin . . ."

"You kept saying 'they' just now," Haden said. "Who are 'they'?"

"People," Leyton said. "Contacts who kept changing. 'Who' was their business. I didn't want to know."

"Have 'they' mentioned Karl Kordt? Especially recently?"

"I was asked to do something," Harold Leyton said. "It seemed my duty, if you'll forgive an old-fashioned word, to do it. No one ever discussed anything, except what I was supposed to pass on to Heinz."

"There's Helen Lloyd," Haden said. "And don't tell me she just happens to know an FBI man at the U.S. Embassy."

"You asked for something. That was all I could think of. The other people, they always contact me. I've no way of getting hold of them."

"She implied she'd had a long-standing affair. Someone who mattered. Who was that with?"

"I've no idea," Harold Leyton said. "She's very efficient, provides useful commercial information, and that's all I know about her. I'm just a businessman."

"Harry," Haden said, "I think you'd go on bleating that you were just a businessman after five years in the Lubyanka."

*T*he hall porter handed him his key and a message slip. Haden glanced at it briefly, saw that it was only from Christa, and stuffed it in his pocket, unread.

"Welcome back, Mr. Haden," the hall porter said. "We've kept the same room for you."

Haden was conscious that the sickly pain in his loins had declined into a disagreeable ache but he still felt very unwell. He stripped, dropped the soiled suit with the ripped shoulder pad in a crumpled heap at the bottom of the wardrobe, and lay for half an hour in a hot bath. The unpleasant ache finally went away but the feeling of malaise did not.

Lethargically, he dried himself, pulled on a terry-cloth dressing gown, and decided to order a light meal in his room and go to bed. The telephone rang as he was about to lift the receiver.

"A call from Switzerland for you, Mr. Haden," the operator's soft voice said.

Stephen Haden did not recognize the voice which came on the line.

"Mr. Haden, we've been trying to trace you, we've been on to your office, eventually we phoned Christa and she . . . "

"Just a minute. Who is that?"

"Your mother's in hospital, Mr. Haden," the voice of the unknown woman said. "I'm one of her neighbors . . . "

NINE

The mountains towered behind the village church, wearing their summer green. Only on the highest peaks did a few scattered patches of snow survive, hardy relics of winter, small reminders that with its return, snow would command the region as far as the eye could see.

Stephen Haden stood beside his mother's grave as the coffin was lowered in. He had been too late, in time only to see a body being wheeled on a trolley away from the ward. Words were being spoken, but he was deaf to them. He watched the polished casket on its short downward journey, until it came to rest. His mother had possessed a simple unshakable faith. For her sake, he hoped she had been right, and was even now joined again in spirit with the man she had loved. He wished he could believe as well as hope.

The cluster around the graveside was small. The village was isolated, at the end of a narrow road which thereafter led nowhere. Tourists only found their way there by chance and turned back. His mother had been happy to live quietly, content with the few friends who were there. Stephen was her only surviving relative.

Flowers and wreaths lay on the grass nearby. There was a wreath from Carli and Anton, another from Anna. A spray of wildflowers bore Christa's name. The plot was the one his mother had chosen many years before. The headstone would be simple, and carry only her name, date of death, and the single word "Reunited," as she had wished.

Anna was there, which was nice of her, considering the two women had never got on. His mother had thoroughly disapproved of Anna, although she had done her best to conceal her dislike, but she had conceived an immediate fondness for Christa, on whom she lavished loving kindness, and was ever eager to have the child come and stay with her in the mountain village, an eagerness which Christa reciprocated.

Christa was there too. She had begged to be allowed to fly back with Haden to see "Nan," as she called her, perhaps in a subconscious attempt to construct a surrogate family for herself. She was standing beside Anna, dry-eyed, but her face taut, her hands clenched tightly in front of her.

Stephen Haden had cried when his mother had sat beside him and cuddled him and stroked his hair, and told him that his father was dead. The tears had been genuine, but they had been a little boy's tears, in retrospect not dissimilar to the bitter tears the same little boy had shed when his dog was run over and killed. His father had gone from his life early, leaving few memories, little more than a series of disconnected mental snapshots, but his mother had always been there, caring for him, chiding him for running wild, but there, a constant, taken for granted even when, in later years, he saw her infrequently. Now he was no longer a boy, half of his life or more had run its course, and she too had gone, unexpectedly, the victim of a massive stroke.

The handful of earth spattered onto the coffin. Stephen Haden found it necessary to keep swallowing. He had experienced many feelings in his life, but not this. For a moment, Harold Leyton's crumpled face and helpless sobs flitted across the background of his mind. So this was what grief was like. Real grief. He did not want it. He did not like it. But he could not help it. It had come.

Stephen Haden realized that it was all over. Elderly

women across the grave were waiting awkwardly, as if for a cue. He turned away, and swallowed again. Anna was looking at him curiously. The mourners were drifting away.

Haden turned to Christa and put his arm around her.

"All right?" The girl nodded. "I shall have to stay for a day or two. Clear up Nan's things." He looked at Anna. "Will you see her onto the plane?"

"Yes, of course," Anna said.

"And arrange for a car to meet her at Heathrow, take her back to school."

"I always do that, Stephen," Anna said pointedly. "You needn't worry about Christa."

"I want to hang on for a bit," Haden said. "So I'll say good-bye now." Christa turned and put her arms around him. "See you soon," Haden said.

"You mean that? You really will?"

"Promise," Haden said. "We'll do something. I'll ring you."

Christa walked away toward Anna's car.

"No one knew you were in London," Anna said. "Christa didn't say."

"Perhaps you haven't spoken to her," Haden said.

"I'm glad you're taking some notice of her at last. Even if a little late. Will you be in London long?"

"I have some business to see to," Haden said. "I don't know."

"I shouldn't have asked. You hate committing yourself. I ought to know that, better than anyone."

With a half smile she touched his hand briefly and followed Christa.

Stephen Haden turned back to the open grave. Beside it was another, well-kept. The flowers in the marble urn were just beginning to wilt. Inscribed on the headstone was the name "Charles Haden."

Until he was in his teens, Stephen Haden had accompanied his mother on her weekly pilgrimages, the bunch of fresh flowers in her gloved hand. He could still smell the stale water as he tipped it from the urn, then refilled the urn from the tap, before returning to the kneeling figure of his mother beside the grave and watching her arrange the flowers to her satisfaction. With the onset of puberty, he had stopped going. By then, Sunday afternoons were for village girls, or catching the bus into Geneva with his friends. It was more years than he could remember now since he had seen his father's grave.

Stephen Haden lifted his head and took a deep breath of the clean, fresh air. The past was dead and gone. He turned his back on the graves and walked toward Schlunegger. Distantly, between the trees, were the glassy waters of Lake Geneva.

Schlunegger had been there when the party emerged from the church. He had stood at a distance from the grave while the coffin was consigned to the earth and was now propped up against his car, arms folded, waiting.

"I told you to let me know where you were," Schlunegger said.

"So you did. It slipped my mind."

"Funny how hard numbers can't resist funerals," Schlunegger said. "Especially their old lady's. You'd have been more sensible to stay away."

"If you just came to needle me," Haden said, grimly, "you're doing well."

"More curiosity," Schlunegger said, unruffled. "See who else turned up besides you."

"All right. You've seen."

"And sniff around a bit," Schlunegger added.

"Okay. Go and do it. Enjoy yourself."

"Sniffed already," Schlunegger said. "Nothing unusual. No strangers. What are you doing in London?"

"Keeping my head down."

"You'd have done better to go to Miami, or better still, Peru. How long are you staying here?"

"No longer than I can help."

"Don't linger," Schlunegger said. "If I knew you'd

come, other people might arrive at the same conclusion. I half expected Carli to be here, Anton Weiss, a couple of your heavies perhaps."

"I told them to stay away."

Schlunegger nodded and gazed thoughtfully at the quiet, peaceful churchyard. Two gravediggers had started to fill in the grave, working unhurriedly.

"Barring unexpected luck, it doesn't look as though we're going to catch the blond young man who shot you."

"I gathered from the papers you were getting bored with it."

"Not bored," Schlunegger said gently. "Technically, inquiries are proceeding. But manpower's limited. Crimes occur every day. Your case is growing whiskers. We've tried to eliminate—or not—all those who were in or visited your house and offices the day before you were shot. Do you know how many there were?"

Haden shook his head.

"A lot. It was a busy day."

"Your staff," said Schlunegger, ticking them off on his fingers. "Domestic help. Two messengers—I'm only talking about those who were admitted to the house. A woman from your accountant's. Your lawyer. Anna called. What did she come for?"

"Lunch," Haden said.

"I know that," Schlunegger said patiently.

"She was leaving for Italy. She'd had the offer of a partnership in a night club there. Thought I might back her."

"Anna knows the night club business," Schlunegger said neutrally.

"If it was such a good proposition, she could have got the financing anywhere. Lending risk money isn't *my* business."

Schlunegger laughed.

"No. You prefer to accumulate it. Sundry visitors," he resumed, "who accounted for their presence in various ways. Whether I believed them or not is neither here nor there. Two men delivered fuel oil for your central heating system, and checked the boiler."

"I'd forgotten that. I'm not sure I knew. Perhaps Carli arranged it."

"She did," Schlunegger said. "Your part-time handyman swears he secured the basement door after they'd left, and switched the door alarm back on. How reliable is your handyman?"

"As reliable as anyone until they get an offer they prefer."

"So you can't tell me, hand on heart, that you'd eliminate any of them."

"You're working on the assumption that the gunman came in through the basement door," Haden said.

"I never assume anything," Schlunegger said. "But I think it looks possible."

"In that case, someone left it open for him."

Schlunegger shook his head.

"It could have beem neglect," he said. "Your handyman may be afraid to admit that he forgot to lock it."

"The guy who shot me didn't wander around the house trying doors on the off chance. He's not that sort. It was a setup. He knew."

"Suppose you're right. Who set you up? Which one, in your heart of hearts, do you suspect?"

"Every single one of them. Look for a motive. That's your trade, isn't it?"

"You attract too many motives, Haden," Schlunegger said. "Greed, money, hatred, revenge, you name it. Nearly everyone can be bought, especially for something simple like leaving a door unlocked. *If* that's how it was done, the accomplice might not even have known the intention was to kill you. In which case, he or she is scared shitless, and is going to cover up like crazy for fear of being an accessory to attempted murder."

"In plain language," Haden said, "you've given up."

"I'm disheartened," Schlunegger said. "I hoped you

might have thought it over and decided to try and help me this time. I still wonder about 'Schmidt.' Heard anything from him since?"

"Not a word," Haden said.

"Listen," Schlunegger said, "I'm going off the record. That means I haven't said anything, and if you ever claim I have, you'll reach old age in prison, and I can fix that, believe me."

"I believe you," Haden said. "I believe you would, too."

"You'd better. I'm just a humble copper," Schlunegger mused reflectively. "Murder, rape, incest, straightforward things like that. But yours was a shooting with possible political implications. We've trespassed into areas we're not usually told about. A team of men out and about asking questions, a lot of information accumulates. Bloody mounds of it, one percent possibly relevant, the rest useless crap. But there are bits . . . scraps . . . hints . . . disconnected, don't add up, don't make sense. But something's going on. I don't know what. I can feel it in my bones. Zurich comes into it. Berlin, East or West, maybe both. There's that dangerous bastard Kurt Gabler. Dropped out of sight before you got perforated. I thought that was an interesting coincidence, and I'll bet you did too."

"It crossed my mind," Haden said.

"He turned up, innocent as you please. Claimed he'd only just heard Interpol were looking for him," Schlunegger said, skeptical.

"Where's he supposed to have been?"

"Shacked up with some woman near bloody Stavanger." Schlunegger sighed regretfully. "What's more, it checks out. His alibi's cast iron, so Kurt is definitely eliminated, I'm sorry to say. He reckons you owe him money."

"He's spreading that around for some reason," Haden said.

Schlunegger gazed around him and sniffed the air appreciatively.

"Lovely spot, this," he said. "Nice and quiet. Restful.

Ah, well, back to the grind." He unlocked his car door, got in, started the engine, and wound down the driver's window. "Kurt's still in Zurich. He was coming on a bit strong about that money you owe him. He might decide to come and collect."

Haden said, "I'll get some beer in."

Schlunegger grinned.

"I don't think Kurt likes you much," he remarked, and drove off.

*T*he inlaid cabinet contained what Haden's mother had always referred to as her private "treasures." He unlocked it with some reluctance. It seemed like prying, yet it had to be done.

Inside the cabinet were a number of drawers and shelves, the latter stacked in a seemingly random fashion with bundles of papers and documents, although the large manila envelope with MY WILL written on it in large ink capitals was propped up prominently and could not be missed. Haden opened it.

The will was brief and formal, and left everything to "my only son, Stephen." Also in the envelope were a bank book, statements, some insurance policies and notes of her investments. The single deposit in the bank book was familiar. The account had evidently been opened to receive the amount Haden had repaid to his mother many years ago, and had remained on deposit, untouched, ever since. Stephen Haden grimaced, and laid it aside. He still felt bad about that episode when he had borrowed money from his mother for a business which had failed. She had lent it without question and had never so much as mentioned it until, eventually, he had been able to repay her. She had first inquired anxiously if he was sure he could afford it before accepting his check. He had, of course, been much younger and more thoughtless at the time. Well, younger anyway, Haden thought, with dry sadness. It was still hard to believe that she was dead.

The largest bundle, tied with string, was at the back of the shelf, and proved to be the annual audited accounts of his father's precision engineering business, "Haden Engineering (Basel)," from the day his father had set it up before the war, until it had been sold following his father's death from cancer. The proceeds from the sale had been sufficient to keep his mother comfortably, and without any financial worries.

Stephen Haden's father and mother had lived in Basel until a few years after he was born. He could dimly remember—or thought he could—being driven to their new home in the village, his father at the wheel, but the former home in Basel was a blank. The house in which he now sat contained the few remaining memories of his father he possessed.

A smaller bundle, this one neatly tied with ribbon, was a collection of letters his father had written to his wife before Stephen Haden was born. They were all dated during the war years when, evidently, his father had often been away from home on business in other parts of Switzerland. A glance was sufficient to show that they were love letters. He wound the ribbon around the package and tied it up again.

Depression gripped Stephen Haden. He was not certain what he was doing, or why. All this stuff related to two people who were now dead. The sensible thing, having located the will and related documents, would be to chuck the rest away without further ado. And yet his mother had carefully preserved it all among her "treasures" for upwards of forty years. Obscurely, Haden felt that he should at least know what had been important to her before treating it as rubbish.

He fumbled for a cheroot and lit it before he remembered that there were no ashtrays in this house. He fetched a saucer, and resumed his self-imposed task.

One of the drawers was devoted to mementos of himself, from baptismal certificate to school reports. Haden threw the lot into the wastepaper basket without compunction. School had bored him, and the undistinguished nature of his scholastic achievements was definitely not worth recalling.

Among odds and ends in another drawer was an envelope. Written on it in his mother's firm hand was "Charles, 1942–1944." Inside were a few faded black-and-white photographs. Haden was somewhat surprised. It had been his mother's meticulous habit to mount carefully all photographs in an album, which lay on the bottom shelf and which he had not bothered to look at, being familiar with its contents, from his parents' wedding photographs to some embarrassing shots of himself as a teenager, alternately moody or grinning fatuously.

The photographs puzzled him at first. He scarcely recognized his father, who wore a full beard. Search his memory as he might, he could not remember that beard. In one, his father was bending over the engine of a vehicle parked outside some sort of hut. In another, he was talking to a fresh-faced young man. Both were heavily muffled against the cold. Snow lay on the ground, and encrusted the trees behind them. Haden shuffled through the prints. All were obviously in the mountains somewhere, and he came to the conclusion that they had been taken during one or more hunting expeditions. In one of them, his father, part of a group, was examining the breech of a rifle, and the other men had guns slung over their shoulders.

Stephen Haden returned the snapshots to the envelope. His mother, he remembered, had disapproved of shooting animals, and hence of his father's occasional hunting trips. Quite likely, she had disapproved of the beard as well and that was why she had declined to elevate these particular snapshots to the dignity of her family album while being unable to bring herself to dispose of them, it being her nature to throw nothing away.

The latter was most certainly true, Haden reflected, as he gazed at the cabinet. It was growing late, and he had scarcely dealt with a third of its contents. He glanced at his watch tiredly, and decided to give it another half an hour.

The discovery of the journal woke him up.

It was not a diary, although each entry, beginning on a fresh page, was dated, but long gaps, sometimes running into years, separated the segments of neat, round handwriting.

Haden flicked the pages and realized that this cardboard-bound exercise book was the refuge to which his mother had turned to record her deepest and most private emotions. Several pages, written the day after his father had died, began, *"Oh, dear God, why have you taken him from me...?"*

Stephen Haden's first instinct was to read no more. This was between her and the God in whom she had so devoutly believed, but as he allowed the pages to fall and reached for the large brown envelope from which he had extracted the exercise book, he found himself looking at another page on which were a mere couple of lines:

"He is my son and I shall love him always, but he is not the man his father was, nor ever will be."

No more. Just that. The date showed Haden that it had been penned when the police were beginning to take an interest in his night club.

Stephen Haden crushed his dying cheroot out on the saucer, and screwed it into a mass of fragments. His face and neck had grown hot. He loosened his tie, and wished he had thought to buy a bottle of cognac. The dead woman's words stared at him like some eternal judgment.

A kind of masochistic curiosity drove him on. He found a more recent entry, when his escape-helper business was flourishing.

"I tell myself he is helping the oppressed. It is true men and women are free through him. Yet it is not for freedom, not for his country. Just money. I wonder what my dear Charles would have thought! Often, I have wished I could

speak out. Perhaps later, when I know I am going to die. Perhaps then."

Stephen Haden's facial muscles were taut with a mixture of resentment and anger. What the hell was she raving about? His father had been no saintly, frugal monk. He had been in business to make a profit, and very successfully too. Everyone did everything for money, his father included.

Mystified, Stephen Haden went back to the beginning. His mother had bought the exercise book on her honeymoon, and it began with a young girl's delight and happiness with her English bridegroom and lover. Haden skipped forward. To read that really would be voyeurism. He passed the somber entry in 1939 recording her first pregnancy and miscarriage, followed by a prolonged period of ill health. Haden knew about that, she had told him, and he skipped forward again to the autumn of 1944.

"My prayers have been answered. He is back! I was so afraid that I would never see him again, but he is with me again!"

Back from where? The cryptic lines stood alone on the page; there was no explanation. Haden sought one among earlier entries.

"He says it is business which takes him away so much. I have tried to believe him. I no longer do so. God, please help me. What shall I do?"

And, later:

"Perhaps ignorance would have been better. Today, I forced him to tell me. No one must know. I can only come to terms with it, and try not to be afraid. I pray it may end soon."

Haden snapped the journal closed. Secrets should die with the dead. Who cared? His father, it seemed, had been involved in a prolonged affair with another woman, finally given her up, and returned to his wife. Such things happened often enough. No marriage was perfect. Parents were only people. It was, however, ironically amusing that his mother should have been so intolerant of *his* shortcomings, and so forgiving of his father's. Perhaps that was the way it was with one's children. He wouldn't know about that.

Haden worked on methodically until he had emptied the cabinet. Nothing more of much interest came to light. The last thing he extracted was a hardback book, which at first he took to be a novel but on glancing at the blurb found was someone's wartime reminiscences. Called *Dragon and the Brave*, it was by J. K. R. Walker and had been published in 1950.

The flyleaf was inscribed:

For Charles:
This may amuse you!
(Sorry about the omissions. Would have wished otherwise, but there it is.)
All good wishes for the future.
Regards,
Jim.

Haden yawned and turned idly to the back of the dust-cover. Underneath the photograph of the author, he read:

"James Kenneth Richard Walker saw action throughout the war as soldier, airman, and resistance fighter. He was awarded the D.F.C. and the Croix de Guerre for his exploits, and . . ."

Stephen Haden closed the book and pushed it aside. His eyelids were heavy. He had made up the bed in the room he had occupied as a boy. As his head touched the pillow, his last thought was that by 1950 his father's future had been decidedly limited.

The dim advance warning of dawn was seeping around the edges of the curtains when his eyes opened as if of their own accord and he considered the unlikely recollection which his subconscious had dredged up. Or, more probably, invented, the product of some forgotten dream. For a moment, he considered getting up to make certain, but the embrace of the bed was warm and comforting, and even as he thought about it, he fell asleep again at once, and did not awake again until after nine.

It was a moment or two before he could place where he was, and why. Stephen Haden, rested, sat on the edge of the bed, and stretched. There were no ghosts in this house.

West of the village, where the approach road looped on its upward climb, was an eyrie overlooking the valley below, shielded by rocks from upward glances from passersby, a solitary, private place.

From behind those rocks, when Stephen Haden was a small boy, he and his friends had been Red Indians and the occasional passing cart the stagecoach galloping into their ambush. They had unleashed arrows from homemade bows and danced around whooping after the receding cart, before retrieving their arrows, which always fell well short. In later years, on sunny summer Sunday afternoons, the eyrie had served the teenage Stephen Haden for more carnal purposes, his heart thudding as his fingers undid buttons, and slipped brassieres from young breasts which needed little support.

Now he sat, propped up against the rocks, reading Walker's book, raising his eyes only when an ascending car appeared around the bend below, and watching it pass before allowing his gaze to return to the page.

The bothersome physical symptoms which had persisted until the day before seemed, he thought cautiously, to have gone. There was no need to see Dr. Hensler. Rudi was a worrier. He was okay.

The account of James Walker's war was told in a no-nonsense fashion, without embroidery. The unpretentious, straightforward style lent it a certain vivid conviction.

Walker had been a pupil accountant and a member of the Territorial Army at the outbreak of war. Called to the colors, he had been sent to France and in 1940 had fought in Belgium before being evacuated from Dunkirk.

Back in England, with a unit which had lost nearly all its arms and equipment, and with the Battle of Britain going on in the skies overhead, James Walker had chafed at the lack of prospect of any further action in the foreseeable future, and volunteered for air-crew duty in the Royal Air Force.

He was accepted, and commissioned on the conclusion of his training as a navigator. During his first tour of operations, he was awarded the DFC for his part in saving a burning aircraft. Early in his second tour of operations, his Halifax night bomber was fatally disabled by an ME110 night fighter and the pilot gave the order to bail out.

Walker parachuted to safety but became separated from the remainder of the crew. He evaded capture by the German search parties, and fell in with a Belgian escape organization.

Hidden in Brussels for several weeks, he was eventually provided with civilian clothes and forged papers, and sent "down the line," traveling with two other shot-down air crewmen and an escort, a Belgian girl. They went first of all to Paris, where they rested in a safehouse for a couple of days, and then were ready to begin their journey south toward the Spanish border, where a guide would have taken them over the Pyrenees into Spain and on to Gibraltar. From there they would have been flown back to England, and resumed bombing operations.

The safehouse in which they were staying overnight, however, proved to be less than safe. They had been betrayed by a German agent who had infiltrated the escape organization.

By chance, Walker happened to be relieving himself in the nearby woods when the trap was sprung, and he got away, although he continued to be hunted by the Germans.

In a bleak, laconic parenthesis, the author recorded that, after the war, he had made inquiries and had learned that the escort had been tortured and executed by the Gestapo, as were the owners of the safehouse.

Walker guessed that the Germans would expect him to head south. Moving by night, he traveled east instead and succeeded in evading his pursuers. His French was adequate. Friendly peasants helped him, although none were in touch with the resistance, and he had some close calls with a German motorcycle patrol.

Finally, after several weeks, a woodcutter who had sheltered him in his hut promised to lead him to a Maquis headquarters.

Stephen Haden raised his eyes as he heard the car approaching. Looking down from high above the road, he could not see the face of the solitary occupant, but the car bore Zurich license plates.

The car drew into the car park of the café on the fringe of the village. The occupant got out and went into the café. A minute later he came out, opening a packet of cigarettes. He lit one, his back to Haden, shielding the flame against the gentle breeze. He did not get back into his car, nor did he walk on directly into the village. Instead, he struck off into a side turning, and was lost to sight.

Stephen Haden marked the page, closed the book, and laid it down. He was still less than halfway through it. The major events were yet to come.

Beside him on the grass lay a short heavy kitchen knife. His mother had liked her kitchen utensils to be of the best. The gleaming, razor-sharp blade tapered to a point.

Haden rose to his feet and tucked the knife into his waistband. He turned away from the road below and began to climb, circling away from the village, keeping out of sight. The whine of a far-off jet on its way into the Geneva airport was the only sound which broke the silence of the encircling woods.

The knife was the best weapon he had been able to find.

TEN

The house was on the far side of the village, and nestled at the foot of the wooded hills. It stood alone, and lacked any near neighbors.

From high on the hillside, Stephen Haden scanned the front and back. No caller stood waiting outside the locked front door, no one was in sight.

Taking his time, he came down through the trees and crouched a few yards short of the garden fence, still under cover, studying the rear of the house. All seemed as it should be. No window was open. But anyone who knew his job, having forced a window, would close it again once he was inside.

Haden stayed where he was for twenty minutes, watching and listening. If he was mistaken, he would only have wasted half an hour of his life. It was a small-enough price. But he could see and sense nothing amiss.

He was about to risk sliding forward and slipping through the gate which led from the garden into the woods when he saw it. A tiny wisp of bluish smoke drifted from somewhere on his left. Haden shrank back. Half a minute later, there was another thin trace of smoke.

Haden melted back into the trees, climbing high up before circling and beginning to descend again, slowly, noiselessly, inch by inch, content to spend minutes to buy silence, to avoid the slightest rustle which might betray his approach to the point where he calculated the man should be.

Whoever it was had chosen his cover well. Haden was jolted to find himself only a few feet away when, sliding from behind a tree, he saw the man for the first time.

The man was waiting on the other side of a tree, his back against it. In front of him were flowering bushes. Through them, he could see the approach to the house while remaining unseen. All of him that was visible to Haden was the shoulder of a dark suit, and part of a trouser leg. As he watched, the unknown man dropped a cigarette butt and trod on it.

Haden did not think much of his chances of crossing the twig-strewn, relatively open ground which separated them without giving himself away in the still and utter silence. And while the knife he held was potentially murderous at close quarters, it was not built for throwing.

Stephen Haden stayed where he was and waited for what he needed. Minutes passed. The shoulder he could see shifted slightly. Another cigarette butt dropped to the ground. Haden swore silently. Finally, it came, the faint whine of the jet approaching Geneva airport. The sound grew, but not as loud as usual, and certainly fainter than Haden would have wished. He listened intently, still motionless, and when he fancied the distant whine was as loud as it was going to get, he moved, taking long, fast strides.

The watching man heard the crack of twigs above the jet whine and began to turn, a gun already traveling from his shoulder holster, but a fraction too late. By then, Haden had the powerful, muscular body clamped from behind, the knife across his windpipe.

"Drop it, or I slit your bloody throat," Haden told him.

"Christ, man . . ." A gasp.

"Drop it," Haden repeated, and emphasized his seriousness with the razor-sharp blade.

"Okay . . . okay . . ."

Kurt Gabler dropped it.

"You stay quite still," Haden said into his ear, maintaining the pressure. The knife had nicked the skin. Blood was running down Kurt Gabler's throat. "And tell me what you're doing here."

"Waiting for you," Kurt Gabler breathed, as still as if every muscle was frozen into place.

Haden said, "You could have driven up to the front door and waited."

"And be seen? I didn't think you'd want that."

"What do *you* want?"

"A beer and a talk . . . that's all, Stephen . . . I swear . . ."

Haden said, "Tell you what we're going to do, Kurt. Take two paces forward, just the way we are. Careful and slow, so this knife doesn't slip. Okay?"

Kurt Gabler refrained from nodding his nead. As they took the second slow pace forward, Haden let him go, and shoved him hard in the back.

Kurt Gabler stumbled forward, regained his balance, and swung around. By then, Haden had the automatic in his hand. Kurt touched his throat, and looked disbelievingly at the blood on his fingers.

"Christ, man," he said, reproachfully. "There was no need for all that."

"Someone waiting for me makes me nervous," Haden said. "It's happened before." With the automatic in his hand, he felt more relaxed and at ease. "All right, Kurt," he said. "Now we'll have that talk. Inside."

Stephen Haden closed the front door. Kurt Gabler stared at himself in the large mirror which hung in the hall, his expression aghast. Large bloodstains disfigured his formerly spotless white shirt.

"Christ, my fucking shirt's ruined, you lunatic." He took the neatly folded handkerchief from his breast pocket and held it to his throat. "It's handmade, you bastard, my favorite shirt," he complained.

"In there," Haden said, indicating the living room with Kurt Gabler's automatic. "Sit in the armchair facing the window."

Kurt Gabler sat as instructed, still holding the handkerchief to his throat. He took it away and inspected it at intervals, in the hope that the steady dribble of blood was lessening.

Haden sat facing him, several feet away.

"You're the one who wants to talk, Kurt," he said. "Talk."

"You owe me money," Kurt Gabler said, sulkily.

"No one's arguing," Haden said. "Go to the office and collect it."

"I've been to the fucking office," Kurt Gabler said, violently. "Anton and Carli say you're keeping them short. I need it now, goddamn it."

"What for?" Haden inquired. "Is your shirtmaker dunning you for payment?"

Kurt Gabler closed his eyes and took a deep breath, as if trying to restrain himself.

"To square those thieving tax bastards," he growled. "Until that's settled, I can't go back to Berlin." He opened his eyes and stared at Haden accusingly. "Some lousy bastard dropped me in it."

"There are those," Haden said, "who thought this anonymous informant might have been you."

"Rat on myself? Why the hell should I do that?"

"Kurt," Haden said, tiredly, "apart from being greedy, vain, and a natural bully, you're as sharp as they come. When you act naive and innocent, it's not convincing, it makes me wonder." Kurt Gabler stared at him sullenly. "Suddenly you have tax problems," Haden said patiently. "You have to drop out of sight. It's a first-class reason. I sympathize. Only once you've disappeared, things happen. That's a coincidence."

Kurt Gabler removed the handkerchief from his throat again and inspected it closely.

"It's congealing," Haden said. "You're not going to bleed to death."

"I had to get out of Berlin and try and sort something out," Kurt Gabler said. "I went to Oslo."

"Why Oslo?" Haden interjected.

"I had money there," Kurt Gabler said. "Not a lot, but enough to see me through for a while. And there was someone in Oslo I could look up. She's no spring chicken, but she's a terrific screw. Besides, she's loaded, which makes it even nicer. I've been giving her one for years, off and on, should her husband happen to be somewhere else. He's some sort of diplomat, so he often is. This time he'd gone to the UN in New York. She'd taken a chalet near Stavanger. It seemed like a good place to let the heat die down. I was there all the time. I didn't read the papers, I didn't even know you'd been shot. When I surfaced, I heard I was on Interpol's books. I came back to Zurich to square things. You can ask that evil shit Schlunegger. He wouldn't let me go until he'd double-checked every dot and comma." A sudden grin creased his normally far-from-amiable hard-featured face. "That'll be one convenient screw down the drain for keeps. Norwegian coppers turning up on her doorstep asking questions, she won't like that one little bit."

"I can't pay you in cash," Haden said.

"Cash is what I need," Kurt Gabler said. "Cash doesn't bounce."

"You can have a bearer check on a Geneva bank," Haden said. He checked his watch. "You'll have time to get there today."

"Do me a favor," Kurt Gabler said. "In this shirt, I'd be arrested on suspicion on bloody sight."

"You can have one of mine," Haden said.

In the bathroom, Kurt Gabler stripped to the waist, washed, dried himself, and slipped into one of Haden's shirts, while Haden leaned on the doorframe, watching him. With the check in his hip pocket, Kurt's humor had improved considerably.

"You're a suspicious sod, Stephen Haden—but I don't blame you," he said generously, as he eased on his shoulder holster. "Oh, my gun, if you've finished with it."

"I'll keep it for a while," Haden said. "My next caller might not be such a good friend as you."

Kurt Gabler smiled at him in the mirror.

"What's going on in London? Anything interesting?"

"Not to my knowledge," Haden said. "Where now? Back to Berlin?"

"Right away." Kurt Gabler patted his hip pocket. "Now I can make a deal with the bastards."

They went downstairs, and Haden opened the front door.

"Anything in particular I can do for you, Stephen?" Kurt Gabler asked.

"Look after Berlin. According to Anton, there's a backlog."

"Anton Weiss is a prick," Kurt Gabler said. "You're the boss, Stephen. You always have been. Sorry about the misunderstanding."

"We'll be in touch," Haden said.

He watched Kurt as he moved away with his easy, silky smooth walk. When he was at some distance, Haden eased the door closed, and followed. If Kurt Gabler knew he was there, he did not look back. His long-legged stride took him through the village and on to the café, where he climbed into his car and drove off.

Haden continued on until he reached the first loop in the road, then climbed back up to the eyrie in the rocks, picked up the book he had left lying on the grass, and settled down to read again.

The declining sun had lost much of its warmth when he finished the last page, closed the book, and laid it down. He fumbled for a cheroot, lit it, and sat staring unseeingly at the distant waters of Lake Geneva.

It still made no sense. There was no explanation he could think of.

*T*he cottage was in the Surrey countryside outside Dorking. It was called "The Elms." Stephen Haden switched off the engine of his Mercedes and sat looking at it. At one time a group of farmworkers' cottages, it had been converted into one picturesque residence a good many years ago, he guessed. The elms after which it had presumably been christened had long since gone, victims of Dutch elm disease.

Haden got out, approached the front door, rang the bell, and waited. The front garden was immaculate, the beds massed with flowers, the lawn perfect with not a weed in sight.

He rang twice more, but there was no answer. From somewhere at the back came an even, rhythmic sound. Haden skirted the cottage and crossed the broad, close-cut lawns, on which stood a garden table, chairs, and sun umbrella, toward an ornamental low wall, after which the garden dipped into a hollow. Standing in the hollow, stripped to the waist, a man was methodically attacking a huge tree stump with a long-handled axe.

Of average height, he was stoutly built, and although a rim of fat rippled around his waist, his sweat-streaked upper body was strong and muscular. Short gray hair half circled his shining bald head. Haden had expected someone more elderly. If this was the right one, he seemed to be in remarkably good physical shape for his age.

The man caught sight of him, lowered his axe, and turned inquiringly.

"Hullo . . . sorry . . . didn't see you . . ."

"I'm looking for a Mr. James Walker," Haden said.

"That's me. Can I help you?"

"I did ring several times," Haden said, indicating the cottage.

"My wife's away, gone to see our grandchildren. Didn't

hear the bell." He bent and picked up a portable telephone. "You didn't phone first, did you?" Haden shook his head. The man looked relieved, and put the telephone down again. "Marvelous things, but they don't always work. Sorry I didn't hear you ring. I suppose I was concentrating too hard on the job at hand."

"There are easier ways to remove tree stumps," Haden remarked.

"I know, but this is personal between me and it. My old enemy." He swung the axe in a semicircle, and left it sticking in the tree stump. "More of an old friend, really," he said, cheerfully. "He's always there, helps to keep me in trim. Anyway, what can I do for you?"

"I wondered if you'd sign this for me," Haden said, showing him the book.

"Good God, that's been out of print for well over thirty years." He grinned broadly. "Long forgotten by one and all, I fear. Where on earth did you get it?"

"I happened to come across it," Haden said.

"Yes, but how did you find me? Not through the publishers, surely? The chap I dealt with must have retired by now, and I've moved since those days, anyway."

"One of their old hands thought you were living somewhere near Dorking. You're ex-directory, so I tried the voters' list."

James Walker studied Haden curiously.

"You've been to a lot of trouble," he remarked.

"Not really," Haden said. "Your book fascinated me. It made me want to meet you."

"Really? Well, that is a compliment!" Walker picked up his portable telephone and climbed out of the hollow. "This calls for a drink. Time for a break anyway. Beer for you, or something else?"

"Beer would be fine," Haden said.

They walked across the lawn toward the table and chairs.

"Sit yourself down," Walker said. "It'll make a nice

change, to look at it instead of working on it. Are you a gardener?"

"No," Haden said.

"You don't know what you're missing," Walker said. "Shan't be long."

Haden sat and waited. The scent of roses hung in the air. James Walker came back bearing a tray with glasses of ice-cold lager. He had donned a shirt and jacket.

"I'm ready for this." He sat down, and handed a glass to Haden. "Your good health."

"And yours." Haden sipped his lager. "The way I read it, your book is really a tribute to the Maquis."

"That's right. The first part just sets the scene. Explains how I came to be involved." Walker gazed at his glass thoughtfully, his eyes crinkled against the sun. "Chaps in uniform like me, if we were captured it was a prisoner-of-war camp, tiresome, extremely boring, but no more. But the Belgians and French who ran the escape routes, those who sheltered us, the Maquis, if they got caught, it was a quick firing squad if they were lucky, and the attentions of the Gestapo first if they weren't. It was that kind of quite extraordinary bravery I was trying to convey."

"You succeeded," Haden said.

"Thank you for saying so, but it could have been done better, and I know it. I'm not really a writer, never was." Walker toyed with his glass, his eyes veiled and distant. "All I was trying to do was get back to England, but after we were betrayed, I was alone, Jerry was on my tail, I'd been forced to travel the wrong way for weeks, and by the time I fell in with the Maquis, I couldn't see a hope in hell of getting to Spain. It was altogether too far. The Maquis were busy fighting their own war. Getting a lone R.A.F. evader hundreds of miles across France to the Spanish border was decidedly low priority as far as they were concerned."

"From where they were operating, I'd have thought you might have been able to cross the mountains into Switzerland," Haden suggested.

"Yes, but Switzerland was virtually cut off, it was hellish to get out again. Thousands of R.A.F. aircrew were stuck in Switzerland, but I wanted to get back into the war, not sit on my rear, twiddling my thumbs. In fact, an escape route *was* eventually set up from Switzerland, across the French Riviera to Spain." Walker chuckled. "Believe it or not, over four and a half *thousand* forged passports were flown out from the U.K. by the R.A.F., dropped to the Maquis, and taken into Switzerland for use by stranded air crewmen on the new escape route. Not as many got out that way as had been hoped, the shape of the war changed, and there were other factors, but just the same, I sometimes think that if we organized ourselves half as well in peace as we did during the war, most of our present problems would melt away. However, I digress."

"Not a lot," Haden said. "And the beer's good."

James Walker smiled.

"Talking about it takes me back. It was a very vivid period of my life. When I joined up with the Maquis, I could hardly believe the extent to which they were in control of pretty well the whole of the Annecy region, and on to Grenoble. Do you know the area?"

"I've driven through it," Haden said, obliquely.

"Then you'll understand. Mountains, woods, valleys, fierce winters, the geography made it possible. The Maquis were very well equipped, arms, explosives, supplies dropped by the R.A.F., they even had their own transport, captured German stuff, made them mobile, able to move fast. It was what we'd call these days virtually a no-go area as far as the Germans were concerned. I thought 'Hell, I'm here, I was a military man before I transferred to the R.A.F., I know a bit about handling weapons and explosives, there's plenty going on here, I may as well stay put and lend a hand.'" He waved his free hand like a windmill, swallowed some lager, and set the glass down. "So I did. And it proved quite lively, blowing up bridges, ambushing German convoys, cutting communications. There was a certain amount of ad libbing, of course, when we saw the opportunity to make life unpleasant for Jerry, but most of the attacks on important targets were carried out on instructions received from London. Naturally, we returned the compliment by way of intelligence reports about German activity in the region."

"How did you communicate with London?" Haden asked. "Do you mind if I smoke?"

"No, you carry on, please. I've given up, but it doesn't bother me." Haden lit a cheroot. "Where were we?" James Walker resumed. "Oh yes. London. We were in touch, one way and another. You mustn't imagine, when I talk of a no-go area, that Jerry sat back and let us get on with it. Far from it. Rooting out the Maquis was the responsibility of the S.S. chief in Grenoble, a certain *Sturmbahnführer*, Horst Bauer. He took his job seriously, too. The S.S. Interrogation Center at Grenoble achieved quite a reputation. I never sampled it, thank God, but a lot did, poor devils. Speaking dispassionately, if one can, *Sturmbahnführer* Horst Bauer was no bad tactician. Nibbled and probed away at the edges; varied his patrols; tried to cut our lines of communication; carried out sudden, unexpected strikes; always aiming to keep us off balance, and force us onto ground of his choosing rather than ours, but thanks to our mobility he never quite succeeded. In the end, we provoked him too much. He demanded and got reinforcements. Carried out an attack in strength designed to wipe us out. Nothing for it but to retreat, harry them as best we could, try not to take too many losses . . . but it was rough . . ."

"And that more or less coincided with the American landings in southern France," Haden said.

"Operation Dragon. That's right. Not that we knew anything about Dragon, but London did, naturally. Every operation we'd undertaken in the preceding months had been designed to draw German troops away from southern France. And it succeeded. A lot of very well-equipped Jerries were chasing us, instead of facing the Yanks. So I think one might say that those Maquis I had the privilege of knowing and serving with saved quite a number of Allied lives. That's why I called my book *Dragon and the Brave* . . . a sort of tribute . . ." He struck his bald dome with the palm of his hand, an expression of comic apology on his face. "My book! Here am I, chattering away, and do you know, I'd quite forgotten why you're here." He took a pen from his inside jacket pocket. "Let me do it now."

"If you would," Haden said, and handed him the book.

James Walker opened it, and prepared to write.

"My pleasure, I assure you, it's . . ." His eyes fell on the flyleaf, and he broke off. "I didn't ask what your name was," he said.

"It's Stephen," Haden said.

James Walker looked up then and nodded, interest and comprehension in his eyes.

"Stephen Haden," he said, warmly. "Well, I'm damned. I don't suppose you remember me." Haden shook his head. "I was at your father's funeral," Walker said. He held his hand out over the grass. "You were only about so high. I didn't know you. You've changed. So have I, come to that. I had hair in those days. Well, well, after all these years. Tell me, how is your mother keeping? I haven't seen her from that day to this."

"She's dead," Haden said.

"I'm sorry to hear it. My commiserations."

"I found your book in her personal effects," Haden said.

"Yes, I see." Walker smoothed the flyleaf flat abstractedly. "Is there anything special you'd like me to say?" He looked up inquiringly, his pen poised.

"I'd be grateful if you'd tell me what your 'omissions' were," Haden said.

"Omissions?" Walker queried, puzzled. He looked at the flyleaf. "Oh, I see." He shook his head. "Do you know, it's so long ago, I've no idea. Simply can't imagine. You must blame my failing memory."

"Your memory has been remarkably good until now,"

Haden observed. "Perhaps these will help you." He took out the white envelope marked "Charles, 1942–1944," extracted the old photographs, spread them on the table. James Walker watched him but said nothing. "Especially this one, of my father with another man." He flipped the book closed and opened it again at the endcover. "The same man who wrote this book, according to the photograph of the author on the dustcover."

James Walker sighed deeply, and worry lines erased his previously genial expression.

"What you're asking may not be possible," he said. "I'd like to think about it, if I may."

"By all means," Haden said. His cheroot had burned down. He looked around for somewhere to dispose of it.

"Chuck it in the flower beds," Walker said absently. "That's what I used to do." Haden twisted around in his chair, flicked the cheroot end at some roses, turned back, and found Walker staring at him fixedly. "I assume Stephen Haden the *'Fluchthelfer'* must be you," Walker said. Haden nodded. Walker said, "Not that your activities make much news in England. The attempt on your life got half an inch in an inside page of the *Times* as I recall. But I supposed it was you. Did you come all this way just to see me?"

Haden shook his head. "I have business in London."

"Concerning your profession, if I may so put it?"

"In a way," Haden said.

"Forgive me if I press you."

"I'd like to trace the man who tried to kill me," Haden said.

James Walker thought about that.

"So today's visit, and your request . . . ?"

"Simply between you and me," Haden said. "Purely personal. A mystery I don't understand, and can't explain."

"Well, it's natural enough to be curious about your own father," Walker said. He brooded for a while, chewing his lip. "Technically, we should have another beer and discuss the weather before I wave you bye-bye," he said. "In reality,

I can't see that it matters any more, but I'm one of those people who go by the book, and the book says 'no.' So it really would have to remain between the two of us. I'd rather like your word on that."

"Very well. You have my word."

"Thank you," Walker said. "My book ends, you may recall, with the success of Operation Dragon, and the departure or capture of the Germans. When I got back to England, I was promoted from flight lieutenant to squadron leader and transferred to the R.A.F. Intelligence Branch, where my experience in Occupied France had a certain value. After the war, I stayed on for a few years, and served for some time at the Allied Intelligence Headquarters in Paris, where, incidentally," he remarked dryly, "we were planning World War Three which, it was supposed, would commence when the Russians kept on coming. Happily, that didn't happen, or at least not in that form. However, it was during this period that I wrote my book. As a serving officer, I was obliged to submit the manuscript for approval. Before it could be published, I was required to make certain deletions."

"The reason being?"

"The passages in question would have breached the Official Secrets Act. That ruling, I have to say, still applies."

"After all this time?" Haden inquired skeptically. "Why?"

James Walker shrugged, turned the pages of the book, and gazed at the flyleaf, penned long ago. "We all make mistakes," he said, pensively. "The reference to omissions was a touch careless on my part, but I assumed no one else would ever see it."

Haden said, "My mother probably found it when my father died."

"Your mother knew," James Walker said. "Not at first; Charles had done his best to account for his absences by writing letters to her in advance, and having them posted from places where in fact he was not, but the time came

•

when the deception was wearing thin. I learned all this much later, of course. He asked her to keep it to herself." Walker gave Haden a rather sad little smile. "I gather she kept her word."

"I found some odd jottings she'd made among her private papers," Haden said. "They imply she thought he was having an affair."

Walker said, "What I was required to leave out from my book amounted to two things. Our safest method of communicating with London, and the source of some of our supplies. The former included our operational instructions and the intelligence reports we sent back, both of which were vitally important and had to be absolutely secure in the run up to Operation Dragon. The latter included gold, which the French respected more than paper money; nitroglycerine, which was too unstable to be dropped to us from the air; and most important of all, spare parts for our vehicles. The strength of the Maquis in that region lay, as I've emphasized, in their mobility, the use of captured German transport, but spares were a desperate problem. They had to be specially made elsewhere. All these things were brought in and taken out by a courier operating from Switzerland. He used a code name. Obviously I met him, but he told me nothing, and in those days one didn't ask questions. Later, when I found myself in Intelligence, with access to secret files, curious about this mysterious figure, I looked him up. He proved to be a Swiss resident, but a British national, named Charles Haden, who ran a precision-engineering business."

Haden sat in the peaceful Surrey garden trying to take it in. An exploring ant crawled across the table, bees buzzed about their business. Walker did not strike him as a man who would lie or invent. And why should he?

"So the spare parts . . . ?" he said, at last.

"He'd take the broken camshaft, worn ball joints, or whatever, make up replacements, and bring them back again."

"My mother wrote at some point that she had thought she would never see him again."

"The Germans had got wind of him. They had standing patrols out. He knew the mountains better than they did, and he kept on coming. In the end, his luck ran out. He was captured and taken to Grenoble for interrogation."

"I take it you mean torture," Haden said, flatly.

"Your father would never talk about it. In his job, ending up with someone like Horst Bauer was one of the risks such chaps took. As it happened, the American forces advanced with amazing speed and took Grenoble. Your father was released and returned to Switzerland. After the war, I looked him up. We cracked a bottle or two of wine."

"What happened to Horst Bauer?"

"Taken prisoner. We all expected him to be tried for war crimes, but the Yanks carried him off with them, and officially he was never heard of again. The French kicked up a bit of a stink after the war, demanded him back, but there was an awful lot of confusion in the postwar years, and they never got him."

"You said 'officially,'" Haden said. "How about unofficially?"

"S.S. officers were often extremely skillful and experienced in intelligence work. Some became poachers turned gamekeepers during the denazification period. They were used to track down Nazis who'd gone under cover. They knew where the bodies were buried, not to mention that they were good at sniffing out communist subversives. I wouldn't be too surprised," James Walker said, cautiously, "if Horst Bauer had not been used in some such capacity. There's no morality in the world of intelligence. But what became of him, I don't know."

"I was grown up before I met my grandparents on my father's side," Haden said. "They made a fuss of me, but they avoided talking about my father. They thought he should have gone back to England and done his bit, instead of sitting out the war in safety."

"You must excuse them," Walker said, tolerantly. "They weren't to know."

"I just thought they were stupid," Haden said tartly. "I wasn't born until after the war. It was ancient history as far as I was concerned. But it mattered to them. Why couldn't they have been told that he *had* been involved after all?"

"It was a bit more than being involved," James Walker said, gently. "We're back to the Official Secrets Act."

"Oh, for Christ's sake," Haden snapped, "the war was long over. What was the bloody difference by then?"

"Charles Haden wasn't some gung-ho amateur," James Walker said. "He worked for British Military Intelligence, an MI-6 agent. His controller was the First Secretary at the British Embassy in Switzerland. Both sides found Swiss neutrality useful, the Red Cross and so on, but neutral *means* neutral. If our embassy ran agents who engaged not only in clandestine activities but warlike excursions into a neighboring country, that could never be openly admitted. Then—or now," he said, pointedly. "That's the way the game's played. Your father knew the rules. Would you like another beer before you go?" he inquired.

"No, thank you." Haden picked up the book, and stood up. "We'll skip the autograph," he said. They strolled side by side across the garden. "Did you stay in the R.A.F. or go back to accountancy?" he asked.

"Neither. I became a civil servant."

"In case you retained any contacts with intelligence, you might be able to help me. Or offer some advice."

"I've been too indiscreet already," James Walker said firmly.

"I'm in touch with some people," Haden said. "I wanted something from them. It seems they want to use me. I'd like to know more about them. Who's behind them. What it's all about."

They skirted the house and approached Haden's car.

"Very nice," James Walker said, admiringly. "I run a

Volvo. My wife's taken it." He gazed down the lane, as if she might appear any moment.

Haden took out his diary and, using the hood for support, wrote in it quickly, tore out the page, and handed it to James Walker.

"A car-hire firm, an institute, a name or two. Not much, but all I know. That's where I'm staying."

"I use the R.A.F. Club when I stay in town myself," James Walker said.

He held out his hand. When Haden took it, his grip was firm and friendly.

"Thanks for the information about my father," Haden said. "It wasn't what I was expecting. I haven't really taken it in yet, but thanks anyway."

"He came across those mountains, time after time, on foot," James Walker said, "with a heavy load on his back which could include nitroglycerine. Summer and winter alike, snow, ice, rain, mist, it made no difference. He dared not use the easier crossings. Treacherous conditions underfoot, bad weather, traveling by night, the Germans hunting him. Just try to visualize it." He opened the car door, and Haden slid behind the wheel. "Glad you looked me up, Stephen. Nice to have had the opportunity to talk to you.

He slammed the door, and stood waving good-bye.

ELEVEN

Stephen Haden opened the envelope which had arrived by messenger. Inside was what appeared to be a photostat of an identification document. All the particulars had been blacked out. The photograph on the document was that of a man in his thirties, unsmiling, with hair receding toward the crown, giving him a very high forehead. All of Christa's sketches had shown a man with a small, polite smile on his lips, but otherwise it could possibly but not certainly have been the same individual.

It was not long afterwards when Helen Lloyd phoned. She sounded slightly tentative and apologetic.

"If we're still speaking, how about meeting me for a drink tonight, seven o'clock at À l'Écu de France in Jermyn Street?"

"Is the drink followed by dinner?"

"Maybe. We'll see, okay? Seven o'clock."

When the taxi turned into Jermyn Street, Haden thought that the Jaguar he saw pulling away from the restaurant entrance was somewhat familiar.

A waiter approached him as he walked into the bar.

"Good evening, sir. Do you have a reservation?"

"I'm meeting Miss Lloyd."

"Of course, sir. This way."

Haden began to move toward the restaurant, and then stopped. The waiter was heading for the stairs which led down from the bar.

"This way, sir," the waiter said, again.

Downstairs, among the wine cellars, were several private dining rooms. The waiter led him to one of the smaller ones, and withdrew after announcing him.

Helen Lloyd turned with a smile of greeting, and offered her hand. She was wearing a white outfit against which her tanned skin seemed to glow.

"Hullo, Stephen. Glad you could make it." She released his hand almost as soon as her fingers touched his.

The table was laid for six. Silverware and crystal glasses gleamed. Bottles of white wine were chilling in ice buckets. The red had already been decanted, the color almost matching the bowls of deep red roses on the table. Behind a small bar, a white-jacketed waiter stood impassively at the ready.

Three men were also present.

"I believe you know Herr Kordt," said Helen, doing the honors.

"Happy to see you once more, Mr. Haden," Karl Kordt beamed.

"This is Andrew Sawyer, my chief, director of the Institute," Helen Lloyd said.

"How do you do, sir," Sawyer said, shaking hands. He had a wayward mass of prematurely white hair, but his face was soft, chubby, and unlined. "What can we offer you?"

"Dry sherry," Haden said. The waiter's hands moved smoothly toward the appropriate glass and bottle.

"And Tom Leeson," Helen Lloyd said, "a trade specialist from our embassy."

"We've met before," Haden said. "Did I get the job after all, Mr. Leeson?"

The American with the blank eyes behind large glasses who had sat beside Haden at Hampton Court smiled vaguely, as at some irony he did not understand.

Sawyer took the brimming sherry glass from the waiter and handed it to Haden.

"We'll look after ourselves until the others arrive," he said to the waiter, who left at once as if expecting the instruction, closing the door behind him. "Not to waste time, Helen has kept me informed concerning her meetings with you, Mr. Haden," Sawyer said.

"In every detail?"

"The essentials," Helen Lloyd said, expressionless.

"Policy is my province," Sawyer said. "Other people look after details."

"Tell me about your policy," Haden said.

"With pleasure," Sawyer said. "Despite its title the International Information Institute is not solely concerned with the provision and exchange of commercial information."

"I'd already worked that out," Haden said. Tom Leeson's glasses glinted as he turned his head, and gazed at Haden bleakly.

"Right!" Sawyer said, with a pleased smile. "We're also in business to build bridges, remove obstacles to trade, ease away misunderstandings. Let me give you an example."

"It would help if it had some bearing on what I'm doing here," Haden said.

"Such was my intention," Sawyer assured him. "There's a huge potential market for personal computers in Eastern Europe. Our friend, Herr Kordt, is eager to buy. There are American and British hardware manufacturers and software suppliers eager to sell. Sadly, in the world we inhabit, there are problems." Sawyer sighed, and pushed back a handful of errant white hair. "Given the rapidly developing state of the art, the galloping advances taking place all the time, how personal is personal? Might they have other applications, for example in the military field? Might they represent a high-tech free gift, as it were? What about the software? Could programs be adapted for other purposes? The difficulties are apparent to you, I'm sure, Mr. Haden."

"I'm listening," Haden said, neutrally. The man seemed to suffer from an overdue admiration for the sound of his own voice, which might or might not serve as a veil for something else entirely.

"Among ourselves," Sawyer continued, embracing Karl Kordt in his sweeping gesture, "we speak freely, and no one takes offense. We share a desire to resolve these problems. The Institute is in a position to listen, to understand, make proposals here, suggest safeguards there, work toward satisfying both Herr Kordt and his people, and those on our side who worry about the implications. Since we have no political connections, we can act as honest brokers, and work toward an agreement which would be to the advantage of both sides."

Karl Kordt nodded cordially, and helped himself to another drink.

"Over and above all that, the parties themselves may wish to agree on certain quid pro quos," Sawyer said, vaguely, "but that is a matter for them. The International Information Institute takes no part in detailed negotiations."

Haden said, "I've been waiting for information myself."

"You should have received it," Karl Kordt said, mildly.

Haden held out the envelope. Karl Kordt took it, produced a pair of spectacles, and moved to a position under a light, which happened to take him to the far side of the room. Haden joined him. The other three remained where they were. Helen Lloyd spoke quietly to Sawyer, who looked at his watch. Tom Leeson's gaze was on Haden.

"This is it," Karl Kordt said. "What you wanted."

"I'm no wiser," Haden said.

"You know he exists," Karl Kordt said.

"Someone who happens to be in your files? Quite a coincidence."

"Dismiss the notion in your mind, Mr. Haden," Karl Kordt said sternly. "My country does not attempt to murder foreign nationals. This individual," he said, returning the photostat to Haden, "is a person of no importance, suspected of various petty crimes, wanted for questioning by our police, but now resident in the West, and therefore outside our jurisdiction. If he is guilty of a crime in Zurich, he should be brought to justice."

"Fine," Haden said. "All I need is the name he uses, and where he's living."

"That is in the hands of others, to be passed to you once your job is done," Karl Kordt said.

"And this job, you'll fix it. I get your help."

Karl Kordt gazed across the room at the group standing at the bar. "The way will be smoothed for you. But you won't be able to sail across our border, pick him up like some international taxi, and sail back again. If it were that easy, the man could be given an airline ticket. Excuse me." He smiled affably, and wandered back toward the bar. "Andrew, my friend, how about another glass of that excellent Scotch?"

"Coming right up, Karl," Sawyer said.

Haden pulled out a chair, sat down where he was, and waited. Tom Leeson left the little group and sat beside him.

"Now you're in the picture," he said.

"Vetted and approved. I wonder what I said that was so convincing," Haden said.

"It was considered, by whoever deals with such things, that your replies were consistent."

"Tell me about this guy in a wheelchair."

"There's a chance his condition could be successfully treated in America. He's been refused an exit permit. Someone in the States who can influence decisions would like him brought out. You possess the necessary skills."

"In return for what? A photostat which could have been forged, with a doctored photograph added?"

"Mr. Haden, we are not in the business of deception. The information is reliable, according to expert opinion, and will be made available to you once your job is done."

"Let's reverse the procedure," Haden said. "Give me the information now. I'll check it out first. If I'm satisfied it's my man, *then* you get your guy in the wheelchair."

"That isn't possible," Tom Leeson said flatly. "I'm sorry, but there can be no delay. The situation has changed. Time is pressing."

"In that case," Haden said, "pass on my regrets to whoever receives apologies."

He stood up. A waiter had knocked, opened the door, and was speaking to Sawyer, who nodded briefly, replied in an undertone, turned, and offered his hand in Haden's direction.

"A pleasure to have met you, Mr. Haden," he said, "and thank you for coming. If you'll forgive us now, business calls. Helen will join you upstairs in a moment, and look after you from here on."

Upstairs in the bar Haden sat and gazed at the three new arrivals, huddled at a table over drinks. When Helen Lloyd came upstairs, she was greeted affably, and there was a brief smiling conversation before a waiter led the three down the stairs.

"I take it I'm not concerned with them," Haden said, when Helen joined him.

"Not unless you're in computers."

"Do you look after me here, or somewhere else?" Haden inquired.

"My place, if that's okay with you."

Outside the restaurant, the Jaguar was waiting. The friendly English driver opened the passenger door with a polite smile of recognition.

"Good evening, Mr. Haden, sir," he said.

Once in Piccadilly, the Jaguar drove to Hyde Park Corner, and north up Park Lane toward Marble Arch.

"Sorry to hear about your mother," Helen Lloyd said.

Haden glanced at her profile.

"From whom?"

"We were trying to contact you. I spoke to Christa. She'd just got back."

The Jaguar turned into Bayswater Road.

"Is your boss really just a windbag?" Haden asked. Helen Lloyd's lips twitched in amusement.

"He's a broad-brush man" she said. "Objectives are his concern. 'How' is someone else's."

"I don't buy blindfold," Haden said. "If a nonevent can take place, that was it."

"Maybe more progress was hoped for, but I guess no one was too surprised you weren't entirely persuaded."

"And persuasion gets delegated to you again, does it?"

"Since I don't know what you're supposed to buy," Helen Lloyd said, "no, it doesn't."

"Pity," Haden said. "You're good at it."

She turned and studied him, as the Jaguar eased forward from the traffic lights by the Royal Lancaster Hotel.

"Whatever it is you resent, Stephen," she said, "stop picking at scabs. Getting angry is a luxury I reserve for my personal life. This evening isn't personal."

The Jaguar crossed Praed Street, the driver a professional deaf mute.

Helen Lloyd's flat was on the ground floor of one of the tall, gracious, early Victorian houses in Cleveland Square. She led him across the hall and into a spacious, tastefully furnished living room which gave onto a patio.

"You left your French windows open," Haden told her.

"I know," Helen Lloyd said.

"You also have an intruder," Haden added.

The portly figure sitting on the patio stood up, and Harold Leyton came in through the French windows.

"I'll leave you two alone," Helen Lloyd said, retreating into the hall. "Drinks on the sideboard." The door closed behind her.

Haden watched Harold Leyton's hands, and unbuttoned his jacket. Leyton spread his arms wide.

"I'm not armed, Stephen," he said. He turned around, and Haden made certain he was telling the truth.

"You owe me for one ruined suit, Harry," he said.

"I need to have a bridge made," Leyton said. "You owe me for that. And I don't like dentists. I'm a coward." He closed and bolted the French windows. "Cognac for you, Stephen?" he asked.

"Last time, you wanted to kill me," Haden said, "not dispense someone else's drinks."

Harold Leyton said, "I was overwrought." He stared at Haden with a meek little smile, as if hoping for some response. Finding none, he said uneasily, "Well, I'm having a whisky." He poured a neat Scotch, and drank half of it in one gulp. "Part of what I said to you was true, Stephen," he said. "I think I know who tried to kill you."

"And now you're plagued with remorse," Haden suggested.

"I was contacted. One of the people I told you about."

"You also told me that was finished, thanks to me," Haden reminded him.

"I thought it was," Harold Leyton said earnestly. "I suppose once you allow yourself to be used, you go on being used. They insisted. They said it was important." Haden stonily regarded the florid face across the room.

Harold Leyton said, "Whatever you've got, let me see it."

Haden showed him the photostat. Harold Leyton nodded.

"That's him," he said.

"I see. And on the strength of that, I sign on the dotted line, is that it?"

Harold Leyton said, "I know where he is, I know who he is." He tapped his head with one forefinger. "It's in here. You get it . . . well, I was told you'd know when."

"I want it now," Haden said.

"My instructions forbid that," Harold Leyton said. "I give you my word of honor that I have what you want, and I'll deliver according to the arrangement."

"You're up against a problem," Haden said. "You're a gutsy bugger, and in a way I quite like you. But I don't trust you."

"Well, I've done all I can," Harold Leyton said. He crossed the room, sat down close to Haden, gazed at his glass, and swirled the remainder of his Scotch thoughtfully. When he resumed, it was in a low, secretive voice. "You didn't talk about my temporary loss of control to anyone, I gather." He raised sad eyes to Haden's. "If you had, they wouldn't have let me near you," he explained. "I owe you for that, at least."

"I don't know what your game is, Harry," Haden said., "but you meant to kill me. That I shan't forget."

"Nor would they," Harold Leyton said. "I'd be written off as unreliable." He swallowed the remains of his drink and put the glass down. "What you're good at is getting people out of places, especially East Germany. You want something, that's what they want. Close?"

"If we're swapping tidbits," Haden said, "you kick off."

Harold Leyton sighed, and shook his head.

"We get nowhere until you talk to someone you trust. Right?"

Haden said, "Someone I could half believe would do. No one in the company you keep ever knows anything."

Harold Leyton said, "How much do the people in your own organization know when you're planning something? Precious little, I'm sure. People who know too much are a danger. You're being unfair."

"They know that if they do the job, they get paid. In this case, I don't. That's the difference."

"There's someone who may be able to satisfy you," Harold Leyton said. He got to his feet. "Since I obviously can't do so, I'm to arrange a meeting."

"Okay, arrange it," Haden said. "When?"

"Now," Harold Leyton said. He opened the door, went into the hall, and called, "Helen, we're leaving."

Helen Lloyd emerged from the kitchen.

"I'm fixing something to eat."

"Sorry," Harold Leyton said. "Another time."

Helen Lloyd looked at Haden in a way which he found hard to fathom.

"Okay. I'll say good-night," was all she said.

Harold Leyton climbed into the Jaguar, sat beside Haden without a word, and remained silent throughout the journey, seemingly deep in private thoughts of his own.

By the time they reached the Kingston bypass, it was growing dark. Halfway along, the Jaguar turned off. The driver, evidently familiar with the route, used minor roads as shortcuts. A considerable number of possible destinations were signposted along the way, but Stephen Haden was not too surprised when the Jaguar finally came to a stop outside "The Elms," in the countryside near Dorking.

Inside, the rooms were distributed off a narrow, zigzag hall in an erratic, homely fashion. An ageing central-heating system was about the only concession to modernity. During the preliminary civilities, Harold Leyton seemed not to know James Walker well, and called him "Mr. Walker."

The living room boasted original ceiling beams, and a large inglenook by a fireplace in which were propped some huge logs.

"Reluctantly yielded up by the old enemy," James Walker said, following Haden's glance. He opened another door, opposite the one through which he had led them. "Harry, I expect you'd rather wait elsewhere. Follow your nose that way, and you'll find the dining room. Drinks on the trolley. Help yourself." Harold Leyton escaped with something akin to relief, although whether out of unease or the prospect of another Scotch was not clear. "Something for you, Stephen?" Walker inquired.

"No, thank you, Mr. Walker," Haden said.

James Walker closed the door.

"I hope we're still friends, Stephen," he said. "Take a pew, anyway."

Haden sat in a chintz-covered armchair, molded by long usage to receive the human form. James Walker shoved his hands in his trouser pockets and ambled about, occasionally removing one hand to gesticulate.

"On reflection, I had no alternative but to report your visit, and what had taken place between us," he said. "Not because of our conversation concerning your father. Had it only been that, I shouldn't have bothered. But just before you left, you made a request and gave me certain information. The fact that you were going around asking questions about something which could be highly sensitive was rather worrying. It was my duty to make that known."

"I wasn't 'going around asking questions,'" Haden said with some tartness. "I asked a man whom, on a very brief acquaintance, I thought I could trust."

James Walker said, "I'd be very sorry if you felt that I had betrayed a confidence. I am still a servant of the Crown."

"Various people have been put up who make vague noises and profess ignorance," Haden said. "Apart from better manners, you're just the latest in a long line."

"They may have been telling the truth," James Walker suggested.

"Puppets don't move on their own," Haden said. "Someone pulls the strings."

James Walker perched on the window seat. A standard lamp illuminated his legs and feet, but his face was shadowed.

"I am still consulted on sundry matters," he said. "In this case, I have been asked to speak with you. The concept of a puppet master somewhere is naive, Stephen," he said, with gentle reproof. "Things aren't organized in that way. Certain information is at my disposal. I am authorized to use my discretion. How frank I can be depends on what it is that worries you."

Haden said, "Who I'm dealing with. British Intelligence? That would give my old man a laugh, I suppose. The C.I.A.? Fringe organizations? Some way-out political outfit? The whole shooting match, mixed up like some kind of stew?"

"As I understand it, you require certain information," James Walker said, still speaking from the shadows. "That information has been located, and the bargain put to you will be kept to the letter. Next question."

"You didn't answer the first one," Haden said.

"A 'stew,' as you put it, has various ingredients. If it's tasty no one worries too much about the recipe."

"It doesn't smell appetizing," Haden said. "Something's off, or the chef's got it wrong."

James Walker said, "Cooperation between disparate bodies is never friction-free, as I know only too well from my far-off days at Allied H.Q. The view is that it would be in the general interest were you to accept the proposal put to you."

"Carting someone confined to a wheelchair across a heavily guarded frontier is about the lousiest proposition I've ever heard," Haden said.

James Walker said, "Your record suggests you'll find a way. The escape has to look good. Your pickup will be eased for you, but after that you're on your own. No one will want to know your intended method in advance. How you do it is your business. Safe delivery is all."

"Karl Kordt suggested a route via Sweden," Haden said.

"That one's out. Not considered wise to deliver to a neutral country. This is too important to risk loss of control. It'd have to be West Germany."

"He also stipulated a side deal. Fifty thousand Swiss francs for him."

James Walker said, neutrally, "Since the identity of your man is already to hand, you don't have to keep any

•

agreement you may have made with him once it's all over, unless you feel honor-bound to do so, should that be what chiefly concerns you."

"It's not, it's Karl Kordt," Haden said. "Is all this stuff about computer sales a blind?"

"Originally, no," James Walker said. "Events have overtaken it. But there's always a price. Anyway, it'll keep. The little matter you're concerned with was slipped in at some point, a pinch of pepper in the stew, if you like." He chuckled gently at his own analogy.

"In which Kordt too is involved."

"He has to be," James Walker said.

Haden shook his head. "It smells worse than cat shit," he said. "Karl Kordt is a big wheel in the D.D.R. I'm supposed to cross into the East for a difficult client I can only pick up with his permission. All he has to do is to forget to make the necessary arrangements . . . "

"He won't," James Walker interrupted.

"Why not?" Haden demanded. "I wind up in prison, or a coffin, Karl Kordt earns Brownie points from his bosses in East Berlin, wraps up the computer deal, and comes out smelling of roses with not one scrap of risk to himself."

James Walker said, "He'll go through with it as planned."

"Why the hell should he? I wouldn't."

James Walker had moved and was standing beside the standard lamp, gazing speculatively at Haden.

"In my judgment, Stephen, your chances of a long life are none too good," he said, "should we fail to reach an agreement tonight."

Haden stared at the honest, avuncular face before him.

"You surprise me, Mr. Walker. Threats? From you?"

"Good heavens, no," James Walker said, a frown rising high toward his bald head. "An assessment. It's time I used my discretion. Are you familiar with Karl Kordt's early history? War service and so forth?"

"Supposed to have been mixed up in the July Plot. I had

one of my people try to check it out. He couldn't find any proof either way."

"A good deal of evidence does exist to support the story," James Walker said. "Although, if traced back, all his best references emanate from Russian sources. That doesn't make it untrue, of course. On the other hand, there is another school of thought to the effect that, while Kordt was certainly a prisoner of the Russians, he was captured at Stalingrad, rather than later in the war. That he was one of those who, whether from conviction or self-interest, was wholeheartedly converted to the faith. This school of thought holds that Kordt was carefully trained by the Russians to play a particular long-term role, returned to East Germany later in that capacity, has done so ever since, and is a Senior KGB officer."

Haden took in the implications of that, and laughed shortly.

"So you cheerfully negotiate with a known KGB man, to sell his country computers."

James Walker said, "When agents use a cover, it's genuine. Your father *was* a highly skilled engineer, for example. Karl Kordt *is* an important man in matters of trade. The doubters may be mistaken about Kordt's KGB function. Your expedition will provide the answer, one way or the other. That's why it's so crucial for you to go."

"If you think that's persuasion, you're crazy," Haden said, derisively. "Set foot across that frontier with the KGB in on the act?"

"Stephen, believe me, Karl Kordt isn't interested in you. It's an intriguing game," James Walker said reflectively. "He's been put in a position in which he must seem to cooperate. How doesn't matter. The truth about him will come from the man you bring out."

"I'm not playing," Haden said. "Find someone else."

"There is no one else," James Walker said.

Haden said, "No one knew I was coming to London in the first place. I make one phone call. Within days, there's no one else but me who can be used to identify a possible KGB officer. And, by chance, I already know him. I had an appointment with him the day someone tried to kill me."

"Chance comes into everything," James Walker observed.

"It's too pat," Haden said. "Life isn't that tidy."

James Walker said, "Given who you are, a bright idea was conceived as a result of your phone call. There may have been reservations concerning any possible, shall we say, informal connections you might have with the D.D.R. State Security Service. Once satisfied on that score, the rest follows. My acquaintance with your father was coincidence. Nothing else."

"Tell me about Helen Lloyd," Haden said.

"Outside my province," James Walker said.

Haden said dryly, "I'd have thought you might have some inkling as to whether the Institute is a front or not."

James Walker sighed. "Front organizations are also genuine, by definition. Which includes most of those employed by them. They're not stuffed with agents, or everyone would know who was which. These things do tend to get awfully complicated," he complained sadly.

Haden stood up.

"Too complicated for me," he said.

"I suppose it's no use reminding you that you are a British national, and you would be doing your country a service?"

"No," Haden said. "I'm not my dear old dad."

"You really haven't grasped what was behind the attempt on your life, have you."

"I'll know that when I find the bastard," Haden said.

"A mere tool, a nobody," James Walker said dismissively. "He wasn't acting on his own."

"I know that," Haden snapped. "He had help. I've ideas about that too."

"Accomplices? You're obsessed," James Walker said. "You fail to perceive the obvious."

"Don't patronize me, Mr. James Walker," Haden
growled. "Recruited from the R.A.F. by MI-6, became a
high-flyer, a behind-the-scenes man, told prime ministers
as much as you thought they ought to know, still regarded
as some sort of veteran mastermind. Since you mention the
obvious."

"You're simply trying to flatter me," James Walker said
meekly.

"Oh, Jesus," Haden said. "You're impossible. Look, I do
realize there was more to it than a killer with a gun."

"So who do you imagine was behind him?"

"The East Germans have tried to put me out of business
before. If it was them, I can't take on a state. But if the
score's evened, they'll back off. Let it drop. They're realists.
I'm not that important."

"No, you're not," James Walker agreed. "But you have
built up an organization, efficient, flexible, its operatives
hard to identify, whose function in life is to smuggle people
across frontiers, unseen and unknown. We know that it has
already been used on an ad hoc basis to infiltrate at least
one agent, Heinz Meyer, and probably more. The possibilities strike me as very tempting indeed for any number of
undercover organizations. Hence, the attempt to dispose of
you. Someone else wants control, Stephen. That's what it's
all about."

Haden stared at him.

"East Germany? They want to take it over?"

James Walker shrugged. "If so, they'd have to use a good
front man. But the same means you've used to get people
out could also be used to take people in. A reliable ferry
service, running both ways, for agents, dissidents, sabo-
teurs—and a parcel service, too, tapes, film, documents.
Why," James Walker said enthusiastically, "the possibilities are endless!"

"Glad you approve," Haden said. "Make me an offer."

"No use with you there, my dear Stephen," James
Walker said kindly. "Not the sort one would choose to

work under instruction at all." He peered at Haden sideways. "Perhaps I should emphasize that the British are most certainly *not* involved."

"But you're hinting that someone in the West could be," Haden said. He wondered if James Walker's openly frank denial could be taken at face value. Stephen Haden had imagined until recently that he was highly skilled in the arts of deceit and deception. Compared with this lot, he was an innocent.

James Walker said, "Undercover organizations, being secret and none too accountable, like to offer results, and tend to accept the 'end justifies the means' philosophy. People can sometimes get carried away. Not so much at the center, at the fringes. That applies to both sides is all I'm saying."

"Karl Kordt claims that the face I'm after belongs to an East German petty criminal on the run," Haden said.

James Walker shook his head judicially.

"Such an individual might be used by anyone," he said. "Karl Kordt may be double bluffing. Who can say? Your trip may provide the answer."

Stephen Haden took out a cheroot, lit it, puffed on it reflectively, and wished he had accepted the offer of a drink.

James Walker said, "While you've been in London, you've had a degree of protection, some of which you've probably been aware of, some you wouldn't know about. If you decide you can't help us, that's it. It'll be open season on Stephen Haden. I'm sorry, but there it is." He checked his watch. "Very soon, I shall be receiving a telephone call." He gazed at Haden inquiringly.

"It'll cost more than expected," Haden said.

James Walker's eyebrows rose.

"I understood the fee had been agreed upon," he said.

"Expenses," Haden said. "A wheelchair means special transport."

"An ambulance you mean?" James Walker queried dubiously. "No, don't tell me," he went on hurriedly. "I'm sure additional transport expenses will be acceptable."

"It'll take time to arrange," Haden said.

"A few days before you need cross over, if all goes well."

"Good enough," Haden said.

There seemed to be nothing more to say. They sat in silence until the telephone rang.

TWELVE

There was whisky on Harold Leyton's breath, and he was a little uncertain on his feet. Halfway along the garden path, he stumbled, and clutched at Haden for support.

James Walker was a silhouette in the open doorway.

"Are you all right, Harry?" he called.

Harold Leyton, still leaning on Haden, looked back, a sickly smile on his lips.

"Fine. Just slipped," he said, slurring his words. As he turned to the front again, his mouth almost brushed Haden's ear, and he whispered, "Ask me in for a drink." The soft, sibilant plea was almost inaudible, even to Haden.

In the rear seat of the Jaguar, Harold Leyton laid his head back and spent the journey with his eyes closed, breathing heavily, only coming to life when the car drew up outside Haden's hotel.

"Already? Must have dropped off," Harold Leyton said as the driver opened the door with his customary mixture of efficient courtesy and dignity.

"Coming in for a nightcap, Harry?" Haden inquired.

"You're on," Harold Leyton said, struggling out after Haden.

The driver displayed marginal indications of unease.

"Excuse me, sir," he said, addressing Haden, "but my

instructions are to take Mr. Leyton home, and I have to go on to another job after that . . . "

"We shan't be long," Haden said.

"The car park's full, sir," the driver protested, "there's nowhere to wait . . . "

Harold Leyton thrust his face close to the driver's with the incipient aggression of the semi-inebriate.

"Listen, driver," he said, loftily, "anyone who can park at London Airport for bloody hours can find a space here for five minutes," and set off after Haden, his short legs moving stiffly.

Inside, Haden paused in the foyer.

"All right, where? My room?"

"Not safe," Harold Leyton said, quietly. "Could be wired."

A fair number of people were scattered around the bar, but a corner table was unoccupied. Harold Leyton stopped beside it.

"This'll have to do," he said. "Mine's a Scotch. Excuse me."

Haden sat down, gestured to a waiter, and ordered. Harold Leyton crossed to the bar, bought something, and headed for the men's cloakroom. By the time he came back, his Scotch was on the table and Haden was sipping a cognac. Leyton sat close beside him, looked around quickly, gulped down most of his Scotch, and eased a cheroot forward from a pack of the expensive Dutch variety which Haden smoked.

"Have one with my compliments. In place of my round. Won't be time for that." Haden accepted the cheroot, lit it, and studied Harold Leyton's face through the swirl of fragrant smoke. Leyton said rapidly in the same low tone, "I want you to do something for me. You won't be far from Dresden. You could see that Heinz gets a letter."

"You must be drunk after all, Harry," Haden said. "Go home."

"You don't have to meet him," Harold Leyton said urgently. "I wouldn't ask you to take that kind of risk. Just make sure it gets to him. I daren't try to contact him in the ordinary way. I'm putting myself in your hands." He glanced around nervously. "If you showed it to anyone here, that would be the end for me. Please, Stephen."

Harold Leyton's doggy, mournful eyes, the lines of wretchedness on his face, gave every indication that he was in earnest.

"Harry, they'll know Heinz Meyer was used," Haden said. "He'll be cleaning out lavatories in some labor camp."

Harold Leyton shook his head vigorously.

"They think his mission paid off. So good, that was why our people got suspicious. He'll be the blue-eyed boy. When there's something else in his line, they'll send him out again."

Harold Leyton had seated himself so that he could see the glass doors leading to the foyer, and his eyes kept flicking sideways to them even as he was speaking.

"Heinz Meyer is a secret agent, assigned to you when they began to wonder about your comings and goings," Haden said. "He doesn't give a shit about you, Harry."

"That may be so," Harold Leyton said, subdued but stubborn. "I'm gambling. I've nothing to lose." He took his eyes away from the glass doors and gazed at Haden. "I've money salted away. A lot. A good salesman can always make a living. Australia, New Zealand, Brazil, it doesn't matter where. He could join me the first time he's at some Western airport. We could have a good life."

"If you're serious, I'm sorry for you," Haden said.

"I'm serious," Harold Leyton said, his glance returning to the glass doors. He leaned even closer. "Do as I ask, and you get the name of your man, and where to find him. Now. Tonight."

Haden said, "If I knew where he was, I wouldn't set foot in the D.D.R., much less go to Dresden."

Harold Leyton said, "You have to go. You must. I'd want your solemn word."

"My solemn word is worth about as much as yours," Haden said.

A beatific smile creased Harold Leyton's face. He stopped looking in the direction of the glass doors, turned the packet around, and began to extract a cheroot.

"Your minder's on his way," he said between his teeth, like a ventriloquist. "It'll have to be on trust, Stephen. Trust. Don't let me down. And don't feel sorry for me. It may hurt like hell, but at least I feel something."

Haden's back was to the doors and he did not hear them open, but a woman's laugh whinnied high from the direction of the foyer.

"No, I don't think I will," Harold Leyton said in his normal, rather loud voice. He pushed the cheroot back. "Don't need any more bad habits." His glance swiveled across Haden's left shoulder, and he beamed broadly. "Hullo, there. Come and join us. What'll you have?"

"I'm sorry, Mr. Leyton," the driver said, "but it's clogged up out there, and they're talking about sending for the police if I don't move."

"All right." Harold Leyton heaved himself to his feet, and patted Haden's shoulder. "My shout next time, Stephen."

"See you, Harry. Good-night," Haden said to the driver.

"Good-night, sir," the driver said.

Haden remained where he was and finished his cheroot over another cognac before he picked up the pack and went to his room.

Sitting on the bed, he opened the pack. He had initially arrived without warning. No one had known he was coming to this hotel. If the room had been wired, as Harold Leyton had suggested, it would have been during his absence in Gothenburg. It seemed extremely unlikely that video surveillance would have been installed as well, but he dimmed the light to the minimum, just in case.

Tucked behind the lower layer of cheroots was an envelope, addressed, marked "By hand," unsealed. Both it and the sheets inside were wafer thin airmail paper.

Stephen Haden read the contents. It was a love letter. Leaving aside the personal endearments, the anguish of separation, the desire to be reunited, it amounted in essence to the same suggestion of a new life together somewhere which Haden had already heard, with a final plea for Heinz Meyer to contact Leyton, " . . . you know how . . . " It was signed simply "H."

Haden folded the sheets, put them back in the envelope, and returned to the pack of cheroots. He found the folded slip tucked behind the silver paper. On it was written a man's name and address. Underneath were listed three cafés located in the same district.

Haden returned the envelope and the slip to their former positions inside the packet, which seemed as good a place as any, and pocketed it.

Haden sat, the dim light playing on his knees for some long time, thinking, until the telephone rang. He lifted the receiver.

"I thought you might be back by now," said Helen Lloyd. "Just calling to say good-night. How are you?"

"Fine," Haden said.

"What are you doing?"

"Thinking about ordering some sandwiches. I haven't eaten."

"Oh." There was a very slight pause. "I turned everything off when you had to go. It wouldn't take long, though."

"Give me half an hour."

"Okay, it'll be ready."

Haden hung up. If the call *was* being monitored, any listener would only have heard exactly what he expected to hear.

As a briefing the exchange which had taken place when James Walker handed him the telephone had lacked detail. Haden was to be in position, his arrangements completed, in three days' time. Twice a day, without fail, he was to call a Frankfurt contact number for further information.

"When we have the go," Tom Leeson had said, "you'll be given a map reference. That's where you pick up. Clear?"

"Hang on," Haden had said. "I'm writing all this down. When I've memorized everything, I'll eat it."

"Please don't be absurd, Haden," Tom Leeson had said disdainfully.

Haden thought that Tom Leeson did not like him very much, a feeling which was pretty mutual.

Stephen Haden drifted into semi-wakefulness to find agreeably smooth, slim arms embracing him, and warm breath brushing his cheek.

He moved his head back and studied her face until she yawned gently, opened her eyes, stretched, and wrapped her legs comfortably around his.

"'Morning," said Helen Lloyd.

"Good morning," Haden said, and cupped the round breast which came to hand. For a while, they lay as they were without speaking.

"Eggs okay for breakfast?" she asked at last.

"I'll get it at the hotel before I check out."

"You're leaving?"

"Want me to tell you about it?"

"No," she said, and shifted her head onto his chest.

Haden stroked her hair and watched the gleaming strands as they fell between his fingers.

Finally, he said, "Who was the one who left you celibate?"

"Why? D'you want to look him up and compare notes?"

"Keep your claws in. I'm interested, that's all."

She transferred her head back to her pillow so that she could see his face.

"Who was the last woman you really cared about?"

"My wife. For a while. Until it went wrong."

"It always does when it matters, it seems." She traced a pattern on his chest with one fingernail. "He was someone who was important to me," she said finally. "The time came when I realized that I wasn't all that important to him. No one ever really knows anyone, I guess. So I called it off."

"How did he feel about that?"

"Not pleased. Hurt pride to some extent, maybe. Also, as an arrangement, it still suited him very well. But it didn't suit me."

"I think I could guess who it might have been," Haden said.

"Forget it. He doesn't matter any more, and from here on I'd lie about it anyway."

"How will you describe me to the next one?"

"I probably shan't bother," Helen Lloyd said. "If pressed, I'd say, 'He was something of a bastard, and he didn't give a goddamn, but at least he didn't pretend to.'"

Stephen Haden smiled, and explored her slender flanks. Helen Lloyd dug her fingernails into him.

"Don't do that if you're going," she said.

"I'm in no hurry," Haden told her. "They go on serving breakfast until late."

"Okay," Helen Lloyd said, and began to fondle him in return. "While you're away," she murmured, "I could call Christa, if you like, maybe go and see her."

"Why?" He was more keenly aware of the urgent sensations she was inducing than anything else.

"She's nice. We get on."

"If you want to," Stephen Haden said. His mind was on other things.

*Haden packed and checked out of his hotel. He decided to skip breakfast after all. Time had slipped away unnoticed, if agreeably, and he needed to use a safe telephone.

He left London and headed for Dover. If he was being

kept under surveillance, as James Walker had told him, it was not apparent. Halfway to the Channel port, he turned off, chose a pleasant hotel at random, ate a leisurely lunch, and made a lengthy phone call to West Berlin before resuming his journey.

He arrived in Heidelburg the following morning, having dawdled his way across France and stopped for the night in a village near the West German border. The bookshop was in a narrow side street, not far from the Neckar River. Haden parked his car nearby and, carrying his suitcase, walked to the shop, which catered largely to students from the ancient university, and pushed open the door.

The quiet, self-contained, middle-aged couple were expecting him. They greeted him courteously but with matter-of-fact brevity.

"Please go through," the man with the close-cropped, steel-gray hair said. "You know the way. He's upstairs."

Haden thanked him, skirted the counter, went through the door at the back, and climbed the stairs.

Christian Weber heard him coming and met him in the open door to the living room with a broad, open smile and a firm handshake.

"You're in the same room at the top," he said. "Let me take your suitcase. Make yourself at home."

He disappeared up the old, winding staircase with light, skipping steps as if the heavy case were featherweight.

Haden sat down in the living room and dialed the Frankfurt number. He had used this place a number of times before. Christian Weber's father and mother kept busy in the shop, left him to his own devices, and asked no questions.

A woman's voice answered. Haden identified himself.

"If you will give me the number you are calling from, Mr. Haden," the woman's voice said, "your call will be returned within fifteen minutes."

Haden gave her the number and hung up. Christian Weber came back and poured a cognac for Haden and a beer for himself.

"Thank you," Haden said. "Any problems?"

"Only with Kurt. He didn't like it. Said there was a job for me and I had no right visiting my parents without giving him warning." He shrugged slightly. "I told him my mother wasn't well. Didn't mention you, of course. I thought it best to say I'd be here, Stephen, in case he took it into his head to start phoning around, checking up on me."

Haden nodded agreement.

"What do you make of Kurt Gabler?"

"Good at his job, no one better," Christian Weber said.

"I ask as a friend, Christian."

"Hard, tough, careful, afraid of nothing, a good organizer."

"You're telling me things I already know," Haden said, quietly.

"I don't like him, but I'm not paid to. Women do. Some women," Christian amended. "God knows why. His macho style, I suppose. Do they bother you? The kind of women he has?"

"Only if our business is put at risk," Haden said.

Christian Weber shook his head.

"He's too fond of money. But so what? We none of us work for nothing." He hesitated for a moment. "I have heard that he's mixed up with some pretty funny people, but that could be just talk."

"Funny people of what variety?"

Christian Weber said, "Groups who call themselves this or that kind of brotherhood. Talk about 'action' and sound like Nazis. Whether Kurt Gabler's really got links with them, I can't be sure. It may not be true."

"It wouldn't surprise me if it were," Haden said. "Kurt's a fanatical anticommunist. He hates the lot of them. Kurt has the perfect incentive. He makes good money and fights his own private war at the same time."

Christian Weber said, "Me, I don't like the system over there, but I can't get excited about it, the way Kurt does. Helping people who want to get out, that gives me a kick, but plenty don't want to. Ordinary people, getting on with their own lives, Germans just like me, whatever the system." He put down his glass of beer, took out his wallet, and extracted a piece of paper. "This appeared a few days ago," he said. "It may have no bearing on anything. Or mere coincidence. Anyway . . . "

Haden took the press clipping. It was from a West Berlin newspaper and concerned a Norwegian diplomat who had been arrested at his summer home near Stavanger and charged with spying for the Soviet Union.

"Kurt was in Switzerland when this happened," Haden said, noting the date of the man's arrest. "He told me about a woman, but not her name."

"Nor me," Christian Weber said. "How many Norwegian diplomats have summer homes near Stavanger? Could be dozens for all I know."

"Kurt Gabler picks up some indiscreet talk in bed from his woman and fingers her husband, that's your theory," Haden said. Christian Weber shrugged. "It sounds in character," Haden said dryly. "Provided Kurt got paid for it as well." He looked at his watch. "Let's have another drink."

Stephen Haden read the press clipping again while Christian Weber poured the drinks. If Kurt Gabler had seized a chance opportunity to put a detested communist agent behind bars, such a piece of politically motivated moonlighting did not interfere with Haden's business activities as far as he could see.

The telephone rang a few minutes later. Haden answered it before Herr Weber could lift the receiver downstairs.

"Concerning your immediate outgoings," said Tom Leeson, "give me a bank in Heidelburg where you are known."

"Crédit Suisse," Haden said.

"The agreed sum for expenses, together with the initial element of your fee, will be deposited there within the hour. Arrangements on the other side are moving forward.

We anticipate collection should be possible in three days' time, but as a contingency, be ready to move in forty-eight hours."

"Forty-eight hours," Haden repeated. Tom Leeson said something irritably, but Haden was watching Christian Weber's face. Christian grimaced, but nodded.

"Forty-eight hours is possible," Haden said into the telephone.

"Continue to check in twice daily as instructed, but we shan't speak again until you have the go."

Haden hung up.

"Let's go for a walk," he said.

They strolled through the narrow streets past some taverns popular with students, and along the riverbank.

"Everything's under way," Christian Weber said. "The transport you specified's no problem. Work's started, a local firm, good people, I've used them before. The documents required, they're another matter, red tape galore, they don't like moving fast over there. Palms need greasing, it'll cost a lot."

"The money's available," Haden said.

"If you want to travel separately," Christian Weber said, "you won't want to take that Mercedes of yours. My Volkswagen be O.K.? Nice and anonymous."

Haden glanced at the young man.

"You've done your bit already," he said. "This one could be trouble."

"That's what I thought," Christian Weber said. "Sounded like a two-man job. Backup."

"You don't have to come, Christian," Haden said.

"That's settled then," Christian Weber said cheerfully.

When they walked into the shop Haden said, "I shan't be staying after all, Herr Weber."

Christian's father nodded. "Another time, perhaps."

Later, Haden carefully inspected the perfect, if false, papers which authorized him to visit a sick relative in Dresden and, satisfied, pocketed them. Sets of such papers were kept in the West Berlin office, ready for instant use. Kurt Gabler was efficient in that respect, as in others. Haden also checked Christian's papers, which showed a different reason for his visit to East Germany.

"You seem to have taken it for granted you'd be in on it," Haden said, eyeing Christian.

"Easy to change, if you'd said no," Christian said blandly.

They went to the bank, where Haden completed the formalities, withdrew some money for himself, authorized Christian Weber to draw on the account, and then drove to the workshop. The modification was going well. Haden examined it, and was pleased with the result.

"Better than I expected," he said. "Well done." Christian Weber was not only utterly reliable, he moved fast, a somewhat rarer attribute in Haden's experience.

"What are we going to do with the cargo when we get it back?" Christian asked.

"Sell it," Haden said. "And if we make a profit, half for you, okay?

"I won't argue," Christian said. "But you don't have to, Stephen."

"Bonus," Haden said.

Back in the room he was not to use over the bookshop, Haden went through his suitcase and personal belongings, and eliminated any evidence of his visit to England. That evening, before he left, he called the Frankfurt number. A different woman was on duty and did not ask which number he was calling from.

"No messages, Mr. Haden," she said.

Haden said good-bye to Christian and his parents, and pitched his suitcase into the Volkswagen. The gun, retrieved from the Mercedes, sat in his shoulder holster.

Unhurriedly, he drove through the night across West Germany, having chosen to cross via Helmstedt. The first dim tinges of approaching daylight began to lighten the darkness of the sky as he headed steadily along the long finger of transit autobahn which led across East Germany to Berlin.

The enclave of West Berlin was more than the western half of a divided city, covered 575 square miles, embraced lakes, beaches, rivers, and enough meadows and forests to allow prosperous West Berliners so inclined to indulge in hunting. The small apartment block was close to the outskirts of the city itself.

Stephen Haden circled the block along adjoining roads, sizing up the layout of the district, while keeping at a safe distance, and eventually found what he was looking for. The filling station offered repair facilities and, to one side, was an old, rambling house with a notice in the ground-floor window, "ZIMMER."

He left the Volkswagen for a service which, as a precaution against the next few days, would do it no harm, walked to the house, rang the bell, and asked the plump, elderly woman who answered if he could see the available rooms.

She seemed glad to comply, and treated him with a kind of motherly cordiality. He chose one high up at the rear of the house with a metered telephone of its own, arranged for breakfast in his room, and said that he would prefer not to be disturbed for the rest of the day after his long journey. She nodded understandingly.

The view from his window was not perfect, but it would have to do. Through his binoculars, he had an angled view of the main entrance to the block, and the windows of the apartments he was interested in.

Coffee was Haden's first priority, after which he felt better. He ate something, and studied the block carefully, only laying down his binoculars to pour more coffee. If the scribbled note could be relied upon, a somewhat large assumption, the apartment he wanted was on the second floor. As far as he could judge, there were three on that floor. Two he eliminated fairly quickly, the first when a dumpy, blond woman, yawning hugely, drew the curtains and turned to speak to a thin, small man, still in his undershirt; the second when he caught sight of two children running across the room.

That left the one on the corner, where the curtains were open and the windows closed. Because of his imperfect angle, he could not see into the rooms. Besides, for all he knew, there could be other windows to the apartment on the side of the block which he could not see.

Haden concentrated his attention on the entrance to the block. Over a period of an hour or so, a steady trickle of occupants came out. Some climbed into cars and drove off. Some hurried around the corner toward the main road behind, along which buses ran. After that, the trickle dried up. None had even slightly resembled the man he wanted.

Haden kept it up for another couple of hours. There was still no sign of life in the apartment on the corner of the block. He set his traveling alarm clock, called Frankfurt, lay on the bed, and slept, exhausted.

He awoke at four in the afternoon, his mind beating the alarm to it by seconds.

He checked in with the Frankfurt number. Again there were "no messages." After that, he resumed his binocular vigil.

The homecoming residents of the block began to trickle back. An hour or so later, some emerged again and set off for the evening. By now, he knew their faces. None included his man.

At eight o'clock, a taxi drew up outside the block and waited. Haden studied it hopefully, but the passenger who eventually came out and got into the cab, exchanging a few smiling words with the driver, was a woman. She looked to be about thirty, and Haden had not seen her before. Black hair framed her immaculately made-up face. Her figure was slim although her dress emphasized her full breasts. She could have been an attractive young housewife dolled up to go to a party. Haden thought it more likely she was in a branch of the entertainment business.

Hunger was biting at the lining of his stomach. He tried

on the hat which he had bought in Heidelburg and studied his image in the mirror. Stephen Haden never wore a hat. He added the pair of spectacles with plain lenses. They gave him an uncharacteristically introspective look which he decided to cultivate. His lost weight had left his face a little more finely drawn than it had previously been, and with his missing mustache and the hat and spectacles, the ensemble could just result in a casual glance skating past him, at least for the second or two that would matter in the event of an unexpected encounter.

Stephen Haden had dwelt on many permutations, among which he considered the front runner to be that the information was pure invention. Another was that it was good, and passed on by a man who was not acting but almost out of his mind with distress, in the hope of securing a favor. It was also possible that the information was good—but that he would be expected.

At the nearest of the three cafés listed, he ordered a meal. All were within comfortable walking distance of the apartment block. His hunger satisfied, he sat for a while over coffee, seemingly immersed in his newspaper. Finally, he tucked it under his arm and paid his bill.

At each of the other two cafés, he sat over a leisurely cognac, smoking. No one took any notice of him. None remotely resembled Ernst Braun—if that was even the name he was using.

Haden made no inquiries. Questions concerning a regular customer would ensure that he was remembered. By now it was late, and patrons were thinning out. Haden left too, before he became one of the conspicuous remainder. He had confirmed nothing and learned nothing.

Eyes alert under the brim of his hat, he turned into the road running alongside the apartment block which he could not see from his room.

The darkness was relieved by intermittent street lights, and there were few people about. Haden kept to the shadows as much as possible, and walked along steadily but unhurriedly. He passed the apartment block, turned away from it, and on toward the filling station and the shelter of his room. He felt unduly exposed, although for no good reason. The windows which might belong to the second-floor apartment on the corner of the block had been closed, the curtains open; no lights had been on.

Haden sat in darkness staring through his binoculars at the now-familiar apartment block. The occasional light went out. Only two or three occupants arrived, among them, by taxi, the dark-haired woman. She was with a man who looked like an Arab in Western dress. They both went inside.

It was 2 A.M. Haden closed his curtains and switched on the bedside light. He had wasted a day. For all his watchful caution, he had established only that whoever occupied that apartment was not there. He still did not even know who the absentee was, much less if it was Ernst Braun, or whatever his real name was. He would learn nothing if he did not expose himself to risk. He undressed and went to bed.

At six o'clock, the alarm clock shrilled. Still half asleep, he turned it off. The water in the bathroom next door was not even tepid yet, but at least the chill woke him up properly.

Just after seven o'clock, Haden entered the apartment block when the cleaner, whom he had seen arrive a few minutes beforehand, opened the front door to clean the steps outside.

"'Morning," Haden said, brightly, like a man who belonged there, and crossed the threshold. The cleaner displayed no particular interest in him, and got on with her job. Who came and went was none of her business.

There was an elevator, but Haden chose to trot up the stairs. On the second floor he passed through the swing doors, and walked past seven and eight to number nine. There was a Yale lock which would present little difficulty but, lower down, was another of the double-locking variety, which it would be impossible to deal with quickly and without noise. He pressed the doorbell just in case the occupant had returned while he was sleeping. He took his hand away from the bell and slipped it inside his jacket where his palm sat on the butt of his gun, against the perhaps remote possibility that a killer with a receding hairline might open the door and recognize him instantly, hat, spectacles, and missing mustache or no.

He listened intently but could hear nothing from inside the apartment. He took his hand away from his gun and was about to stoop to examine the double lock more closely when the door to an apartment a little way along the corridor and on the opposite side opened. He pressed the doorbell again instead.

The Arab in Western clothes gave Haden a quick, darting look, turned away, and hurried toward the elevator without speaking to the woman who had seen him out. Now wearing a flimsy negligee, her makeup was still complete if growing somewhat tarnished. She remained in her open doorway, eyeing Haden speculatively.

He gave her the most agreeable smile he could muster and pressed the doorbell once more.

"Doesn't seem to be anyone in," he remarked, walking toward her.

"He's probably away." Her voice was low and rather pleasing. She smiled back at him in a friendly fashion. Her lingering perfume was seductive. So was her expression in an automatic kind of way.

"Are you a friend of his?" Haden asked, nodding toward apartment number nine.

"Him?" There was amused contempt in her tone. "He likes little girls."

Haden nodded, wondering if that fitted or not.

"Suppose I come in," he suggested.

"I don't usually have gentlemen callers here," she said, becoming prim. Haden glanced at the Arab, who was stepping into the elevator. "He'd been drinking," she explained, following Haden's eyes. "His family are very strict. They're all in the same suite, and he didn't want them to know. I let him sleep on my couch until he'd sobered up." Her mascaraed eyes were large and ingenuous.

"Be kind to me too," Haden said.

"Okay," she said, after a perfunctory moment of hesitation.

Haden went inside and into the living room. The door to a bedroom was open, and he could see the double bed with its crumpled pillows and bedclothes.

Pushing back her straying black hair, she followed him.

"This'll have to be a quickie though, darling," she said, businesslike suddenly. "I'm tired. Sorry, but you understand."

Haden sat down in an armchair.

"I only want to talk," he said.

"Oh, you're one of those," she said. "It's still the same as for the real thing though."

"Going rate," Haden agreed.

"Okay. What is it you like? You want to watch me make myself come while we talk, or what?"

"About your neighbor," Haden said.

Her expression changed.

"Look, darling," she said, "I mind my own business. "You're no cop, I can smell those bastards, so on your way."

Haden took out his wallet, and fingered the notes inside suggestively.

"I represent a loan and finance company," he said. "My job is dealing with difficult clients."

"Uh-huh," she said noncommittally. But she sat down opposite Haden, although her eyes were wary.

"When the sum involved is large, we appreciate any help we can get." He laid a hundred-mark note on the coffee table between them. She eyed it with interest, but did not take it.

"I wouldn't want it to come out that I'd talked to anyone," she said cautiously.

"We'd never get any information if we didn't treat our sources as entirely confidential," Haden assured her.

She leaned forward, picked up the note, and slipped it into the pocket of her negligee, which was the only place she could put it. Underneath the filmy garment was nothing but her. Even without a brassiere, her well-formed breasts stood up. Haden remembered the Arab, and stopped looking at them.

"My sessions come to more than that," she remarked.

Haden said, "I'm not even certain this is the right man. The name we have is Ernst Braun." She nodded to that. "A pretty common name, though," Haden said. "Can you describe him?"

"Oh . . ." She screwed her eyes up. ". . . thirty-four, thirty-five, around your height, sort of lightish brown hair but losing it at the front, a sharp dresser, you know, likes good clothes . . ."

"What about his face? Any distinguishing characteristics?"

"No . . . nothing special . . . except he's got a funny little smile . . . polite but creepy . . ."

Haden held up the photograph he had been given.

"Is this him?"

She bent forward and studied it with a frown which aged her.

"Yes, that looks like him," she said, but without total conviction.

"He may have changed his occupation since first dealing with us. What does he do for a living, do you know?"

She shook her head.

"Some sort of representative, I suppose. He spends more time away than he does here."

"What about cars?"

"Oh, yes. He likes nice cars too."

"A white BMW?" Haden asked.

"I've never seen him with a BMW."

"Perhaps he sold it without notifying us," Haden said. "What's he been driving lately?"

"A red Manta Berlinetta coupé," she said promptly. "Very smooth."

"You wouldn't happen to remember the registration number, I suppose?"

"Jesus," she said. "I have enough trouble remembering my own phone number."

"These young girls he likes, the same ones? Or various?"

"Different ones."

"Apprenticed to the trade?"

"Darling," she said, derisively, "sweet seventeen they may be, but they know the trade."

During the next ten minutes, she relaxed and talked more freely, but the more willing she was to talk, the more the law of diminishing returns set in. She thought that Ernst Braun might rent his apartment, furnished, but she was not certain. She did not know how long he had been there, having only moved in herself a few months ago. She was not sure when he had left, and had no idea when he might come back. Haden decided that the session had run its course, topped up the initial hundred marks to her satisfaction, and stood up to go.

Before she opened the door she handed him a card.

"If you're ever in town and you don't just want to talk, I might be free, if you call me," she said, coquettishly.

The card informed the recipient that Eva was a masseuse, skilled in relieving nervous tension of all kinds, and provided her phone number.

"Thank you, Eva," Haden said. "I may well do that."

Haden returned to his room. On the face of it, he now knew where Ernst Braun, who had changed his appearance sufficiently to be described as a blond young man, resided. Yet on what was that supposition based? Christa's speculative sketches, a photograph from Karl Kordt, a name and address provided by Harold Leyton. Of the three sources, Christa had been guessing, the other two were untrustworthy. Yet so much added up, if not conclusively. Was he carrying caution and suspicion to extremes? One thing *was* certain. Someone badly wanted him, for reasons he knew not, to fetch a man out of East Germany.

Haden sighed. He had set out to use, and was being used instead. His choices, however, seemed to be limited. If James Walker was to be believed, his life depended on going through with it. But was he?

Haden worried over that for some time before he called the Frankfurt number.

"If you will give me your number, Mr. Haden," the woman's calm voice said, "someone will call you back in fifteen minutes."

Haden gave her the number, hung up, and sat waiting for the phone to ring. The familiar mixure of excitement and apprehension knotted his stomach.

It was on.

That pain in his loins was coming back again. Perhaps it was just imagination. He examined his fingers. They were trembling. He felt cold, but that was sweat on his face. Not now, for Christ's sake. Not now.

THIRTEEN

The following day, having spent most of the intervening hours in bed, Haden drove across the city toward the checkpoint, his car radio keeping him company as he weaved his way through the heavy traffic.

He was nearing the checkpoint when the program was interrupted by a news flash. Yet another high-ranking West German counterintelligence officer had disappeared from his desk some time ago, since when his whereabouts had been anxiously sought, and surveillance at airports, ports, and road crossings stepped up. The reason for now revealing this to the public emerged as the newscaster went on. Gerhard Friedrichs had surfaced in East Berlin, having eluded the net, and asked for political asylum. East German radio had just announced, tongue in cheek, that his request was being considered. The hunt was still on for a male secretary from the same department who had vanished at the same time.

The same kind of revelations had cropped up often enough before. Haden sometimes thought, with sour hyperbole, that the blandly, euphemistically titled Office for the Defense of the Constitution of West Germany appeared to be almost exclusively staffed by agents from the East.

Stephen Haden had a personal if tenuous interest in the

matter. Most of his business was connected with the Federal Republic, one way or another. However, the very West German policy which made his activities possible and not illegal—that Germans were Germans and automatically entitled to citizenship—also opened up a leak in the side of the ship of state, and provided a convenient means of infiltration, gratefully taken advantage of in the silent, continuous intelligence war by the East German espionage service and, no doubt, by Big Brother in Moscow as well. The one was an inevitable part of the other, a kind of Newton's Law about which he could do nothing. Haden switched over to another program.

When he arrived at the crossing, the queue of traffic was longer than he had expected and inched forward with unusual slowness. Haden got out of his car and peered ahead. The holdup was on the Western side. Looking for the missing male secretary, Haden supposed. The shark had eluded them, but they were still trying to net the minnow.

He got back in, switched off the radio and, along with the other would-be travelers, tried to contain his impatience.

Tom Leeson's message had been clear and concise. Too concise, Haden had thought.

"You've left out any means of identification," he had reminded Leeson.

"Not necessary," Tom Leeson had said laconically. "You'll know." Haden did not like it, and said so. "Haden," Tom Leeson had said, with that edge in his voice which Haden seemed to generate, "for once in your life, you are invaluable. This is much too important to take the slightest unnecessary risk. Identification will not be a problem. Neither side will be in any doubt. Okay?"

Grudgingly, Haden had supposed that Tom Leeson knew what he was doing. In his own rather more minor way, he often took the same view: that the less his agents knew, the less danger there was to themselves and the operation.

He had telephoned Christian Weber, and they had agreed that since Haden was already halfway there, no point would be served by his traveling back to Heidelburg, which Haden was disinclined to do anyway. He hoped that the tremors which shook him would pass off, but he wanted as much rest first as he could get. They had briefly discussed taking C.B. radios, and quickly rejected the idea. Apart from the risk of confiscation and attracting unwanted attention upon entry, the only occasion when they might need them would be in the East, when their use would constitute a hazard rather than an aid. They had agreed on a rendezvous and fixed times instead. If either of them did not show, the other would abandon the operation and return to the West. Christian would use a checkpoint across the "green frontier" to the south.

Haden had dragged himself out of bed occasionally to stare across at the apartment, but there was no sign of a returning occupant, nor of a red Berlinetta coupé.

Haden's gun and shoulder holster were inside his locked suitcase which he had left in the wardrobe of his room overlooking the apartment block. He had told the woman that he would like the same room for another week or two and would be back in a day or so. Since he had also paid in advance, the woman had been only too pleased to oblige. There was no point in crossing into the East armed, and Haden had never done so. Should anything go wrong, he was certainly not going to compound it by shooting anybody, and while much could be explained away, given sufficient ingenuity, the possession of a gun most certainly could not.

Haden finally made it to the head of the queue, where he was asked to get out, his appearance and papers scrutinized carefully by a couple of policemen and a man in plainclothes, and his Volkswagen Golf subjected to the kind of examination more usual in the East.

Finally, he was allowed to drive on. By comparison, the formalities on the Eastern side were almost languid, and not long after, he had left East Berlin and was heading toward Dresden.

Halfway, he turned off the main road and continued in the general direction of the map reference, which he had been given. When he had looked it up, the point seemed to be in the middle of nowhere with not so much as a village within miles.

There was still a fair amount of holiday traffic. He passed a couple of camping sites, tent cities with their adjoining cars and bicycles, and turned off again. The traffic diminished to almost nothing. He drove along dusty roads and through dusty villages, until the landscape changed to one of gently rolling pine woods.

From the crest of a rise, he caught sight, between the trees, of the dull sheen of a large and distant lake, stopped, and studied his map again.

Despite the unexpected delay at the border crossing, there was plenty of time at his disposal. Although Christian Weber would have left considerably earlier that morning, his was a much longer journey, and he would not be in position yet.

Haden drove on slowly, along twisting and turning narrow, unmetalled roads, scarcely a car's width wide, keeping the lake, which he only glimpsed now and then, on his right. Several times he stopped, switched off the engine, looked around him carefully, and listened intently.

No vehicle could possibly have followed him unnoticed, he knew that for certain. A helicopter could have, but if so it would have lost him when he entered the shelter of the pine trees, and would now be quartering, searching for him. In the silence of the woods he could have heard the clatter of rotor blades many miles away.

At last, Haden completed his circle of the lake. He had not encountered another living soul. He pulled off the road, stopped, picked up his binoculars, and walked through the trees.

From the bank there was a drop of several feet into the

water, which was so dark as to bespeak considerable depth, even here. Pine trees grew to the very edge. One or two had fallen and lay canted, half underwater.

His calculations had been slightly out, he had emerged at the point where the lake was at its widest, and he could only just make out with the naked eye the single building away to his left and on the opposite side of the lake which was the only form of habitation in sight. Haden raised his binoculars and focused them.

The distant shape grew into a single-story wooden lodge of the kind which might be a weekend retreat or holiday home, set in a clearing. Behind it, a rutted track led into the trees and was lost to sight. The tip of a car's bumper just protruded from behind the lodge.

Between the lodge and the lake a stretch of green grass completed the idyllic setting. Parked on the edge of the bank was a wheelchair. The man sitting in it was holding a fishing rod.

The distance was too great for Haden to make out the man's face, or whether he was old or young. Haden meticulously traversed the area to either side of the cottage without finding anything to disturb him, and returned his binoculars to the fisherman in the wheelchair. Nothing had changed. No one else had appeared.

Haden remained where he was for another ten minutes, his binoculars glued to the lodge and the stretch of grass fronting it. Once, the fisherman landed something, stunned the fish casually, dropped it in a basket, rebaited his line, cast it back in the water, and settled down again. That was the only sign of life.

Haden walked back to the Volkswagen Golf, threading his way through the pine trees. As yet, he was not committed. If he did not like what he found on the other side of the lake, he could claim to be lost. Even here, that was no crime. He was nowhere near any restricted area. That was the first thing he had checked.

Stephen Haden reversed the Volkswagen and drove back

the way he had come. After a while, he slowed to a crawl, searching for the track leading to the lodge, which should be somewhere to his left. Even so, he passed it before he belatedly realized it was there. He dabbed his brakes, backed up, swung the wheel, and bumped slowly down the winding slope. The lodge only came into view when the track turned back upon itself, and he found his hood pointing at it. The car parked behind it was a brown Audi 100 Quatro, its four-wheel drive no doubt useful on frozen tracks during icy winters.

He parked beside the Audi, got out, prepared to ask for directions, and walked around to the front.

The man in the wheelchair had heard the Volkswagen arriving. Still holding his fishing rod, he was looking back at Haden over his shoulder. He was either in his thirties or a young-looking forty, with dark hair and a round but firm face. He continued to look at Haden curiously, but did not call or make any gesture.

Haden heard the door of the lodge open, and turned to look at the man standing there.

"Please come in, Mr. Haden," said Karl Kordt courteously.

Haden stepped inside. Karl Kordt closed the door, which gave into a large living room, furnished in Scandinavian style.

"Very nice," Haden said, looking around. "One of your fringe benefits along with the Audi?"

Karl Kordt said, "Somewhere to recharge the batteries in peace and quiet." He was wearing an open-neck check shirt and cord trousers.

Haden looked out the window. The man in the wheelchair was facing the lake again, his hands delicately manipulating the rod.

"And the fisherman?" he inquired.

Karl Kordt said, "My son, Hans. Something of an athlete at one time."

"Your son who would like to become an athlete again," Haden said.

Karl Kordt said, "To stand, to take a few steps, even with crutches, would be a triumph for a man with his condition. Hans is a realist."

"I see," Haden said noncommittally.

"It sounds like very little, but it is very much to a paraplegic," Karl Kordt said. "However, even that was just a dream. He will not be traveling with you after all." That was the last thing Haden had expected to hear. "You must return to the West alone," Karl Kordt said. "I am truly sorry we cannot proceed. Our friends too will be disappointed, but there it is."

"They may not believe I've even been here," Haden said pointedly. "They're expecting delivery. They've laid out a lot of money."

"Do sit down," Karl Kordt said. "Smoke if you wish, of course."

Haden sat in an unlikely chromium and leather creation which was more comfortable than it looked. He took out a cheroot, lit up, and studied Karl Kordt, who had remained on his feet.

For all his easy cordiality, Kordt showed signs of a man under stress. He was restless in an uneasy fashion, his gaze frequently turning to the window, and to the man in the wheelchair.

He said at last, "In fact, our friends will understand."

Haden drew on his cheroot.

"I don't," he said steadily. "Although if I'm due to get picked up and put away when I leave here, that doesn't much matter."

Karl Kordt said, "You may rest easy as to that, Mr. Haden. Were you to be apprehended and questioned, how could I account for your presence? To protect myself, I have to protect you."

"Okay," Haden said, unmoved. "But I'd feel safer if I

knew what was behind it all, and I'm not leaving until I do."

"You know too much already for my peace of mind, Mr. Haden," Kordt said, after a long pause. "There is perhaps less to add than you imagine. My work entails much travel in the West. I am never accompanied by those for whom I care most. My wife, when she was alive. Now, my son. It is a well-understood convention." His tone was without irony.

"Otherwise, you'd have defected long ago, I suppose," Haden said.

Karl Kordt said, "You may cease trying to test me by provoking me, Mr. Haden. No. I would not."

It would be simpler, Haden thought, if intertwined with his instinctive distrust there was not a strand of equally instinctive liking for the big old German. It made the cold assessment he needed elusive.

"What changed your mind?" he asked, more neutrally.

"My son," Karl Kordt said, "has been told that nothing can be done. He heard of a clinic in Boston which claims to have had some success. I was abroad at the time. He made a serious mistake. He applied for permission to go to Boston for treatment, without consulting me. Permission was naturally refused. From then on, he stood no chance of being allowed to travel abroad, even to Czechoslovakia."

That fitted with what Kordt had said in Gothenburg. Another part jarred.

"So it was all for love of your son," Haden said.

"You're doing it again, Mr. Haden," Karl Kordt said mildly.

"You stipulated a side deal. Fifty thousand Swiss francs for yourself," Haden reminded him.

"At the time, I dared not tell you his identity," Karl Kordt said. "You wouldn't have believed me anyway. Because I demanded money, you were at least half-prepared to think I might be in earnest. When dealing with those from the West, it is as well to remember Western values," he said, with detached contempt. "It doesn't arise now, but I wouldn't have taken your money."

Haden considered that. Again, it failed to match the adjoining piece of the jigsaw.

"You'd have taken it for that antiques deal," he remarked.

Karl Kordt gestured dismissively.

"Channeled through me," he said. "That would have been a useful source of good Swiss currency, badly needed here."

"You mean it was all official," Haden said.

Karl Kordt said, "It could not be official. The state could not be seen to be involved in any such enterprise."

"Approved, then," Haden said. "With you as an instrument who could be disowned, if necessary."

"If you wish," Karl Kordt said tiredly, "but it has nothing . . ."

"Others could have known of your appointment with me the day I was shot," Haden interrupted.

"Mr. Haden," Karl Kordt said heavily, "because of that, a means of acquiring significant sums in hard currency came to nothing. In practical terms, there was no reason to have you killed."

"Had our meeting taken place, were you going to ask me to smuggle your son out?"

Karl Kordt shook his head.

"That thought only began to emerge later," he said. "Trade discussions with the British and Americans, of which you are aware, had been going on for some long time. I put out feelers concerning Hans. The eventual response was favorable. But there was a condition. In exchange for getting my son out and to Boston, I was to defect."

"Why do they want you?" Haden inquired.

"They seem to think I can tell them things." Karl Kordt

smiled slightly. "I suppose I would be quite a catch. I've moved in high circles."

"You don't sound madly enthusiastic about the prospect," Haden said.

"I have no idea if this Boston treatment would work or not," Karl Kordt said. "But if there was only a slender chance, I could not deny him that chance. Much of his life is before him. Most of mine is behind me. Once he had been taken to the West illegally, I would be finished. It made a kind of brutal sense. So there you are. Now you know."

"Except why you want to call it off," Haden said.

"The timing was critical," Karl Kordt said. "Everything had to appear normal. My son spends much of the summers here. Myself also, as much as I can. So far, fine. The date was set. Today. Tomorrow I was due to fly to Brussels, from where I would be taken to England and apply for political asylum. These arrangements had to be made in advance."

"Then what's gone wrong?"

"A certain Gerhard Friedrichs failed to appear at his office in Bonn, and was thought to have gone into hiding."

Haden said, "Your friends would have kept this plan of yours well away from him."

"Unfortunately, he had good personal relationships with his American and British counterparts. Some hint might have come to his knowledge. Just the same, since we thought he was still in West Germany, we decided to go ahead. Today was the only possible day when everything fitted. But this morning . . . "

"I heard it on the radio," Haden said. "You can't be certain he knows anything. Even if he's picked up a whisper, he can't have the details. I could have your son across the border within hours."

Karl Kordt said, "The defection of Friedrichs is an important matter. I would expect my office to have informed me before it was officially announced. They did not do so. I too only heard about it on the radio."

Haden eyed the silent telephone.

"Have you checked if it's working?"

"I don't have to," Karl Kordt said. "An hour before you arrived, it rang. My trip to Brussels has been postponed."

Haden's cheroot had burned down. He stubbed it out. "I wasn't followed here. I made certain of that."

"Friedrichs doesn't know any details, or we wouldn't be sitting here peacefully talking," Karl Kordt said. "Something though. Enough for precautions to be taken. My Brussels trip 'postponed,' a clampdown on all exits. No matter how cleverly a car has been modified, they'd find him. I suggest you use some other means to return to the West. Abandon your car somewhere a long way from here, if you please."

"You'll still be left under suspicion," Haden said.

Karl Kordt said, "If no attempt is made, it denies the suspicion. If we do nothing it will all fade away."

"With Hans still in his wheelchair for good," Haden said.

"Better that than in prison," Karl Kordt said. "I refuse to risk that."

"There was always a risk," Haden said. "Does he know it's off?"

Kordt shook his head slowly.

"He's pinned everything on this. He'll take it badly. When you've gone. It will need time, a lot of time."

"May I speak to him in private?"

Karl Kordt stared at Haden.

"What purpose would that serve?"

"I don't know," Haden said. "Do you have some objection?"

Karl Kordt sighed wearily.

"So long as you don't tell him," he said. "That's my job." Haden nodded, got to his feet, and moved to the door. Karl Kordt watched him. "An impostor would have been carefully chosen and well-briefed, Mr. Haden," he said sardonically.

"I'm sure," Haden said.

The man in the wheelchair heard the door open and, by the time Haden had walked to the bank, he had reeled in the line and was deftly dismantling his fishing rod.

"Do you know who I am?" Haden asked.

"My father said it was best I didn't. Is it time to go?"

"Not quite yet," Haden said. He squatted beside the wheelchair. The face which turned toward him was guarded although not suspicious. The shoulders were broad, the arms strong. "Your father says I can talk to you," Haden said, pointing toward the open door of the lodge where Karl Kordt was standing.

Hans twisted his head around. Karl Kordt raised one hand with a bright smile, nodded, and went back inside.

"What about?" Hans asked then.

"One or two things I'd like to know." Haden laid his hands on Hans's thighs. There was no response to his touch. Underneath the man's trousers, the thighs were wasted, unnaturally thin, little larger than a normal man's biceps. "What did you do before?" Haden asked.

"Full-time coach. The junior national athletics squad."

"Did you travel with them?"

"Often. The Soviet Union, Poland, Rumania, Czechoslovakia. Not the West."

"Your father said you were an athlete yourself."

"Previously, yes. A middle-distance runner. Not of the top rank on the international level. A silver medal in Moscow once. A few bronzes, Budapest, Sofia, Bucharest. Nothing outstanding. I am better at coaching. I have a degree in physiology. I know how to obtain the maximum performance from others."

"What happened to put you in a wheelchair?"

"A car accident. I was driving my mother to meet my father at the airport. A speeding truck jackknifed and hit us. My mother was killed outright. I was trapped in the wreckage. When they cut me free, I was like this."

"You could still go on coaching from a wheelchair."

"So they tell me. People who say that do not understand. I want to stand. I want to walk again."

"How did you hear about the clinic in Boston?"

"There was an international medical convention in Leipzig. I obtained a ticket for a fringe meeting on paraplegia. An American doctor showed me the report in a medical journal."

"You have some medical knowledge. Do you believe the treatment could be successful?"

"I'm not a neurologist. I know it's experimental. My eyes are open. What can I lose? Let them experiment on me. Let me be a guinea pig. It might work."

"You'll have to stay in America," Haden said. He was watching the somber face closely. "Won't you miss your father?"

"Yes. But he says that he hopes to be able to come and see me later on."

"Time I had a word with him," Haden said.

He walked toward the lodge. All the alternatives offered their own dangers, for he had nothing to guide him but his own imperfect instincts. Given time, it would be easy enough to check the validity of everything the man in the wheelchair had told him. Time, however, was not at his disposal. The only advantage he could perceive lay in a proposition which no one had put to him. That struck Stephen Haden as a very large plus indeed, especially since the risks would be equally shared.

Karl Kordt must have been watching through the window. He emerged from the lodge and joined Haden as he strolled toward the two cars, half hidden under the pine trees.

When they reached the Volkswagen Golf, Karl Kordt stopped and offered his hand.

"I shall wish you a safe return journey, Mr. Haden," he said.

Haden ignored the outstretched hand.

"Suppose I got you both out at the same time," he said.

Karl Kordt's hand wavered. He used it to scratch his large nose instead. His eyes strayed to the Golf.

"Two of us? In that? Not one chance in ten million. I've told you, at the border crossings they'll be taking suspected cars to pieces."

"Let them," Haden said. "The Golf's clean."

"Then how?" Karl Kordt demanded.

"You don't have to buy sight unseen. It'll mean half an hour's drive. I'll take you. I think it's on."

"At what risk?" Karl Kordt inquired.

"The same to which you were willing to expose your son," Haden said.

Karl Kordt continued to rub his nose thoughtfully long after any itch must have subsided. "What is this, Mr. Haden?" he inquired ironically. "The ultimate test of my credibility?"

Haden looked at his watch.

"You don't have time to debate it," he said. "Another few minutes and it'll be too late. You can forget it."

Karl Kordt massaged his ear instead of his nose.

"This magic carpet you have tucked away somewhere," he said at last, "should I not share your faith in its flying characteristics . . . ?"

"I'll bring you back again, and no harm done," Haden said. "But if you do go, you go as you are. You can take money and papers with you, small valuables, a few clothes, but no suitcase. Well, Herr Kordt? Do you want to go window shopping, or not?"

Hans looped his arms around Karl Kordt's neck, and took the strain. Kordt lifted him into the front seat of the Golf, and settled him. The folded wheelchair went in the back, as did Karl Kordt, sitting on the few clothes which Haden had allowed. Slowly, they bumped and swayed along the track, away from the lodge.

Once he gained the narrow, unmetalled surface, Haden drove as fast as he dared and, when he turned onto a wider but still lonely road, increased his speed again.

His evident urgency infected his passengers. Neither spoke. Hans, although strapped in, clung onto a grab handle. In the mirror Karl Kordt's face was taut, and he kept turning his head and looking out of the rear window.

They were nearing the edge of the densely wooded area when Haden saw the pulloff up ahead. It was empty. He swore silently, changed down as they passed the pulloff and trod on the throttle hard as they entered the bend beyond. Protesting tires screeched as the bend sharpened, then twisted the other way. Anxiously, his eyes searched the winding road ahead.

The trees were thinning into scattered clumps, with open countryside and a village in the distance, when, lurching out of another bend, Haden saw the horse trailer, towed by a Land Rover far ahead. He flashed his headlights. Again. Again. The third time, he saw the answering wink of brake lights, and relaxed, content to leave it to Christian.

He had closed up, and was driving sedately behind the horse trailer, when the brake lights ahead came on again and the horse trailer slowed to a crawl, turned off the road, and eased between the trees to their right.

Haden followed, and saw that Christian had spotted a clearing, deep in the clump of trees, where he came to a stop. Haden followed suit and got out. Karl Kordt was gazing at the horse trailer.

"Inspection time," Haden told him. There was the sound of an approaching vehicle and Haden swiveled apprehensively, but the passing car was little more than a flicker of bodywork between the trees. The clearing was well concealed from the road, and Haden tramped across to the horse trailer.

"Well done, Christian," he said.

"Sorry," Christian Weber said. "I left it as late as I could . . . "

"My fault, not yours," Haden said. "Cut it too fine. Let's open her up."

Christian Weber opened the doors of the trailer. The bottom half lowered to form a ramp. Haden gestured to Karl Kordt, and they walked up the ramp and inside.

"We'll make it easy for you," Haden said. "No straw on the floor."

Kordt studied a rack of tools, and chose one he liked the look of, his eyes glinting. Evidently, he regarded the challenge as a personal one. He walked around slowly, his head bent, studying the floorboards. He began to probe the boards here and there. After a while, he got down on his hands and knees and started an inch-by-inch examination until he had probed every board.

Some ten minutes later he stood up, a film of sweat glistening on his face. He gave Haden a look and went outside. Haden followed him.

Karl Kordt was standing, assessing the trailer. He walked around it twice, very slowly. Then he crawled underneath and remained there, grunting now and then.

Haden smoked a cheroot and waited. Hans, still seated in the Golf, was watching the proceedings intently, his head angled forward, peering through the windshield.

Karl Kordt slid backwards from under the trailer, stood up, brushed pine needles from his trousers, and went back up the ramp.

Haden finished his cheroot, trod it into the ground, and joined Kordt, who had taken to rapping the floorboards with the handle of the implement. His face was flushed and wore an expression of frustrated irritation. He rose to his feet, breathing hard.

"All right, Haden," he said, belligerently. "I say it's not here at all. It's in the Land Rover."

Christian Weber looked pleased and twisted one of the metal rings on the side of the vehicle. There was a rattle of bolts being withdrawn, and a section of the floorboards rose the thickness of one board.

Haden lifted the section which, when in place, had been sitting on small coiled springs. Two bolts had formerly secured it in place. Underneath was a shallow oblong cavity.

"The passenger can operate the bolts manually from inside," Haden said, "which overrides the system. Safety reasons, in case of accident and the driver's hurt and can't reach him, for instance. For use in a life-or-death emergency only."

"Put it back," Karl Kordt said.

Haden replaced the square of boarding, and stood on it. Christian Weber twisted the ring. There was the snap of the bolts ramming home.

Now that he knew where it was, Karl Kordt crouched and examined the cracks minutely, but they ran along the natural line of the planks. There was nothing to show the "trapdoor" was there. The work had been painstakingly done, and Christian Weber had supervised it well.

This time, when he had finished his inspection, Karl Kordt pushed and twisted the ring himself. The "trapdoor" rose. Kordt lifted it off and gazed into the shallow cavity.

"Like a bloody coffin," he said.

"The folded wheelchair goes in first," Haden said. "Your spare clothes spread across it. The compartment was made a little larger than usual, in view of the prospective passenger's condition. There's room for two, just about."

"With straw on top," Karl Kordt said, eyeing the sacks. "For what purpose, I'm almost afraid to ask."

"A fine mare from one of your excellent breeding stables," Haden said, "not very far from here."

With some difficulty Kordt eased himself, feet first, into the compartment, slithering, wriggling, grunting, until he was lying on his side. The compartment sat above the axle. Kordt's head and feet were out of sight; only his midriff was visible.

"Put the lid on," Kordt said, his voice muffled and mildly sepulchral.

Haden obliged. Christian Weber operated the ring. The

bolts snapped home. For a while, there was silence, followed eventually by the sound of fingers scrabbling, and half audible angry mutters. Finally Kordt located the bolts, and the square rose on its springs. Kordt pushed the square aside himself and, panting and puffing, managed to crawl out in an undignified manner.

"It'd be a bloody tight fit for two of us," he complained, rubbing one knee where he had scraped it.

"You'll probably suffer from cramp," Haden agreed. "And I can't promise you won't get horse piss over you. The odds are you'll get through. If that's what you want."

"Unless we suffocate on the way," Karl Kordt said, wheezing.

"You do fuss about details, Herr Kordt," Haden said.

"I know," Karl Kordt rumbled. "That's why I'm still breathing and I'd prefer to continue doing so for another few years yet. I say we'd suffocate."

"If you'd feel under here, sir," Christian said, guiding Karl Kordt's fingers under the boards to one side of the compartment, "you'll find a button. Have you got it? Press it."

A soft humming noise commenced, emanating from the compartment.

"Two mini-ventilators," Haden said. "Only to be used when you're in motion, and as little as possible. They're powered by batteries."

Karl Kordt switched off the ventilators, stood erect, and gazed at Haden.

"Very well, Mr. Haden," he said. "You know your business, that I grant. But so do they."

"Their attention will be elsewhere when you arrive," Haden said.

Karl Kordt glanced at the Golf and then his eyes sought the dark, shadowed entry to the compartment. "Let me speak to my son," he said at last, and clumped down the ramp and across to the Golf. Haden leaned against the side of the trailer.

"We'll use the Bitstedt crossing, Christian," he said.

Christian Weber pursed his lips doubtfully.

"I always avoid Bitstedt, Stephen," he said, carefully. "Not much traffic, too quiet for comfort, and if they're on the lookout . . . "

"I know," Haden said. Karl Kordt had straightened up from his position at the open passenger door of the Golf and gestured. They clattered down the ramp and walked toward him. "If we get our timing right, they won't pay much attention to you, Christian," Haden said.

Karl Kordt was taking out the wheelchair and their few personal belongings.

"Give me a hand," he said.

"Your keys first," Haden said. "Your car and the lodge." Karl Kordt handed the keys over without word or query. "Once I've left to shut up shop with these," Haden said, "you're committed. No turning back."

"We've talked. We've decided," Karl Kordt said. "Let's get on with it."

Stephen Haden drove back to the lodge and went inside. Karl Kordt had taken the telephone off its rest before they left. Haden left it where it was. Hans's fishing gear had been put away. Satisfied that everything inside appeared normal, he checked that the windows were secure and locked the door.

Haden half-considered driving the Audi to the edge of the lake and tipping it into the deep waters, but he decided not to risk some chance forest worker in the surrounding dense woods witnessing such a curious act, certainly worthy of a phone call to the police.

He compromised by leaving Kordt's car keys in the ignition which would, he hoped, indicate to any visitor that Karl Kordt was still around somewhere with his son. There was a chance that someone trying to reach Kordt on the phone could decide to call on him instead, but even if they did all that would take time.

Stephen Haden left the lodge for the last time, drove

toward the road which Christian Weber would use, and joined the stream of traffic. Half an hour later, he chose a suitable inn, sat at a table outside where he could see the road, and ordered coffee and something to eat. When the horse trailer passed, he paid his bill.

Christian Weber was driving sedately and Haden did likewise, hanging well back and allowing cars and trucks to pass him. Only when he reached the prearranged point did Haden increase his speed until, one car in the faster-moving stream, he passed the horse trailer and settled down to his new cruising speed. Quite soon the trailer disappeared from his rearview mirror, but from now on Christian, like himself, would be using agreed landmarks and adjusting his speed accordingly.

When the road curved away to the north, taking the greater part of the traffic stream with it, Haden took the exit which led eventually to the Bitstedt frontier crossing. He checked his watch. Within half a minute, he was on time.

The swath of cleared land separating East and West came into sight in the distance, along with the watch-towers straddling the countryside. On the Eastern side, the Bitstedt crossing was a huddle of buildings and a barrier. Haden drifted to a stop, and switched off.

Ahead of him were a Polish truck and a French car containing a family, its roof rack piled high with camping equipment. Soon, the barrier rose to allow the Polish truck through, but some sort of problem developed with the innocent French family, possibly some minor breach of customs regulations complicated by language difficulties, Haden never knew. He tried to contain his unease at the passing minutes as the French luggage was unloaded and opened, and resisted the temptation to look back at the road behind him.

The East German officer in charge had, however, clearly been very aware of Haden's arrival in the first place and had cast several stony looks in his direction. Eventually, he lost patience, snapped something which evidently settled the problem, walked toward Haden, and curtly invited him to pull over to an inspection area and get out.

Haden did as he was told, and his papers were scrutinized closely while the resigned French family repacked their possessions and eventually drove off.

The officer studied photograph and face, as if comparing one specimen with another, but gave no indication that he suspected Haden's real identity. The "wanted" photograph which was no doubt in his office was years out of date and Haden, with his hat, glasses and missing mustache, no longer closely resembled it. Haden's papers, too, stood up to careful examination but, not unexpectedly, the officer viewed his quick dash into and out of the D.D.R. with some reserve.

Why was his visit so short? Haden explained that he had visited his relative prior to an operation, and was forced to return at once by urgent business. An operation for what, and where? Haden offered appendicitis and the name of a Dresden hospital. Why was he returning via Bitstedt, when he had crossed into the country at Berlin? An appointment the following day in Heidelburg, Haden told him. Could he confirm that? Haden offered a business card and a diary entry.

Predictably, the officer found all this less than conclusive and nodded to the inspection team, who went to work on the Volkswagen Golf with considerable method.

The seat and back cushion came out, carpets were lifted, and men with flashlights and measuring equipment went underneath, paying particular attention to the wheel arches.

Haden was more than a little relieved to see that the reliable Christian Weber was approaching at this point. In truth, the Golf was far from being an ideal car in which to construct a hidden compartment, and it could not have taken too much longer before the team came to the same conclusion.

Christian Weber got out of the Land Rover, and asked, politely and apologetically, if he could possibly be dealt with on the grounds that he was transporting valuable livestock.

Two of the inspection team were detached and opened the door of the horse trailer. The white mare, nervous and not enjoying her ordeal, displayed her displeasure, stamping her hooves, whinnying, and attempting to rear. The two men stepped back smartly and left it to Christian, who led the horse outside. With no discernible enthusiasm, the two assigned to this duty began probing around in the malodorous soiled straw. One soon decided that he would sooner inspect the underside of the trailer. The other muttered something surlily and carried on inside.

Christian Weber looked the part of a stable hand, but was not having much success in controlling the still nervous horse, and perhaps was not trying very hard.

The officer clearly found the wild-eyed prancing animal distracting.

Giving Haden a hard look he became impatient, strode across, looked over the Land Rover, and gave a sharp order. Christian managed to persuade the mare back into the trailer and went to retrieve his papers. The two men went back under the Golf.

Haden watched the trailer recede toward the distant West German side. It was done. Let them dismantle the Golf into its component parts, if they wished; there was nothing to find.

The inspection team evidently agreed, and had lost their enthusiasm. The officer reluctantly admitted defeat, and walked away irritably. The team started putting the Golf back together again.

Over on the other side, Haden could just see that the horse trailer was still there. He supposed the delay must be due to the formalities relating to the import of livestock. Christian would not reveal the presence of his passengers and embarrass the West German frontier personnel. They would be released from their compartment at the rendezvous, some fifteen minutes' drive into the Federal Republic.

By the time the barrier was raised, and Haden had driven through and begun to traverse the open stretch between East and West, the horse trailer had gone. It had been, Haden reflected, a clockwork operation, a good piece of teamwork.

On the Western side the formalities were brief, and he drove on, choosing the prearranged minor road. Reaction was setting in, but there were only a few details left. Phone the Frankfurt number, arrange his cargo's collection, and that was it. Afer that came finding a buyer for the mare, but he would welcome a couple of restful nights' sleep before he returned to West Berlin. That nagging ache in the loins was still there, although the feverishness had subsided.

Away in the far distance, across the rolling countryside, he could just pick out the autobahn they would use once Karl Kordt and Hans had been released from their confinement and transferred to the Golf to resume their journey in somewhat more comfort.

The horse trailer came into sight a long way in front, as it topped a rise, and then disappeared over the other side. The distance between them was closing. It was not far now.

Haden gained the crest of the rise himself. Before him spread a panorama of rich farming country. The trailer was slowing as it approached the pulloff where they were to meet.

From his vantage point as he began to descend Haden could see for miles. Other than the trailer the only other vehicle in sight was a small truck, the rear portion covered in tarpaulin, traveling slowly in the opposite direction.

As Christian Weber's indicators winked his intention to turn into the pulloff, the truck ambled into a turning which forked off to the right and climbed the gentle side of the valley overlooking the road.

When the trailer came to a stop in the pulloff, the truck

stopped, too, and Haden thought he saw the tarpaulin move slightly, and something metallic.

Stephen Haden jammed the accelerator to the floor, sounded his horn in a continuous blast, and screamed a useless warning as the Golf hurtled forward.

He saw the driver's door of the Land Rover open. He saw the distant white blur of Christian Weber's face as he leaned out, looking back toward Haden. In the same second, the air between the truck and Christian seemed to shimmer, almost imperceptibly.

There was an ugly blinding orange flash followed by an expanding ball of black smoke and Stephen Haden could see neither trailer nor Land Rover, as the missile struck home.

The truck began to move, gained speed, and disappeared from sight.

FOURTEEN

Stephen Haden skidded to a stop, jumped out of the Golf, and ran forward on legs of jelly which threatened to give way under him.

The pall of black smoke was dissolving and drifting lazily away. The Land Rover was a mess of tangled metal. The wooden horse trailer had been blown sideways, the top half roofless, the structure shredded by the blast, the chassis canted at a crazy angle. There was the smell of gasoline.

The body mixed up in the remains of the Land Rover had no face. Scorched tatters of what had been a stable-hand's clothes clung to what was left of the torso.

Haden turned away, gulping back vomit, ran around the shattered trailer, and forced his way in through the splintered timbers. The once-white mare was dead, spilling blood and entrails, her belly half gouged out, and had fallen on her side. The straw was smoldering, giving off choking, stinking smoke. What had been the floor seemed to be reasonably intact, but for a moment, Haden could not locate the compartment. Then he heard the sounds of weak scrabbling, and someone retching. He also heard the commencing crackle of flame.

He groped around and found a spade which had become detached from its rack. By standing on the dead animal's back, he could reach the canted compartment. Squinting through the billowing smoke, trying not to breathe, he forced the blade of the spade between the boards and levered, leaning on the spade with all his strength. The board snapped. One bolt had come away with it. Through the gap, he saw Karl Kordt's pale face, eyes blinking, coughing and trying to speak.

Haden jammed the spade in farther along the crack, and levered again.

"Push!" he gasped. "Push!"

Karl Kordt understood, and managed to maneuver his broad shoulders under the jammed "trapdoor." Haden strained, and between their combined efforts, the remaining bolt gave with a snap. Haden wrenched the "trapdoor" aside, grabbed Karl Kordt by his arms, and pulled him free. Kordt fell sideways across the dead mare but scrambled up at once, his feet sliding in her blood.

"My son . . . ," he choked.

The flames were taking hold, dancing fingers igniting more of the straw. Eyes misting, hardly able to see, Haden frantically found an arm, Karl Kordt grabbed a handful of clothing, and they heaved out the dead weight of Hans, his paralyzed legs trailing, lifted him, and stumbled clear of the trailer.

The final whoosh came, the blur of heat, the roar of flame, as the gasoline went up. As one, they flung themselves to the ground. For a moment, the air was an oven-hot gale, and then it passed, and there was only the raging roar of the flaming trailer and the stench of roasting horseflesh.

They dragged Hans a few yards farther away and laid him down. Haden collapsed, gasping for air, simultaneously choking and heaving, tears streaming from his eyes, bile running from his open mouth.

When at last his breathing became less agonizing, he spat out the remaining bile and sat up.

It took Karl Kordt a little longer to recover. When he did so, he seemed at first not to know where he was. For a while, he simply gazed dully at the trailer, still burning steadily.

Stephen Haden said nothing. There was nothing to say.

Eventually, Karl Kordt's expression changed, and he looked toward Hans, who was lying on the ground where they had laid him. Karl Kordt's gaze became fixed. He turned his head away, and began to rub his smoke-blackened face slowly, with both hands.

In the back of Hans's head, there was a hole, the size of a man's fist.

The naked body lay in the mortuary under the harsh fluorescent lights, as if illuminated by spotlights in some grim theater. Stephen Haden's burns were not serious and had been treated, along with the cuts from splintered wood. His hands were bandaged. The mortuary was in a military hospital near Darmstadt, to which the living and the dead had been transferred by helicopter.

Tom Leeson and James Walker were murmuring quietly to the pathologist. The pathologist looked at his watch, nodded, and went out. Walker and Leeson had arrived together, either working in close harmony or, perhaps, to ensure a fair division of the spoils. They spoke briefly, in undertones, out of earshot, and then walked across to Haden.

"It is only a formality, Stephen, but if you'd be good enough to oblige?" James Walker gazed gravely at the corpse.

"It's Hans Kordt," Haden said.

"I doubt you can be that specific," Tom Leeson said. Haden turned slowly, and stared at the American in a way which left no room for misunderstanding. "On the other hand, your judgment may well be sound, Stephen," Tom Leeson said hurriedly. There had been a marked change in attitude on the part of both men, especially Leeson. General approbation hung in the air, the feeling that Haden had shown admirable initiative. With this more or less open apreciation of his achievement had come a difference in treatment. Stephen Haden, it seemed, was no longer a single-purpose useful outsider, but an insider, implicitly a splendid member of the team who, by his resourceful individual play, had turned the game when it seemed to be lost. "We wouldn't have Karl Kordt now, if it weren't for you," Tom Leeson said placatingly. "We thought we'd have to write the whole thing off when Friedrichs showed up in East Berlin. You did one hell of a fine job," he said warmly.

"I know," Haden said. "And only two corpses."

"Everyone's sorry about that," James Walker said gently.

"Whether or not this is Kordt's son makes a difference," Tom Leeson said, looking at the body dispassionately. "We need to know his game plan. Happily, certain sources may have been able to obtain Hans Kordt's dental records. If so, we'll soon be in a position to confirm for sure, and if you're right, great, we know the score."

"In which case, since he's dead, you've lost your stranglehold on Karl Kordt," Haden said. "Unless you can perform like Jesus Christ."

"We have physical possession of Kordt," Tom Leeson said confidently. "We have time. They'll be shitting bricks on the other side. We'll play it as it comes. Get as much as we can from him, and then maybe do a deal with them, we'll see."

"It was never going to be straightforward," James Walker said. "Anything Karl Kordt says would have been subjected to the most stringent analysis, anyway."

"You can never buy outright what a defector tells you," Tom Leeson said judicially. "By definition, a defector is also a traitor, whatever his reasons. It doesn't do to forget that."

Haden said, "I want to know who ambushed us."

"The West German police have found the vehicle you described, abandoned not far away, but after that the trail went cold," James Walker said.

"Luckily, we've been able to keep the event under control," Tom Leeson said. "It's being reported as a terrorist attack on the wrong target. Real names won't be mentioned, of course, least of all yours. You needn't be concerned about that."

Haden said, "Christian Weber was about as near to a friend as I've ever had. That's what concerns me."

"It's a complete mystery," James Walker said frankly. "Please don't think it isn't being taken seriously, but there's nothing to go on. Besides which, it doesn't make any kind of sense."

"It made sense to whoever fired that missile," Haden remarked.

"Maybe the cover story is right," Tom Leeson said. "Some crazy man shot up the wrong thing. The fact remains, we have Kordt, alive and safe," he said with satisfaction.

"I hope you'll be very happy together," Haden said, and walked away.

Tom Leeson shook his head at Haden's prickly and unreasonable attitude, and gave Walker a look of mute appeal.

"Stephen, just a moment." James Walker hurried over and caught up with Haden as he reached the door. "We'd very much appreciate your further help," he said, quietly and with some urgency. "It's too soon to expect much from Kordt yet, of course, but his attitude is unhelpful, one might say hostile. You may be in a position to gain his confidence."

"Me? I'm the one who got his son killed."

"Try to keep an open mind about that," James Walker said soberly. "If he was a substitute, they'd have chosen a paraplegic, they'd have trained him meticulously. Kordt's reaction could be merely to the death of a colleague. Bear that in mind for the time being, at least."

"I've had to tell Christian Weber's parents he was dead," Haden said. "I wish I'd turned you down flat, Mr. Walker."

"Don't," James Walker said, with unusual forcefulness. "Karl Kordt could be the biggest prize we've laid our hands on in a decade. No one regrets the cost more than I do, but now let's try to make sure it was worthwhile."

"Delivery is all," Haden said. "I delivered, I've been paid. End of transaction."

"Kordt seems to have a curious liking for you," James Walker said. "That's a relationship we could use. Spend time with him, talk to him, induce a more relaxed frame of mind, that's all we ask." Haden shook his head wearily. James Walker gave him a benevolent smile and a pat on the shoulder. "You're tired," he said. "Get some rest. We shan't be moving him today." He opened the door for Haden. "No one expects something for nothing," he said. "Valuable services attract the recognition they deserve. Think it over, Stephen. We'll talk again."

Stephen Haden returned to Heidelburg. He was using his Mercedes again. Christian Weber's car had been handed over to his parents. He had felt obliged to tell them face to face that their son was dead. They had listened, dully shocked, but seemed not to hold him responsible.

Christian's father forced a smile when he walked into the bookshop.

"Someone phoned for you, Mr. Haden," he said. "Twice. He said there was no message but he would call back. I said you would return soon."

"Who was it?"

"I don't know." Haden nodded, and moved toward the stairs. "Oh, Mr. Haden," Herr Weber went on, "my wife asked me to say, you are welcome to stay, if you wish. The funeral will be a private occasion, his fiancée is coming from West Berlin, naturally, and if you would like to be present . . . "

"Thank you," Haden said. He searched for something else to say. "Thank you." Herr Weber turned to serve a customer.

Haden tramped heavily up the stairs, bubbling with suppressed anger. Had he not, without a second thought, accepted Christian Weber's offer of help, their son would be alive now. He wished they would say so. Not politely invite him to the funeral, an honored guest at the "private occasion."

Haden lay on the bed and tried to think. The workshop where the trailer had been modified was the only weak link he could find, where others, even though trusted by Christian, knew that an escape was being planned. Yet even if there had been a leak, deliberate or inadvertent, no one could have known the return route. Haden had decided to use the Bitstedt crossing himself and without prior discussion with anyone. But that slow-moving truck with the missile launcher under the tarpaulin had, in retrospect, been patrolling the road, waiting. Who could have known, or been almost certain? And how? Or could it really have been a mistake, an attack on the wrong target?

The bedroom door was open and he heard the telephone ringing in the living room. After a few seconds, it stopped. Christian Weber's father had answered it downstairs in the bookshop.

Moments later, Herr Weber called up the stairs.

"Mr. Haden. Telephone."

"I'll take it up here," Haden called back.

He went into the living room, lifted the receiver, and heard the click as Herr Weber hung up. The voice at the other end was male, neutral, and spoke levelly and without emotion.

"Am I speaking to Mr. Stephen Haden?"

"Yes. Who is that?"

"There is a call for you, Mr. Haden, but you are using an extension. It is very important we are not overheard."

"The phone in the shop has been replaced."

"Very well. Hold on, please."

There was a brief silence.

"Hullo, Stephen. It's me."

This voice was unnaturally taut.

"Christa," Haden said blankly. "Where are you?"

The line went dead at once. Seconds later, the neutral male voice came back.

"No questions, please, Mr. Haden. She will speak, you will listen."

"It's me again, Stephen," Christa said. "This is what happened. At lunchtime, there was a message. I thought it was from you. I went outside." Her tone was stilted, as if repeating rehearsed phrases. "Someone there said you wanted to see me at once. That it was important and no one must know, except I could leave a note. I wrote it, and left it in the office. There was no one there. I got in the car. No one saw us leave." She paused, and the rest was unrehearsed, as she began to sob. "I'm sorry, Stephen . . . I know it was stupid . . . but I thought you needed me . . . I thought you were in trouble . . . "

"Don't cry," Haden said helplessly. "Are you hurt? Have they done anything to you?"

"No . . . Stephen, I can't help it . . . I'm frightened . . . "

"It'll be all right," Haden said, as reassuringly as he could. "Don't worry. I'll see you soon. Just do as they tell you. Is there anything else?"

"No. I'm not to say any more." She sounded a little calmer. " 'Bye, Stephen. See you."

There was a considerably longer pause during which Haden listened intently, but could hear nothing, before the neutral male voice spoke again.

"She can no longer hear us, Mr. Haden. She is being well looked after. Provided you cooperate, she will come to no harm."

"What do you want?"

"As to that, you will be contacted shortly. Assuming you agree, all will be well. If you refuse, you will be responsible for the consequences. Is that clear?"

"I hear you," Haden said. Christa had been repeating

what she had been told to say. There was no guarantee it was true. But if it was close to what had happened, she had not mentioned returning to her dormitory. In that case, she would not have her passport with her. She must be somewhere within an hour or two's drive of the school . . .

"Should the police be informed, or it became known she is missing, she will not be seen again," the monotonous voice went on.

Haden said, "How do I get in touch with you?"

"That will not be necessary," the voice said, and the owner hung up.

Slowly, Haden returned the receiver to its rest. He did not have to wait long.

"Mr. Haden. Mr. Haden," Herr Weber was calling.

Haden went out onto the landing. Christian's father was halfway up the stairs.

"Someone wishes to speak to you, Mr. Haden," he said.

"I'm coming," Haden said, and began to descend the stairs.

"The man suggested you meet at the café near the bridge." His face, already drawn with grief, wore a look of anxiety as well.

"Did you recognize him?" Haden asked.

"No. But I realize now, he followed you into the shop. I thought he was just browsing, at first, but I noticed he was watching me when you received your phone call. I think perhaps he is from the police. Is there to be more trouble, Mr. Haden?"

Haden managed a smile, as he shook his head.

"Nothing to concern you, Herr Weber," he said.

Christian's father stood aside to let him pass.

There were few people inside the café. He recognized none of the faces; no one looked toward him and caught his eye. He sat at a table outside, ordered a large cognac, and lit a cheroot.

The waiter was setting the glass down when the man

wearing sunglasses detached himself from the strolling passersby, walked over to the table, and sat down.

"Make it two," said Heinz Meyer. He gave Haden one of
his agreeable and still youthful smiles. "Quite like our first
meeting, Mr. Haden," he murmured. "I enjoyed the excitement of that escape. Now, we shall plan another one."

"Your people seem to have solved the problems of out-
of-work actors," Haden said. "Use them for spying, abduc-
tion, blackmail, and threatening to kill a child."

Heinz Meyer said modestly, "Since I once enjoyed some
slight acquaintance with you, it is considered that I may be
qualified to help resolve the difficult situation which has
arisen. One hopes for your agreement, Mr. Haden, without
crude threats."

He saw the waiter returning, sat back, accepted the
glass, and sipped his cognac in a leisurely fashion before
leaning forward toward Haden again.

"The only difficult situation I know of," Haden said
tightly, "is that a young girl has been kidnapped."

"There is another side to the equation," Heinz Meyer
said softly. "Karl Kordt is being detained against his wishes.
Once his freedom has been secured, the young lady will be
returned to your care. An eminently fair and reasonable
proposition, as I hope you will agree."

Haden could see no advantage in trying to pretend
ignorance.

"How do you know about Karl Kordt?" he asked directly.

Heinz Meyer said, "He did not return to his office. He is
not at his lodge. He has disappeared. Also his son. There
was some sort of accident, curiously played down. You are
here. Simple addition."

Haden listened but did not believe. Someone had
known where to telephone him.

"You could be wasting your time," he said. "If Kordt
were one of the casualties."

"Now you are wasting time, Mr. Haden," Heinz Meyer

said, an unpleasant edge entering his quiet voice. "It is known he is alive. It is known where he is."

Which confirmed that Heinz Meyer, or more likely his superiors, had access to a very well informed source indeed. Haden had no idea who that source might be, nor would it help much if he did, but the fact that it existed made him feel exposed and defenseless.

"Kordt is not 'detained,'" Haden said. "He defected of his own free will."

"I wonder," Heinz Meyer mused. "Or did he act under extreme duress, in exchange for a promise concerning his son's welfare? Now you find yourself in a similar position. Is it really so very different, Mr. Haden?"

Haden watched a police car as it cruised toward the café. Heinz Meyer followed his gaze.

"If I flag them down," Haden said, "I think they'd be very interested in who you are and what you're doing here."

"I should deny everything and appeal to my embassy," Heinz Meyer said. "But still, you could put me in a lot of trouble. Only you wouldn't see Christa again."

"She's not my bloody child," Haden said brutally. "I hardly ever see the girl. She's nothing to me."

"Then you won't mind what happens to her," Heinz Meyer remarked. His eyes switched to the police car, now receding. "Too late," he said with mock regret. "But I expect the waiter would telephone for the police, if you asked him." He looked back at Haden. "Your face gives you away, Mr. Haden," he said. "I have seen you and your step-daughter together. She was obviously very fond of you. There was certainly the possibility that you felt nothing in return. Had that been so, we'd have been no worse off. When one can only gain, the bet is a safe one. Let us now talk business."

"Where is she?" Haden asked, drained and beaten.

"In good hands. No one wishes the girl any harm."

"What do you expect?"

"Delivery of Karl Kordt."

•

"He'll be under guard, watched all the time. He won't be kept here. They'll move him. God knows where, America, anywhere. I don't know."

"Kordt's new location will be convenient. We do not expect the impossible. There is one absolute imperative. You must not travel with him. Find some excuse which will not arouse their suspicions. Leave the following morning. Drive. Use your own car. Follow the shortest route."

"The route to where?"

"Your friends will have told you that," Heinz Meyer said patiently.

"When I arrive, what then?"

Heinz Meyer's face had been serious and businesslike during the exchange in undertones. Now the agreeable smile reappeared on his lips.

"Then, we shall proceed further, Mr. Haden." He glanced at his watch. "Soon, within the hour, you must speak to Christa's school. Account convincingly for her whereabouts for, perhaps, the next week or so. Bear in mind that should her absence be reported to the police, her temporary guardians will be obliged to act on their instructions."

Haden picked up the packet lying on the table, eased back the silver paper, and took out the wafer-thin sheets.

"I have a letter for you," he said. "I was asked to have it delivered, but I couldn't."

Heinz Meyer looked surprised. He took the letter and read it in silence.

"Dear Harry," he said eventually. "I shall keep this, if I may."

He folded the letter with care, and tucked it meticulously into his wallet.

"If you want to take up his offer," Haden said, "I could help you. Arrangements. Contact Harry. Money too. As much cash as I can raise now. More later. Just tell me where Christa is being held."

"A generous offer, Mr. Haden," Heinz Meyer said, after a long pause. There was a strange expression on his face.

"But we are both caught up in the same process. It cannot be changed. There is only one way open to you to secure Christa's release. Please remember that two things could endanger her life. Should anything happen to me. Or should you talk to anyone, her mother, a friend, anyone, which would lead to the slightest suspicion."

Haden abandoned his confused, tentative half-thought that he might speak obliquely to Helen Lloyd. Besides Meyer's threat, she might be their source, or even the unknown person who had collected Christa. No, somehow, if it were possible, he had to see this through alone.

"You may be asking too much," he said, as Heinz Meyer stood up to go. "I'm not sure it can be done."

Heinz Meyer bent down to speak, his lips close to Haden's ear, the passing scent of his musk aftershave in the air.

"Some things will be on your side," he said softly. "Karl Kordt is valuable and will be treated accordingly, not as a prisoner. They want his cooperation and will not wish to offend a man of such importance. He will be protected, yes, but also allowed a certain apparent measure of freedom. You must take advantage of that. And when the time comes, you will not be without help." He straightened up. "Remember, Mr. Haden," he said, "it has been achieved before, in similar cases. Take heart from that."

*T*he steps laid down by Heinz Meyer were self-checking, as Haden well appreciated, and he hastened back to the bookshop, where he called the school and spoke to Mary Turner. The connection was admirably clear, and he told her that he was speaking from London. Some relatives, he said, had unexpectedly arrived in England for a short visit. Christa was on her way with them to Dorset where she would be staying with them for about a week. Mary Turner was duly outraged at this cavalier arrangement, made without seeking permission or even informing the school in advance, and he allowed her indignation to flow, apologizing abjectly in such few brief intervals as occurred. In the end, reluctantly, she accepted the fait accompli, and he agreed to write a note absolving the school from all responsibility.

He hung up and scribbled the note. He would be able, he suspected, to post it so that it carried an English postmark in the pretty near future.

Then he called James Walker.

A self-contained section of the top floor of the hospital had been set aside to contain the very important patient. Haden rode up in the elevator. When he stepped out, unobtrusive men in plainclothes eyed him, but made no attempt to approach him.

It was James Walker who strode forward, smiling widely, hand outstretched.

"Welcome aboard, Stephen," he said. "Delighted. Couldn't be more pleased. A chip off the old block after all, eh?" His eyes twinkled knowingly.

James Walker led the way. No one suggested that Haden should be searched, or an electronic body scan used. He wondered if that would last.

"You won't be disturbed," James Walker said. "Talk about anything you think he might respond to. Entirely up to you. Take as much time as you like."

Haden went into the private ward and closed the door. It was pleasantly furnished, with an adjoining bathroom. Karl Kordt was alone. He was sitting up in bed, wearing hospital pajamas, scanning a newspaper.

He looked up, and studied Haden ironically.

"Well, well," he said. "The hero of the hour."

Haden placed a chair at the bedside and sat down.

"How are you feeling?" he asked.

"Bored," Karl Kordt said. "This place is populated by tiresome cretins."

"I'm sorry about your son."

"Other people seem less sure of his identity," Karl Kordt remarked. "Have you seen this?" He stabbed a stubby forefinger at an item in the newspaper. "I thought there was no censorship in the West."

"There isn't," Haden said. "It's known as manipulating the news."

"What an end," Karl Kordt said. "Murdered, and then cut up and the pieces examined, like some laboratory specimen."

"I'd like to find out who killed him," Haden said. "Would you?"

Karl Kordt folded the newspaper with care, laid it aside, and removed his spectacles.

"Why should that concern you, Mr. Haden?" he inquired distantly.

"My friend was killed, too," Haden said.

Karl Kordt studied him for a long moment, and then nodded. Bitterness etched his face.

"They were waiting," he said. "Arrangements had been made. Someone knew. But who? I considered your friend . . ."

"It wasn't him," Haden said.

"Certainly highly unlikely," Karl Kordt agreed. "Since he was one of the victims. Then I thought of you, Mr. Haden. You selected the route. You were not with us. But yet you chose to risk your life in an effort to save him. Why would you do that if you had set us up?"

"I thought it might have been your people," Haden said.

"It wasn't," Karl Kordt said. "You may be quite certain of that. Which seems to leave your employers."

"The arrangements were left entirely to me," Haden said. "They didn't know the means, they didn't know the route. Besides, they want you alive, not dead."

Karl Kordt nodded reluctantly.

"There has to be an answer," he said.

They talked for an hour. No answer emerged.

Stephen Haden joined James Walker in a small room in which electronic equipment had been installed. Tom Leeson had arrived and was sitting, wearing earphones, listening intently to the tape. He lifted a hand in a cordial gesture of greeting toward Haden, but did not stop listening.

"Well done, Stephen," James Walker said warmly. "An inspiration, your choice of subject. A masterstroke. Perhaps it really was his son," he said thoughtfully. "Anyway, you've begun to pry him open nicely. If we can build on that, guide him in other directions . . . he trusts you, and that's what we need . . . I take it you can make yourself available? Given some suitable financial arrangement, of course."

"I'm not sure," Haden said. "My step-daughter's staying with relatives in England," he said, casually. "I really must go and see them, if only for a day or so."

There was no perceptible reaction from James Walker.

"We can fit that in," he said. "We're moving him tomorrow. You may as well travel with us."

Heinz Meyer and his associates had a deadly accurate line through direct to someone at the heart of things.

"I'll join you the following day," Haden said. "I can't travel tomorrow, Mr. Walker."

"It's *James*, please," Walker said. "Why not?"

"I have to attend a funeral," Stephen Haden said.

FIFTEEN

Stephen Haden had skirted Rheims and joined the Paris-Calais autoroute when it hit him.

His hands began to tremble, at first almost imperceptibly but quite soon in spasms which he could only control by gripping the steering wheel hard. Not long aferwards, the tremors began to affect his legs as well. There was dull, sickening pain in his loins.

The previous day, James Walker had telephoned, made sympathetic noises about the funeral, and suggested a flight which Haden might care to catch. When told that he intended to drive, Walker raised no objection, but asked which ferry he intended to use, and from where. Haden chose a sailing time from Calais which would allow him plenty of time for the journey.

"Fine," James Walker had said. "Won't ask you to stay with us. Best if our friend regards you as a welcome visitor. Have you booked in at your previous hotel. Convenient all around, yes?"

Later, Heinz Meyer had phoned with the same inquiry concerning his travel arrangements.

"Don't miss it," he had said, before he hung up. "Under any circumstances."

The bookshop had been closed for the day. One of Haden's priorities before that had been to search Christian Weber's bedroom and remove the .22 Beretta he found inside the lining of the valise which Christian had brought with him from West Berlin. Christian had not been overfond of firearms, but had usually kept one around somewhere as a reluctant precaution. Haden had transferred the slim automatic to the compartment in his Mercedes. It was loaded, but there were no spare clips in the valise. He did not want Christian's parents to find it, and having it in his possession made him feel marginally more comfortable against he knew not what circumstance.

He had felt lethargic when he got up, his limbs heavy, but he had tried to put that down to a sleepless night, the stress laid upon him by an insoluble problem, and the general strain of the funeral, which had included trying to talk with some semblance of normality to Christian's fiancée from West Berlin. She was a pretty, young brunette who had tended to start crying in the middle of a sentence. When it was time to go, he had settled himself behind the wheel with relief, glad to get away. But he had not anticipated anything as bad as this.

For a while he slowed down and kept going, but the tremors, although intermittent, became worse and he was aware of increasing light-headedness. He turned off at the next exit, and stopped in the first village he came to.

Gray stone buildings lined a broad street once busy with constant traffic now diverted since the autoroute had been built. Now the place was somnolent and almost deserted. He asked at a small garage where the village doctor lived, followed the directions, and hammered repeatedly on the door of the large house until an elderly woman opened it. Her expression was less than welcoming. She began to tell him sharply that if he wished to see the doctor he must come back that evening during surgery hours, but when she looked at him more closely, her manner changed. She showed him into the surgery, and told him to wait.

Haden sat, his hands clasped, gazing vacantly at the floor. Some minutes elapsed before the doctor, as elderly as the woman, entered. His collar was crumpled, and he wore the bad-tempered look of a man who had just been woken up and did not like it. He was wearing bifocals and the first things he focused on were Haden's hands as he unclasped them.

"Minor burns. Is that what is so urgent?" he demanded aggressively.

"No," Haden said. He had removed the bandages, and his hands were sore and inflamed. He handed over Dr. Hensler's note. "It's not in French . . ."

The French doctor took a second, more careful look at Haden's ashen face, pursed his lips, and read the note in silence, his lips moving as he mentally translated it.

"Let's take a look at you," he said briskly, when he had finished.

Haden shook his head.

"All I want is something to be going on with . . ."

"Not until I've examined you," the doctor said firmly. He waved at the couch. "Over there. Strip off."

Haden submitted, undressed, and lay on the couch. Gentle and considerate now, although his eyes contained a detached alertness, the doctor prodded and probed, took his temperature, asked questions about his symptoms, and finally disappeared with the urine sample Haden had given.

Haden dressed clumsily, and fretted about the passing time. The doctor came back.

"No wonder you feel ill," he said, crossing to his desk.

"Just give me some drugs to keep me going," Haden said.

"Going? You are going nowhere, my friend." The doctor smiled paternally. "You belong in the hospital. I'll have you admitted." He reached for the telephone.

"No! I can't!" Haden said violently. Hand outstretched, the doctor looked at him compassionately, and began to say something soothing. "I'm booked on a flight from Paris to

Zurich," Haden said, struggling to steady his voice to that of a rational man in full possession of himself. "In Zurich, I shall go straight to the hospital." He pointed at the note. "They know all about me. In a few hours, I shall be there."

The doctor made it plain that he was less than happy with this arrangement, but in the face of Haden's obstinate insistence, he capitulated and wrote a prescription.

"Be clear," he said, gazing at Haden, "these drugs will merely relieve the symptoms temporarily. We are dealing with a condition which is certainly serious, and could be dangerous. You must get yourself into a hospital without delay. Is that understood?"

Haden made the required promises, and the doctor saw him to the front door. He was so concerned that he almost forgot to ask for his fee.

In the local pharmacy, Haden swallowed the drugs dispensed and obtained a copy of the prescription. Soon after, he had regained the autoroute. He was less aware of his surroundings than he should have been and was granted more than his fair share of luck that day. He was neither stopped for speeding, involved in an accident, nor booked for recklesss driving. He arrived at the car ferry just before the ramp was raised.

*T*he crowds which thronged the ferry largely comprised foot passengers. Haden climbed to the upper deck, where he could get some fresh air, and found a seat near the stern, where he was soon surrounded by a bunch of French teenagers who chattered continuously like magpies. When the engines began to throb, Haden closed his eyes. After a while, the machine-gun French and youthful bursts of laughter diminished in volume, and finally faded into nothing.

When he awoke, not much more than half an hour had passed, but the involuntary tremors had ceased. Cautiously, he thought that he felt more like himself.

The white cliffs were near enough to be a spectacle. The French teenagers had gone, either into the bows to stare at the dramatic, sheer fall of the chalk cliffs, or to queue up to disembark.

Heinz Meyer sauntered along the deck and sat beside Haden.

"We nearly sailed without you," he said reprovingly. "That would have been very bad for all concerned."

"I want to speak to Christa today and every day until she's free," Haden said.

Heinz Meyer's face became stony.

"Mr. Haden, if you have some silly notion about having phone calls traced, that would not be good for Christa."

"For all I know, she could be dead now," Haden said. "Every day. Without fail. If I don't, I talk."

"You're not going about this the right way, Mr. Haden. You know what the consequences of that would be."

"So do you," Haden said. "If I talk, you don't stand a chance in hell of getting Kordt."

"I'll try and arrange it," Heinz Meyer said. "But no fixed times, nothing like that."

"Day or night," Haden said. "So long as I hear."

The ship's engines grunted and slowed. They were approaching the harbor.

Heinz Meyer said, "Your initial task is to learn all you can about Herr Kordt's place of confinement. Then, perhaps in a day or two, we shall discuss his onward transmission."

"Jesus," Haden said, "he's not a bloody letter to be forwarded. He's a valuable property. I don't even know where he's being kept. He'll be surrounded by security staff. Who's going to deal with them?"

"You will have access to him. The aim is for it to be accomplished without violence. Neither side will wish for a diplomatic incident."

"And I'm supposed to rely on your word that Christa will then be released."

"No, Mr. Haden, she will be handed over to you personally, alive and well. You may believe that. It is in our interests to do so."

Haden said, "If you're expecting me to work out some way, I don't know if I can, and if I could I don't know when. Even if I knew where to contact you, I may not get the chance."

"You don't have to worry about that," Heinz Meyer said. "Time you got down to the car deck, Mr. Haden."

Haden was not certain if Heinz Meyer remained on board, or disembarked among the jostling throng of foot passengers. He did not see him. Perhaps Meyer was taking precautions in case whoever was sent to meet Haden might recognize him.

Haden was waved through Customs. When he drove out of the shed, Harold Leyton was waiting. Haden stopped, and Leyton climbed in.

"Head for Arundel," he said.

"I need some more of these," Haden said. "I don't want to see a doctor."

He passed over the copy of the prescription. The French doctor had only prescribed a day's supply. Harold Leyton looked at it with some surprise.

"Are you ill, Stephen?" he inquired.

"Half the Western world takes drugs all the time," Haden growled. "Why should I be ill? Can you fix it or not?"

"All right. No need to bite my head off."

They drove on for some long time in silence.

"Glad you're okay, Stephen," Harold Leyton said eventually. "I gather it was a bit rough."

"That's why I couldn't deliver your letter," Haden said.

"Ah. I wondered about that." Harold Leyton fell silent.

The country house was a graceful Georgian structure, set in extensive grounds. Facing across a valley it commanded a distant view of Arundel Castle. In terms of the landed gentry of the time, it had probably been regarded as a relatively modest manor house, the residence of some knight of the shires. The tall wrought-iron gates were locked, and Harold Leyton got out and rang the bell.

The custodian who emerged from the adjoining gate-house had the erect bearing of a former soldier, was expecting them, and called them both "sir." He opened the gates, handed Haden a pass, checked the inside of the Mercedes, apologetically removed Haden's suitcase, saying that it would be returned to him when he left, and asked him to use the visitors' car park.

The long drive looped around ornamental gardens. Haden followed the signs until they diverged. The staff car park was out of sight somewhere. The visitors' open car park adjoined a walled garden at the rear of the house and was sparsely populated, with only a few cars there, including Harold Leyton's cream Sierra.

There were tennis courts and a croquet lawn nearby. Beyond was a large ornamental lake, after which the land fell away in a gentle slope. Alongside the car park a path meandered down to the ornamental lake. Toward the house the path was covered, and led to a door.

The door was not locked, but when they walked in their passes were checked in a brief, matter-of-fact, routine way. Harold Leyton's pass was a different color, and well used.

"Ignore the front door," Harold Leyton said, as they walked along a carpeted corridor. "That's kept locked. Everyone's channeled through the back. Helps save on staff and stretch the budget, I suppose."

He showed Haden into a small book-lined library cum writing room, indicated a sideboard, invited Haden to help himself, and left.

Haden wondered if cognac would mix with his pills and tried it, finishing his supply. He hoped Harold Leyton would remember.

James Walker was his usual breezy self when he arrived.

"Ah, Stephen. Good journey? Oh, you've given yourself a drink. Good man." Haden thought that he was only supposed to listen, and let him ramble on. "Our guest's having a full medical at the moment, but he's looking a bit tired, so with your by-your-leave, we won't trouble him tonight. Might look a bit contrived anyway, your popping up at once. Tomorrow p.m., if that suits you. I expect you'll be glad of a good night's rest yourself." Haden nodded. He had no need to feign weariness. "Suppose I show you around, so that you know where everything is, perhaps have a bite to eat afterwards, if you like. Quite a nice place, I think you'll find. We strain every nerve to make our guests feel at home, and generally loved and wanted."

James Walker gave him a conducted tour which was confined to the more public rooms, dining room, billiard room, morning room, conservatory, picture gallery, and the like. Haden commented on the apparent absence of staff.

"Deliberate," James Walker said. "Can't have our guests feeling they're being watched all the time, escorted everywhere, nonsense like that. That would never do. Free to wander where they will, without question."

"Trips outside? Shopping? Theaters? Anything like that?"

"Ah, well, no," James Walker said. "Anything they want, we'll get it, but as for excursions . . . some of them are potty about the ballet, you know, but regretfully we're unable to oblige in that direction until the process here is completed. We'll take a turn around the grounds while it's still daylight, shall we?"

They descended the main staircase and crossed the hall toward the rear exit.

"There are a number of backroom staff," James Walker said, resuming his previous train of thought, "but no point in bothering you with their whereabouts. Except the cashier's office, which is there," he said, pointing. "Pop in when convenient, sign a chitty, and they'll look after your expenses, et cetera." They paused at the porter's desk beside the rear door, flashed passes, and walked through. "Bit of a farce, really," James Walker said, putting his away. "More to keep people on their toes than anything. Our guests don't carry passes of course. That would be quite wrong. Don't want to make them feel like prisoners. No one's going to mistake who they are. A responsible officer—not the porter—discreetly logs them in and out, but otherwise . . ."

The "turn around" the grounds was more of a solid tramp. By the time they were returning past the ornamental lake, Haden noticed that his hands were beginning to tremble again. He shoved them into his jacket pockets.

"He's being very cautious," James Walker said, reverting to Karl Kordt. "As one would expect. He knows the score better than anyone. I'm not going to attempt to brief you. We don't expect him to tell you anything significant. But at least you seem able to get him talking. A point of leverage may emerge. Some aspect of him we can work on to speed up the process a little."

They turned into the car park. Haden had declined the offer of "a bite to eat."

James Walker admired the Mercedes again, abstractedly.

"I always liked this model," he said. "My old Volvo's getting on a bit too. Don't hold with changing cars for the sake of it, myself."

A chauffeur-driven limousine had arrived. Tom Leeson emerged from the house and hurried toward it, pausing only to greet Haden briefly with his newfound cordiality.

"Hi there, Stephen . . . maybe we'll find time for a chat tomorrow . . . must rush . . . "

"How's Helen Lloyd?" Haden asked.

"Okay, I think." Tom Leeson spoke over his shoulder as he was turning away. "Haven't seen her since that evening at the restaurant."

He climbed into the limousine. Haden noted that the

cream Sierra had gone. Harold Leyton carried a permanent pass, but was not on the staff. He was not quite the insignificant unwilling tool, working his passage, which he liked to make out.

"I take it Harold Leyton has now provided thc details you require," James Walker said. Haden nodded assent, without elaborating on when. He wondered if Walker was gifted with thought transference. "I want to be as fair as I can with you, Stephen," James Walker continued. "The information concerning your man came from Karl Kordt. At the time, he was very anxious to progress the escape. To that end, his identification of . . . Ernst Braun, was it? . . . may be accurate. But we can't guarantee that."

"Does such a man even live at the address I've been given?" Haden inquired.

"Routinely validated as part of an assessment of Kordt's sincerity or otherwise," James Walker said. "Braun is of East German origin. The West German police have nothing against him, nor is he suspected of criminal activities. He works as a courier from time to time for a commercial firm of couriers. Nothing known against them either. His tax affairs are in order. That is all I can tell you. It was not possible to establish his whereabouts when you were shot without interviewing him, and it was thought you wouldn't like that."

Haden said, "Right man or not, I'll know that when he sees me."

James Walker eyed him with speculative diffidence.

"Guilt or innocence is the business of the police and a court of law. I take it one may assume your intention is to assist the course of justice."

"I couldn't have put it better," Haden said. "Anyway, he's only part of it." The first flimsy dawning of how and why had come to him, paradoxically, unasked, during his earlier spell of light-headedness, a condition which was threatening to return. He strove to steady his hand as he took out his car keys. "He'll keep," he said.

James Walker seemed satisfied with this, and stepped back.

"Good-night, Stephen," he said.

Before the gates were unlocked, the custodian took Haden's pass from him, returned his suitcase, and handed him a package.

"From Mr. Leyton, sir," he said.

Haden stopped half a mile along the road and ripped open the package. It contained the drugs he had asked for. He swallowed a dose at once.

Darkness fell as Haden drove with infinite caution to London, while the drugs took effect. Stationed in the slow lane, he was no danger to anyone. It also served to establish that neither side considered it necessary to have him followed.

At the hotel, Haden drove straight into the car park. He reversed into a space and doused his headlights. From the deep shadows in an unlit corner, a waiting figure detached itself and walked toward him. Haden unlocked the passenger door. Heinz Meyer got in beside him.

"Your telephone calls are not being monitored," he said. "So, as an indication of our goodwill, it has been agreed. Christa will know what to say. Any attempt on your part to gain information, any slip . . . well, I needn't labor the point. You will hear this evening, and at some time tomorrow. After that, one hopes, it will not be necessary."

Stephen Haden stared through the windshield at the rows of cars, dimly illuminated by infrequent moon-shaped lights on the concrete walls. A gun lay at his fingertips. With any ordinary man he would have used it to extract Christa's whereabouts. But Heinz Meyer was a professional, trained in the last resort to endure and die if necessary. As was Harold Leyton, as were they all. His fingers left the carpet which lay over the small compartment.

"Kordt is being kept at a house not far from Arundel," he said in a flat voice. "He won't be allowed out. There's only one vehicular access. It's locked. Everyone needs passes. The boundary is a thorn hedge. In it is an electrified barbed-wire fence, randomly patrolled on the other side. It can't be done. Let Christa go."

"Were it, despite all our combined best efforts, to prove impossible, we shall do so," Heinz Meyer said, quietly. "No one wishes to harm a child. But that will only be contemplated when we have tried and failed."

"It's my trade," Haden said. "I've tried to think of a way. There isn't one. Tell them to let Christa go."

Heinz Meyer said, "Mr. Haden, I traveled across the Swiss frontier in this very car."

Haden turned and looked at the pale shape of the handsome face beside him. "Kordt is a big, heavy man," he said. "I'm supposed to club him unconscious, try and carry a dead weight to the car, and fit him in somehow, all without being seen? Do you think that's a practical way?"

"No, not very," Heinz Meyer agreed. "Show it to me. I only occupied it. I didn't see how you operated it."

Wearily, Haden got out and lifted the tailgate. Heinz Meyer studied the interior, felt around the ribbed floor for a while, and gave up. Haden showed him the catch, which was beside the spare wheel. Once undone, a section of the ribbed floor lifted and gave access to a space in which a human being, half doubled up, might travel. Leaning inside, Heinz Meyer played about for a while, doing it for himself.

Haden stood outside, watching him. In the earlier days he had used that compartment to house refugees two or three times, before deciding that the Mercedes was becoming conspicuous. By then, he was attached to it. It was a comfortable and practical vehicle, for, among other things, taking his dogs out. The last time the compartment had been used was when he had taken Heinz Meyer into Switzerland, "technically illegally." Heinz Meyer straightened up.

"Tomorrow, find out all you can about the routine of the place," he said. "For now, I shall say good-night."

———

*H*aden wasted no time in getting into bed. The drugs staved off the worst of it but he felt as if he was running down, like the mechanism of some tired, worn-out clock, although sleep was a million miles away.

He lifted the receiver a second after the telephone began to ring.

"Hullo, Stephen. It's me," said Christa.

"How's everything in Dorset?"

"Oh, fine. Hoping to see you sometime, though."

"You will, soon . . . "

They talked inconsequentially for another minute or so, but Haden was anxious not to risk an accidental false note in the conversation, some "slip."

"Let's have a chat another time, shall we?" he said. "Only I've had a long day."

"Okay. Good-night, Stephen."

Haden hung up. To his ear, and probably to his alone, there had been an unnatural note in her voice, but she had sounded in better spirits than the day before. He was certain that she could not have approached such a degree of normality were she being ill-treated, which was something at least . . .

The next thing Stephen Haden knew his eyes opened, and daylight was edging the curtains. He had slept the night through.

*H*aden met Karl Kordt over afternoon tea, served in the drawing room, with James Walker and Harold Leyton. As a social occasion it was not a success.

"I don't like tea, I can't stand tea," complained Karl Kordt. "I told one of your menials that this morning."

Coffee was hurriedly substituted.

Kordt continued to rumble and grumble. After one glare, he ignored Haden. James Walker kept a flow of genial conversation going which was virtually a monologue, since Kordt's only response was to grunt and raise his bushy eye-

•

brows derisively. For Harold Leyton, he reserved a special hostility, making one offensive personal remark after another. Harold Leyton smiled weakly, and tried to find safer conversationl ground.

Finally Kordt stood up abruptly.

"I'm going for a walk," he said aggresssively, and strode out.

James Walker sighed, and watched him go.

"Log him out, Harold, please," he said. Leyton stood up and strolled slowly after Kordt.

"Our guest isn't in a very good humor today," James Walker said, shaking his head sorrowfully. "They're often like this, you know, until they get used to the idea of being free." He gazed at Haden significantly.

Haden found Karl Kordt sitting on a bench beside the ornamental lake, hurling pebbles at cruising ducks, who maintained course with lofty indifference. Haden sat down beside him. It was one of those sun-veiled English summer days, pleasant enough as it went, although the risk of sunstroke was negligible.

Kordt began to get the range, and the leader of the duck formation squawked as an inexplicable waterspout rose from under its beak, and took off hurriedly in alarm. The remainder took up the cry and followed their leader.

Seemingly satisfied, Karl Kordt leaned back and clasped his hands across his stomach.

"So you have joined with them, Mr. Haden," he said. "You are to play the friend in need in whom I am supposed to confide. Very well. Time drags. You have been sent to do what?"

"Pander to your bad temper, I suppose," Haden said.

"They know I know," Kordt grumbled. "If I talk in my sleep, it's recorded and analyzed. I am to feel free, do as I wish, go where I please, so long as I don't go anywhere and merely chat to charming chaps now and then. Even here, if I prefer, far from the house, where their directional microphones can't reach us." He eyed Haden. "Although body tape recorders or transmitters are not unheard of."

Haden said, "Check if you like. You'll find nothing."

Karl Kordt gazed at the circling ducks coming in to land. "I really don't care," he said. "It's just all so bloody predictable. Like some old-fashioned, stately, and ultimately tiresome quadrille. Everyone knows the steps. Everyone obediently goes through the same motions." But he smiled in mild appreciation of his own analogy, and was evidently feeling better.

"You chose to dance," Haden said. "You can either lead or follow."

"On or off the record, Mr. Haden, where do you really stand?"

"I come from a neutral country," Haden said. "I think like a neutral."

"Bullshit," Karl Kordt remarked. "You're a people-smuggler. But only one way. You took sides the day you began."

"They only want to go one way," Haden said. "If anyone wanted to travel in the opposite direction, I'm open to suggestions."

Karl Kordt sat for a while, apparently lost in thought, but if he perceived the invitation, he chose to ignore it.

"Do you have a family, Mr. Haden?" he inquired, at last.

"A divorced wife. A step-daughter."

"That doesn't count," Kordt said. He sighed. "A man expects to outlive his son. But I can't change that. I have a practical nature. However many years I have left, I must live for something."

"Name what you want," Haden said.

Karl Kordt smiled.

"Ah, we are to play at negotiating. Let me see," he said dreamily. "A million dollars in cash. A ranch house in California, fortified, naturally. Armed protection. A supply of compliant young women. An income of two hundred and fifty thousand dollars a year. Automobiles? Perhaps a white Ferrari to begin with. And the resurrection of my wife and son."

"You won't get them all," Haden said.

"Strike the last one," Karl Kordt said. "I'm willing to be reasonable."

*H*aden stayed for supper that evening. After the prolonged and useless play-acting beside the ornamental lake, Kordt had declared that he would eat in his room, and once the duty moron had talked to him he could watch obscene videos in peace.

"They're about as fruity as *Gone With the Wind*," James Walker said as he led the way into the dining room. "I wonder if he would like some raunchy ones," he pondered. "Perhaps we should slip a few in for him." They sat down. "I don't agree that it was entirely play-acting, Stephen," he said, studying the menu. "Our duty moron, as he's pleased to call the poor chap, reports that for the first time Kordt let drop something promising during their chat. No, I think the process of bargaining is gently under way, and he's decided to use you. Offer some juicy tidbit in parallel to whet the appetite in support of his outrageous demands. Kite flying, naturally, but we'll reach agreement in the end, we always do. I'm anxious that should be sooner rather than later. Under our agreement, Tom Leeson's people have sole access after a given period, and we want as large a bite of the cherry as we can get. So, same again tomorrow, Stephen, if you don't mind, let's try to close the gap fast. I'm having the lamb chops. What do you feel like?"

Haden had not seen Tom Leeson that day. When he left, the cream Sierra was still there.

*I*n the hotel car park, Haden switched off his headlights. No figure emerged from the shadows. He walked up the ramp and toward the front of the hotel. As he was passing a taxi waiting to one side, its "For Hire" sign off, the passenger door opened. Haden got in. The taxi moved forward and joined the traffic stream.

Heinz Meyer made certain that the glass panel separating them from the driver was firmly closed and sat back.

"The routine of the place, mealtimes, things like that," he said.

Haden told him. Meyer listened and asked a few questions. The driver seemed to know where he was going.

"Tomorrow," he said, when Haden had finished, "behave as today. Make sure that you back your car up against the wall in the car park."

"It sounds as though you've been there," Haden said.

Heinz Meyer smiled wryly in the half darkness inside the cab.

"A pleasure I am never likely to experience," he said. "I am too unimportant. Your tailgate is to be unlocked. Leave the premises at eight o'clock exactly. Take the shortest route toward the London road, but stop for gas at the second filling station. No variations, please. You will be observed. Clear?"

Haden nodded.

"What else?"

"Nothing. You will receive further instructions then, depending upon circumstances." Heinz Meyer leaned forward and slid open the glass panel. "You can put me down here."

Heinz Meyer got out and disappeared into Earls Court Station. The taxi returned to Haden's hotel.

Haden spent some time in thought, largely wasted. There were too many speculative imponderables, and even if he guessed right, he did not know the details. He studied his clothes, and experimented with various ways of taping or suspending a small, slim automatic, but eventually decided not to be clever. The kind of people he was dealing with were not going to miss a gun about his person, no matter how artfully concealed, and he did not believe for one moment that they would not check him at some point.

He went to bed, and tried to get as much rest as his overactive mind and indifferent physical condition allowed.

*T*here was a brief phone call from Christa soon after he got up, and the day passed much like its predecessor. Haden drove into the car park, and reversed into position so that the tailgate was close to the wall. When in that position, he noted, the car was shielded from the house and the porter who manned the desk just inside the rear door, as well as a considerable section of the grounds.

He forced himself to spend two hours in mock serious bargaining with Karl Kordt, this time during a lengthy perambulation on the grounds.

"At least I don't *feel* so confined out here," Karl Kordt rumbled.

Presumably that was the intention. No one followed them around. No obtrusive "gardeners" happened coincidentally to be working nearby. Given the commanding position of the house, possibly surveillance was being conducted from inside, but when they walked the farthest boundaries and sat down on the grass for a while, they were in "dead ground," a combination of the lie of the land and green-mantled intervening trees, and must have been out of sight of the house for nearly half an hour. Still no one appeared, or passed on patrol the other side of the dense thorn hedge. It was perhaps conceivable that a radio bug had been planted on Kordt, but Haden doubted it. The old fox beside him would have been up to that one, and they must know it.

Finally, Karl Kordt said, "I've had enough. You go in. I want to walk on my own."

Haden returned to the house, went to his car for some cheroots, and half-smoked one outside before he showed his pass and went in. As far as he could tell, Karl Kordt had been left to his own devices.

He was glad to accept the offer of a cognac from James Walker, and tried to appear to enjoy the early "bite to eat" which followed. He had glimpsed Harold Leyton once or twice, but had not spoken to him. Karl Kordt had come in and joined them briefly for a lager before going to his room, where someone would have a chat with him.

James Walker excused himself for five minutes before they sat down to eat. When he came back he was looking pleased, and confided that the "chat," in the opinion of the experienced interrogator concerned, showed Kordt to be adopting a more amenable attitude. He had offered portions of several tempting delicacies, while withholding the substance.

"He's holding out for all he can get," James Walker said tolerantly. "Can't blame him. He's got a lot to give. But we're getting there, Stephen. Another day or two, with any luck . . . "

The main course had arrived when Harold Leyton sidled into the dining room and spoke quietly to James Walker.

"He's eaten, sir, and gone for his evening stroll."

"Okay, Harry, we've finished with him for the day. So long as he's logged back in before dark." Harold Leyton sidled out again. James Walker turned to Haden. "With your permission, Stephen, now that we're getting down to brass tacks, I'd like to guide you about the approach you should take to him tomorrow . . . "

Haden nodded, watched the man's lips move as he continued, and hoped that his occasional responses, when they seemed to be called for, indicated that he was taking it all in.

Just before eight o'clock, Haden declined coffee and brandy, and made his excuses.

"You're looking a bit under the weather, Stephen," James Walker said. "Sure you're feeling all right?"

"Nothing an early night won't cure. See you to-morrow."

Haden was intercepted outside the dining room by Tom Leeson, who had just arrived. For what seemed an age, he made small talk as convincingly as he could, before bidding Leeson good-night. Leeson joined James Walker and their heads bent close together.

Leeson's chauffeur was sitting talking to the porter. Haden showed his pass and walked out. A layer of cloud obscured the declining sun, but it was still daylight.

It was three minutes past eight when he surrendered his pass, and the soldierly custodian checked the interior of the Mercedes before unlocking the gates.

The second filling station was half a mile short of the intersection with the main London road. Haden filled the tank and paid at the cashier's window. Several people were browsing along the shelves in the self-service accesssories shop. When Haden walked back to the Mercedes, one of them followed him. Heinz Meyer got into the passenger seat.

"Follow my directions," he said.

They weaved along a network of meandering minor roads, out of Sussex, and across Hampshire. Twilight became night. Haden switched on his headlights.

A minute later he said, "We're being followed."

Heinz Meyer turned his head and stared back for a long time. Haden was obliged to concentrate on his driving along the twisting, narrow lanes but from occasional glances at his rearview mirror, he thought that, while the headlights behind disappeared from time to time when S bends intervened, they always reappeared.

Heinz Meyer eventually faced the front again.

"Keep going," he said. A map was on his knee. Some time later he spoke again. "Take the next turning right, and then fork left."

This was unfamiliar country to Haden and he had not

previously known exactly where they were, or were heading. Now, though, they were skirting a forest. So far as he could recollect, the only one which seemed to fit their general direction and journey time was Savernake Forest.

"Slow down," Heinz Meyer said. "There should be a very narrow turning to the right, no signpost. There it is."

Haden swung the wheel. They entered the forest itself, and drove deeper into it. Until now, Haden had not realized that it was so extensive.

"Dead slow," Heinz Meyer said. "Just around the next bend there's a track on the left."

Without the advance warning, Haden would have passed it, unnoticed. The track was rutted and uneven. The headlights illuminated nothing but trees and undergrowth as they wound their way on until the track finally ended at an old, single-story stone cottage. The windows were barred, no light showed, and it appeared to be deserted, but deep in the trees beyond was concealed some sort of vehicle.

"Switch off," Heinz Meyer said. "Lights too."

Haden complied. The darkness was absolute until his eyes began to adjust. In the complete silence, there was no sound of any approaching car, but Haden heard the faint squeak of hinges, and then saw a dark shape approaching the car.

"Out," Heinz Meyer said, and got out himself. Haden opened his door and stood erect. "Turn around," Heinz Meyer said. "Hands on the roof."

Haden did as he was told. The man from the house searched him with no regard for modesty or privacy, then moved away, satisfied, to help Heinz Meyer, who had the tailgate open.

Haden leaned inside the driver's door, looking back at the two men. His fingers sought the compartment under the carpet.

"Do you need a hand?"

"No. Stay there."

When Heinz Meyer removed the section of ribbed flooring, soft moans of pain could be heard. The two men heaved unceremoniously. The grunts and moans became louder. When Haden straightened up, the .22 Beretta was in his pocket.

"Inside. Walk ahead," Heinz Meyer said.

Haden approached the cottage. Behind, Heinz Meyer and his companion half-dragged, half-carried Karl Kordt. A woman opened the door. He was aware of the flicker of distant headlights somewhere between the trees but did not turn his head. He entered the pitch blackness of the cottage. A hand guided him into a room. Behind, footsteps stumbled, and the burden continued to moan.

When the light went on, Haden saw that he was in a living room, the window heavily curtained, the furnishings basic, a table, kitchen chairs, a sideboard, a couple of spartan armchairs with wooden arms. There was a door to another room, a key in the lock. The woman who had let him in was in her thirties, with rather severe although not unattractive features. Like the man who was helping Heinz Meyer, she was tall, with fair hair, and said little. In one corner of the room was a telephone.

"Sit there, please," Heinz Meyer said to Haden.

Haden sat in the indicated armchair. Karl Kordt had been put on one of the hard kitchen chairs, and was doubled up, his eyes screwed tight with pain, still involuntarily groaning as he tried to ease the agonizing cramps. Haden took the opportunity, while no one was paying any attention to him, to slip the automatic under the chair cushion.

After a while, Karl Kordt opened his eyes, stood up unsteadily, winced, cursed under his breath, leaned on the back of the kitchen chair, and began to stamp his feet.

Finally, as the spasms of cramp eased, and became bearable, he stood erect, took a deep long breath of relief, and shook Heinz Meyer by the hand.

"Well done, Heinz," he said.

Haden had not heard a car draw up outside. Perhaps any sound had been obscured by Karl Kordt's deep-throated moaning and groaning. But now the front door closed and Harold Leyton entered the room.

"And you, Mr. Leyton," Karl Kordt said. "My thanks."

An affectionate smile appeared on Heinz Meyer's face. He moved forward and kissed Harold Leyton on the cheek.

"Dear Harry," he said.

SIXTEEN

"Business first, if you please," Karl Kordt said. He sat down again, moving stiffly, and gazed at Harold Leyton. "Once confined in one of Haden's appalling contraptions, one knows nothing."

"You know that the most dangerous part passed off safely," Harold Leyton said. Haden knew what that meant. He could visualize doing it himself. But, briefed by Heinz Meyer on the operation of the compartment, Leyton could have had Kordt inside and the compartment closed up again in less than a minute. "In fact, Mr. Leeson's car arrived unexpectedly. Had he turned up half a minute earlier, we wouldn't be here. That was the only serious risk, that someone would see us. No one did. Or Mr. Haden would never have been allowed to leave."

Karl Kordt said, "Suppose they let him go, and tracked him in some way?"

"You're too valuable," Harold Leyton said. "They'd never chance that."

"I bow to your special knowledge," Karl Kordt said. "Go on."

"A piece of luck which will help," Harold Leyton said. "The porter was gossiping to Mr. Leeson's chauffeur. I was able to log you back into the house at ten past eight without his noticing. I signed off duty myself at eight-twenty. Your absence will have been discovered at nine-thirty when the room check is made. They may waste as much as an hour searching the house. No one followed our cars. They can have no idea where you are. You're safe."

"Good," Karl Kordt said. He turned his head and gazed at Haden. "Under the laws of my country, you are nothing but a common criminal, Mr. Haden" he said. "However, even criminals can be quite agreeable fellows. You have been of service to me twice. You have acted bravely, and kept your word. For that, I respect you."

"I could have got Hans out alone," Haden said. "You didn't have to come. Why all this? Why go back now?"

"Only if I delivered myself and turned traitor would the bastards treat my son," Karl Kordt said bitterly. "For him, I agreed. Now he's dead. It was always a dirty bargain. No reason remains why I should keep it."

"You know what'll happen to you if you go back," Haden said.

"I have committed a grave subjective error," Karl Kordt said. "It is my duty to correct it. If I stay, even if they do not break me in the end, they would use me in some other fashion to their advantage. The only remaining way I can serve my country is to remove myself from the hands of the enemy. I told you, Mr. Haden, I must have something to live for. My son is gone. My country remains." His tone changed. "However, I regret the necessity to use your step-daughter."

He gestured to the woman. After a glance at Heinz Meyer, who nodded, she unlocked and opened the door. Haden saw part of a small bedroom, simply furnished. Christa came in hesitantly. Her eyes were wide and apprehensive as she stared at the strange faces. Haden stood up. She saw him, turned, and flung her arms around him.

"It's all right," Haden said. "It's okay now." He could feel the rapid beating of her heart, and the smear of tears against his cheek. She was wearing unfamiliar clothes which did not quite fit. Someone must have bought them for her. He held her at arm's length and searched her face. She was unmarked, her skin clear, her color good.

"You don't look too bad, considering," Haden said lightly.

Her smile was almost a laugh of relief.

"I'm fine, honestly," she said. She glanced quickly at the man and woman. "They've been quite kind, really. Can we go now?" she appealed, looking back at Haden.

"Not yet," Heinz Meyer said, taking charge again. "We leave first, and I think that should be soon, Herr Kordt." His tone nicely indicated that he was both servant and captor. "The aircraft will be standing by."

"Of course," Kordt said obediently. Heinz Meyer gestured at the telephone. "We were only to phone if anything had gone wrong," he said impatiently to the tall fair man.

He bent down and ripped out the wires.

"You will not object to being left locked inside the house, Mr. Haden," Heinz Meyer said. "It will take some while for you to force your way out. You may then search for a telephone, if you wish. There isn't one for miles. You will find your car parked in Marlborough. So will you, Harry."

"Me? My car?" Harold Leyton's expression was blank, uncomprehending. "What do you mean?"

"You are not coming with us after all," Heinz Meyer said.

"You promised . . ." Harold Leyton stared at the gun which had appeared in Heinz Meyer's hand.

"Forgive this, Harry, dear," Heinz Meyer said. "Application was made, but refused on the grounds that your presence would serve no useful purpose to the state."

"You promised . . ." Harold Leyton said, disbelievingly. "When you contacted me . . . you swore . . ."

"Sit down, Harry," Heinz Meyer said. He gave Harold Leyton a hard shove in the chest.

Leyton sprawled backwards into one of the kitchen

chairs. Tears welled in his eyes. The tall fair man bent over him, took car keys from his pocket, conscientiously searched him, and shook his head in Heinz Meyer's direction. Harold Leyton's face had collapsed into ashen, puffy folds. Hands dangling limply, he leaned his elbows on his knees and stared sightlessly at the floor, his mouth hanging open like a broken doll's. Saliva began to dribble down his chin.

The tall fair man walked toward Haden, who took out his car keys, gave them to him, and sat down again in the armchair. The woman had gone into the little hall, where packed suitcases were standing ready. The man joined her and, each carrying suitcases, they went outside.

Heinz Meyer put his free hand under Harold Leyton's chin, lifted his head, closing his mouth, and gazed seriously into his eyes.

"Some things are possible, Harry," he said, quietly, "some are not. There is no further function you could perform for us. Try and see that."

"You promised . . . ," Harold Leyton mumbled again. His eyes were as dead as those of a corpse. Heinz Meyer took his hand away. Harold Leyton's head sank into its former limp position.

"If you are ready, Herr Kordt . . . ," Heinz Meyer said, with the same odd mixture of deference and authority.

"Get our transport ready," Karl Kordt said. "I would like a brief private word with Mr. Haden." Before Heinz Meyer could utter the negative on his lips, Karl Kordt went on, sharply, "I have voluntarily placed myself in your custody, Heinz, but kindly remember that for the time being I am still your superior officer."

Heinz Meyer stiffened automatically, nodded respectfully, and walked out.

"You can start getting your things together, Christa," Haden said. "Close the door, and stay in there until I call you, okay?" Christa looked at him, puzzled, but did as she was asked. "Some things I'd rather she didn't know,"

Haden said to Kordt when the bedroom door clicked shut. "What our broken-hearted friend hears doesn't matter." Outside, he heard an engine start up behind the cottage.

Karl Kordt glanced at the unaware Harold Leyton with a thin smile.

"Mr. Leyton seems to be hearing very little anyway," he said. He turned and pushed the door to the hall closed, continuing as he did so. "Mr. Haden, you have your step-daughter. I must tell you, before I go, to leave it at that. Should you make any attempt to . . . "

As he began to turn back toward Haden, he stopped speaking, his lips froze. Haden was no longer seated. He was at Karl Kordt's side, and the Beretta was jammed into the fleshy folds under Kordt's chin.

"You're not going, Herr Kordt," Haden told him softly. "One sound and I'll kill you. Understood?"

Kordt moved his head very slowly and very cautiously in assent, and opened his mouth to shout anyway. Haden slashed him across the temple with the automatic.

It was not a heavy weapon, but the blow half stunned Karl Kordt, the incipient shout turned into a strangled gurgle, and he reeled back against the wall. Haden caught him before he fell, and heaved him into the other armchair.

Harold Leyton had lifted his head and turned it toward Haden, although his eyes were glazed and vacant. Haden moved swiftly into the hall. The front door was ajar. He eased it closed, as quietly as he could. The squeak of the hinges was lost in the rumble of the vehicle moving around the cottage. Haden slipped the bolts home and went back into the living room.

Harold Leyton was still in the same position, his slack face puzzled. Haden stood over Karl Kordt, who was shaking his head as he regained his senses.

"Try again, and I'll put you out," Haden said. "Please yourself."

"I was wrong," Karl Kordt said thickly, nursing his head. "You are not a man of your word."

"Nor are you, Herr Kordt," Haden said. "I know it all, or most of it. You set me up in Zurich. The appointment you never kept was to make sure I was there when the killer came. I know why. Then, all at once, things changed. You made a deal with the other side. You needed me to get your son out. You identified the hit man. What the hell, you were handing yourself over, too. Why not, if it would hook me? But Hans died. After that, it was all different. All bets canceled. You decided to be a patriot again. I know too much, Herr Kordt."

"What you know is unimportant, provided you let me go," Karl Kordt said. "Put that gun away and open the door, for if not, very soon . . . "

"I think I also know who killed your son," Haden interrupted.

"Who?" It was a whisper. Kordt's hand gripped the arms of the chair. "Tell me."

"When my guess is proven, I will," Haden said.

Karl Kordt leaned his head against the back of the chair and stared up at Haden.

"Even for that knowledge, even if you could obtain it, there is no turning back now," he said finally. "Outside are two guns in the hands of trained men."

"If they try anything, I'll kill you," Haden said. "I mean that."

"I believe you."

"Right. That's what you tell them."

"You do not understand, Mr. Haden," Karl Kordt said. "If they cannot take me home, it is their duty to kill me. Not as punishment, but to deny our enemies further access to me. They will not go away and leave me. They may force the doors. They may smash the windows and start shooting, but one way or another . . . "

"Stephen." It was a frightened gasp. Christa stood in the doorway to the bedroom, a cheap suitcase in her hand. "Stephen?"

Someone rattled the front door. And again, harder.

"Stay in there," Haden ordered sharply.

Christa retreated, but did not close the door. Karl Kordt looked toward her sadly.

"When the shooting starts," he said, "there will be innocent victims. I can't guarantee her safety. Can you? You have not thought this through, Mr. Haden."

Someone banged on the front door.

"Herr Kordt. Herr Kordt."

Haden's shoulders sagged. He put the gun away, defeated. Kordt was right. Originally, the Beretta had only been intended for use if Christa had been harmed or killed. Then he had seized what seemed to be a chance opportunity. But he had not thought it through first.

"It's all right," Kordt called.

Haden went into the hall, unbolted the door, and opened it. The tall fair man walked in, a pistol in his hand.

"What's going on?"

"He's in there," Haden said.

Outside, a large unmarked van was reversing across the front of the cottage. Haden went first, the pistol in his back, into the living room. The tall fair man stared at the bruised swelling on Karl Kordt's temple.

"What happened, Herr Kordt?" he demanded.

"Nothing of consequence." Karl Kordt levered himself to his feet, swayed, and steadied himself. "I'm all right. There is no call for alarm, but Mr. Haden has a weapon in his right-hand jacket pocket."

The man swung around. Haden had his hands in the air. The man moved toward him. Next second, a kitchen chair smashed down onto his head. He fell heavily to the floor without uttering a sound.

Harold Leyton dropped the remnants of the wooden chair he was holding, knelt down, and picked up the pistol which had fallen from the man's hand. Harold Leyton had come to life again.

"Now there's only one gun outside," he remarked.

Blood stained the tall man's fair hair. A thick, spreading puddle oozed over the carpet.

Christa was staring at the blood in fixed horror. She gagged, her face deathly white. Haden thought she was going to faint and moved toward her.

"Christa . . . "

Harold Leyton, kneeling, was extracting two sets of car keys from the man's pockets. Karl Kordt chose that moment to run, ungainly and stumbling but surprisingly fast, and by the time Haden had swung around to go after him, and Harold Leyton had gained his feet, Kordt was in the darkened hall and out of sight. The front door slammed.

Haden reached the front door first.

"Careful!" Harold Leyton warned sharply, crouching down.

Haden dropped on one knee and cautiously eased the door ajar. Harold Leyton inched beside him. Outside, Kordt had stopped running, and was standing some distance from the cottage. The engine of the van was still idling monotonously. Kordt was looking at something on the other side of it.

"Heinz," Karl Kordt said clearly. "It's no good. Go. I order you to go."

There was a moment's silence, followed by a single shot. Haden and Leyton ducked instinctively. There were no further shots. A door slammed, the engine revved up, the van began to bump away.

Karl Kordt had fallen backwards. His right eye was a bloody pulp, and there was a jagged, uneven hole in the back of his head where the bullet had emerged.

Haden stood up, steadied himself in the doorway, and aimed at the receding van. Harold Leyton grasped his wrist.

"No," he said. "Leave him to me, Stephen."

Haden went back in. Christa had not moved. Haden took the small suitcase and put his arm around her.

"Come on, darling," he said.

The woman had sidled cautiously in. She saw the man on the floor, cried out, and fell on her knees beside him. She began to try to revive him, whispering choked endearments, tears running down her face. Christa hesitated as they skirted her kneeling form.

"Stephen . . . she was nice to me . . . "

"We'll send for help," Haden said.

They went out into the cool night air. Harold Leyton was waiting. He locked the front door, pocketed the key, and handed Haden his car keys.

"I'll make a phone call, have them collected, and everything tidied up," he said. "You won't hear anything more about it, Stephen. Nothing's happened. Do you understand that, Christa?" She stared at the prone form of Karl Kordt. Haden could feel her body trembling under his arm. "Nothing's happened," Harold Leyton repeated. "It's very important you realize that."

"I'll try to explain to her later," Haden said. "What about you, Harry?"

"Go after Heinz," Harold Leyton said. "I know where he's heading. I know the registration number of the van. Once I've phoned, they'll catch him, but I want to make sure."

"Harry, forget it," Haden said. "Get on a plane. Go anywhere. Let someone else deal with him."

"Heinz is my business," Harold Leyton said.

"If you hang around, they'll find out everything. They may know already. They'll crucify you."

"I lost my senses," Harold Leyton said. "Because I wanted something so much, I turned traitor. But I'm not one really, you know, Stephen."

"I know," Haden said.

"Whatever they do to me, I want it," Harold Leyton said. "I've deserved it. You follow me and I'll put you on the right road."

Haden followed the cream Sierra along the track when it turned left and after a while into another turning marked

Private Road. They passed the dark silhouette of an old mansion which was a preparatory school, and came out near a hamlet called Durley. The cream Sierra drew up at a public telephone box outside one of the scattered cottages, and Harold Leyton's arm waved them on.

Stephen Haden followed the signs for Marlborough, where he took the road to London.

SEVENTEEN

The phone call came while Stephen Haden was opening his suitcase.

He had not really believed that he would not hear any more about it. A man had been shot dead; his killer was loose or, if Harold Leyton had been genuine for once, had been captured, and confined somewhere; a kidnapper had been left badly injured and conceivably dying. Yet the police had not arrived, no one had contacted him. So far. This was probably the desk to say that someone was on the way up. He lifted the receiver.

"Good morning," said Helen Lloyd. "You're back, then. How're things?"

"Marvelous," Haden said. "I'm packing."

"Whenever I call, you're always off somewhere."

"I'm just a visitor. Visitors come and go."

"Mostly go, it seems to me. Listen, I'm at home, just leaving for the office. How about meeting me in the park, where we talked before, opposite the Dorchester? Just for a few minutes. Say in around half an hour. Okay?"

Haden walked along the corridor, tapped on the door, and went in. Christa was sitting up in bed, her breakfast on a tray. She was eating with relish.

"This is great," she said. "We don't get breakfasts like this at school."

"I have to go out for an hour or so," Haden said. "Will you be all right?"

"Yes, fine. I want to have a lie in the bath anyway. They didn't have a bath at that place. I'm really looking forward to it."

She speared the last piece of bacon and sighed with satisfaction.

She bore every sign of a sound night's sleep. Her eyes were bright, her face dewy and refreshed. The resilience of the young was incredible.

"See you later," Haden said.

"Stephen. Can't I even tell Paul? Just a little bit?"

"Not even Paul," Haden said. "Not a little bit. Not anything."

"Well, all right," Christa said, regretfully. "If you say so."

"Last night, you promised. I want you to keep that promise."

"I shall burst," Christa said. "It's such a terrific story."

"No one would believe you anyway," Haden said.

He left his Mercedes in the cavern of Hyde Park underground car park and walked. Helen Lloyd was sitting on a park bench. She waved, and came to meet him.

"Hi," she said. They strolled deeper into the park. Heavy clouds were rolling in from the west, threatening rain. Hyde Park practically belonged to them.

"Are you okay?" she asked. "You look dreadful."

"I haven't been sleeping well," Haden said. He came to a stop and faced her. "You said you were going to phone Christa. Arrange to go and see her. Did you?"

"I meant to, but things have been pretty hectic at the office."

"I don't know if it would have made any difference," Haden said. She just looked at him. "I have things to do,"

Haden said. "You called me, I didn't call you."

"Tom Leeson phoned early this morning. He said there'd been the biggest foul-up in history with the Anglo-American trade deal he's been working on. He seems to think it was all your doing. His British colleagues are mad about it too. You appear to have a minus popularity rating."

"That's the message you're to pass on from Tom Leeson and others."

"I guess," Helen Lloyd said. "I've never known him so angry. If I value my career, I'm to have nothing more to do with you." She looked at her watch. "After that, there was another call. I'm to see my chief in ten minutes' time. More of the same, at greater length."

"How much have you been involved, Helen?"

Helen Lloyd held his gaze. Her eyes did not waver.

"Not as much as you imagine," she said. "I have a job. Some things are part of it. Why, I'm usually not told. That's how it is. Can I say you're going back to Switzerland?"

"Yes," Haden said. "You can say that."

"Shall we meet again, do you think?"

"And screw up your career?"

"That's business," Helen Lloyd said. "This is personal. Shall we?"

"I don't know," Haden said. "I can't tell you."

"Okay," Helen Lloyd said. "Remember me to Christa. Nice to have known you."

She turned and walked away toward Park Lane.

*H*aden collected Christa and took her back to her school. They arrived at lunchtime. Groups of youngsters were drifting toward the main building. Christa took her suitcase and turned to Haden.

"I'll never talk about it again, Stephen," she said. "But I just want to say . . . oh, gosh, I don't know what I want to say . . . something like thanks for looking after me . . . and for taking me on in the first place, I suppose . . . " She kissed him quickly on the cheek with a sharp hug. "Hey, there's Paul." She ran toward the boy, calling, "Paul. Paul."

As Haden got back into his car, he could just hear their young voices.

"Did you miss me?"

"Not a lot. Have a good time?"

"It was all right. I'm glad to be back, though. Have you eaten yet? I'm starving."

Stephen Haden drove to Heathrow, left his car in the long-term car park, and bought a ticket for the next flight to West Berlin. He was ignoring the instructions on the containers and taking the drugs with increasing frequency. He felt like death.

*T*he woman greeted him and showed him up to his former room, assuring him that of course it had not been used during his absence and, fussing maternally, seemed disposed to linger. Haden got rid of her, and took his suitcase from the wardrobe, set it on the bed, and unlocked it. He strapped on the shoulder holster and checked his .38 Smith and Wesson revolver carefully. Then he sat down and focused the binoculars he had brought with him.

Apartment nine still gave no outward sign of being occupied, but a red Berlinetta coupé was parked outside the apartment block. Clouds mantled Berlin, but as yet it was only evening. He considered waiting for darkness, but the sickening pain in his loins was returning, and his hands shook as he lowered the binoculars. He swallowed more of the drugs while he dialed the number.

When the voice answered, he said, "It's Stephen. I'm in Berlin."

"Stephen!" Kurt Gabler said warmly. "No one seemed to know where you were. Why didn't you let me know you were coming?"

"I couldn't. I'm calling from the airport on a private line. I've just got in. Listen, Kurt, I need your help."

•

"Anything, you know that."

"I know who shot me in Zurich."

There was a slight pause.

"Are you sure?"

"Ninety percent. If the information's good, I can't take him alone. Two of us could. It'd be worth a lot, but if you'd rather not, I'll understand."

"You're crazy," Kurt Gabler said. "Try and stop me. What do you want me to do?"

"There's a Shell filling station at the far end of Taubenweg. Do you know it?"

"No, but I'll find it. Is that where we meet?"

"If it's him, he lives not far away. I need to grab something to eat. Can you meet me at the filling station one hour from now?"

"I'll be there. Do you have your gun?"

"No. Bring one for me."

"See you in an hour," Kurt Gabler said enthusiastically.

Haden hung up, fished the card from his wallet, and redialed.

"This is the man from the finance company," he said.

"What?" Then she laughed. "Oh, it's you. In the mood for some more talking?"

"No talk this time. Are you free now?"

"As it happens, yes. And in the mood," she said coquettishly. "How soon is now?"

"I'm just around the corner. When's your next appointment?"

"I'm available all evening, darling," Eva said. "Hurry up. You're getting me excited."

Haden rather doubted that. He hung up, donned his hat and glasses, and went downstairs and out into Taubenweg, where he turned right and walked some distance before he chose the side turning which would bring him out where he wanted to be.

He reached the road, crossed it, and turned right again. Even though he was walking fast, he had been out of sight of the apartment block for some five minutes. Now he could see its roof. The red Berlinetta coupé was still parked in the same place. He slowed down to a normal pace, breathing hard. From this direction he was approaching under the lea of the block as it were. The windows of apartment nine were at the far end. No one in there could see him without opening a window and leaning out. Just the same, it was with relief that he gained the shelter of the canopy over the front entrance. He pressed Eva's bell and spoke into the entry phone. There was an answering buzz, and he pushed the street door open.

He walked up the stairs to the second floor, went through the swinging doors, and tapped lightly on Eva's door. It opened at once.

Eva was either still in her working gear, or had stripped down to her filmy negligee ready for action. She gave him an inviting smile.

"Come on in, darling."

Haden moved no farther than the doorway, where he could keep one eye on the door of apartment nine.

"I see our friend's car is outside," he murmured quietly. "I think I'll see if he's at home first."

"Pleasure before business, darling," Eva said coldly, losing her smile. "I've just turned someone down for you."

Haden pressed some notes into her hand. "Waiting time. Keep yourself warm for half an hour, okay?"

"Okay, darling," Eva said affectionately, having glanced at the notes' denomination, and closed the door.

Haden retreated behind the swinging doors and stood watching the corridor through the glass panel. No one came out of apartment nine. Minutes dragged slowly past. The big woman and her husband came out of the adjoining apartment, walked to the elevator, pressed the call button, stepped inside, and the elevator door slid closed. The whine of the elevator stopped, and he heard the street door slam shut. Otherwise, the corridor remained empty.

Icy perspiration streaked Haden's face. The intervals of

relief were growing shorter and shorter. It was coming back again. The pain in his loins, the wooliness in his head, the tremors. His legs were signaling that they did not wish to support him for much longer. He leaned against the wall, wiped the smear of perspiration from his face, and kept his eyes on the doorway of apartment nine. His vision seemed to be filming, and he took off his glasses.

Downstairs, he thought he heard the sound of the buzzer. Almost immediately, the street door slammed. The elevator began to whine. Haden tensed himself, and stood up straight. The elevator door opened. Kurt Gabler stepped out and turned along the corridor.

Stephen Haden slipped gently through the swinging doors. The elevator whined upward. His footsteps were noiseless on the carpeted floor, but some sixth sense, or inherent caution, made Kurt Gabler begin to turn his head.

Haden jammed his gun against Kurt Gabler's cheek, forcing his head back and his eyes wide.

"Stephen . . . " It was a strangled whisper.

"Quite still, Kurt, or I'll blow your head off," Haden murmured.

Kurt Gabler remained quite still. Haden relieved him of the Colt .32 revolver Kurt Gabler loved and cherished, and slipped it into his own shoulder holster, not for a fraction of a second taking his eyes from Kurt's. The small .22 Ruger he found in Kurt Gabler's jacket pocket was little more than a target weapon, had presumably been intended for him, and might be loaded with blanks anyway. Haden did not bother to find out, but put it in his breast pocket.

Haden slid his gun along Kurt Gabler's taut skin until it rested in his ear.

"Nice and slowly, along to number nine, Kurt," Haden said.

Kurt Gabler was sweating too. With infinite care, he took the few, slow steps to the door, Haden's gun lodged in his ear as he went.

"Stand in front of the peephole," Haden said softly,

nudging Kurt Gabler's head with the Smith and Wesson until he was satisfied that he was in the right position. "In ten seconds," Haden said in a whisper as rough-edged as a saw, "you ring the doorbell. If you make a sound, or so much as blink, you're dead. Start counting."

Kurt Gabler licked his lips. Haden withdrew the gun a few inches until it was out of range of the door viewer, but still aimed at Kurt Gabler's head. Haden put his weight on his left leg, poised himself, and waited.

Kurt Gabler extended an arm which was not fully under control, and shakily pressed the doorbell. Haden heard the ringing inside the apartment. Kurt Gabler took his finger off the button and it stopped.

There was no answering sound of movement inside apartment nine. Haden strained his ears listening. Ernst Braun had to be in there. Eternity followed. Still there was not the slightest sound. Kurt Gabler's expression was unnatural, his eyes staring fixedly, his lips parted showing his teeth, his face pale. Perhaps the look of him had warned Ernst Braun. But yet, why should it? If Kurt Gabler had phoned him with bad news, he would expect Kurt to look anxious.

Haden's gun hand was beginning to tremble. He considered shooting out the door lock before Kurt Gabler noticed that. But the door would almost certainly be chained as well. And while Kurt Gabler did not want to die, and was at present in a state of near-paralytic fear, he was still, given the slightest opportunity, a dangerous bastard. To shoot out the lock, Haden would have to stop aiming at Kurt Gabler's head, if only for moments. That would be quite sufficient opportunity for Kurt Gabler who, given the condition Haden was in, was by far the more powerful man.

Haden tried to think, but his brain was incapable of calculating alternatives. The bizarre tableau had to come to an end very soon, one way or another. Haden's gun hand was already beginning to waver.

Then something broke the endless silence which had

lasted for less than thirty seconds. Inside the apartment, on the other side of the door, was the rattle of a chain.

The door began to open. As soon as the gap widened to a few inches, Haden kicked it savagely as hard as he could while at the same time clubbing Kurt Gabler across the back of the head with the barrel of his revolver.

From inside, there was a yell of pain as the door hit something. Kurt Gabler let out a deep groan and stumbled forward. Haden helped him on by charging him bodily. The door was flung wide open by Gabler's weight, and he continued across the room, hit the corner of a coffee table, and finished up on the floor against the radiator under the window.

Haden had used his own impetus to get into the room nearly as fast as Kurt Gabler. Ernst Braun too was on the floor, halfway across the room. The edge of the kicked-open door had caught him across the face. Blood was pouring from his nose and seeping from his mouth. He was lifting himself on one elbow, and was by no means unconscious.

Carried forward by his own penultimate exertion, Haden had one momentary glimpse of the thirty-five-year-old man with the receding hairline who had shot him in Zurich. The instant light of recognition in Ernst Braun's narrowed eyes left no remaining doubt about that.

In that same frozen moment, Haden saw that Braun's free hand had already traveled to his shoulder holster, and the 7.65mm Mannlicher he had drawn was swinging in the required short arc toward Haden as he came through the doorway.

Haden was off balance, and had no chance of aiming and firing in time. He kept going, and lashed out with his foot savagely. The point of his shoe dug into Braun's gun hand as though it were a football, so hard that pain flamed in Haden's ankle.

The Mannlicher flew from Braun's hand, skidded across the carpet, and bounced off the wall. Kurt Gabler flung himself sideways, clawing for the butt. It was in his hand, when Haden, forcing his protesting limbs into another lurch forward, stamped on Kurt Gabler's wrist with all his weight.

There was the sound of something snapping. Kurt Gabler screamed, and the Mannlicher fell from his fingers. Haden kicked it somewhere, anywhere, staggered around to meet Ernst Braun's onslaught, and pulled the trigger.

In the confined space the explosion was deafening. Ernst Braun's legs ceased to function and gave way as the .38 bullet tore into him at close range. His torso kept on coming. Haden stumbled aside out of its path. Ernst Braun hit the floor with a thud, and lay motionless.

Haden collapsed into an armchair. His legs, no longer under control, refused to support him further. Gasping, he tried to force air into empty lungs which his madly pounding heart was intent on bursting. Through eyes which seemed not to be focusing properly, he peered at Kurt Gabler.

Kurt had propped himself up against the radiator. He was holding his cracked wrist against his body and moaning.

Vaguely, Haden became aware that someone was standing in the doorway. He turned his throbbing head around, and his wavering revolver.

Eva retreated, wrapping her diaphanous negligee around her as if that would protect her.

"Send for the police," Haden gasped.

"What the hell is going on?" The meaningless query was high-pitched, semi-hysterical. "Are you fucking insane or something?"

"Get them here." A spasm of coughing racked him. He struggled to resume. " . . . do it, woman! Now! Do it!"

Eva retreated out of sight toward her apartment. Haden's skull seemed to be several times as heavy as normal. He leaned it against the back of the armchair, which made it easier to turn his head and find Kurt Gabler with his eyes. The coughing fit had passed. The sense of heaviness was not unpleasant; in a way it was rather comforting.

"You killed Christian Weber, Kurt," he said. He discovered that if he rested his wrist on the arm of the chair he could keep his revolver aimed more or less at Kurt Gabler.

"Me? No. You've got it wrong, Stephen."

"It took a long time," Haden said, dreamily, "before it came together. At first, nothing fitted. The trip . . . the ambush . . . how could anyone know? But Christian had told you he'd gone to Heidelburg. You checked. Maybe you own someone in the workshop. Maybe someone just talked out of turn. Once you knew the trailer was being fitted out, you could put the rest together."

"I didn't," Kurt Gabler protested. "I didn't know anything about it."

Haden ignored the words and concentrated on the blurred face of Kurt Gabler.

"What threw me was how anyone could have known I was going to use the Bitstedt crossing." He frowned, as if still wondering. "No one could have read my mind. Except you, Kurt. You know the way I think. You couldn't be certain, no, but it was an odds-on chance, and you took it. You waited. You knew roughly where we'd stop, because that's where you'd have stopped. We've both done it so often, Kurt. And you knew the vehicle you were looking for. There aren't too many horse trailers around."

Haden tried to concentrate his thoughts. He seemed to be rambling.

Kurt Gabler was still in pain, but he managed a half laugh.

"Come on," he said. "You've invented a fairy story. Me kill Christian Weber? I wouldn't do that. He was our best agent in West Berlin. He was too valuable."

"No, you didn't want to kill Christian," Haden agreed. "You thought it would be me driving. You were after me."

"What's happened to you, Stephen? Are you delirious? How many years have I worked for you?"

"You helped set me up in Zurich, Kurt," Haden said. "Karl Kordt was empire-building. He wanted control of the business. You'd be the front man. You were going to run it for them, their way."

"Don't be bloody stupid," Kurt Gabler said, offended. "Me work for any commie? I hate the bastards."

Haden said, "You love money more than you hate them, Kurt. They'd give you the business provided you did what they wanted. You'd been in touch with them for years. It was you who betrayed refugees to them for blood money."

"Be reasonable, Stephen," Kurt Gabler urged. "I shopped that Norwegian bastard when his wife talked too much and I realized he was a shitty commie spy. That proves how I feel about them."

It vaguely occurred to Stephen Haden that Kurt was being uncharacteristically calm and reasonable, at least in his terms, and seemed surprisingly content to sit where he was and discuss the matter. Haden was not positive, but he had the impression the doorway was occupied.

He rolled his head toward the door. Through the veil, he saw that several people were standing there. Some of Ernst Braun's neighbors, he supposed. They were staring into the room in fearful fascination.

It took Haden a second or two to find Kurt Gabler again. Perhaps Kurt had moved sideways a bit. With an effort, he shifted in the armchair so that the muzzle of his Smith and Wesson was pointing in Kurt Gabler's general direction. What had they been talking about?

"Oh, yes, the Norwegian diplomat," he said, pleased at recollecting it. "And his wife, the woman you were screwing. Perhaps you were. Perhaps not. You didn't shop him, Kurt. He just happened to get caught. He was one of your contacts with the other side. Like Ernst Braun. I wasn't really positive when I phoned you. But you turned up here.

He knew you. He let you in. Explain that away, Kurt." Kurt Gabler did not seem disposed to try. "Anyway, we'll let the police handle it," Haden said, drowsily. "See what they can find out."

There was no reply from Kurt Gabler, who simply sat on the floor, staring at him. Had Kurt not been leaning against the radiator previously? Haden could not remember. It did not matter. Nothing to do now except wait for the police. It was all over. Nearly all over. There was still Zurich. Plenty of time for that later. Plenty . . .

Stephen Haden felt better than he had for days. Warm, thoroughly relaxed, content. The strange sensation that he was floating somewhere, almost weightless, was very agreeable. He felt at peace, fulfilled.

His chin was resting on something. He wondered what it was, and found that he had to open his eyes to find out. Of course. His chest. He thought he heard, somewhere a long way off, a collective gasp of fright and someone calling out. He lifted his head and searched for the cause.

Through the haze, he saw that Kurt Gabler had certainly moved this time, and was kneeling beside a glass-fronted cabinet which stood on curved wooden legs. His right arm hung at his side, but his left hand was coming out from underneath the cabinet and in his hand was Ernst Braun's 7.65 Mannlicher.

Everything, it seemed to Stephen Haden, happened very slowly. His wrist, he found, was drooping over the arm of the chair. He attempted to cock it, lift the revolver still clenched in his fingers. The gun was a lead weight, and resisted his efforts to raise it the necessary few inches.

Equally slowly, or so it appeared to Stephen Haden, Kurt Gabler's dimly perceived kneeling form twisted around and his left hand rose in an arc.

Haden's right hand was finally overcoming the massive weight. With detached interest, he watched the ponderous, slow-motion race between the two hands, his and Kurt

Gabler's. He supposed that, some time or another, his brain should issue instructions to his trigger finger. Difficult to tell when. The shape which must be Kurt Gabler had begun to flicker and dance slowly, rather like a lazily rising cloud of wood smoke. Perhaps he should wait until it cleared . . .

But the haze which his blinking eyes could not clear was thickening. He fired into it before it became opaque. There was a kick against his hand, so the bullet must be on its way, but the explosion was oddly dull and muffled, as if heard through cotton wool.

From some far-off place, a woman screamed. Darkness had set in, his chin was resting comfortably again. From out there somewhere, he detected the crash of splintering glass, and a thump as some heavy object hit the floor. Perhaps the bullet had found Kurt Gabler. He had no way of telling. Nor, if he had, how much damage it had done. He rather thought there was no lead weight in his right hand any more, although he could not be quite certain. His entire body was leaden.

Perhaps there had been an answering shot, which his dimming senses had not noticed. Perhaps he had been hit and did not know it, receding as he was into some unimaginably distant galaxy.

Later, when he had rested, and perhaps Rudi Hensler had fixed him up again, he would sort out Carli. Although probably she had gone already. Anton Weiss had merely cooked the books and creamed off cash. It had been Carli who had left the basement door open that day, ready for Ernst Braun.

For a long time, he had thought that it must have been Anna. That the night club business had just been an excuse to gain entry to the house. He felt shame about that. He wondered if she still wanted to invest in that night club. He must ask her. She could have the money. If it mattered to her, why shouldn't she? Money no longer seemed as important as it had.

Carli had left that door open. She was one of Kurt Gabler's women. Quite likely, she had not known the real reason. Kurt could have fed her some story she chose to believe. Perhaps Ernst Braun had intended to make it look as though robbery had been the motive, until he had discovered Christa's unexpected presence in the house. It mattered little now. Carli was the final small link in the chain.

Apart from Carli, it was done, finished. Strange things had emerged along the way. Things he had never expected to learn. That he could love someone. Christa. He loved that girl, who was not his child. He loved her more than he loved himself. How strange it was to discover that. He was glad, though. It was a good feeling. He wondered if he loved Helen Lloyd, too, in a different way? Perhaps he should find out about that. It might be important.

The last thing which intruded on his consciousness was a peculiar wailing noise. It was very faint and distant, although coming closer. His mind solved the strange puzzle moments before everything was switched off.

The faint sound, becoming fainter, was the ear-splitting scream of arriving police sirens.

The two policemen followed Eva's pointing finger, edged cautiously to the open door of apartment nine, and put their guns away.

Two men lay on the floor. One was flat on his face. On top of the other, a bookcase had toppled, its glass front shattered.

The third man was slumped in an armchair, his eyes closed, as if he had fallen peacefully asleep.

*T*he place familiar, been somewhere like this before. No slight sticky pressure on the eyelids, though. No monotonous *shush-click, shush-click* . . .

Voices speaking in German. One, a stranger's, curt, insistent, something about the patient not being disturbed. The other, the well-known one, arguing. Schlunegger must have flown in from Zurich. Feel exhausted, wrung out, glad to be in bed, but no pain. Kurt Gabler must have missed. Or got him first. Doesn't matter.

The doctor saying what? Come back tomorrow? Schlunegger protesting. Schlunegger, who had instinctively got it right at the very beginning. Done his bloody job for him, though.

Stephen Haden kept his eyes closed. Schlunegger could wait.